Boundless Alberta

Boundless Alberta

EDITED BY ARITHA VAN HERK

NeWest Press

Edmonton

Canadian Cataloguing in Publication Data

Main entry under title:

Boundless Alberta

ISBN 0-920897-41-X

1. Short stories, Canadian (English)—Alberta* 2. Canadian fiction (English)—20th century.* I. Van Herk, Aritha, 1954-
PS8329.5.A4B68 1993   C813'.010897123   C93-091714-6
PR9198.2.A42B68 1993

Every effort has been made to obtain permission for quoted material. If there is an omission or error the authors and publisher would be grateful to be so informed.

Editor for the Press: Aritha van Herk
Cover design: Bob Young/BOOKENDS DESIGNWORKS
Interior design: John Luckhurst/Graphic Design Limited
Financial assistance: NeWest Press gratefully acknowledges the financial assistance of The Canada Council; The Alberta Foundation for the Arts, a beneficiary of the Lottery Fund of the Government of Alberta; and The NeWest Institute for Western Canadian Studies.

Printed and bound in Canada

NeWest Publishers Limited
Suite 310, 10359 - 82 Avenue
Edmonton, Alberta T6E 1Z9

Contents

Introduction

The traditional expectation of the regional story collection is that it will magnify a small and rather limited place, reveal the seams and fissures in an inevitably parochial world. But the thirty-six short fictions gathered here configure Alberta quite differently from its ubiquitously ascribed gophers and grain elevators, prairie and sky, oil wells and Rockies. Once again, Alberta becomes an exotic location, a window on the world, a literary telescope.

In publishing this anthology, NeWest Press, in its fifteenth anniversary year, is building on the success of its two earlier collections, *Alberta Bound* and *Alberta ReBound*, both of which convinced an enormous readership that short fiction in this province is undergoing not so much a renaissance as an explosion of talent. The stories included in *Boundless Alberta* were obviously chosen for their quality and their range, but also for the unique vision that they present, a re-reading of this place in relation to the larger world. Rather than closing the borders of the imagination, this collection invites us to cross them.

Once again, the selection process was difficult. There are so many excellent writers working in this province that making choices became an editorial torment, but I settled finally for a combination of superlative and evocative stories. I only hope that the end result will encourage readers to search out not only these writers but the many, many others who make culture in this province so rich.

I completed the textual editing of *Boundless Alberta* while I was working as a guest professor of Canadian literature at the University of Trier in Germany. Far away from home, living in a language other than English, I was struck by the powerful immediacy of these stories. As a counterpoint to the Canadian literature that I was teaching to German students (who view Canada as unbelievably exotic), these stories grounded me, reminded me not to underestimate the literary sophistication of my home province. And although I travelled to cities like Berlin and Vienna, working on this collection in trains and in airports, in my small flat in Gusterath, and in my office at Trier, I felt both homesick and at home, a part of a community of words that can traverse the world and hold its own, but that still comes from the heart of where we live.

Part of the virtuosity of these thirty-six fictions is the way that they range over time and space. Whether set in Canada or internationally, in the past or in the future, the situations that the reader will discover are those of the imagination on a journey, a journey that does not necessarily conclude with an expected destination, a journey that begins to challenge all perceptions of the imagination.

Most obvious is the cultural diversity of this anthology. Albertans are from Japan, Italy, New Delhi, Toronto, Trinidad, China, Holland, and heaven. Their literary travels take them not just back to earlier homes, but on first-time journeys to Prague, India, Germany, Zaire, Iceland, New York, and the moon. And what experience these travels offer is not always comforting, not merely indolently exotic. Characters discover the shifting nature of what we call home. Canada as a desirable address is called into question; any assumption of Alberta as a provincial safety zone, predictable and well-fed, is challenged. We are now part of the global community, and our literature reflects that connection.

These stories question the social and the political and the domestic worlds that might at one time have seemed metaphorically unshakable. But their questions do not merely destroy or negate, they ultimately suggest alternatives, possibilities, transfigurations. Out of passionate concern for a fragmenting and uncertain narrative, these writers bring together the edges of both questions and answers, posing with language profound epiphanies. And yet they do not confine themselves to straightforward realism. There is surrealism and magic side by side with history's repeated shuffle, philosophy's questions, humour's quick bite. Some of these pieces are tragic, some are light as air. But all invite the reader to come in, to sit down, to forget daily routines, and to enjoy, even momentarily, the configurations of a different life.

Begin perhaps with Lobe's "Two Enormous, Dazzling Statues." A typical prairie town is visited by two marble statues who bring with them happiness and prosperity, but also the dis-ease of cultural licentiousness. In a delicious send-up of our conservatism, our dour and stringent ways, the story pokes fun at the pessimism of the rural prairie community, its refusal to embrace optimism, its marvellous carnivalesque convolutions. From there, Mulcahy's "Texas Two-Step" literally embraces the tension between neighbourliness and social responsibility, when an environmental activist must practice dancing with a feller-buncher who works for the mill that she opposed. In such contradictions do Albertans locate themselves: desiring but resisting, antagonists but partners, prepared for doom but always optimistic.

And what does home mean to us? These stories make strange the familiar, make us question the home we take for granted. In Bowers' "At the Trailer Park" a man tries to reconcile his work in a "mobile home community" with his family's lost P.E.I. farm and his own lost hopes; mending the roof of his house, a single father in Hollingshead's "Walking on the Moon" suddenly sees his neighbourhood completely afresh, full of the spirit of love. When Dutch immigrants move in next door, a young girl in Bachmann's "Splitting Hares" gains a new perspective on displacement and survival. Home is not so predictable a place, but it is still a concept that we inhabit, and a place that we begin from.

The domestic world is no less a site of change and contention. Whether potentially claustrophobic, as in Trigueiro's "The Poisoning" or horrifically frustrating for a classic mother and wife whose family is mad about hockey, as in Stenson's "The Hockey Widow," marriage is subject to the gentle fissures of laughter and resistance. In Badami's "Jhoomri's Window" set in India, marriage becomes a metaphorical window, a space that can both open and close.

Home is more than house and family. Characters try to find ways to feel at home in different elements, the challenge of experience extra to grounded reality. Sherman's "Wire Act" balances an entire life in the air above a high wire; while Simmons' "falling angels/have this memory" tries to clear space for a busy mother to undertake a skydive. In both these stories, air is breathless and beautiful, an element of risk and desire. Sacuta's "Earth Moving" enters the density of earth as if it were permeable, despite its setting in the developing suburbs. And van Herk's "At Land" questions the hospitable element of water through a contemporary re-telling of the Jonah story. These immersions suggest a reaching beyond the recognizable, to a glimmer of transcendence. How to transcend this earthbound earth? Perhaps it is only possible through the magic suggested in Chan's "The Ways of Luck" where, through the instrument of a mah-jong game, the winds regenerate good fortune.

Tied to the desire for escape is the confinement of language itself, and characters locked in one inarticulacy or another. Chow's "Graves-in-Waiting" questions the ironies of language through a child who feels excluded from Chinese: how can we begin to understand the language of our ancestors, if we do not live in their sphere? And how can we speak when we have always been silenced? Frey's "The Tastee Freeze Man" metaphorizes that mufflement through a character, who, because she has never been able to say what she thinks, has a tree growing in her throat. The terrifying inarticulacy of love can sometimes only express itself through displacement or anger, as in Wiebe's "Sleeping (uneasily) with Franz Kafka." Love becomes an ambiguous space, a measurable weight, a chasm of words, between father and son in Hilles' "Horse," and between mother and son in Howes' "Entry Site."

And the body too is anarchic, a planet, a yearning space, whether as nude model in Huser's "Nudities" or as one of the handicapped people struggling to manage an unforgiving world in Megann's "The Missing You." The characters of

Dorsey's "What We Wore" clothe themselves in an alternative sexual orientation; the black woman of Mayr's "Scalps" resists accommodating physical characteristics that do not fit a white notion of beauty; the traveller in Haynes' "Krishna saw the universe in his mother's (father's mouth)" wrestles physically and spiritually with the dysentery that may bring about her death. And the body serves as its own mirror in Murphy's "Balancing Act," about an abused child's double, and in Bishop's "Rose," where a voyeur watching a woman who is watching for her child is both marked and unmasked.

Revision becomes both playful and a strategy for survival, for coping with a never-predictable world. History is reversed in Sproxton's story of the rebel Mickey Marlowe, "The Redheaded Woman with the Black Black Heart," just as the character in Riskin's "Men, Boys, Girls, Women" rebuilds her journey so that she will be able to call her story her own. And Rawdon's "Mapping Toronto by Darkness" is a test of consumerism and its games. Even death becomes a revision, a welcome space, in sorrow the forgiveness of memory, as in Krahn's "The Mother Died" and in Gunnars' "Dreamwoman."

And death proposes other transitions, the transition of immigration between Trinidad and Canada in Harris' "And The Heart Pauses for Breath," as well as the transition two people from completely different cultures who make a new life, make strange a familiar world, achieve in Crate's "Betwixt and Between." Although a return to a real or imagined past can auger desire, it can also outline sacrifice, in Edwards' "On a Platter," or alienation, in Zachariah's "Soap Bubbles." Goto's "Tilting" remembers the blur between geography and climate and culture and how travel erases difference and memory, both. Finally, Nixon's "Preparations" addresses the futility of the missionary position for both body and soul.

Boundless Alberta is exactly that, a boundless collection of fiction that speaks to a newly voiced maturity in the writing of this province. Here is fiction both transparent and tantalizing; both deeply felt and rollicking with laughter; both determinedly regional and elegantly sophisticated. The writers of Alberta speak out of an experience of this place in all its complexity, and with brilliant observation. The pleasure the reader will find in these pages is indeed boundless.

Aritha van Herk
Calgary, Alberta

Texas Two-Step

BARBARA MULCAHY

I can tell we both feel awkward when the dancing instructor says, "Ladies move forward to the next man," and I walk up to him. I recognize him from the public meeting—the one where I mouthed off to Forestry about furans and dioxins. He's a feller buncher—that's what I call the catskinners and the loggers and the truckers and the feller-buncher operators that got all this work when the pulp mill got built. We were real small-time before that. There were cats and trucks and people logged but no one had a feller-buncher because it was too big and expensive for this area. Now things are different. Anyway, I saw him at the meeting. He was sitting in the back with his buddies. They didn't join in the applause for my outburst.

Now, here, I can tell he recognizes me too, but he smiles and puts his left hand out. I place my right hand in it. Then I put my left hand firmly on his shoulder blade. I stiffen my arms way too much. "Pressure," I joke. Because that's what the instructor keeps saying, "Starch." "Pressure." "Firm up." He wants us to feel "the framework of our bodies." Well, that's what he says. I've never thought of my body that way, like it has a structure. But it is fun to have to think something different. And it is fun to hold onto a man, although it does make me a little nervous. Just when I'm beginning to feel that way holding on so close to the feller-buncher, the instructor says, "One and a two, quick-quick . . ." and we start moving. We're learning the Texas Two-Step. The instructor says it's an easy step and I can see some people around us are catching on already.

The feller-buncher has a nice way of holding me. Close but not too close. There is one man at the dance class who pulls me right up to his chest—so my breasts touch him, and holds me there. I don't like that but when I try to pull away he says, "Not so much pressure." He's been taking the class for several years and he thinks he knows a lot.

But the feller-buncher, he isn't a grabber. He leaves a comfortable distance but still holds me so that I know he's holding me. And he smells nice. Like a person. The dance class is held in the evening and a lot of the married men smell like dinner. Maybe their wives are safeguarding their marriages, I don't know. It's not something I do. And the unmarried men, they smell like aftershave.

I've been married a long time but I never knew how to dance so it's been forever since I held a man other than Marty. And, to be honest, a long time since I've held him when he didn't figure he had more important things to do. Its been quite an experience taking dancing lessons, let me tell you. Someone once told me that you exchange some kind of energy when you touch people; when you don't, you get "out of touch." And that's the way I felt after the first class, like I'd never known my neighbors before. At first when I smelled these young guys I wondered if they had been drinking aftershave. It took me some time to remember that that's the way men do things, you know—overdo things, when they don't have a woman to advise them.

But the feller-buncher, I've been told he's newly married—so he's been set straight about how much aftershave is needed. And I guess his bride hasn't wised up to the old wives' trick of garlic, onion and grease for dinner. Still, I bet she doesn't like me. I remember her, too. She was sitting by his side at the hearing and I noticed her bristle when all the environmentalists interrupted my comments with enthusiastic applause. "There goes my new double-wide and the trips to Vegas," she was thinking. She didn't realize like I do that these public meetings are a farce. The government waives any legal requirements that get in their way; a little meeting in a little hick town in northern Alberta simply isn't going to get in the government's way and that's the only reason it holds them. The environmentalists let off steam and nothing else happens. When I came home all worked up my husband said, "Just face it. You're gonna get screwed no matter what. You might as well pull down your pants and bend over and get done with it."

And he was right. The mill got built and the highway's full of logging trucks. You know how when you suggest doing something and people figure there's nothing better to do, they say, "Can't dance, too wet to plow, might as well." I don't know. It doesn't really have anything to do with it I guess. But anyway around this time I got it into my head that I wanted to learn how to dance. Dancing's popular up here. Marty said I was getting menopausal but as it happened one of his buddies signed up so he said we could go too.

Really, though, I'm no good at dancing. I don't have an ear for the music. In fact, at class I prefer it when we're just going through the steps and the music system's turned off. Pretty bad, huh? When I was a teenager I used to keep an eye out for the toe-tappers so I could tap my foot at the same time as them and no one would know what a tin ear I had.

At dance class I don't even try to pick up the beat. I just try to dance with whatever partner I'm holding on to. And men are so different. Probably that's another reason I'm no good at dancing. I'm not really interested in music. I'm just interested in holding on to these different men and trying to figure out what they're like. It's not sexual. I guess I just married so early that I never really got to know that people are different. But that doesn't mean I'm looking for trouble.

And it's interesting because all these men are my neighbours so I always thought I knew them. But when you dance with someone its like you have to dance from the inside. And I've only known them from the outside, which guys have the new four-wheel drives with the quads permanently loaded in back, which ones have eight quarters and new machinery, which ones spray and which ones go organic. You think you know someone and then he puts his arm around you and it's like diving—whooh!—someplace new.

Well, the feller-buncher seems relaxed. I tell myself, "Of course he's relaxed, he sits in a machine all day moving logs from here to there and when he goes home he doesn't think about how things are going to hell. He just goes home." But still, it is nice to be with someone so relaxed. He can't dance either, so when we get out of step we just stop in the middle of the floor.

That's interesting, too, to be held and not moving. And the rest of the class keeps dancing all around us. Like we aren't there. Like we're somewhere else. I like it. The feller-buncher doesn't notice. He only apologizes, says his wife always calls out the beat to him. I smile at him and admit my husband does the same for me. Marty gets mad at me for that. I don't "try to feel the music" is what he says, I'm a "deadhead." We fight a lot when we dance. The last time I said if he didn't shut up I was going to punch him in the nose. I meant it and I suppose I should have gone ahead and done it because he didn't stop. My feet are "in the wrong place." That's why he steps on them. I should "just learn how to dance right."

So I really like it when it's time to change partners. People give you more leeway when you're not married to each other and they know they don't have to dance with you for very long.

And the feller-buncher, well, he's good looking. I don't wear blinders just because I'm married. I can see. And even if I don't do anything, I can still feel. Hormones—that's what Marty calls "whore moans." It's funny, you know, I didn't feel anything till I was in my thirties. Then—wham, bam— it was like I got socked when I finally weaned my last kid. Suddenly I realized what it was like for Marty when he just couldn't keep himself back. And I was sorry I'd been so unfeeling. But it was too late. Marty couldn't feel it anymore. Not with me at least. Anyway, the feller-buncher's not so good looking that he's a jerk, just kind of comfortable-good-looking. And he's distracted, trying to listen for the beat, which means I don't feel pressured by him. Well, I know I should pay attention and try to learn how to dance but it's just so nice to be held like that. So very, very nice that when he gets the beat I've forgotten how the steps go—slow . . . slow, quick-quick—and I step all over him. We have to stop again while he catches the beat.

I look around, feel like it's the first time I can just see things. There we are in the middle of the community hall. The basketball hoops are pulled back up against the walls. The floor's kind of rough. They don't wax it except for real dances because otherwise the kids from the school across the road fall down too much when they're here for gym. There are bright coloured tapes going this way and that way across the floor. Red for basketball, white for volleyball, orange for god knows what other sport the kids play during the day. The tape is rough and it's hard to slide your feet across it while you dance. The lights are bright now. Not like a real dance and the music is not so loud because we need to be able to hear the instructor cue us. There we are in the middle of the community hall and he's holding me again while the rest of the class dances around us. And I'm just soaking it up. Then someone bumps into us and I'm pushed against him. My forehead against his chin, my breasts against his chest. I lose my balance for a moment and I have to grab him. And when I do I feel his muscles—I've grabbed his arms—he's strong. It's a surprise, I don't know why. Marty's strong. He works all day. But somehow this is different and something inside me opens. And I look up at him. And it's the way he looks back. Like I've annoyed him. The way Marty looks at me when we're in public and I've said something and he's got to be polite.

It's awkward when I come out of it. I feel embarrassed. I let go, say "sorry," and stand back. We arrange our hands and arms together without saying anything. His arms feel a little more stiff this time.

They're playing a song I like, something about "little sister." I know there's a beat somewhere and when we finally start again I say, "slow . . . slow, quick-quick" along with the feller-buncher. I make myself concentrate on that and where to put my feet.

"Up," the instructor says. "On the balls of your feet."

"Slide. Slide."

~

Barbara Mulcahy was born in Trinidad and raised in India, Greece, the United States, and Israel. She has lived with her family near North Star, Alberta, for fifteen years. Her work is included in The Road Home: New Stories by Alberta Writers (1992) and 200% Cracked Wheat (1992). She was a winner of the 1992 Write for Radio Competition; her radio play, "Bird on a Branch," will be broadcast on CBC's "Studio 94." "Texas-Two Step" was first published in the NeWest Review.

Walking on the Moon

GREG HOLLINGSHEAD

Sunday, and Martin had to go up onto the roof again. At least we don't have skunks, he reflected. Mammals are smarter than water.

Martin's daughter Janey, who was thirteen, was still in the bathroom.

"The goons are up early," she said through the door, meaning their neighbours to the north. "Hey Dad."

"Did the goons go to bed is the question. What?"

The newspaper, emerging from under the door. Martin squatted in the hall to squint at it.

BUTT TAX HIKE EYED, he read.

"Oh I get it—"

"I'm going to be a journalist," Janey said.

"First you're going to have to come out of there. I'll meet you downstairs."

Martin's son Ben was in the kitchen feeding his slime mold. The stuff flows in one mass through soil and rotting leaves, over and around all obstacles. Ben kept his in a Mason jar. He was dropping in oat flakes.

"A perfect day for the roof," Martin said.

"What's it going to do, Dad?"

Ben was four.

"Raise me up. What do you feel like for breakfast, Ben?"

"What have you got."

The toilet flushed. Janey started down the stairs.

"Wash your hands!" Martin shouted.

Janey returned to the bathroom.

"Froot Loops, bagel, oatmeal, nice soft bread, scrambled egg, peanut butter, jam, that's it."

The dog crept in looking shamefaced.

"You," Martin said.

The dog went down carefully onto its elbows and nestled its singed torso into the crook of its big disc thighs, its muzzle low down and parallel to the floor, eyes upraised.

"Answer," Martin said. "I'm waiting here."

"Umm—"

Janey came into the kitchen.

"And you Dog," she said and squatted to scratch its ears. "You don't have to worry. It'll grow back. Pelt-o-genesis."

"Stop being nice to him, after last night," Martin said.

"Aw, Pooch feels terrible about being insane."

"Grambled egg," Ben said.

"Achingly beautiful out there," Martin muttered, glancing towards the window, which was wide and high and in fact showed only the wall of the house next door, the goons' house.

"What we need is a visitor," Janey said.

"Not wet," Ben said.

"I never do your eggs wet," Martin replied.

"*She* does," Ben said.

Janey jumped up, "How can you say that!" The dog's tail whalloped the floor.

"We had a visitor last night," Martin reminded Janey.

"Fifi LePew."

"*Hey*."

"*Your* visitor," Janey said. "I was conversation fodder. Let's see which of us is more alive to this teen disaster."

"That's enough."

"She pass?"

"Yeah, on out the door."

"Roof," Ben said.

"*She*," Martin added, "had a name."

"Gwen. I know. For Gwyneth. You introduced us, remember? Where's the cereal? Hey Dad?"

"What *what*? I'm right here."

Martin was standing with the fridge door open, staring at the empty egg rack on the inside of the door.

"No eggs," he murmured incredulously.

"Check inside. Maybe I didn't put them—Hey Dad?"

"W*hat!?*"

"In England you know what they've got a special tax for?"

"Uh—Poles? Pole tax, get it? Funny accent, funny nameski, Brits tax ya."

"Nope. 'Edible pets.' Isn't that perfect?"

"It is, actually," Martin replied softly and slammed the fridge door with his foot. He then turned, watching his balance, to open a carton of eggs, like a rare book.

"Ah," he said. "Eggs. And for starch, Ben?"

"What's 'edible'?" Ben asked.

"You," Janey told him.

The dog wagged.

"Not y*ou*, Doghouse Demento," Janey said. "I don't care how well you self-cook."

"So anyways," Martin said.

"So anyways," Janey said.

"A perfect day for the roof."

"Oh gawd," Janey cried. "Not the roof! Not the friggin' roof!"

"Language," Martin said. "Bagel or soft, Ben? Use your words."

"Soft."

~

After breakfast Martin, followed by Ben, went for the ladder, which hung on the inside wall of the garage. Next yard over, the goons were gathered in the spring sun. The head goon, Gary, the one with an edge on him, had lately taken down the back fence in order to roll two pickups into the yard. Out of these he was assembling a third, from the wheels up. In a row against the rear wall of the goons' house, a two-storey white clapboard half as big again as Martin's, the goons and their girlfriends had ranged, as against a stage flat, the two seats from the trucks along with a number of steel-and-vinyl kitchen chairs. Here they sprawled—the women on laps, an arm, sometimes two arms, around a goon neck, when they weren't fetching more beer—in desultory banter with Gary, at his labour. Big speakers had been set up outside, so the heavy metal and old Creedence Clearwater was not muffled or otherwise diminished by walls.

Martin's aluminum ladder with its bright blue cord and sixteen-foot capacity fascinated Ben. When Martin clanged the end of it trying to manoeuvre it out the side door of the garage, Ben put his hands over his ears, blinking. If the goons were watching, Martin didn't look to see.

"Here we go," he said.

"Hey Dad—" Ben was walking quickly to keep up, looking to the next yard.

"Yup?"

"Are those lady goons?"

"Keep your voice down, son."

"Are they?"

"I suppose they are."

Martin carried the ladder onto the back step and set it on end. Having never figured out the blue cord, he extended the ladder by hand. The claws slammed each rung as the ladder went higher. At full extension the end just made the second-storey eavestrough and this was from the elevation of the back step. Martin understood that really he ought to have a longer ladder.

He stuck his head in the back door. "Hey, Janey!"

Ben appeared, moving fast from around the side of the house.

"Know what, Dad?" he said in a loud whisper.

"No, what."

"I just saw into the goons' house!"

"Good work, Ben. Any sightings?"

"What?"

"See anything?"

"No."

"Huh."

"It's old in there."

"Yeah, it's an old house, Ben. Like this one."

"What one."

"Ours. Our house."

"Our house is nicer. Dad?"

"Yes?"

"Do the lady goons live there too?"

"Some of them."

When Janey appeared her nose was red.

"White spray on the mirror?" Martin inquired.

"Don't be gross."

Janey scowled as she stood with one foot and both hands on the ladder while Martin crawled upwards. From his left wrist he had slung a yellow plastic Safeway bag containing tools and materials for patching the eavestrough and a rotted place in the facing behind it where water had been coming in, again. With both hands he held tight to the ladder. He did not like the spring of the thing. Finally his eyes were level with the edge of the shingle, but the ladder did not extend far enough beyond it to be grasped while he stepped off with dignity like a proper Mr. Fix-it. Instead, he had to throw the bag up and crawl, clawing gritty shingle, over the end of the ladder—across the abysmal clinging terror of being on neither ladder nor roof—and onto the gentle, fortunately, slope.

"That's it, Janey!"

"Tell me, OK?"

Last time she'd caught him trying to ease down alone.

"So listen," Martin said.

Squatting on the edge of the roof, Martin could see Ben walking around the yard jabbing his shovel into the grass, stopping every once in a while to stare at the goons. Some-times Martin felt so much love for his son that it threatened to throw him down from a high place. A little dizzy, he squatted. As he did so he saw that on his garage roof a cat belonging to the old lady on the other side from the goons paced with its tail whipping. A blue jay watched from the grass. In the goons' backyard Gary was talking on a cellular phone as he worked. The man was constantly surrounded by friends and followers. Of course, it's the rare individual who can turn two old wrecked trucks into a perfectly good truck in front of everybody's eyes. While talking on the phone.

Martin stood up. A tour of the roof. The slope was gentle by the eaves, steeper towards the central ridge. Martin stepped along close to the eaves. A little dizziness from the height. How much of vertigo is knowing you just might throw yourself over? Below, on Martin's right, the neighbour lady's roof, a quilt of windstorms and partial measures. She was old; a new roof had not been worth it to her for a long, long time.

And then Martin was crouched at the window of his dormer, gazing in at a pink sea of government insulation. Last month he'd been up here to measure a pane for an air vent and up again to install it. The salesclerk at the building supply, a guy with Orange Crush hair, had kept bringing the wrong design, shape, size. As the guy was on his way to the back for the fourth time, Martin had turned to a couple of clerks smirking at the transaction and said, "The man is a fool."

The smirks vanished, the guy heard the remark. He paused, kept going. Later, as he handed Martin the correct vent, he said, "I hope you choke on it."

Fair enough, Martin had thought, nodding as he took the vent from the guy's hand. Fair enough.

On the other side of the ridge, the goon side, the sewer stink of the septic tube. Higher up the slope, the shining globe ventilator, casting its flickering shadow against goon clapboard.

And so full circle. Martin came around the blanched, eroded chimney, looked at the Safeway bag, and kept going. One more time for the difference and remove. He was conscious now of the views, back and front, down through gaps in the leaves to the clipped grass, the street with its margin of dust and oil stains where the cars parked, and he got the longer ones too: the skein of trolley lines two houses over, office towers downtown in Sunday quiet, a small plane crawling the blue sky.

But mostly what Martin got was the difference, how he could never imagine it. You climb a little. Suddenly you're in the trees, new breezes. Same world, different world. Like when a cloud darkens the sun. You can't conceive how everything will be once the cloud moves away. And then it has, the sun is back, and you can't conceive how everything will be once the next cloud arrives. Sun's out, sun's in, sun's out. Inconceivable. An astronaut comes back to earth, and after all that training, all that simulation, how could anyone have known beforehand the reality of walking on the moon?

"How was it, Captain?"

"Awesome, Sir."

"Any ego effects at this point in time you're prepared to report on?"

"Yes Sir. Hunger for love, Sir."

"Well, Captain. [Clears throat.] I'm sure we can scare you up a woman."

"No Sir. My hunger is for the love and respect of my fellow creatures."

Full circle once more, and Martin was kneeling to dump the contents of the Safeway bag.

A car, a Trans-Am sort of thing, had pulled into the

goons' backyard. Gary's girlfriend was at the wheel. It seemed that she was on her way somewhere but had failed to clear this first with Gary. It wasn't that she couldn't go, she could. It was something else. The speakers happened to be silent for a moment and Gary was five feet from the car, so Martin heard what it was.

"Your problem," Gary explained to his girlfriend, "you fuckin' snivel too much. It fuckin' grates on my nerves."

The way she sat there in the driver's seat looking up at Gary, Martin was glad he could not hear her apologizing. And then her head bowed and a metal shriek went up. She'd turned the ignition with the engine idling. That got a big cheer from everybody except Gary, who watched from deep in an aside to a buddy as she backed, goon reckless, into the lane and pulled away with a little wave of her fingers. Gary and his buddy laughed, from the stomach, at something meant to sound dirty, and Gary turned back to his work. Over goon speakers Creedence Clearwater hit the opening chords of "Proud Mary" for the nine trillionth time in the history of the world, on the garage roof the neighbour lady's cat continued to pace, and Martin thought about his dinner last night with Gwen. She'd worn a bottle-green cashmere suit and left with it dusted in ashes. *Clack clack clack clack* went her high heels down the walk to her car.

Gwen was older than Martin by four years, six months, and two days. He knew this because he'd found her by going though the personnel files at work. Gwen was easily the most desirable unattached forty-seven-year-old woman in the company. There was only one thing, and Martin had found it out last night.

Under Gwen's house there lived ten to fifteen skunks. She'd had the City after them, but nothing worked. Skunks are too smart for traps, and you can't poison them because they go back home to die and suddenly your live-skunk smell problem (the spray permeates joists and wallboard and cannot be removed) was nothing. Gwen got Martin to put his face in her purse and sure enough. They were having a drink before dinner, single malt, a fire going in the grate. She was telling him the skunk story, in episodes, like a fantastic, comic outrage against herself. Each episode seemed to be the last, and then there was another, more outrageous. The woman was like a magician, pulling more and more impossible objects from a hat. It was a wall of performance, seamless and hard. She was still at it when Martin's dog walked in, took a look around, whined, sat down, got up, sniffed, howled, and threw itself into the fireplace.

Billows of smoke and ash. With an arm over his face, Martin kept grabbing at the blurs of the dog's legs while Gwen exclaimed and cried out. At last Janey ran in with a big pot of cold water and tossed it on the dog, which scrambled to its feet in a fit of uncontrollable sneezing. As soon as that subsided, it shook the water off, pelt-cracking dog style, everybody springing back, and walked out of the room, stumbling a little on the way from a kick in the ass by Martin, who turned to Gwen and said, "Look, I've been at this a long time. I don't know why it shouldn't be easy by now. I don't know why a person shouldn't be allowed to get back to something they can fucking relate to."

Gwen stayed for the meal, but she was gone right after coffee. Martin did the dishes. Then he put on his winter coat and went out into the backyard.

No stars. Too much light from the goon's backyard floodlights, the light over Martin's own back porch, the light from the dining room, the light from Janey's bedroom, the yellow light of the city sky, and the lights of the back lane. Night was aspiring to day, but it was cold. No goons out back. They had all gone to the bar. One of Gary's admirers had arrived mid-afternoon in the brand-new cab of a sixteen wheeler, now parked, minus rig, right up against the two old pickups, what was left of them, and the new one being born. The monster was silent, candy apple with silver sparkles at various depths, gleaming. It had come from another dimension. It was twice as tall as Martin's garage, half the length of the goons' backyard. It was enormously large, way, way out of scale. Martin stood and looked at it for a long time, and then he went back into the house.

Next day, Sunday, on his roof, squatting with his Safeway bag of trough-patching materials, Martin lifted his eyes to see how the goons' backyard looked in daytime containing the absence of a sixteen-wheeler cab. But the movement of the neighbour lady's cat on his garage roof stopped his eye, and that was when he understood what the animal was doing. Six or seven feet away was a shed roof it wanted to jump to. Would it make it? The cat didn't know. It paced and crackled. Tail switching, it returned again and again to study this problem. The knowledge it needed was more than distance, than relative heights and traction of surfaces, than force and direction of breezes. It was muscles and sinews. It was all the other jumps. Some cats do fall. It was, Exactly how much do I want this thing? It was, When will I want it enough? You focus and focus, you stoke your energy, you're practically out of your mind.

But does it really have to be this way? Look at slime mold. The kid loses interest, things dry out, there's no hesitation—up a tree, a building, up the side of the fridge. At rest in your elevated position you stretch out and wait. A breeze will come, it always does. That music you hear, the backbeat? That's not "Proud Mary," that's the sound of flowers bursting from the surface of your body.

≈

Greg Hollingshead *teaches English literature and creative writing at the University of Alberta. He is the author of two story collections,* Famous Players *(1982) and* White Buick *(1992; winner of the Howard O'Hagan Award for Short Fiction), and a novel,* Spin Dry *(1992; shortlisted for the Smith Books/Books in Canada First Novel Award and winner of the Georges Bugnet Award for the Novel). He is working on a third story collection and a second novel. "Walking on the Moon" was published in* Malahat Review 97.

Two Enormous, Dazzling Statues
(nihil obstat)

CLIFF LOBE

It was impossible to tell where the marble man came from. He might have been burped up to us through the river's primal muck, or floated downstream from upriver somewhere. It was a problem we couldn't solve. But we were sure of the terrestrial shudder he created when he rammed himself into our bridge. The collision set up waves of geological convulsions that spread through the land that we farmed, causing the rich river-flats of our valley to behave like an ocean. For a moment, the knees of our strongest men buckled, our heaviest women couldn't keep their eyeballs from shaking. While our world bounced in and out of focus, we lived in a town that was made up of strangers and filled with the music of shattering plates.

We stumbled together, that morning in June, like drunks on a corduroy map. Our natural reflex was to remember the end, the biblical catastrophes we had read of as children: cataclysms, plagues, apocalyptic horsemen, horrors that would signal the beginning of the end of the world. That was the fate we expected. And our most pious believers were ready, they had been waiting for this sign all their lives. But the rest of us were reluctant. Imminent judgement made our souls edgy, there were too many things we hadn't done yet, too many sins we'd committed then swept under the carpet. So we joked with each other. This was probably an earthquake, a tectonic adjustment. How could the world end, here, on a Thursday? History wasn't that literal.

But the heaves in the centre of town were authentic. They fractured the artificial ice in our new hockey rink. Even the obelisk in front of the First Mennonite Church, polished black, like a coffin, crumbled. The inscriptions it bore were reduced to Scrabble-sized pieces of granite. It was the only real monument we had.

Our streets contracted and expanded, like muscle. There was no place left untouched. Recent leaves twitched and then rained to the ground, as if surrendering, in advance, to inevitable seasons. Young magpies were thrown from one branch to another, while lost engagement rings and spent .22 casings spilled from their nests in the denuded trees. The flowers we grew in our gardens fell apart, they would have to start blooming all over again. Veterans in the Legion Hall saluted each other across tables of tepid beer. "It's the Soviets," they said, "it's their clandestine underground nuclear tests."

Even the gerontological surface of the Home For The Aged was disturbed by the seismic tremors. A few of the ancient inhabitants thought that the vibrations were caused by yesterday's supper of lentils, and they complained about this while they gummed down their Rolaids. In the Sun Room, the tremors caused the record-player to skip, to skip at 11:22, as it played "Shall We Gather At The River." Not one of the listeners got up to coax the needle into the next verse. Some were too old to notice the lurch. Some were just glad for a diversion. The endless repetition stretched the hymn past its regular ending, and for the first time in years Mrs. Harder caught her breath and matched the words in her mouth to the words on the record. The rest of the residents were oblivious. Their ears were filled with cheap hearing aids that were forever breaking down or needing new batteries.

They were difficult to surprise, most of these old folks, accustomed as they were to the alchemy of calendars. "Oh, statues," they said, nodding wisely, as if statues, or angels, were commonplace. They lived in a slow chaos of identical days and nights, far away from their children, and the river that traced through the aluminum-haze of their ancient memories was an innocent channel of blue; if it delivered a marble man, so much the better, the world was an unfinished puzzle. For the rest of us it wasn't that simple. The marble man arrived with the magnitude of Christmas, we still talk about that uncanny shudder. He slammed into the concrete piling under Gabriel's Bridge with an iceberg's invincible blindness. His ribs had the look of a full skin-wrapped cage, not a mortal Homo sapiens' chest. And though he kept his Greek head under water, we could see the root of his Olympian neck, as shiny and thick as a thoroughbred stallion's. But even with his overgrown shoulders and his waist like a funnel, the marble man still looked pathetic. His large wrestler's legs were jammed up into the bridge's steel girders, and he hung there, precariously, like a failed acrobat whose habit of working alone had finally got him into trouble. Of course, there was no question, now, that this out-of-place show-off had finally learned his lesson. The impact had broken off most of his genitals and taken a substantial chunk out of his shin.

It is true that the marble man caught us off guard; he turned up without warning, an unmerited bruise. But the arrival of the marble woman, later that day, astonished our purblind community the most. She gave the whole scene a sense of completion. Even Li Chang (whom we called Sammy) closed the Lucky Dollar and joined us down at the river. There were no clouds in the sky, and the sun was relentlessly bright. But the air smelled like ice, and soon we were surrounded by drizzle. We could see the statues, but it was as if we were looking through bachelor windows. Before long, it was raining large fists of water that punched at our shoulders and occluded the sun. Our town sat under a halo of chromatic rings. By supper-time the fists turned to thin mid-air puddles, and eventually continuous streams. It became impossible to tell where the sky actually ended and the river began. This confused not only us farmers, but the jackfish and sturgeon and mud-coloured suckers that lived in our river. For the first time in their marine lives, the fish swam up through the watery ceiling of their world into a heaven of road signs and barbed wire fences.

The fish were too disappointed to notice the marble woman's contortions, how she slid up the torso of the man and stayed there—parallel—in a shameless, inverted embrace. They were enjoying the new spaces that were unfolding before them, and the strange upright beings standing around them, like piers. The fish had heard rumours about vertical creatures like these, with long bony limbs and ugly digits for fingers, with vertebra spines but with no dorsal fins. Of course, most of these stories were thought to be fables, of sunken-eyed monsters with flesh-ripping pliers. These beings looked benign, or perplexed. Some of them even looked tasty.

The mis-matched lovers were just as oblivious. They held onto each other with naked affection, pressed their bodies together like the ends of an hour. Clinging to each other in pre-marital bliss, they looked a lot like overgrown children. Some of us responded by acting like new parents.

Even in the rain, the gymnastic body of the marble woman made quite an impression. Our fathers' weather-tooled faces reddened. Younger men squinted and held their athletic breath while they imagined the rich mineral taste of her stony cleavage. To be honest, she shocked our male sense of tradition. We were stunned by her poise—undoubtedly urban—and her obvious disrespect for gravity. But even if her behaviour seemed like an insult, we had to admit she was by far the most beautiful creature we'd ever seen naked. She was the purest thing to float down the river in years.

Although the river had once been clean, no one dared to swim in it now; it was out of the question to fish. The only bodies that turned up in the water were dead ones—soft soggy corpses that hung up on the piling and fell apart like reheated oatmeal when they were rescued. The river had turned into a defiled topographical artery, a petrochemical ditch. In fact, it could hardly be called a river at all, except perhaps in nostalgic revision (and that talent was almost extinct). For most of us, the river was an industrial conduit, filled with pestilential liquids, a contaminated place to avoid. It was the fault of the cities upstream. They cared less for the water than their own stinking urine. They flushed their neat toilets into invisible sewers, sending us their turds and their unwanted pets. As children, we made games out of classifying their effluent: torn jackets, used rubbers, flat bicycle tires, the occasional Harlequin romance. We compared the decadence the city folks practiced to what we knew about Sodom and Gomorrah.

It was a mess, our poisoned river, as professors on the CBC reminded us each week. So of course we were twice as surprised when the statues arrived. They didn't look filthy or malignant. They seemed unconcerned about the invisible carcinogens leeching into their skin, or the hundred diseases that the river incubated. In fact, they composed the picture of health, which made us all the more anxious to rescue them quickly. How long could they last in that corrosive solution? How long before they would grow weak and let go, only to float downstream and be claimed by the next major city? Our estimates ranged from an hour to a week, but most of us bet that they'd drop off by nightfall.

So we kept a close vigil that evening, above the unearthly couple whose immortal contortions no one dared to explain. Families piled into their new station wagons. The Vietnamese refugees we sponsored came down to the bridge on their bicycles. Even pedestrian bachelors turned up. Suppers cooled and chores went undone on the farms that surrounded our town. Our valley was filled with the complaints of hungry roosters and unmilked Holsteins.

And as the municipality assembled, the garbage in the river began to clot around the statues. All manner of junk collected: old fence posts and warped shiplap boards, a worn-out hide-away-bed. By this time, the rain was beginning to let up, stranding fish on the road or in the eavestroughs of our houses. We could just make out the moon overhead, but our eyes were hardly reliable. We saw huge bulging outlines creeping up to the statues, or thin slimy snakes, shapes that rightly belonged in our nightmares. Before long, the debris would clog the river and we'd be up to our necks in a flood. Sid, the Twenty-Four-Hour Wrecker, was called in that night, to untangle the mess with his new one-ton tow-truck.

It was dawn when Sid got down to the bridge, and two hours went by before he realized the statues were heavy. Sid pulled at the levers and adjusted the hydraulic valves on his tow-truck with a neurosurgeon's dexterity. But when Sid finally set his grapple-hook under the woman's armpit and sturdy left breast, nothing much happened. Not even when he revved up his engine. Her mass was too much for Sid and his eighth-grade calculations. Before she would budge, Sid's tow-truck would flip. Humiliated, Sid released his cable and gummed out a string of curses which no one on the bridge could translate.

It wasn't Sid's fault, or a flaw in his winch. The lovers simply didn't want to let go. Sid wanted to explain that to the crowd on the bridge, but he had been missing his tongue since the day he turned six. On a January morning, in 1967, Sid licked the school's wrought-iron flag pole. Thermometers, that day, could only be measured against Kelvin's Absolute Zero; the Fahrenheit and Celsius mercury had disappeared. Sid was left with a nub of scar-tissue at the top of his throat that wobbled when he wanted to speak. What came out of his mouth were guttural sounds—misshapen vowels and half-frozen syllables. Sid heard these as perfectly elegant words; we heard a village idiot.

The deformity Sid suffered on that patriotic birthday turned his life into a perpetual misunderstanding. He became as grotesque as his sea lions' language. But we loved him as much as we hated his sounds, and we pitied his luck at the same time that we feared him. He helped us to forget our own slight imperfections. When we asked Sid questions, we laughed on the spot, and we aped his responses when he wasn't looking. We behaved as if Sid had frozen his ears off too, along with his primitive feelings. Of course, we didn't laugh at Sid's curses that Friday morning, even if they spilled out of his mouth like linguistic dumplings. We were too busy waiting for the rain to quit, and swatting at nibbling fish.

When the rain stopped falling, later that day, our intestines were empty and grumbling. We'd been down at the river for a day and a half, and in the excitement we'd neglected to eat. More than half of us smelled like fishermen. Instinctively, we gulped down the smell of the just rinsed-out world, as if that would fill our stomachs. We argued: why stay out here, catch our deaths? If the statues were nothing but the wreckage of some solstitial parade, forget them. We'd look pretty funny written up in the papers, all worked up about nothing but junk. But our wives and our mothers brought us thermoses of coffee and yesterday's kommst borscht, and two-inch-thick slices of bread. We ate in the darkness without table manners; we feasted like ravenous prisoners. The food helped to allay our osmotic doubts, and when the sun we had all but forgotten reappeared we dried out our water-logged bones. Gladly, we resumed our vigil.

Not one of us could interpret the statues. Were they delivered to us by a spasm of nature? or by divine intervention? They were a sign that could have meant anything. We wanted to share our summer with these cosmopolitan strangers. So we quit thinking narrow thoughts about curling or fastball, we even curtailed our interest in the Stanley Cup play-offs. Instead, we turned our attention to our new cultural centre, the one that the Women's Auxiliary had been quietly planning for years. It would house a museum, an art shoppe, and a Victorian tea house, to begin with, and sell crafts to rich travellers from the city who were convinced that anything purchased in the country was antique. We thought of the crops we'd just seeded, with the threads of our dreams tangled up in their roots, and the softball we would normally play while we waited for harvest. We planned an incredible rescue.

We would need a crane from the city to untangle the lithic couple, a crane and a thick wire-rope cable. But that would cost money, and the town had no budget to speak of for art. That was when we decided to hold a non-profit marathon bingo. We bolted a chain to the bridge and wound it around the two lovers; we wanted them to stay put. For a week of nicotine days and nights, we jammed ourselves into the Legion Hall, where we learned how to gamble. We sent prayers up in clouds of cigarette smoke, begging that no one would win.

Eight days after the marble man hit the bridge, we returned to the river with a crane we had hired for two hundred dollars an hour. Sid was annoyed at the size of the thing, to him it was only a jacked-up tow-truck. He was sure his unit could match that city contraption if he burned a new high-octane fuel, if we gave him just one more chance. But the crane freed the statues without a mechanical hiccup.

When we saw the bleached bodies up close, they were lying in state on two flat-bed trailers. It was the first chance we had to touch them. We filed past them in funereal style, but none of us felt we were mourning. It was as if we had witnessed the birth of two royal people, possessed of superior virtue. Their bodies were perfect: ancient, solid, and bright. So bright that we couldn't stop blinking. The two elegant strangers commanded respect, even if their faces displayed some disinterest. No doubt they were weary from centuries of travel, or a long-suffered cosmic jet-lag, it's hard to be certain with statues. What we really wanted to do most was wake them up and ask questions: about where they were from and the places they'd seen, information they kept stored inside them.

We imagined what their mountainous voices would sound like, but the answers would have to wait. There were complex new problems that we had to solve. What would we do with such unadorned objects? Where should the statues go next?

We probably would have argued about it for weeks, trading insults and caustic remarks with our neighbours, if the minister of culture from the capital city hadn't showed up. He insisted, from the half-open window of his Cadillac limousine, that the statues belonged to the province. He cited a Maritime Salvaging Act to prove it. To strengthen his case, he'd brought the attorney general along, and a curator from the Provincial Art Gallery. It was the curator who stepped out of the car and began to read us a speech. He encouraged us to think of ourselves as patrons, as beneficent rural aesthetes. He called the statues *objets d'art*, and he cited our town as a place of great vision. He promised to reimburse us for all of our troubles.

It was a speech we had heard in a thousand variations. Most of us drove rust-eaten vehicles. If we bought art, it came in the mail from Sears' Catalogue. Quite simply, these civil servants annoyed us. We had gambled for a week to get the lovers extracted, for some at great moral expense. We were tired of the city getting everything. We said as much to the minister.

We rocked his great car, the way they do in televised revolutions. If he thought he was going to take anything away, he was greatly—and gravely—mistaken.

The curator continued his lecture; he addressed us as if we were children. We were incensed by his mellifluous words, they had too many syllables to trust. We heard enough sermons like this on Sundays. So we began, systematically, to abuse his logic. Over-taxed farmers snorted and booed in disgust. For years they'd squirmed under debts owed to banks from the city. "People in suits like you fuck up the world," we shouted, shocked at our own filthy language. Hired hands joined to express their contempt: "Boars will grow tits before we own our own places; your taxes and lawyers keep us oppressed!" Boldness and solidarity beamed from our faces. We shouted: "How stupid do you think we can possibly be?" The curator said nothing. He was up against decades of distrust, not to mention generations who were tired of aesthetic condescension. "Go back to the city," we hollered together, collecting our rustic outrage, "and keep your cushy artistic development grants. We do honest work here, we know how to grow things! Beat it you pompous magpies! You incredibly stupid vultures! Do us a favour, go back to your mental art gallery and stay there, keep your lily-white hands in your own pants! Art is for faggots. Sculpture is for unemployed welders."

Such was the passion we felt. It is likely we would have tied up that trio of over-paid civil servants and sent them downstream. But Siemens, our mayor, prevailed. He knew how to speak the discourse of cities; he'd been born in the East himself. But that was a far as his urbanity went. Years ago he'd bought a barn full of hogs, at a time when the world still enjoyed bacon. By now, there was no way to tell that he was once urban, except for the traces of some former habits—like using a Kleenex when his nose needed blowing, or refusing to spit when ladies were present—but even these habits became weaker each year. He was as much a farmer as any of us.

It was during the time that the statues arrived that Siemens was trying to retire. He had sold his farm and bought a house at the edge of our town, where he was trying to teach himself to do nothing. "The problem," he said, "is that I only know how to work. I am unable to quit, or do anything else. A hobby is nothing but work that doesn't earn money."

It was a problem that plagued most old Protestants in our area. Even though Siemens had sold off his quota for pork, the hog-smell of his past on his skin drove him crazy, crippling him with pangs of pungent nostalgia. But he had a community college degree, and he knew *Robert's Rules of Order* precisely (he used them to raise his twelve children). So when Schlegel, our mayor, died of cancer, we asked Siemens to run for election.

It was a perfect arrangement. We respected that erstwhile farmer, whose success with hogs was impressive. And everyone knows that a town should be run by a man who knows how to make money, with savings and a decent RRSP. And Siemens made the transition easily. "A town full of folks is no different than a barn full of swine," he declared on the night that he was campaigning. "That is what I have come to believe. Each has its appetites, each has its needs. People are simply pigs who can think."

The statues were Siemens' first civic test. Crowds excited him in a way that the fattest sow couldn't. A sow might be loyal, but people know how to believe. "Of the people, for the people, by the people!" Siemens proclaimed, "though not necessarily in that order." Then he scrambled up onto the trailers, and then onto the abdomen of the prostrate marble woman. "These remarkable statues belong in the centre of town! Of that I am perfectly clear. The people have spoken. Why else would the statues stop at our bridge in the first place? Does anyone need to rebut?"

The first thing we needed to find was a pedestal. The Masons drew up an elaborate blueprint, with florid rococo chisel-work and deep bas-relief, but not one of them knew how to cut stone any longer. As a guild, the Masons were useless. While the Masons accused one another of being unworthy, the Knights of Columbus purchased an old granite base from the Department of Warfare. The base had once held up an Unknown Soldier in the capital city, in front of the Parliament buildings. But the cenotaph had been knocked over years ago by a back-hoe operator who'd lost one eye in the war and stayed drunk to correct his perception. We hauled in the base and levelled it at the gate to the Jubilee Cemetery, across the street from Centennial Park. We recalled the crane for Erection Day.

Not all of our citizens were happy. There was room on the base for the man and the woman, which made the Mennonites worry. "Would the statues be standing together? If they did, would they touch? And why did they have to be naked?" A delegation of Mennonite elders complained to the mayor: "This kind of art sure isn't Christian, there is something pagan about these graven images! Idolatry just isn't biblical!"

The Mennonites didn't approve of the project, and they made up most of the town. But they didn't run everything, even if they were all related. The Uniteds, the Lutherans, and all of the Catholics lacked such puritan fears. The Hutterites who lived on the other side of the river shook their heads as they drove by in their grain trucks, hurrying back to their colony. The statues would revive the town's sagging image, maybe stop the bleed of young people into the cities. It had very little to do with religion. Maybe the supernatural mass of the statues would encourage tourists to stop in, and that would mean jobs and external revenue. Perhaps, in the future, there could be a shrine, and a service station which sold humanist paraphernalia. At some point, our town might become a holy place just off the highway, for the world's richest and sickest pilgrims.

We celebrated the day that the statues went up with a parade and a come-and-go picnic. We thought of the statues as our non-biological ancestors, as harbingers of wealth and success, and we placed them with pride in the centre of town. We fastened ribbons to their heads, which our children wove into a colourful shroud that encompassed, for the moment, our life-like May Poles.

Since the Catholics had grown up with icons, they approved of the statues from the beginning. The marble lovers brought a classical feeling to the area, a feeling that had always been missing. But after a week, there were complaints. The Catholics didn't like the location. The statues cast long shadows across the graveyard at sunrise, which offended the Catholic dead who faced east, waiting for resurrection. "Our faithful parishioners deserve more than a shadow," said the Catholics, and they wrote letters complaining about this to the archbishop. But the Mennonites, with their majority voice, were generally unsympathetic. They made up jokes about dwarfs and apostolic midgets, in their practical Low German accents. The couple made the crosses and Virgins on the Catholics' headstones look like puny and amateur fakes. The Catholics would have to adjust.

By this time we quit trying to figure out where the statues had come from, and turned our thoughts to finding them suitable names. The names "Adam" and "Eve" were out of the question, though a biblical aura surrounded the couple, despite the fact they were naked. "Isaac Bourne" was a popular suggestion. He was the township's first homesteader, a Russian Mennonite who had arrived more than a century ago with a two-bottom plow and a sack of seed-wheat. Though we owed our existence to that patriarch's migration, we couldn't remember the name of his wife. Some thought that her name was Rebekah. Others thought it was Esther or Rachel or Hannah or Sarah. The debate would have extended into the New Testament if Alderman Fast hadn't produced a hospital ledger of polio victims that proved her name to be Lucy—the first of six wives that Isaac outlived. The matter was tabled until the fall plebiscite.

We took to the large white rock bodies immediately, they really didn't need names. We saw ourselves in their unblemished faces, in their permanent limbs born of stone and bleached clean by aeons of sun. In fact, we were so pleased with our new monument that we began to feel cleaner and bigger, pleasantly full of ourselves. We moved quicker, with confidence, and we spoke with meticulous diction. Each saw the statues carved in his own perfect image. We no longer bothered to consult the mirrors in our houses. Some said that they felt at least ten years younger, or that their postures began to improve after years of neglect and the attrition of gravity. Hypochondriacs (and our town had more than its share) claimed to feel organs growing in holes left by old surgeries: new appendixes, kidneys, and spleens. But as we all generated cathartic bodies, not one of us noticed how fast things in the fields of the township were growing, turning an obscene and wonderful green, even though it hadn't rained since the day that the marble woman turned up.

It was old Blind Martens who said: "Things feel green, but I haven't smelled rain. It's high time for precipitation."

Blind Martens sat out his life on the Anglican pew in front of the Wheat Pool Hall, sniffing at history as it twisted and looped past his useless blue eyes. The old man had been there so long he knew all our genealogical odours. He greeted the pool-sharks who reeked of snooker; he sorted out travellers who waited for buses, and wished each one of them a safe journey. If he was in an especially good mood, he'd call to blushing young lovers on their way to the post office: "Check your postage, young lady, it smells like you're two-cents short. Don't forget that stamps went up a cent in April."

For the first time in his life, Blind Martens' venerable sense couldn't help him. He'd heard all about the marble people, he even claimed that a cold flinty weight had flattened the air the day the statues arrived. Martens debated going to touch them himself, and he tried to explain to himself the logic of miracles. In the end, he was too old to waste energy on frivolous hope. "What's with all this fuss, with these stony colossi? Ach, it all to me smells so unnatural! Can they really make blind people see?" Waving the cane that grew out of his palm, he wheezed: "I am old, what good will eyes be? What's left that I need to see?"

Not much, we were sure. Martens was finished. We were no longer interested in his Germanic mumblings. He was hardly a seer, maybe just a good guesser. And we were tired of his short-sighted, Prussian nose. If we listened to him now it was mere toleration, the charitable habits of a town full of Christians. We speculated that Martens had finally gone crazy, that his life had turned into his death. In fact, rumours went around that Martens' arse had turned into petrified wood, that his brain was cottage cheese. He belonged in an intensive care unit, not sitting outside on a bench. His body was so decrepit it was beginning to stink up our streets, to fill the rooms of our houses with a hospital smell—the reek of stale urine and sour, fouled sheets. While everything else in our world was replenished, we choked on the stench of his decaying body. Schoolboys crept up beside him and poked him with sticks, or made fart noises by sticking their hands in their armpits. It was clear that Martens was a victim of life. He could no longer move his own ancestral bowels, and he barely knew how to breathe anymore.

It was Balzer, the agent for Imperial Oil, who connected the statues and the green crops and the rain that was late. He studied the weather charts in *The Western Producer*. He marked the day the statues were found. "I don't believe it," he told his wife, "but it's right here on paper. Just look, I've based my theory on triangulation."

The revelation of Imperial Oil's agent filled the cafe with opinions. The waitresses poured coffee until all four of their wrists ached. The unemployed continued to complain, while they sipped coffee and blamed everyone but themselves and the statues for their unemployable state. The Monthly Ecumenical Society called an emergency meeting in the non-smoker's Green Room. "The statues are powerful," Pastor Janz informed the group, "of that there is no question. But what do they mean? Why are they here? Who could possibly have sent them?"

The society had no answers. Pastor Janz was vexed. After a long phlegmatic silence, the most recent addition to the group spoke up. The monotone voice of Chief Trumpet Bugler filled the Golden Valley Cafe. "They did not come from Ottawa," he said, "which is something, though they still may be subject to surtaxes." We nodded our heads at this incontrovertible wisdom.

Not Janz nor the ecumenical leaders nor the biology teacher at the high school could explain the way things were growing. It was hard to believe that Imperial Oil's man Balzer could be an expert on weather and art. It was his job to sell fertilizer or herbicide or anhydrous ammonia, to force crops to increase. Even on Sundays his hands reeked of leaded gasoline, and pellets of granular fertilizer fell out of his ears when he bowed his head to hear the benediction. He was too local to know anything about classical sculpture, much less organic chemistry.

In the end, none of that really mattered. Our farmers were happy, spending the money that was growing in their fields. They were busy imagining themselves in new John Deere tractors, in combines with air-conditioned cabs. Their crops were filling out so well they would each need a dozen new grain bins by fall. Even the ditches that separated their fields were filled with the sounds of this wonderful growing—a low-pitched echo that sounded a lot like a choir of Gregorian angels, or a five-speed transmission jammed in reverse.

The economy in the township over-heated. It was a time of cooperation and conceivable plenty. Only Travel Agent Dirks and the Funeral Friesens found that they weren't doing any business, and they talked about amalgamation. We lived with one foot in a prosperous future, one foot in an exotic present. But as our barley lodged under its own fertile weight, and as our canola flowered, turning the air sticky and yellow, six Bergthalers and six Mennonite Brethren began a fast to protest the odious surplus. They sat and joined hands at the base of the statues, feeling proud of their stern, skinny bodies. At the feet of the full-bodied marvels, the fasters looked more like twelve living corpses, twelve frustrated Caucasian Buddhas. As the sun set that evening, sliding down the horizon like a mandarin disc on a seamless, stained-glass blue dusk, somebody saw tears the size of potatoes roll down the cheeks of the couple and land in pillows of dust.

But the boycott was fruitless: schoolboys threw rotten apples at the fasters, interrupting their meditative vigil; schoolgirls hurled precisely metred abuses at the dissenters, in the form of hopscotch rhymes. The fasters were simply an eyesore, a blight on the progressive and prosperous image our town was projecting. There was no question that they would scare off the tourists. So the RCMP intervened at dawn on Day Three, instructing the fasters to go home to their families. While the fasters shook dew out of their ears and wailed like newly-wed widows, they prostrated themselves on the wet morning grass. They shouted out socialist slogans, and prophetic threats about sin-weakened flesh. The Mounted Police had no choice but to arrest all twelve malcontent men and stack them up in their cruisers, like a shipment of frozen beef tongues.

If anything, the fast was a religious disaster. We were embarrassed by our self-righteous neighbours. The district was blanketed by a primal fog of contentment, vaster than any of us could remember. Age-old grudges were being dissolved with hand-shakes on our main street, and even the paint on our buildings looked brighter each day. Our neighbours no longer annoyed us. Before long, we forgot that our town had ever been run down. We lived, for that time, inside an ecological prism. Crocuses bloomed in the cracks of our sidewalks, in oranges and reds as continuous as lipstick. Leaves duplicated themselves every couple of hours, and hung on the trees like wet tropical laundry. The marriage counsellor gave up his part-time job at the abattoir, to cover the backlog of couples deciding to marry. Nurses scrambled at the medical clinic, scheduling new pre-natal classes every Monday evening. We slept out of habit, not because we were tired. Each new morning had the rhythm of a long paid vacation.

Sister Keehn from Our Lady of Perpetual Repression was the first to notice that the marble man's organ was growing, about a centimetre and a half, each day. She had been warned about this kind of behaviour at the convent. When she was sure this not merely some autogenous replacement, she alerted the mayor about the development. By this time it was clear this was a marble erection, curving away from the statue like a perverted rainbow. The town council was racked by paroxysms of worry.

Respectable women feigned disgust when they heard of the problem, but peeked through curtains and shutters while they mashed potatoes for supper. "What a delicious young body," they said to themselves, slamming the doors of their cupboards. They thought about the wide shoulders their husbands once had, and the flat hairy bellies that time had mulched into the soft flesh of over-ripe pears. As hard as they tried, they couldn't remember why they had married these scrubby, small men, these degenerate bulges of skin.

Girls, on the other hand, dreamed, while they polished the silverware and pianos they would one day inherit. Where on earth (except perhaps in the potash mines of the south), would they find a man like that to marry? A man of such obvious density. The boys they would wed drove hopped-up Chevrolet pick-ups with chromed exhaust pipes. They had dirty fingernails and almost no buttocks, and were trapped inside contracted vocabularies. For the kind of potential the girls saw in the statues, they knew they had no choice but to travel.

The cemetery became the most beautiful place. Mothers and daughters spent entire afternoons strolling among graves, carrying rakes and hedge-clippers and canisters of weed-killer. They happily tended the plots of atheist strangers, or third cousins who had been forgotten three or four times. Mothers and daughters worked gladly together, in a productive feminine solidarity. They brought lunches in baskets, picked at low-calorie salads, while they kept an eye on the statue's immodest development.

There was nothing left for the men of the town to do but grumble. We felt offended, not to mention inadequate and shiftless and cruel.

Only young children and the oldest widows could afford to be amused. They hung streamers and colourful ribbons from the organ; they wove wreaths out of dandelion and sinuous brome grass. The most brave and ambitious children climbed the statue, as if he were a common playground apparatus.

In a few days our aldermen had had enough. The mayor called the town council together for an emergency plenary session.

The Mennonites insisted the town break up the statues and bury them. They didn't belong above ground, we'd seen enough smut already. The Catholics suggested a loin cloth of canvas, but birth-control was out of the question. The coach of the hockey club thought something athletic would work, and he sketched plans for a jock-strap of Kevlar. The fire chief proposed an artesian well-water shower. While the aldermen deliberated, the marble woman turned her hips slightly. Her nipples and lips bloomed corpulent red. The statues were imperceptibly swivelling toward one another, before long they would be touching.

It was a cataclysm of shame. A pornographic re-play of the Original Sin.

The Catholics covered the eyes of the Blessed Virgins and Fathers in the cemetery with toques. The Mennonites threatened to exhume their dead and start their own cemetery. They wanted nothing to do with this pageant of flagrant carnality. Dukhobors danced in the streets. As the aldermen hardened their hearts in anticipation, the RCMP cordoned the area. The Catholics opened their confessional to everyone. It was only a matter of hours before the igneous lovers would end their subtle foreplay, and maneuver themselves into some coital position up on the pedestal. That was all that we needed, statues coupling like beasts of the field.

Enough was enough. The voluptuous choreography could bring nothing but trouble. It was obvious the statues knew way too much. As we concealed our fraternal embarrassment, the marble man showed no signs of restraint. He slipped his left hand onto his partner's unaging buttocks. The next day he began tracing the geometry of her neck and her shoulders and the grid of her torso with his own, realistic fingers. There was no end in sight to the ductile appendage.

"This behavior is unedifying, selfish, corrupt," the mayor declared, "they've got to come down. Let's forget that we've ever seen them."

The crane returned and pulled the lovers apart like bad children. But not before we scrubbed the red off the marble woman with industrial strength Dutch Cleanser. Then the mayor ceremoniously knocked the offensive member off the marble man with a nine-pound fencing sledge-hammer. It took the once robust ex-pig farmer several whacks, and he ended up with a blister. The statues were hauled to the dump north of town and cast among the rusted refrigerators and empty pesticide drums.

That night an infectious white light lit up the sky over the dump. The light illuminated the garbage, making the dump look as clean as a novice priest's collar. Filthy nocturnal rats were forced out from under the refuse. They left in a disorderly exodus, blindly winding their way to nearby haystacks or granaries. Coyotes howled at what they took to be aurora borealis, while they feasted on disoriented rats. Dogs barked at the coyotes. A galaxy of moths swirled over the dump, deafening the families who lived nearby.

The Union Hospital filled. Once again, people felt they had always been sick. A myriad of cancers and ulcers and the ugliest rashes began to grow in and on their indecent bodies. Women who thought they were pregnant realized that their stomachs were full of misbegotten dreams, that their bodies had become swollen with lust and the saccharin taste of imprudent desire. Men remembered their bulbous pot-bellies, and the metallic odour of chronic bad breath crept back up into their teeth. Most people blamed the statues, it was obvious that they were guilty. Some might have toyed with the idea of keeping them, but they couldn't come out and say it. The town didn't appreciate perversity. We had no place for that sort of naked fornication.

So it went. Our town gave up its wonderful colours, faded each day like an unread newspaper. Our faces grew tight and wasted. Instead of laughing at Sid, or inviting him to dinner, we kicked and we punched him when we passed him on the streets. Farmers were ashamed of the size of their crops, and their premature spending on credit, but they still kept one eye on the clouds while they secretly prayed for continuing good weather. We'd never seen a bumper crop like this before; we expected the harvest of harvests.

But the light from the dump continued to shine, and no thunderheads boiled on the horizon. The sky stayed full of an opulent light—day and night—and it remained that way for most of a month. We found ourselves longing for a week of deep shadows, for an extended solar eclipse. In vain, we tried to remember the black grain of darkness; we wore hats with large Spanish brims. But even with our eyes closed, our heads were full of annoying spot-lights—stars that refused to stay buried. Before long, flowers began to grow in the dump's abused ditches. Grass-blades shot up in ground that had been saturated by used motor-oil. Roses and lady slippers and fragrant lily of the valley took root in old washing-machines. In no time, birds of all countries arrived and began to build permanent nests. The dump was becoming a recycled garden.

It was the Mennonites who came up with the idea to put the statues back in the river. The brilliant dump was a blight on the entire township, not to mention a source of temptation. It would only be a matter of time before someone reconsidered and tried to rescue the pair. Then what? Go through this abomination again? The Old Testament showed clearly enough that people can't resist the lure of prosperity, and they never learn from their mistakes. Of course, as the Mennonites had warned us when the statues were standing, people can't live with prosperity either.

When the statues were pulled from the pit, they were as clean as the day they were found. Perhaps they were even cleaner. At the river, most of the same people who witnessed the arrival of the statues were present. It was a dull and hot day, with no rain in sight, and the air was completely worn out. It had been breathed too many times. Most of the town was happy, glad to see the last of the promiscuous sculptures. But some were quiet as the crane-hand fashioned a cable noose with the precision of a skilled executioner. As the first statue was suspended out over the water, a few people (mostly our teachers) whispered their liberal complaints. "It was only an erection," they muttered to each other, "and that's hardly new, no reason to get bent out of shape." But most of the town agreed: "This is best, we don't need our noses rubbed in that . . . thing!" they said, "It's disgusting," angling their heads in the direction of the truncated organ.

At a signal from the crane-hand the marble man dropped into the water and disappeared, hitting the bottom of the river with a thud that shook the plank deck of the bridge. The falling statue shattered the still surface of the river, breaking its surface into a thousand pieces of malleable mirror that distorted the reflections of our faces, then smoothed themselves back into one molten plane. His descent startled the fish who slept in the riverbed muck, including arthritic sturgeon who hadn't been angled for two hundred years. The fish were still dreaming of the things they had seen on the day that they swam up into heaven.

The aftershocks spread out into our valley, in trivial, expanding circles. When the tremours reached the Home For The Aged, they jarred the stylus in the Sun Room loose, bumping it into the final Amen of "Shall We Gather At The River." "It's about time," the old people cried in relief, "We're sick of that hollowed-out record."

The marble woman followed, creating her own epicentre. She disappeared, and the river closed over her head, like an oily, adhesive solvent. Only then did the town feel vindicated. Only then did we begin to feel safe. As we watched for signs that the statues would re-surface, we coughed forgotten summer dust up out of our lungs. We noticed the polluted water was becoming quite blue, a colour that made us all thirsty.

～

Cliff Lobe, like many Albertans, was born in Saskatchewan, on a farm near Thirteen-Mile Corner. He has published one other short story, in Grain, *and currently lives in Edmonton, where he is working on a Ph.D. in English at the University of Alberta.*

And the Heart
Pauses for Breath

CLAIRE HARRIS

Blood. Circles. Hatched in old thunder. Sinews. Names.
Lines. Charged, linked by terrifying energy. And converging.
Try to spit on such a space, even in another landscape, the spit
blows back through the hole in your face. In spite of northern
pines. A white geometry. New tongue. *Que sera, sera.* . . .
   Stop it. STOP IT.
   Here in Calgary she has lost Aunt Camille, *admit it,
child,* misplaced her as one misplaces a tune. All these words,
like fleas in the air, will not hinder, reverse her going, *say it,
Girl,* her *death.* If she pays real attention she can slice the
silences as thin as Camille's. Delicate brown onion circlets
to decorate the pork before she stores it in the deep freeze.
Careful, watch your fingers. Up through down up
through . . . an earthquake, deathlight, aftershocks, the ground
refusing to settle. She clutches at the counter. A faded
Camille dissolves, wavers in the garden house her brother
designed for his bride from China. He had drawn from a
sketch. Crouched over a book in the high-ceilinged Victorian
Public Library of Trinidad and Tobago, not knowing that he
had chosen a Thai spirit house, seeing only a fairy, feathery
green delicacy so like his woman.

Sulyn slips the onions onto a saucer, adds sliced garlic, a few cloves, walks over to the counter. Now if she does not remember every curve, wrinkle, wry twist, Aunt will not come. To her left a wide window frames a view as northern as precise as a Harris. Strange how familiar all the names are. Fool you into thinking you're speaking the same language, living in the same society.

She begins to remove slices of lemon from slits she has made in the picnic butt; it is enough for two meals, and there'll be lots of crackling. Rob loves crackling. Sonny loves everything Rob loves. At the moment. The girls will slice off skin/fat and weigh themselves in the morning. She smiles imagining what Aunt would say. She sticks cloves into slits, drains off all but a teaspoon of marinade, pours on two capfuls of rum. Everything she does, she does as Camille had done. This necessary precision to keep her to the sweet harshness of the path she must walk. As if she were in a tropical kitchen, she brushes a damp strand of hair off her forehead with a wrist. *A sprinkle of sugar in everything salt; a sprinkle of salt in everything sweet. That's reality, Su-child; reality!* There is no time to make a prune sauce. She takes sixteen prunes out of Towne plastic, makes a circle around the roast. *What goes round comes round* . . . lemon juice, sugar, cinnamon. *Watch yourself!*

She watched herself. Yessirree! Under grieving roofs, they smile often at their naïveté. She and Robert. Neither had dreamt, come near to dreaming how much it took, so much energy to avoid erosion of the self in Peking eyes, Ashanti cheekbones. Now under careless capes of snow stitched with sunlight, their linked fluent African stride moves against mountains.

And once again, nothing is like itself. Or even as she had imagined it to be. She covers the dish with tin foil, pops it into the oven. Three down, one to go. Moving towards the cubed lamb, her hands pause in the act of tipping marinade into the sink, frozen, listening. She stands at the window hearing her silence flow through nails, knuckles, bone. She'd thought, at first, that the house was too noisy, that when Rob left taking the children with him, Aunt Camille would come. It does not seem possible that she can simply leave. Without a sign. The last word has always been her prerogative; why should she change now? Perhaps the whisper of the radio is too much. She takes the lamb with her to the island, reaches up to turn off "The Homestretch." Surely this is quiet enough.

Two years ago over these same pots in a shady grey kitchen, stone floors giving onto verandahs which in turn give onto inch-cropped grass dotted with timarie, starred with tiny yellow, blue flowers disappearing under a belt of banana trees. She and Camille . . . her proud boast that she had never slapped you. As if she'd had to. Tongue like a cokiyea whip.

Absentmindedly she pours two cups of dried coconut into the blender, adds a cup of water, sticks the lot onto liquefy and waits over the opened earth. She sees the first thin earth-splatter crush the blood-red, the white anthurium. Then the dull thud of stones against wood. The coffin jerks, stops its descent, starts again. Cracking voices bounce against casuarinas in the last hymn. The blender peaks into a scream of protest. She startles, switches it off, stands with her hand on the jar, wanting. Anything. Any thing. Eons ago, the pain, the childish pleasure of the long silence. Her own silence, Camille's, echoing back, forth, back and forth across the Caribbean. Till six weeks ago.

KITCHEN—LATE AFTERNOON

A small boy, Sonny, sits at the breakfast bar driving a racing car in tighter and tighter circles. Sulyn stands in the door of the laundry room folding clothes. The phone rings.

> SONNY
>
> I'll get it.
>
> SULYN
>
> Leave it alone!
>
> SONNY
>
> Mommy!
>
> MESSAGE
>
> (A MAN'S VOICE) No one is available to take your call at the moment. Please leave a message after the beep. Thank you.
>
> CAMILLE
>
> So is how it is all you never home? I can't stand talking to machine. . . .

Sulyn darts across the room, grabs the receiver.

> SULYN
>
> Aunt . . . Auntie . . . I'm so glad to hear your voice.
>
> CAMILLE
>
> If you so glad is why you not available? Put Sonny on for me please. . . .

SULYN

Aunt . . . the machine is not for you. . . .

CAMILLE

You throw net for sprat an' you catch shark. Put
Sonny on for me please.

Sulyn shrugs, hands Sonny the phone.

SONNY

Grantie we have it to catch the
boys . . . yeah . . . yeah . . . no . . . no . . . call us
names an' say Klu Klux Klan coming. . . .

Sulyn grabs the phone whispering "please" to Sonny.

SULYN

Aunt is nothing to take serious. . . .

CAMILLE

But is why you can't let the child talk to me? You
afraid he tell me what really going on? If you want
to talk why you don't phone?

~

She wants to talk; she wants Camille to come. She pours off
the bacon fat, adds garlic, onions, two heaping tablespoons of
curry powder. All exactly as Camille would have done.
Perhaps now. . . . Now it will have to burn just a little, or
rather she will get to it just before it burns. She adds a dry
pepper. But she is too restless, her longing too great. She
can't wait for the sharp sizzle and tang that means the curry

is ready. In truth not even Meilyn's palate will notice the difference. Not any more. She's a fast-food girl now. When she isn't trying to shed Ashanti hips. Her mouth twists into Camille's wry smile. She dumps the lamb into pots, taking care to measure equal halves then coconut milk, thyme, onions. Moving almost frantically she covers both pots, turns the stove to simmer, wipes her hands.

Dammit it's not all her fault.

The cool Camille-taunt delivered evenly with a sure-ness born of the nursery. Her own swelling rage finding the first, the deadliest weapon: Please remember, you're only my father's maiden sister. Drowning, she rushes to the book-rack, the Bible she has placed where it infringes only on the corner of an eye. A cable marks the "De Profoundis." She holds the thin sheet between square hands the colour of brown onion skins. Hesitating, she taps the telegram against the counter, then because she must, opens it again.

Sympathy 15635 Camille heart attack. Funeral 21430 Sacred Heart. Come. Nila.

Because some words are impossible, their timing all wrong. Because *words like skin teeth; not every skin teeth is smile.* An undefined doubt rises in her gorge. Camille would not do this! As if she can thrust through rock, across thousand mile prairie, woods, water, wrinkled Atlantic to the house with bright ixora hedges, its deep avocado trees shading the quiet street in Trinidad, she stares through her kitchen windows. Unconscious of sparse Alberta grass, of Sonny's cart, Joni's flipflops emerging from weary snow, she tries to call beyond the thin line of life. Once she trained herself to proud skepticism, insisted on the walk under heavy breadfruit trees to the boys' college for Rob, chemistry, the wintry logic of numbers, physics. Now every muscle strains towards the spirit house.

LIVING ROOM OF ISLAND HOUSE—NIGHT

Two small matching suitcases, one scuffed black leather, the other newish matching green stand in a corner, packed, waiting.

> CAMILLE
> I don't understand what you think it have there, you can't find here!
> SULYN
> You don't get tired of people knowing your business? This whole place like some village.
> CAMILLE
> Robert, I hope you understand all society is village society. People don't live isolate. It don't matter where you live in the world. Human being like to talk.
> ROBERT
> Aunt Camille, I'll never be able to really practice my skills here . . . or stretch them. We talk 'bout this before. Besides I may not get the job. If I do you'll visit and we'll visit. Every year.
> SULYN
> And all the opportunities for the children! Com pared to Trinidad varsity education is free! Here everything limited. Is no joke.
> CAMILLE
> Stretching your skills! Why you can't invent here?

If is invent you want to invent! The trouble with all you so . . . you read so much book 'bout England, U.S.A., those big countries, you think here ain't real.

≈

"Sulyn!" A lostness so complete she is seven again in the slithering, chittering dark of island forest, her back pressed against knobbly roots, too lost even to wail. Her aunt's arms, her father, the lantern travelling down her body, slow comforting country voices.

"Sulyn?"

She surfaces abruptly. Cold. Wraps her arms around herself.

Shelagh is shaking her gently, "So what's wrong? I saw you through the window! Su, I phoned, but you didn't answer. Su . . . Su?"

She realizes suddenly that her face is wet, her nose running. She makes no attempt to hide grief. "My aunt is . . . dead." She starts for the washroom, turns back, "Sherry in the cabinet, brandy. Help yourself, please."

When she returns, Shelagh is perched at the end of the breakfast bar, her hair flaming in last sun, two glasses of brandy poured. "I'm so sorry ! Is this the aunt who was coming to visit? Oh my dear! Look here, can I do anything to help?"

As if she has not noticed the mute head-shake, the closed face, she says, "I see you've been cooking for the regiment; it smells great. How long are you going to be away?"

"I'm not sure; Camille was the last of my father's sisters.

When Mom died, she looked after us. It depends . . . ." She wants to say on whether she comes, but dares not. . . . *cheeks wet, she is standing looking into the coffin. She is saying "Ma, Ma." She stares intently. Ma does not move. In the flickering light of great candles, she sees cold rise from the box. Looks up into the shadowy room. The old women are asleep. They are supposed to be watching. They are asleep. Ma is alone. They promised. She begins to scream. Aunt Camille gets there first. Finds her struggling in the arms of old ladies.*

Shelagh's prompt is gentle, "Sulyn? Rob going with you?"

Sulyn's eyes go opaque. She takes a sip of brandy, "No. My brothers will be there." As if there must be men.

"She was home, wasn't she?"

"Exactly."

"When Ma died I felt abandoned! I remember thinking, 'I can't go home anymore.' I'd lost Ireland. Thomas couldn't . . . wouldn't take leave."

"I'm taking Joni with me. I want her to know . . ."

"Don't worry. I'll keep an eye on them for you. Why do I think Rob is helpless?"

"Because you know Thomas?"

They laugh, say together, "Educating Thomas/Robert." Laugh again.

Sulyn says, "Rob phoned Mrs. Lomans immediately. She'll come every day at one, stay till Sonny's in bed, housekeep."

"You're really lucky. How did you find her, again?"

"Voodoo."

Shelagh grins puts her glass down, begins to walk towards the deck, "OK? When do you leave?"

"Eleven forty-five tonight. I'll get there about six P.M. island time."

She stands at the door watching Shelagh till she disappears through the weathered gate let into her fence. Two children search for golf balls along the water course. High snatches of conversation and what sounds like scuffling reach her. The Miles jog past in perfect rhythm, wave in complete harmony. Hard to believe she has a lover stashed away. One of the Gardiner children, Terry, budding ski champion, and very sweet on Meilyn, calls out a greeting as he wheels his bike in.

To her continuing amazement, Rob seems to be busy turning into her father. "Boys and books don't mix; you understand what I'm telling you? Answer me girl!" She finds herself playing Camille's role, resolving the mutinous silences by ordering Meilyn to her room. It's why she'd believed you could take the man out of Trini, not Trini out of the man. Yet now he will not go home with her.

She turns into the house trying to still her mind, to concentrate absolutely on clearing up, wiping down counters, stacking dishes in the machine. Camille, we must talk! Please!

TROPICAL KITCHEN—LATE AFTERNOON

Camille sits at the table shelling peas into a battered enamel bowl. Sulyn is stacking dishes on to a tray preparatory to laying the table.

CAMILLE

You going there to make more money! Why you can't

admit it? Is because you know it going cost you
youself! And the children! Why you can't leave
them here?

> SULYN

We're not going up there as domestics, Aunt. We're
educated people. They came here head-hunting.
They asked Robert!

> CAMILLE

So educated you lose all you commonsense. Head
hunted is right. After they chew you up they going
spit out the bones. Is Sonny and Meilyn and Joni I
feel for.

> SULYN

Robert and I can take care of our own children.
Thank you very much.

> CAMILLE

Write on their forehead: We ain't like the rest!

~

The realtor in the brisk voice one uses with children: "Here
we have the kitchen and the family room. Notice how the
architect has carried the vaulted ceilings idea through in the
doors. Now this is the view I really love, our famous Rockies.
Of course because the slope is protected and you've got the
golf course—practically your backyard—you never have to
worry about anything blocking you out. Course fees are very
expensive out here. But I don't suppose you play." Sulyn had
glanced at Rob and smiled. Slightly flustered, the woman—
"Oh, just call me Jane,"—had begun pointing out the beauties
of the kitchen, the island, the high quality of the appliances—

"all Jenn-Aire, Maytag,"—enumerating and explaining. "This is the garburator. You just chuck the food scraps in, bone, soft garbage, no paper. Don't ever put your fingers in, dear. You switch on here. Dish washer, the dishes go here, glasses on top, the soap goes here; remember it must be dishwasher detergent. And you can use any cycle. . . ."

Sulyn had finally put a stop to it. "Where's the trash compactor? Is the laundry room on this floor? By the way, before we go any further, does the maid's room have its own facilities?" In fact Sulyn had been determined to buy the house as soon as she'd seen the deep window seats in the small open sitting room off the hall. She had imagined drawing velvet curtains, sitting in unseen quiet, reading and looking out over an exotic winter landscape: snow-roofed houses, the frozen lake through hoar-frosted trees, robins, rosy children muffled against cold—Sonny and Meilyn among them—hot chocolate steaming in the kitchen, although privately she drew the line at marshmallows, blue flames, apple wood in the fireplace. Now from the front window she stares on the unpeopled silence, the terrible emptiness of a Canadian bedroom suburb, as if all the people had been abducted without warning.

"Camille!" Not a whisper, no shadow. "Okay! You win! You win!"

She flees upstairs to their bedroom and its small sitting area. From the old, old prie-dieu, she removes the potted plants, places the lovely matching table in the corner. Then races down to the basement. In the store room she finds the box unopened. She'd known as soon as it arrived, six months after they did, exactly what it contained. She had told herself it was one of the things she wanted to leave behind; told Rob kids that enough to contend with without dragging "all that" with them. Rob had shrugged, "Your Aunt."

She takes the box upstairs, and quickly, almost frantically, releases the latch. Under layers of foam, a wooden statue of an African Virgin with Chinese eyes. Trust Camille! A white rush of anger flares. Her face burns. She might have broken the image, but *Aunt's hands tremble a little as she clears away onion skins, lemon rinds, dasheen eyes, stems, carrot tops, all the debris of cooking. Her face marked as if the words had been a leather belt. She turns, walks to the door in the noisy quiet of the tropics. Someone across the way laughs. Camille stands in the doorway looking at her. "Sulyn!" Of course she wants to take the words back; of course she could bite off her tongue . . . well not really. Camille just doesn't like the taste of her own medicine! Only there is a glimmer of tears in the round black eyes still fine at seventy-three.* The remaining weeks passed in a silence as absolute as the grave. For Aunt she had ceased to exist.

Perhaps she still doesn't. Exist. In her hands, the silverplated cross from her mother's coffin; crystal vestal lamps, their supply of white and red candles; a very old brass Chinese taper lamp she'd always coveted; four real wax candles sculpted by flame and dripping, wrapped in linen. *Used at a High Mass.* At the very bottom of the box, framed and wrapped in sheets of bubble foam, a painting of the Last Supper: John looking like Rob, Mary from her own graduation photograph, Joni's head on a serving maid.

It occurs to her, as at last she hangs the painting and steps back to admire the whole, that Jesus looks suspiciously like the fading daguerreotype of Camille's fiancé. He had died on his first mission of the Second World War, a young bomber pilot, terribly dashing and vulnerable in his uniform.

It is here that Rob finds her, a figure glimpsed by lightning, caught in some intense secret prayer. The room full of shadows, candle-light. From the windows votive flames call.

"Sulyn? Su-girl?" His chin nestles on her shoulder, his arm around her waist.

"Sh! She hasn't come yet, Camille. . . ."

Startled, he half lifts her to her feet. "Su! Come on, girl, I"ll get you a drink.

"I'll . . . I . . . just . . . w. . . ."

"No! Come with me!"

∾

Dragged back, the evening becomes a whirl of supper, helping Joni pack, clearing up, writing her boss, completing last tasks, explaining to Sonny who, sensing unusual goings-on, decides to go noisily nuts. Finally bathed, calmed down, he listens intently to their tale of God wanting Grantie, then insists that he travel with Sulyn.

"I want her myself! He didn't even ask us! Did He, Mommy?"

"You remember when your fish died?"

Sonny is outraged. "Grantie's not a fish!"

She has to deal with Meilyn and Joni. Rob can field this one. The child is standing on his bed with a face like bewildered thunder. Still she turns at the door, "Are you sure you won't come with me?" She is addressing Rob, unable to keep the pleading from her voice.

"I will!" Sonny.

"Look, Girl, I can't. I tell you so already, you know. Is how many times I have to say that?"

"Two years and eight months! You're more Canadian than Canadians!"

"Dammit Su, I've explained!"

She slams the door shut, but not quickly enough to avoid the image of Sonny collapsing slowly onto his bed as if he had been struck behind the knees.

She slips into her chapellette. *Dies irae, dies irae* the tune rises unbidden into her mind, and she sings it through in a mournful whisper. But there is no scent of roses, no warm indication of presence. The room is empty. She gets up slowly, goes to the girls.

When she wakes minutes before the alarm shrills, Robert is watching her, a curious pity in his eyes. She turns from his look and begins to get out of bed. He holds her back gently, bends to kiss her, "Come on Su, this has to last a long time." She slips out of his grasp.

~

In the end it's a mad dash. In spite of all she's done to ensure calm. But sooner than she dared hope, they are standing in the driveway. She is wholly reluctant to leave. She hugs Meilyn again, gives Sonny a magic kiss to keep in his palm. Robert begins to hurry Joni into the car. The children retreat into the house; Meilyn looking very Chinese in the brilliant red kimono; Sonny worried.

"Daddy'll be back in a couple of hours. Don't forget the latch!"

Meilyn casts her eyes up to heaven, "Motherrr!"

Sulyn laughs, "Okay, okay!" Then wickedly raising her voice, "I'll be blowing a kiss to you every night, little Mei!"

Meilyn shuts the door, goes to stand in the window.

Robert is ostentatiously leaning against the car. She may as well. She is just about to get into the car when the man walking his dog crosses over. "Hello, is this the De Souza House?"

"I'm Robert De Souza."

"Mark. We live on the lake. This letter was delivered to us. Thought I'd drop it in your box. Faster than the post, eh?"

Finally they are off, the letter in Robert's pocket. The dog in a frenzy on the sidewalk. "Okay, Joni?"

"I'm so excited, I can hardly wait! Sorry, Mom. You know what I mean."

She nods. Bare. Fading days yawn. Behind her. A chasm.

The macadam flows, channelling them under yellow fluorescent lights, irrevocably through a hushed wintry world. Robert glances across at her. "Yo! All right?"

"Yes, yes." What is there to say? The swish of tires on pavement carries her towards absolute. . . .

His glance anxious, Robert is handing her the letter, "From Camille."

She tears it open, reads the greeting: *Su-love, my child.* The car fills with the scent of roses, with a presence warm as a lap, shifts tangibly. And Aunt, she herself, Robert, Joni are. A clear exhilarating wave. Complete. Scattered.

~

Claire Harris was born in Trinidad and came to Calgary in 1966. She is the author of Fables from the Women's Quarters

(1984), Travelling to Find a Remedy *(1986),* Translation into Fiction *(1984),* The Conception of Winter *(1990),* Drawing Down a Daughter *(1992), and, with Edna Alford, the anthology* Kitchen Talk *(1992). She is the recipient of several awards including a regional Commonwealth Award, and the Alberta Culture Poetry Prize.*

The Hockey Widow

FRED STENSON

SEPTEMBER

Sid and Jarvis, Digger and Steadman were down in the basement drafting players for their hockey pool. This meant it was September.

Rita pulled a sheet of home-made pizza from the oven and slid it across the burners. She considered how many trips it was apt to take her to get the pizza, plates and napkins, and four cold beer downstairs.

Her recently-deceased mother's voice: *If they want food let them come and get it themselves. What are you, their donkey?*

She imagined going downstairs (why not take the pizza?) and saying this, how they would all either not look at her or, if she bellowed, how they would look up in a lost daze, the way kids look when awakened in the middle of the night.

What about your kids? Pianos tied to their bums?

As if on cue, Lisa entered the room. What she had tied to her were her neon green, street-hockey goalie pads. In one hockey-gloved hand, she carried a plastic goalie stick. On the other hand, her baseball mitt. She was heading for the door.

"It's dark out," Rita said automatically. The TV is on. School starts at nine. It's snowing. She wondered when she would stop saying things like this.

Rita examined her daughter. Hair chopped short, sweatshirt and jeans. No trace of feminine adornment. Lisa would be eleven in a few months and, with pain, Rita remembered her saying recently with a kind of exasperation, "I guess I'll get breasts soon." That this should be viewed as such a negative development, an impediment in her daughter's war to be as good as any boy in the most male of all arenas: the hockey one.

Rita's thoughts, as usual, had gone on too long. Before she could ever decide what it was she needed to say to her daughter, her daughter was gone. Looking through the darkened living room and out the bay window, she could see the ball hockey game in progress, could faintly hear it between the shouts from the basement.

And she wouldn't ask Willy to help. He'd be in his room, reading or drawing, or cutting things out of magazines to paste in his scrapbook. She wouldn't do it: make him a victim of his own absurd good will again.

Rita chopped the pizza into large squares then put her oven mitts back on. Please, Mother, not another word. She carried the pizza downstairs.

The air in the rumpus room was blue-grey. Through the gloom, she saw that her husband Sid had re-arranged his baseball cap so the visor sat in the middle of his head, pointing up. She wouldn't ask. The card table was covered in newspaper clippings, note pads, ashtrays, beer cans (some of them were crushed). It was apparently Sid's turn to pick and the others were grinning at him with hyena-like anticipation.

"This is the pits," he exclaimed. "You've got me cornered."

Rita set the pizza on a metal, floral-designed TV tray, rolled it up to the table.

"Burns, then! I'll take bloody Burns, the wimp." The others guffawed. Steadman, wearing a cowboy hat, reached up and put a hockey card in the band.

Rita was on the stairs again, headed for the napkins, plates and beer. It angered her that she knew exactly what Sid's words meant. Sid hated the local NHL hockey team, the Bisons, like poison. They were losers. Doug Burns was the team's highest scorer and the vicissitudes of the draft system had just trapped Sid into picking Burns against his staunchly held policy of never drafting Bisons players. The hockey card Steadman put in his hat band was likely one of Burns so that Sid would have to look at it throughout the rest of the evening.

I told you. Don't tell me I didn't tell you. Nip it in the bud, I said.

For crying out loud, Mother, you did say that but I never recall you saying how.

Rita was back with the plates and the beer.

"Rosteen."

"Digger, you jerk, he went two rounds ago."

"Ya, get in the game, Dig."

Digger was from Australia. He was expected to screw up like this. But, through a series of what the others called flukes and examples of dumb luck, Digger had won the $450 last year. No more nice guy from the others.

Rita looked at the cluttered table and began clamping together more TV trays. She rolled them into place, set out the plates and napkins, scooped out pieces of pizza, snapped the beer cans and put them on the trays. She reached in for the empties and even dumped the ashtrays. Still, not one of them acknowledged her presence or touched his pizza. Living in the land of the cliché: a hockey widow.

"All right, all right," said Digger. He reached up under his Los Angeles Kings jersey and scratched expressively. "Forbes ain't gone. I'll take Forbes."

"Perfect, Digger. But just so you know, he's got collateral damage in his left knee and probably won't play until Christmas."

"I read it was a third-degree strain. In which case he'll be back by December, unless the anthroscopic surgery shows up complications."

"Who's turn is it?"

Rita almost yelled *pizza* but was glad she didn't. If she had to tell her children that it was dark, snowing or Saturday, she refused to do the same for her husband and his dumb friends.

"I hope you all get third-degree fractures in the collateral ventricles of your skullbones." She wasn't more than three feet away when she said this, picking up some crumpled balls of notepaper, but there was no pleasure in it. Like screaming *you deaf old ninny* in the ear of a deaf old ninny.

Back upstairs, Rita tiptoed to her son's closed door, listened guiltily to the silence within. Willy was thirteen. He didn't listen to music on the tape deck she'd got him in hopes that he would. To please her he had used it once to record the audio off "The Nature of Things." She wished she wasn't hoping that the silence meant he was masturbating.

"Willy? Are you busy?"

"Not really, Mom. Come on in."

She pushed open the door. Willy was spraddled on his bed, cosy against a backrest of bunched pillows. He was reading a library book, one that seemed too thick and dun-coloured for a boy so young and thin.

"What are you reading, Will?"

"Aw, just some more about the ozone layer thing. You know, global warming." The smile on Will's face, so dependable, had the recent worry shining through.

Rita thought the line that would follow if this were a TV situation comedy: *What's that got to do with you?* She felt as if she had said it. In one way or another she was always pushing her son toward things that seemed more suitable to the interests of a boy his age—except hockey; she had not and would not push him there.

"It's pretty bad, Mom. I'm not sure the world's going to get it together in time."

"It might though, Will. When I was a girl, people didn't even know about the dangers and now I think most everyone does."

"But it says here. . . ."

"Will!" She hated the tone, stopped herself. It was the tone in which the TV Mom would ask what that had to do with him.

"It's okay, Mom," said her Will, smiling dependably. "We don't need to talk about it all the time. What are the others doing?"

"Dad and his crew are still at it downstairs. Lisa's out playing street hockey."

They shared the moment then, the one that Rita had to admit was the best these days had to offer: she and her son sitting on his bed with weary, knowledgeable smiles on.

Smiles that said what? What did they say? Here we are, trapped in the hockey nut house. Or: kids will be kids.

"Don't stay up reading too late, Will. You don't want to wake up with a headache."

"Sure, Mom. Thanks." And boom. He was back into the disaster-filled pages: watching the plumes of combusted fossil fuels rising into the damaged sky.

JANUARY

On an ice cold day, Rita was downtown, shopping from an endless list. A cheque book register in her head had been subtracting steadily from a not very big balance.

The cold half of the year had turned into a time of financial disaster for her family. Back-to-school items and Sid's fall hockey pools were just the beginning. Then came the six-month bill for his welding truck insurance, new hockey gear for Sid usually too. Then Christmas. Pretty soon it would be Lisa's birthday, then Sid's, then Will's.

But the huge one, the cost that Rita couldn't believe Sid saddled them with annually, was his season ticket to watch the Bisons, a team he hated. When she complained about the season ticket, Sid would fly off on a tangent as predictable in timing and direction as any migration of birds. He worked hard, he would say; he had few amusements; he was awfully lucky to have the season ticket and, if he gave it up, he would probably never get one again.

Five years ago when the Bisons started up in their city, Rita had been caught up in Sid's childish delight over it all. She had agreed about the season ticket, had even felt a measure of anxiety when he took his sleeping bag down to sleep outside the Bisons ticket office. What if they ran out just as his turn came? She had accepted it all so easily because, back then, Sid did work hard as a welder and had all but paid for his welding truck. And really, at that time, he didn't have many amusements.

Well, things had changed. They had changed so completely it was impossible to believe Sid had failed to notice. *Few amusements?* Relative to whom, Rita wondered. Prince Andrew? His hockey drafts, his "fat man" hockey team, his going out to watch Bisons home games and all the other games he watched with his buddies on the big screen down at the bar. Then there was his hockey card collection and his careful supervision of Lisa's.

Sid played constantly, as far as Rita could see, but she also realized that, somewhere along the line, Sid had ceased to view any of it as play. The season's ticket and the hockey cards were *investments*. The hockey pools were *business*. The fat man recreational hockey league (in spite of the gallons of beer and all the cigarettes afterward) was *exercise*. And the proof that none of it was play was that *none of it was fun*.

In the morning when he read the newspaper before leaving for work, Sid would usually curse and swear, really angry, over the latest Bisons loss or his having slipped down in any of his hockey pools. He and all the other guys on the fat man hockey team took it so seriously that they booked ice in the middle of the night to practice. During the games, they fought.

≈

Rita stopped herself. It took some exertion. *Look at yourself*, her mother was saying and she did.

She was standing in a hockey card store. She had been standing over one of the glass cases for a long time, who knows what crazy expression on her face. It was even possible that she'd talked some of her diatribe out loud. A young kid in a baseball cap was on the opposite side of the glass case, looking bemused and superior.

"Something I can help you with, ma'am?" he asked.

"I'll let you know," Rita snapped.

The kid drifted off to a boy Will's age and they argued over whether you could spot a rare premium card by its colour through the edge of the plastic wrapper in Super Pro Series I. Rita had heard Lisa and Sid debate the same point at home and wondered when these two would get around to the related topic of weighing the wax packs of another set to detect which ones contained the holograms.

Rita tried to decipher Sid's writing on a piece of soiled notepaper: directions on what cards to buy Lisa for her birthday. Some Russian player's rookie card, "but make sure it's centred." Any Guy Lafleur cards from the mid-1970s. There was a list of prices for these that she wasn't permitted to go above. "Mint!" God help her if she failed to notice a wax deposit or a nubbed corner.

Rita had stood here for so long she was getting embarrassed. She kept losing focus on the cards in the case, seeing instead the fray on the cuff of her winter coat. And now there was a man standing beside her at the same case, a fact that exerted another kind of pressure on her to leave. But she had to get the cards, either that or come all the way down here again before Lisa's birthday.

Having looked so long at her own cuff and sleeve, she couldn't help but notice the sleeve on the man's coat. He had on a fine dark-blue overcoat, good wool and brand new. His hand lying on the case close to hers, fingers gently drumming, was hard to figure. It looked like a rich person's hands, the nails so clean and carefully clipped, but there were also little nicks and bruises on it. When she was pretty sure he was looking elsewhere, at the kid who ran the store, she chanced a look up at the man's face.

It was a nice face, clean-shaven, a well-defined angle of jaw. Then she saw that it was also a familiar face, very familiar, and when it came to her that it was the face of Doug Burns, the Bisons centre, it came with such a rush that she said the name aloud. "Doug Burns."

The next few seconds were bad. He swung round to her. He looked startled, even frightened, she thought.

"Yes?" he said, and he said it so timidly, as if he were a child caught fooling around behind teacher's back. Rita tried to think why. They were in a hockey card shop, he was a hockey player; maybe there was something odd, embarrassing, about his being in such a place.

"Oh," Rita said. "I just recognized you and your name popped out." It was the truth.

He smiled at her, risked a smile you might say. His face really was very pleasant. There were hardly any marks on it and his smile was full of wonderfully white teeth. Rita was encouraged by the smile and, with a sort of what-the-heck feeling, she asked, "But what would you be doing here? Do you collect cards?"

She had not intended for him to become as badly rattled as he now became. "No, I, I, just sort of, came in." He was so obviously lying that she became desperate to stop him, to protect him. "Oh, never mind," she said. "It's not that important."

Perhaps grateful to her, he didn't ask the same question back. But he seemed to want to say something. He looked around, his feet might have been glued down. The kids in the store, the one running it too, they were all watching them now. Burns seemed afraid of them.

Rita took control. She called the bemused, superior kid and she asked him, "Do you have a Doug Burns card, his rookie?"

"Ya, I do. It's here."

"Is it mint?"

"I'd say so, ya."

It was four dollars.

"A bargain," said Rita and bought it.

Then she turned to Doug Burns and she said, "Would you join me for a cup of coffee?"

"Ya sure," he said and they left together with the group in the store circling round into a scrum to discuss who that was and what they might have done in the way of an autograph if the bimbo lady hadn't beaten them all to the rookie card. Then again *Beckett's* only listed Burn's rookie at two bucks, mint. Even signed it probably wasn't worth the four she paid.

That part of town was a former slum. It had been rescued from the wrecking ball about the time the city got its NHL franchise. The upper floors of the reclaimed brick buildings were spartan still and rented cheap: perfect for marginal businesses like card collector shops. The main floors were fancier: import boutiques, book stores, vegetarian restaurants and gourmet coffee bars. Into one of the latter, Rita bravely led Doug Burns.

She felt strangely courageous and, in her head, the worn

knee-length winter coat was transforming into something smart and furry. Her battered car full of groceries at the soon-to-be-expired meter had become the possession and problem of someone else, someone with a less attractive coat and manner. In fact, Rita felt the way she had before she met Sid, when she had been in university for social work and the future had always seemed fuzzy but bright, like a sunrise in a snowstorm.

She went straight to the counter and, turning to Doug Burns, asked, "Cappuccino?" He nodded. She took a table next to the curved window, facing right onto the street. She was determined not to lose momentum. Everything she had ever heard about Burns was sharp and ready in her mind, every belittling thing Sid and Lisa had ever said about him, and there'd been plenty.

"My name is Rita," she said, extending her hand through the frayed sleeve. His hand was cool and rough, without any macho grip in it, she noted. Everyone Sid had ever introduced her to, man, woman and child, had tried promptly to break her hand. Burns mumbled something about it being nice to meet her too. He really was very shy.

"Do you like hockey, Doug?" This was a crazy question, impertinent too, but there was considerable doubt in her household that he did.

"Oh, I don't know," he said. The question was certainly a tough one for him. "It's a good job, I try to look at it like that. I don't know what else I would do."

"You don't like hockey as much as most players, then."

He winced but then he seemed to gather some courage of his own. He asked, "What about you, Rita? Do you like hockey?"

"I hate it with all my soul."

Burns laughed, suddenly and loud, like he'd been jabbed with an electrical prong right in the little zone of his brain labelled "Laugh Centre." His laugh had the same effect on Rita: zing to the laugh centre and the only trouble was what they were going to do when the laughing stopped. Things did become silent but Burns was every bit as determined as Rita was to get over this obstacle and go on.

"Why would you be in a sports card store then?" he asked.

Rita's mother started up, something about being absolutely frank about who you are, about your status. Status in her mother's terms meant nothing for a woman but marital status. Shut up, Mother.

"A birthday present for a child I know. You know how it is, it's a hockey-mad city." Rita enjoyed the fact that, technically, no word she had said was a lie. "And you, Doug?"

"Same thing. A kid I'm related to wanted my rookie card and I didn't have one."

"Oh, oh," said Rita, partly in recognition of her having snaffled the card he wanted, partly registering concern that the kid he was related to might be related to him as Lisa was to her. She raced through her mental file on Burns—unmarried, she was almost certain. And that brought up the fact of his being probably a decade younger than her. She cut off both thoughts with the appropriate apology for taking the card he came to the shop to buy. But she didn't offer to give it to him.

"Oh, not to worry," he said. "There must be others around. I guess I hope there are. I'm not that hot an item."

"No? You're always the top scorer, aren't you?"

"On one of the worst teams in history. But how do you know that if you don't like hockey?"

Another challenge. Another order to her mother to keep silent. "It's like if there was a war on," Rita said, amazed at how easy this was. "The news is all around you all the time. You can't help but know things."

"Ya, I see what you mean." He was shy again and then: "Did you want the card autographed? Kids usually like that. It ups the value a bit."

"Of course." She produced the card and she noted for the first time how very young Doug was in the picture. It was an action shot, the fake kind with the helmet off. He had longer hair and a sort of frightened look on his near-adolescent face. He signed it with a special kind of autographing pen that lets you see the picture through the writing.

"Nice signature," she said. The writing had large loops and the *B* in Burns looked like it had breasts. Oh, dear.

"Do you ever think about things like global warming?" she asked. Another insane question but the instinct was a good one. He brightened right away.

"I sure do. I don't know why but I think about those kinds of disasters all the time lately, more than I should, I guess. Why?"

"I do too, that's all."

Rita felt a pressure building, a pressure to leave and a sense that she shouldn't fight this one. It was timing. To stay too long would be to invite some kind of complication she couldn't weave her way around. She took a last drink of her coffee and pushed the cup an inch ahead. She was certain that, with this man, this Doug Burns, the action would be read precisely as meant.

"I guess you have to go," he said, with just the right amount of regret.

"Yes, I do but I wanted to ask, how is it that you have such nice teeth?"

This caused another strange flurry in Burns. His hand started toward his mouth. Then it stopped and was pulled back to the table by some opposite force.

"They really look okay?"

"Really. They're great teeth."

"One of the front ones is a fake."

"I'd never have known."

"It's new. I lost a tooth in Montreal awhile back and had to get this false one." He pointed up at his mouth. She couldn't tell which tooth he was pointing at. She told him that and he rewarded her with an enormous smile that did, frankly, reveal a little something, a wire maybe, over the top of his left front tooth. She tried desperately not to even think this aloud, so perceptive was the communication between them.

"I really want to thank you for the coffee and the talk," he was saying. "It gets pretty lonely sometimes when all people want to talk about is hockey."

"I know what you mean. It's great to find someone who actually plays professional hockey who knows it isn't the whole world."

"It sure isn't."

A lull into which both of them wanted to leap. At the same time it mattered a great deal who did the leaping and how. It was him. There was a sort of silent consensus about that before he spoke.

"Do you think it would be possible for us to have dinner sometime?"

"Yes, it would be possible," she said. "How about the sixth of February?"

Burns popped a little hinged card out of his inside jacket pocket and looked inside it. "That would be great. Well, maybe not. We're in town that night but we've got a game. A late dinner, maybe?"

"Perfect. Have you got a number? So we can figure out where and when closer to the date?"

He gave her another card from the same pocket, a simple one with just his name and phone number. Having put that in her purse, Rita got up quietly and was suddenly outside and walking fast.

All the way back to the car she had to put up with her mother. Once she had the ticket picked off the windshield and was in the car, she put a stop to it. *You always said I should do something about it, didn't you, Mother? Well now I am.*

FEBRUARY

"Care for another glass of wine, Doug?"

Doug Burns had just finished a giant piece of lasagna (his favourite, he said) and he dabbed neatly at his mouth with the cloth napkin before saying that, yes, he thought he could have another glass. Rita reached with the bottle and poured until he held his hand out flat. He was being very careful about how much he drank.

Rita fingered the pearl necklace she had put on for the occasion and watched him take a tiny sip. What a really delicious man he was. It was a real shame what she had done to him but, really, what other way was there?

"How about you, Sid?"

Sid had taken Lisa to the Boston game. This being her birthday, he'd talked Steadman into giving her his ticket.

Sitting on the same side of the table they were both quiet and still confused. "I'll stick to a beer," he said grumpily.

"Will, would you help me for a moment in the kitchen?" She looked at her son and mouthed the word cake. While they walked out toward the kitchen there was silence behind them. But before the kitchen door swung shut, Rita heard Doug ask Lisa what she thought of the game.

Will hadn't been in on the secret either and he was beside himself, as delighted as Rita could remember him being. While plunking wax candles into the chocolate icing, he whispered, "How did you do it, Mom? How did you *meet* him?"

"Just bumped into him one day and we went for coffee." She was retaining her mystery.

"It's great. I thought Dad was going to blow a vessel when he came to the door."

It had been quite a moment. Sid and Lisa had only been back from the game fifteen minutes. Rita had told them there would be a mystery guest, coming late for dinner and cake. "What the hell have you done now?" Sid had asked. He was in a slightly blacker mood than usual because the Bisons had not only lost but had been shut out. He specifically complained about Doug Burns. "He's the guy supposed to score for that crowd."

Then the doorbell and Doug Burns in person, already looking a a bit troubled. He was wearing a suit and bearing gifts: flowers and a bottle of wine. The only really sad part came next, when she'd had to step outside, to whisper to his ear, "I'm sorry, Doug."

She hadn't underestimated him, though. After only a few seconds of looking hurt, Doug rallied. Rita led him in, introduced him to her open-mouthed husband and daughter, to her broadly grinning son, and he'd been very polite, as if the scene was exactly what he'd expected. The flowers were a problem. He was holding them low and slightly behind him. Rita leaned down and took them from him. "Doug, you really are sweet." She swung around and placed the bundle in Lisa's arms. "Mr. Burns brought you roses for your birthday, dear. Wasn't that nice?"

Now Rita carried the flaming cake into the dining room with Will walking ahead carrying the presents and starting the song. Doug sang with gusto, Rita noted. Lisa blew out the candles, Rita cut the cake, Lisa opened her gifts. She opened the little flat one first: Doug Burns's signed rookie card.

It was in that moment that Lisa departed the camp of her father, and perhaps, though it was too soon to say, from the camp of all those who give their lives to hockey. Almost tearful, she said, "Ahhh," the note rising sharply at the end. "Is that ever neat?" And she got up and walked to Doug Burns, and gave him a hug.

Absolutely without doubt now, Rita passed the plates of cake around, serving Doug first. Then she sat back and watched and listened for the short time that Doug could stay. Touching her flowers and the rookie card, ignoring both her parents, Lisa asked Doug a few things about hockey players that she'd always wanted to know. For instance, did hockey players really high stick each other so often deliberately, or was it just their sticks getting bumped up high by accident. Doug said that, whichever it was, he wished he could afford to wear a spherical helmet of clear indestructible plastic like an astronaut. Lisa laughed. Will managed to get the topic around for awhile to the atmospheric effects of aerosol cans.

Doug said that he didn't understand the connection between aerosol and ozone but he was always careful to use the stick kind of deodorant all the same. Given the amount of deodorant a hockey players uses he reckoned his contribution was significant. Everyone laughed, even Sid.

At one point, Doug asked the mostly silent Sid if he had any interest in hockey; Sid had certainly given the impression tonight that he might not have. Sid, for the first time in memory, did not know quite what to say on a hockey topic. "Oh you know," he said, finally, "I guess I have an average interest."

It was about then that Rita paused to address her mother. *See*, she said. *It worked, didn't it*? What's more, Rita suspected it was going to keep on working for awhile. Not that this night would ever be replicated. She was realistic enough to know that Doug and she were very unlikely to meet again. But the effects, they might go on.

While Will and Lisa tried to talk to Doug at the same time, while he took the politest look at his watch, while Sid sat looking down at his uneaten chocolate cake (his favourite, in fact), Rita took the opportunity to have a long last look at Doug Burns. There was more than a little halo of regret around her heart as she did. *To be a mother and a wife is to sacrifice for your family.* That was one of her mother's nuggets. *To a point.* That was another.

When she stopped looking at Doug, Rita noticed that Sid's attention had moved from his cake over to her. She looked Sid right in the eye, right where the little worry was centred, and she repeated that thought very loud. *To a point!*

≈

Fred Stenson *is a resident of Calgary. He grew up on a farm in southern Alberta. Since 1976, he has been a full-time freelance writer. His fiction titles include the short story collection* Working Without a Laugh Track *(1990), and the novels* Last One Home *(1988) and* Lonesome Hero *(1974). His short fiction has appeared in national magazines and literary quarterlies across Canada. He has written over ninety films and videos. He has edited two anthologies of Alberta writing:* Alberta Bound *(1986) and* The Road Home: New Stories by Alberta Writers *(1992).*

Graves-in-Waiting

LAURALYN CHOW

How can Auntie Moe stand living with a grave-in-waiting? How can she take it? That's what I want to know. I think about that every time we go to the Chinese cemetery. Auntie Moe is Mom's baby sister and she doesn't drive, so Mom and I drive her, once a month, on school days off, as long as there isn't snow on the ground.

Auntie Moe is cool. The clothes she buys me for my birthday are always "cutting edge," as she puts it. Lately, she's started wearing miniskirts under her midi coat. And vinyl boots with square heels. Imagine. Boots when it isn't snowing or even raining outside. Auntie Moe is really with it. So what is she doing with a grave-in-waiting?

I bet that's what all of us are thinking, Mom, Auntie Moe, me. That is what's on all of our minds as we stand silently in front of Uncle Louie's gravestone. Gross. A big dark grey stone, bigger than most of the ones around it. On the left side of the stone, it says *Chan Gee Gum Kwee*, underneath that *Born May 20, 1917* and underneath that *Died March 13, 1964*. All the lettering is chiselled right out of the stone, and the insides of the letters and numbers are painted white. So the stone doesn't just say things, it says them forever. Underneath the dates, there is a bunch of Chinese writing in four long columns, saying God knows what. But then, on the right side of the stone, it says *Maureen Lily Chan*, and underneath that *Born July 23, 1938-* . The rest is blank. Shiny, polished, grey-grey blank. That blankness always gives me the creeps. Auntie Moe stands there, her mouth an upside-down sausage painted frosty pink. Mom balances garden shears, a water jug's handle, and some flowers from home in one hand. The other hand grips Auntie Moe's. But like always, Mom lets go of Auntie Moe's hand, squeezes her around the shoulder, and says, "Well, the sooner we start."

Then, and this part always kills me, Mom will walk straight up to the stone, right over that big rectangle of ground that any fool can see is slightly lower than all the ground around it. Oh, the grass may look the same, but the ground is clearly dipped down in a square-edged plot. And even that rectangle of grass is off-centre, a little bit more to the left than center. Come to think of it, the firm ground on the right, the Auntie Moe side, makes it even more of a puzzle as to what Auntie Moe is doing with a grave-in-waiting. But my point is, how can Mom do that, walk right over a rectangle of the dead? Me, I can't even put my toes near the edges of those rectangles. I get dizzy thinking about it. I know *that* dirt is softer, shifting. Restless. Somehow, I know that dirt will move. Dirt isn't solid powder. Dirt is little round pebbles, marbles that will roll, give way to running shoes and almost weightless eight-year-old legs. This is serious stuff, not just walking on sidewalk cracks. Even Auntie Moe, who was married to the man, stands outside the foot of the rectangle and watches Mom lower herself down, her hand holding the top of the tombstone for balance. Mom plucks dry, straw-brown flowers left over from last time out of two green cone-shaped metal vases. The vases have big coat-hanger wire stems that push into the ground. Mom pulls the vases right out of the ground, turns to me and Auntie Moe, smiling. "Well?"

Auntie Moe, who hasn't said one word, has her arms wrapped around her. She walks along the left edge and crouches down beside my mom, who squats dead centre at the top of the rectangle.

Mom washes out the vases with a little water from her jug. She dampens a rag and starts to rub at the bird poop on the stone. Auntie Moe still has her arms wrapped around her as she rocks on her square heels. Auntie Moe has excellent balance.

"Well, run along," Mom says to me.

Right. Like I'm going to run in the cemetery, let my feet step all over these grave tops. Sure. Maybe it's just her way to say "get lost," but maybe, maybe the obvious doesn't occur to her at all.

Actually, I don't mind. Heel toe heel toe heel toe. I watch my feet and walk slowly along the higher ridges of grass. The ridges are continuous and they intersect, sideways with up and down. They make a grid pattern, like streets on a city map. In between are the grave tops. So each gravestone sort of becomes a little house with a sunken front yard. Some of the gravestones have flowers set out, real ones and fake too. A few of them have oranges and incense and burnt papers with Chinese writing scattered in front. And almost empty Crown Royal whiskey bottles, which, Mom says, are not left by drunks, but are probably just filled with coloured water. I picked one up once and it smelled like the real thing to me. All of the stones have flat polished fronts with those chiselled-in figures. Almost all have dates. Some of them just have Chinese writing, or just English writing, or a combination of the two.

I read silently as I walk along. If there are dates, sometimes I do the math to figure out ages. *Jonathan Wong Gee, Born December 22, 1949, Died December 29, 1959.* Oh. Ten years old. That's awful. There's a bunch of little oranges set out in front of the stone. How sad. There are baby ones too, like six months, or eighteen months. Skinny little gravestones that I try to avoid. Now here's one of my favourites, *Wee Lee, Born October 21, 1901, Died April 10, 1959.* Fifty-seven. And the last little piggy went Wee Lee all the way home. I laugh, but quickly stop, remembering where I am. Right beside Wee Lee, I look down and just watch my feet. Left right left right. I am in front of one of those gravestones with a photograph, like a cameo locket, imbedded front and centre. I always get prickly ears looking at those little photos. Because then you've got a face to put on what's underneath that rectangle of grass.

Looking up the hill at Mom and Auntie Moe, I can see them talking. Auntie Moe still has her arms wrapped around her, but she talks when Mom's hands and mouth stop moving. The flowers lie beside Mom's feet. So do the green metal vases.

Uncle Louie was older than Auntie Moe, even older than my Dad. He was tall and skinny and his skin looked like old waxed paper. He kind of looked like what Herman Munster would look like if he was Chinese. Yeah. Chinese Herman Munster. He wore a man's felt hat, even in the house, and he always had these bruise-coloured rings around his eyes. I can picture him, hitting the top of their old console television, then sitting in that flesh-tone La-Z-boy, never taking his eyes off the screen. Wearing that hat. Looking at the wide white television tower, just outside of the cemetery, I have the idea that Uncle Louie must be doing OK.

On that TV tower side of the graveyard is a shrine. It's this garden shed with a Chinese-y looking roof, and, instead of walls, there are no walls, there's support beams and a ledge running all the way around it at about my eye level. From the car, and I'm always telling Mom, "Slow down. Slow. Down," I can see burnt paper banners with Chinese writing hanging down from the ledge. And sitting on top of the ledge are little glass cups filled with amber liquid, oranges, incense sticks, and red paper envelopes for lucky money. I'd like to check out this great stuff, but right beside the shrine is where the recently dead have been buried. There isn't even grass on the rectangles. Just lots of flowers, or paper banners laying over soft, rounded piles of dirt. Fresh graves.

I keep walking the other way. The further along I go, the longer the tombstones have been here. Here's a double. On the Uncle Louie side, it must be the man, Wah Keen Sang, 1953 minus 1890. Sixty-three. And, Wah Ng Lee, 1963 minus 1891. Seventy-two. Good on her. Old Wah waited, let's see, ten years, which is nothing when you compare that to poor old Ng Lee having a grave-in-waiting for the same period of time.

Some of these stones now are really old. They even have rusty cauliflower-looking crud stuck on them, where the paint in the letters has chipped away. Some just have one date on them, like 1924, and a bunch of Chinese writing. Or no dates at all. Out here, all the double graves are full up. There are hardly any flowers or oranges or little red envelopes by the gravestones. I guess there's no one left to bring stuff to them.

We don't put oranges, or incense sticks, booze or Chinese fake Monopoly money out for Uncle Louie on account of God. That's what Mom says. We don't do ancestor worship, Mom says, because we believe in God. I'm not going to ask Mom, but what about the graves where there's oranges and incense *and* flowers and chiselled-in words about God? I think that is what's called dealing from both ends of the deck.

I think about God here, near the end or I guess the beginning, the boundary, of the Chinese graveyard. I don't think about Him much at church. We go to the Chinese United Church and the whole service is in Chinese. I don't understand word one. It's mostly old Chinese people who go. Hymn singing sounds like cats being tortured. After and before, the old ladies pinch your cheeks and ask you things in Chinese. You smile like an idiot, until usually, your Mom says something in Chinese. I can't stand it, the worst, longest sixty-minute hour in the world. But my point is, out here, alone, surrounded by these rectangles of the dead and the chiselled words about God, such as *The Lord Is My Shepherd* and *He Is Risen*, well, I must admit, He occupies your mind.

I look across the cemetery road to the Ukrainian cemetery. Their stones are massive, like six feet tall. They have graves-in-waiting too. Some of the gravestones have just one word, a name written on them, as far as I can see. Kureluk, Holubitsky. And sometimes that word isn't spelled in the English alphabet, but that alphabet with the little curlicues and backwards image letters. The Ukrainians are buried in one cemetery, and on the other side of the street, here's all the Chinese.

And I finally put God and religion and the afterlife all together. When you die, you go to heaven, fine. But, you live in heaven with the people you're buried with. Sure, that's why the graves-in-waiting. It's like putting a sweater on the seat beside you at the movie theatre while your mom, or your boyfriend when you're older, is out buying the popcorn. It's just saving a space for someone.

The traffic whizzes by on the other side of the cement barrier. Although the leaves are gone from the trees, the sun is out, and I have that warm feeling from figuring something out, like learning how to add fractions. But as I look at the rows and rows of tombstones in the Chinese cemetery, I figure something else out. One day, I'm going to spend the rest of eternity with a bunch of old Chinese people who don't speak English. It will be like going to church every day for the rest, well, beyond the rest of my life. I mean, this is where they bury the Chinese-Canadians, which is what I was told to write on the card at school, Chinese-Canadian, beside Nationality. Everyone in my heaven will be Chinese, and hardly anyone will speak English. Probably no one. They won't have had to speak English for years, so they'll have lost it. I am, as Grandpa holds over my head, the only Chinese child in the entire city who doesn't know word one of Chinese. My stomach twinges. My armpits feel warm and greasy. What am I going to do? If I get there before Mom or Dad, who will interpret?

What kind of heaven is this, anyway?

"Kelly, we're going."

My feet come off the ground. Mom and Auntie Moe are standing up. Mom waves her garden shears at me. "Kelly. C'mon."

What kind of people would bury a child in the Chinese graveyard?

My eyes burn holes in the back of the driver's seat. Auntie Moe is sitting way over in the front seat. We're driving her home to Grandpa's. Auntie Moe works at Village Books on Thursday and Friday nights and all day Saturday. She takes the bus there and back. Whenever I'm out with Mom and Dad at night and see those buses riding around, all lit up inside with one or two passengers sitting by themselves, I think of Auntie Moe. She must be as lonely as those people look.

And why she moved to Grandpa's when Uncle Louie died is anyone's guess. Well, he's her father and everything, but he's such a grump. He looks exactly like the porcelain Buddha doll Dad's cousins in Saskatoon have in front of their fireplace. He's got the round, round bald head, white Chiclet teeth, and jiggly fat that gives him an enormous gut and those floppy breasts. In the summer, when Grandpa wears just undershirts, you can even see those little dots around his nipples, just like the Buddha doll's. But that Buddha doll is sitting there with these smiling children climbing all over him, and I don't know any kid in his right mind who'd come near Grandpa. And not just because his breath would knock a cow over. He is just plain mean. He doesn't know much English, but what he knows is pick-pick-pick. You'll be over visiting, having a chat with Auntie Moe, and he'll be talking with your Dad, and all of a sudden, he'll interrupt you and say something like, "Aiya. Childen. Be Seeing. Not hearing." If he were that Buddha doll, he'd be swatting those kids away like flies. What an old fossil. But one thing about Grandpa. At least his daughters can speak Chinese. They're all set. It feels like someone is dragging a teabag soaked in vinegar across the bottom of my stomach. I don't know what I'm going to do.

"You're quiet today, little one." Auntie Moe turns and smiles at me. She is really pretty. "What are you thinking about?"

"Mmmm. Nothing."

I wish I said, something. Auntie Moe shrugs her shoulders and turns around again.

"Well, what are you thinking about?" I ask.

"Nothing too."

"Next month, maybe Auntie Moe will have time to go out for tea," I hear from the back of Mom's head.

"I don't think we need to do this any more," Auntie Moe says, looking straight ahead.

"Well, we'll keep an eye on the weather," Mom says.

"No." I have to lean forward, I can hardly hear Auntie Moe. "I mean any more."

"Oh?" Mom has that bug-eyed tone that means she's not really asking.

"Brian says this just prolongs the mourning period—"

"Who's Brian?" I ask, perching my chin over the front seat edge.

"—but I told him, three years, mourning isn't what it's about. But maybe he has a point."

"Well maybe," Mom says, "maybe Brian doesn't understand things like Duty. Or prior loyalties."

"Who's Brian?"

"I explained that to him, but Brian says it sounds to him like I'm doing this more for Dad," Auntie Moe says, turning her face toward Mom, "and you, Wendy."

"Oh. Well. You tell Brian, you don't owe me anything. All this time, I thought I was just helping you. But look, if you don't want to do this any more, you tell Brian. You tell him

I'm not going to drag you to the cemetery each month, kicking and screaming. I don't need to help you and then have you tell me you're doing this for me."

"Who is Brian?"

(one-two-three-) The front seat goes Chinese. Like the film at school on the UN Assembly, your translation headset cuts out, pauses. And then all you hear is Chinese.

This happens all the time, particularly at the juicy bits. My eyes go back and forth between Auntie Moe and Mom. It always sounds like Chinese people are arguing, but I don't need a translator to know this is the real thing.

I listen carefully. Maybe those words, one word, one syllable will turn sideways for a second, reveal meaning to me. But they talk so fast, the words pour out like jelly beans from a jar. "Brian" is peppered through the Chinese. I listen harder. Wait.

This is useless. My head hurts. They could be talking about space travel for all I know. Who's Brian? And, if I don't learn Chinese, I'll be the village idiot of heaven. Worse. I'll starve. I don't even know how to ask where the bathroom is. I wonder if I'll have to go in heaven.

Already in front of Grandpa's house. We usually stop and visit, but Mom holds onto the steering wheel, looks straight ahead. The car engine rumbles.

"I'll call you," Auntie Moe says, "See ya."

"Mmm."

"See ya Auntie Moe."

Mom takes off without asking me to come up to the front. We ride home in silence. I pretend to be a lady of leisure being driven home by her cranky chauffeur.

～

"How was school today?"

"There wasn't any school. We went to the cemetery."

It's so quiet at dinner tonight, you can hear the knives and forks click clack against the plates. The three of us sit in the kitchen. While Mom made supper, I went to the den and took down these old paperbacks of my dad's with all Chinese writing. They'd been in the den since I remembered, in the little gold metal bookcase. I never thought to look at them before. I was trying to figure out what the squiggly characters meant, looking for patterns, repeated figures. Maybe there was a code, and if I broke it, those squiggles and lines could move around on the page, form letters spelling words with the English alphabet.

"What have you got there?"

I didn't know Dad was already home. Actually, it was getting dark. And cold on the floor where I was sitting, my fingers running lines over the writing.

"Just some old books I was going through."

"Anything interesting?" He put his chin over my shoulder.

"Not really."

"Might be more interesting if you start at the beginning of the book, not the end." He moved the pages from under my fingers.

"Oh?"

"And each page," he said, running his fingers to the bottom of the page, "you read the rows bottom to top, right to left."

"Oh."

~

Mom dabs the napkin at the corners of her mouth, signalling me to clear the table.

"Yes," she says, "we went to the cemetery today." The Chinese starts again. Even sounds like the same conversation, like a needle on a sewing machine madly piercing the fabric, "ne-ne-ne-ne-ne-ne-ne-ne-Brian-ne-ne-ne-ne-ne-ne-ne-Brian-ne-ne-ne."

Dad massages his jaw with his left hand. He talks. A question? No? I stand between them, my hands curved around the plates stacked at the table. The talking is a volleyball, back and forth, over me, I first think, like a net. Then, through me, as if I am not there.

"ne-ne-ne-ne"

"What are you talking about?"

They keep talking.

"Who's Brian?" ne-ne-ne-ne-ne— "What are you talking about?"

Back and forth. Back. Forth.

"I said. What are you talking about?"

"Clear the dishes."

"You heard Mom. Clear the dishes."

"Will you at least answer my question first?"

"Young lady!"

"This always happens. You talk Chinese. You know I don't understand—"

"Kelly—"

"You talk right in front of me. Don't you know that's rude?"

"Go to your room." Mom points down the hall.

~

I had this terrible dream last night. I was walking in this big green field on a sunny day. Alone. Someone tapped me on the shoulder from behind. When I turned around there was an old Chinese man in a white turtleneck. He didn't say a word, but I knew it was Wee Lee, bugging his eyes at me. I started to run, but I tripped, and kept falling. I screamed. Out loud, I think. My eyes opened. My hair felt hot and stuck on, like a rubber bathing cap. I had a droolly pillow and crusts in my eyes. I was still wearing my daytime clothes, in bed. The whole house was quiet. And dark. No one came to see if I was all right. I got up and changed in the dark.

All day long, I have ridden in silence. They have finished all their Saturday driving errands. I'm never going to be as boring as they are. They make a point of speaking English all day, turning their heads toward the back seat as if to include me. I'm no fool. It just means what they're talking about isn't important. Not that I care. I haven't been listening. The car stops at Pinder's house. Mom went to school with Barbara Pinder, who still lives at home, taking care of her mother. Just the two of them, mother and daughter, in the house. There's an awful thought. The Pinders live about three blocks from Village Books, where Auntie Moe should be today.

I slam the car door shut. "I'm going to the bookstore," I say, not even looking at them.

"Kelly, where are you going?" Mom asks. She doesn't even listen.

"Let her go," Dad says. "Call us at the Pinder's and we'll come and get you. Kelly?"

"Mmm."

~

Auntie Moe is at the counter, helping a customer. His back is to me, and he leans over so she doesn't see me come in. There's no one else in the store. I'm not to bother her while she's working, so I browse a shelf of books off to one side. She still doesn't see me.

Is she arm wrestling? They both have their elbows on the counter and their fingers make a big ball fist. But, she is pretty puny. He could easily win, and yet they just look at each other. Wait. He wraps his other hand around and lifts their ball fist to his face, never taking his eyes off her. He kisses her knuckles. Each one separately. This is better than television. She smiles and half-closing her eyes, turns her head toward me.

The way Auntie Moe's head and my head both move back, you can tell we're related. She undoes her hand from the ball. I don't know what to do. Or say. She looks at the man and then waves me over. He turns to face me. He's very tall.

"Kelly, this is my friend, Brian. Brian, this is my favourite niece, Kelly."

"Your only niece," I say.

"But, still my favourite." This is our routine.

His camel's hair coat goes on forever. But he has nice eyes. Soft grey-brown eyebrows and long eyelashes like a pony. The point of his nose matches the points of his shoes matches the blunt tips of his outstretched fingers. The ones that were so close to his lips.

He has warm hands.

"What's up, little one?" Auntie Moe asks me. She looks so pinky clear.

"I need to talk to you," I whisper.

I like that Brian. Without asking even, he just wanders off to the shelves.

"Why so glum chum?"

Auntie Moe crosses her arms on the counter and looks at me seriously. She should be a mother.

"Auntie Moe, I need to learn Chinese."

"Oh. How come?"

"I just have to."

"Right away?"

"Well I think that would be best."

"It's not so easy, you know. What kinds of things do you need to learn first?"

"Well, like, 'Where is the bathroom?' and 'Do you have chicken sandwiches?' and 'Go away. I don't know.' Like that."

"Come with me," she says. We walk by Brian who smiles at us. Auntie Moe has her hand around my shoulder. She stops in front of Travel, picks a book off the lowest shelf, and hands it to me, *Berlitz Chinese for Travellers: A 40-Page Guide.*

"You're lucky," she says, "There's not many of these around."

The book cover shines in my hands. As we walk slowly back to the counter, I open the book. The pages are thick and cream-coloured. There's a column of phrases in English, and then another column, English letters spelling Chinese words. I try one out.

"Joh Sun."

"Good morning to you too," Auntie Moe gently tugs a piece of hair by my bangs, "but you're about eight hours late—"

"I knew that," I shout, "Yes, good morning. I knew that."

As if she were reading my mind, Auntie Moe reaches under the counter and takes her wallet out. "Don't worry," she says, punching the till buttons, "think of it as an early Christmas present." She flips the clip down on the dollar bills, and fishes some coins out of the little compartments.

~

The three of us ride in Brian's car. Dad said it was OK. We are going out for spaghetti and then play it by ear, Auntie Moe says. I sit in the back seat. The car has leather upholstery which smells like forever. They reach across the front seat and hold hands.

"Or, we could go get doughnuts," Auntie Moe says.

"Or, we could go bowling," Brian says.

"Or, we could drive out to the Stardust Drive-in, park off the road, and make up the dialogue for the actors on the screen."

They keep talking. And every idea sounds better than the last one. I fold the paper bag carefully around my book, which I hold in both hands. And as Auntie Moe and Brian make plans, all of a sudden I start thinking about Uncle Louie. And I'm thinking, what would it be like, you tell everyone in heaven that you're waiting for someone, "Yup, she's coming," you say, but no one ever shows up. I mean, you're there for eternity, and everyone knows you're waiting and you know everyone knows you're waiting, you've told them, after all. But no one ever comes. How could Uncle Louie stand waiting for eternity like that? That's what I want to know.

~

Lauralyn Chow is a lawyer who was born and raised in Edmonton. She has lived in Calgary for the past nine years. "Graves-in-Waiting" is her first published story.

What We Wore

CANDAS JANE DORSEY

We used to make a joke together, that he'd have the pick of the boys among the new students, and I of the girls. We used to go as a couple to the faculty parties and the department picnics and the school dances, and those who knew about us kept quiet. He was a natty little fellow, always was, and I was tall and chunky and didn't know enough not to dress like a man, which wouldn't matter today but in those days we had to pay lip service to the rules, even if we were living in another country in our own minds. Not that I wanted to be a man, no, that wasn't it, but it seemed my big body looked foolish disguised as a fashion plate, and after a few tries at it I went back to the outfits that felt comfortable. I guess to those who knew about us we fit into the right preconceptions—a man who cared too much about his clothes and a woman who cared not enough. I couldn't care more, and Sal couldn't be less than dapper, I think it physically hurt him to wear a shirt without a tie, unless it was worn as a jacket over a sweater. He used to do that. Here is a photograph of us at a faculty picnic. You can see there what we wore.

What we wore. Was it important? At the time we used to think so. Once I'd given up the blouses with the little Peter

Pan collars, and the grey flannel pleated skirts, I spent a lot of time looking for clothes that wouldn't make me look like a lumberjack. He'd lie back on my bed, legs crossed, and say, "You should wear burgundy more. It will make your skin glow," and I'd say, "Burgundy, by God! And you with no better sense than to wear a sienna tie with a red shirt!" and we'd go out in fine good spirits, he in his pointed neat shoes and me in my Russian boots, me laughing at him when he couldn't avoid the slush which stained the pale leather and made the fine shoes squeak until they dried. He hated his shoes to squeak, especially in class. He thought the students would laugh.

Not that he didn't enjoy making them laugh, as long as he was in control of the event. He'd do anything to make them giggle, short of stripping his clothes off, and that only because he knew how far he couldn't go. I just frightened them into respect, but he loved them, and they'd go to him with their troubles, the girls shy and not used to talking to a man about their boyfriends, and the boys shy and not used to talking about their feelings to anybody. There he is with one of the graduating classes; see how they clustered around him.

He'd wipe their eyes, and teach them it was fine to be sensitive, and tell them that's what the theatre was all about, and send them away feeling better, and loving him.

And come to me. "That young man is going to be something someday," he'd say, and shake his head, and if he was particularly lonely he'd have to cry, for the handsome young ones going by, falling in love with life and with women. And he was getting older, and so was I, and sometimes we managed to make each other laugh a little. It was that kind of time.

Now when I look at these photographs I see us without the spirits, and he looks dapper and I look foolish and large, and there's no sense in his clown face, and no feeling in my wide one. I suppose we don't control the impressions we give to posterity.

We used to walk down the hill from the campus, and across the river, and on the other side we would sit on the bank and watch the water. That's a picture I took the day he told me he was leaving the school, and that's one he took of me. We look happy, don't we? That was before he told me. We'd been playing in the fallen leaves and were exhausted. It was a place we could play like that, let go, be young if we felt like it, though our bodies were getting older and older despite us. He felt that, I guess, and he felt he had to try before time overwhelmed him to find something more to his liking than a riverbank refuge from an unbearable shared solitude.

"The cats will think you've left me," I said, lying back with my hands behind my head, watching the clouds.

"Tell them I'm gonna send for you. Then you'll have an excuse to quit at mid-term and do that cruise you keep maundering about."

"And the kids will miss you."

"Sure. And keep sneaking into the dorms with their little girlfriends, and what's it to me anyway?"

"Who is it this time?"

"Who isn't it? It's nothing. Knowing my routes are all cut off, no place to go. Well, I'm gonna go someplace."

"What will you do?"

"I was thinking of prostitution."

"You're too old."

"But I'm willing, and cheap."

"And eager."

He looked out over the river. "Oh, God, Sandy, what will happen to us?"

"We'll live," I said, and kept the fear out of my voice.

"Oh, you can't fool me," he said, and he held his damaged hand across his eyes, and I put my large hand on his back, and we sat for a while. We sat watching the river dapple in the fall sun, and I thought, someday, when I have time, I am going to paint some of these moments, I'm sick of wasting my time teaching stage design to supercilious would-be actors. And I turned around so that I touched him, and he put his hand on my hip, and leaned against me, and shook a little with the fall chill.

"Come too," he said. "You're my only friend."

"Oh, sure, Sal," I said. "You want a large woman of forty to stand beside you on the street and negotiate rates with your customers."

"You can wear a leather jacket and go to bars and pick up married women."

"I've had an offer like that in the last week," I said, and missed keeping my voice light, and he turned to look at me.

"Oh, yes," I said. "Our chairman's young wife wonders if I am truly happy, and don't I need the kind of love that only a woman can give another woman. I wouldn't have known what the hell she was talking about if I hadn't seen her fawning over Dulcie MacLean, and heard the same thing, and then had Dulcie tell me what happened when she spent an afternoon there, with soft music and all."

"She's a handsome enough woman," he said, "well-dressed."

"What, Dulcie? She sure is. It must be quite a come-down to proposition me."

"I meant the missus," for that was how the chairman talked of her, the missus this, the missus that.

"Sure, if you like vampires."

"Beggars can't be choosers," he said cruelly and accurately, and I laughed.

"You turned down Iveson," I said, and he said, "Yes, but that was different," and I said, "How?" and he laughed and said, "Don't you even want to know how it feels?"

"Not with her," I lied, and shivered myself, and told myself it was the cold, and he put his shirt around me and we huddled together in our awkward way, and dusk came.

"How about with me?" he said, and I was half asleep and didn't for a moment know what he meant, and when I did remember what we'd last said, I shook my head and half-laughed.

"Too much of a cliché," I said, "the misfits finding each other. And besides, I thought you didn't love women."

"But I love you," he said, and I put my head in his lap and wept.

"Am I that bad?" he said eventually, with a brave voice on.

"Oh, no, it isn't you," I said. "You heard young pretty Dulcie call me a great lumbering Cossack of a woman, and she wasn't far wrong. And I don't look like a man either, like that slim-hipped child you thought had cured you."

"I know how you look. We could all kill ourselves with unkindness. Am I such a bargain to woman or man, with my hand scarred and my little leprechaun body, that phrase is courtesy Dulcie, as I'm sure you realize, my dear, and my fossicky insistence on the right knot in my tie?"

"You set those student hearts a-flutter."

"Unfortunately, the wrong hearts. And what about your heart? You're the only one I've brought myself to love in this whole blank comedy. If it doesn't matter what we are, as we've reassured each other dozens of times, can't we extend that and say it doesn't matter who we are?"

"You'll have to give me a little time to think about it."

"And that's why you played dumb with the missus, and I with Iveson. How much longer? Why do you think I'm leaving?"

"All right. All right. You won't let me off easy, will you?

We went back to my house, and under the dim lamp in my sleeping room and study we undressed together in the same swift way as always, but without the unselfconsciousness. A hundred days I'd changed my clothes before him knowing it didn't matter, but on the hundred and first day I couldn't convince myself that it meant nothing, though I went through the motions easily enough.

We lay down together gingerly as if we were a scientific experiment, and tried to prove something to each other. That didn't work, but finally we got tired, and that made us more relaxed, and somehow we got more interested in each other after that. We made a lot of jokes, and laughed, and took each other seriously and were afraid and all.

It was really rather fine, though I'm afraid we still wished a little that we were with our fantasies instead, the women and the men who still propelled us. This is the picture I took in the morning. He sat by the window with the sun across his face just the way you see it there, and said, "Sandy, I love you."

"But." I said.

"Never mind that now," he said, "That's reality, and

comes back to haunt us later. This has been very happy, don't you think?"

"Yes, I think," I said, and took his picture, and he laughed. This is the one he took of me then, after he wrestled the camera away. He developed them himself in the drafting department's darkroom. He supposed that the corner drugstore would have destroyed the film, as they had done with one of his student's youthful experiments in anatomical study.

"You've made me brave," I said.

"You've made me happy," he said again, and came back and rubbed my neck, around and around, until I turned to him and kissed him, which was a first time for both of us, despite our night of passion. Somehow that made us more tender than all the rewarding acrobatics had been, and we were almost late for class, running like schoolkids down the hill to the bus, not hand in hand because our steps have never matched in length, but comfortable with each other in a new way. When you've told a lover what makes you happy, what intimate touch that you've practised on yourself for years and finally have a chance to share, when you've tasted each other and abandoned dignity, there's a chance for embarrassment or for intense comfort, and we were friends, and didn't care for what we'd given up, so we were cheerful and zany together.

In the afternoon the missus, whose name was Janet and who used to come to the school every day to drive her husband home, and wander around the studios and practice rooms until he'd finished whatever was keeping him late that day, came to my drafting table and said, "I haven't seen you for a week," which was not a surprise, as I'd leapt into corridors and crowded classrooms at the threat of her approach ever since her veiled conversation. We had been for lunch downtown several times, talking intensely over grilled cheese sandwiches at the American Dairy Lunch, walking back across the bridge, me in time for my late class and her to drive home her Thespian-handsome husband. She wore tiny perfect suits and I felt bovine beside her, though I liked her well enough. But I had not expected those subtle words, made into something more than their bare meaning by Dulcie's innuendos and my desperate wanting.

So I looked around the classroom to see that it was empty, and reached across the corner of my drafting table, and put my hand on her wrist, and said, "What do you want? What do you want?" and she turned white, then red, then put her hand over mine and said, "Whatever you want." Somehow that seemed clear to both of us, and I bent my head down—she was so small, here's a photograph of us together, her head came barely to my shoulder—I bent my head down and kissed her dangerously on the mouth, a closed and terrified kiss, and she sighed, and leaned against me, and I looked beyond her to see Sal quietly closing the door, winking at me with a serious face, and I burst into a sweat at how stupid I had been, what if it had been her chairman husband who walked by? And I put my arm around her, and held her to me for a clumsy minute, and then pulled away.

"What's the matter?" she said.

"Nothing," I said. "Do you know I was a virgin until yesterday?"

"What?"

"Never mind. Is your husband such a bad bargain, then, that you have to go to faculty wives and the like?"

"No. No. I can't. . . ."

"Never mind, that was rude of me."

"If I had the guts I should leave him, is that it?"

"Who am I to say? I haven't had any guts all my life. But you were a damn fool to go after Dulcie MacLean, she has a vicious tongue and she keeps it moving."

"I'm not very wise, about this, this, whatever I am."

"Who's wise? Do you want to leave him?"

"No. Not very much."

"So don't."

"And you?"

"Oh, I'll be your mistress, a secret, on the side. Why not do it like the men do it?"

"I want you to be my friend. If this is going to spoil that, I'll live without it."

"No you won't," I said. "You'll die without it. You'll watch me, though God knows why it should be me, I'm the last one I'd want as a lover, you'll watch whoever it is, and you'll be lonely no matter how many meetings at the American Dairy Lunch, you'll be angry with yourself for doing nothing and me for being a stone in your way, and your body for turning on you when you want it to be indifferent and you'll begin to think you're wrong, you're sick, you'll get tired and you'll give up and you'll never have any courage again. You might as well make your mistakes and get it over with."

"Like you?"

"No, like I didn't, until today, didn't dare."

"What changed you?"

"I'm still terrified, what do you mean, change? But I'm getting older, and my best friend's leaving town, and you only live one time, they say. But why me, woman? Why me?"

"You don't believe in yourself. I see you, I see everything

about you. Do you think I do this to everyone? And Dulcie's a liar."

And the door opened, and this time it was the chairman, seeing only us talking and saying, "Janet, ready to go?"

"I'll see you for lunch tomorrow," I said. "We'll go over to my place. I don't have a class until four."

"Sure," she said, looking at her husband, but he was beaming at us. "Good to see you girls getting acquainted," he actually said. "Janet needs more friends." And she looked at me in some kind of shock I think I understood, but I'm more cynical, I've been wearing men's clothes for years, so I grinned at her and said to him, "I'll take her under my wing," and thought, she hasn't got a friend in you, boss.

Sal came in later with the film dripping in a clip in his hand and said, "What a coincidence. I called Iveson today. He has a loft in Toronto. I asked if I could stay with him. He said he was alone right now, and I said good, and he said what do you mean, and I said, it depends on whether your offer is still open, and so it went. I sweated like a teenager. Do you get the feeling we are rushing headlong into life like a couple of clichés?"

It seemed like that at the time, life turning out like an under-the-counter version of those soap operas I've never gotten around to enjoying, either then on radio or now on TV, but that was only one day in a lifefull. Janet had children, and left me, not in that order, and Iveson got sick of himself and committed suicide, and Sal lives alone now in a hand-built house with framed photographs of the stars who were his students, and some of himself when he was onstage before the war, and one of me by which I should be flattered, especially as it is a copy of this one, the one he took that morning. "It's when we were at our best," he said. "You were brave and I was happy. That didn't happen very often."

And I have finally decided to sort these photographs and make and album of them, while I have the time. Here's another of the two of us, Sal and I, when we lived in New York. That was ten years later, just after Iveson died, and we went out there to have a holiday and stayed for two years. He was always a good influence on me. Look at that suit he had! It cost him six hundred dollars, when he didn't have a penny, but he managed it. And that was the cape he bought for me at the same time. I wore it all that winter.

"I knew I could get you to wear burgundy," he said when he gave it to me, so to retaliate, I bought him a purple shirt and a pink tie, and he wore them, by God, one night when he went to an off-Broadway show with a boy he'd picked up. When he got home the next day he told me, "I've always liked your taste in clothes," and we laughed. Here's a snapshot I took. I'm sorry, it's a little blurry. But it gives you an idea, how it was for us then.

~

Candas Jane Dorsey *is an Edmonton-based writer whose twenty-five years of writing have included mainstream and speculative fiction, poetry, drama, non-fiction, and journalism. She has published four books of poetry, one book of short stories, and co-edited an anthology of Canadian speculative fiction. In 1994 one of her short stories will be included on a CD-ROM travelling on a spaceship to Mars. "What We Wore" first appeared in* NeWest Review, *vol. 9, no. 10.*

The Tastee Freeze Man

CECELIA FREY

"Have you had these symptoms long?" Dr. Ptyszkptyszch asked, peering with the help of his little flashlight into what I could only assume was the virgin pink lining of my quaking throat.

I tried to speak but I nearly choked on the flashlight. Dr. Ptyszkptyszch seemed to become aware then of the impossibility of his demand. He pulled out his gadget and held it before him, like a gun, I thought. From his high stool, one heel hooked up onto the rung, he directed its powerful single beam first into my right eye, then into my left.

"What do you mean?" I got out.

For some reason, this question seemed to anger him.

"I mean, what do you mean 'long'?" I quickly added. I sincerely believe that I was not *trying* to be difficult. After all, long is a relative term and what is long to Dr. Ptyszkptyszch may not be long at all to anyone else, including me.

"When did you first notice them?" He rephrased his question.

"Them?" I said and immediately regretted the word.

He snapped off his light. For a moment we stared into each other's eyes. His were blue. Cool blue. I happen to have hazel eyes. Sometimes the green surfaces, sometimes the brown, depending on the light and my mood. I felt sure that, at that moment, the doctor was seeing the dull, stupid brown.

"The symptoms." I could tell from the tone of his voice he was going to try patience.

I tried to think, but my mind flew about like a wild bird I was helpless to catch. The problem was the white coat. White coats always had this effect on me. That uniform of no-nonsense demand for me to supply correct answers. Which, I should point out, was not at all like my father. Oh, my father wore a white coat. He had to. He was a Tastee Freeze Man. But, let's face it, a Tastee Freeze Man hardly wields much authority.

No, when I think of the Tastee Freeze Man I hear a sound in my head, a forlorn, sad, little song trundling down the hot, summer afternoon street, deserted except for a small group of children staring after him, all their desire in their eyes but no change in their pockets.

My father, now that we're on the subject, was a gentle man, although perhaps cold, or not cold so much as distracted and, therefore, seemingly withholding of his affections. I always tried to please him; I was very attached to him, which likely explains why I adore white coats.

"Scratchy throat . . . ," Dr. Ptyszkptyszch was prompting me. ". . . the feeling that something is caught in your throat . . . ," he kept on, ending with a little curlicue of question, ". . . that you can't swallow?"

". . . that I'm always on the verge of choking . . . ," I added, triumphantly. "That something is taking root. . . ." Into the swing of it now, I could have, actually wanted to, keep going.

"Yes." The tone, crisp as his curly hair, brought me down.

"Hmmm," I frowned. I mean, how can you be sure of something that insidious, that creeping? How can you possibly know when you first detected the first sign? I mean, it could have been there from birth for all I know. Like, maybe what I thought was normal wasn't normal.

Impatiently, Dr. Ptyszkptyszch changed tactics. "Is it painful?" he shot out briskly.

"Only when I speak."

He nodded thoughtfully.

"Or eat," I said, trying to be helpful. "Or drink."

He stood up, a tall figure hovering over me. Across his shoulder, above his head, his shadow cast in subdued light loomed on wall and ceiling, a phantom virtually filling the examination room.

"You should have come sooner," he said gravely.

All very well for him to say. It was my body up for inspection, not his. My inadequate body, I might add. For I feel sure that I could have faced those Ptyszkptyszch years with more aplomb armed with a perfect body, one without hips or cellulite or those fleshy appendages hanging around, bouncing in the breeze as my sister, the irreverent one, used to put it.

"Once something like this gets a head start—" he broke off abruptly and changed direction. "Oh, don't think you're unique." His powerful head swung down. "There is, was, one once. Not a patient of mine. . . ."

I held my breath.

I've never actually *seen* one. . . ."

"One?"

"But documented, in the literature. . . ."

"What is it?" I was finally able to whisper, but as soon as the words were out, I didn't want to know.

~

"A tree," I said. "Would you believe? Apparently." I kept my eyes on my plate of untouched leafage. I couldn't bear to see the lovingly condescending smirk that would be on Kirk's face, the smirk that gently teased, "I know you. You just want attention." After two years of marriage, it was clearly apparent that Kirk thought that for one's own good, attention was a commodity to be administered in small doses.

That was why the interest in his voice took me by surprise. "What kind of tree?"

I hadn't thought to ask.

"You mean to say," said Kirk, in disgust, "Some doctor tells you you have a tree growing in your throat and you don't even ask what kind?"

"I guess it threw me for a bit of a loop," I defended, chancing a look across the white linen, through the sparkling crystal.

Steak knife and fork precisely in hand, Kirk was in the act of dissecting the specimen on his plate. As he sliced into his rare find, he might have been measuring lava flow, calculating pleasure in the accuracy of his predictions.

"It makes a difference," he said, lifting his fork with its hunk of flesh speared on the tines. "Poplar's pretty big. Deep roots. On the other hand, a willow can easily be ripped out."

His words agitated me, the same way they had when we first met across a lab bench in Earth Sciences. Oh, not the words in themselves so much, but the way Kirk delivered them. He was just so damned sure of himself. He always knew the answer, if there was one. If there wasn't, that was all right, too, because then you knew. As Kirk explained it, if an experiment doesn't have the expected conclusion, that's just about as good as if it does because then you can cross that possibility off your list. My problem, he said, was that I always try to find a solution, even if there isn't one. My female lack of reason, he enlightened me after class over screaming hot chicken wings and cold beer.

What I learned with Kirk was not to let him get to me (I hadn't as yet arrived at that state of perfection) but, rather, to pretend. Becoming agitated was to fall into his trap; he loved to see my temperature escalate, the simmer and seethe of eruption after the low, warning rumbles. Rather than give him that satisfaction, usually I either ignored him or held myself in check. This had the wonderful, unexpected result of agitating him.

I counted to ten, listened to Muzak's computerized version of "La vie en rose" and watched the waiters, brisk as penguins, swoop and glide. We were in Kirk's favourite restaurant, clean and bright as a research laboratory.

Kirk was completely focused on his steak. There was something appealingly young, even boyish, about such concentration. I had an impulse to reach across and run my fingers through his neat, short curls. I envisioned myself jumping up, running around the table, throwing my arms around his wide, muscular shoulders, nuzzling my face into his deep, fleshy chest. What would he do? I restrained myself.

Instead, I said, "Dr. Ptyszkptyszch says 4-D Killer should get it. I won't even have to miss a day's work."

For the second, or perhaps it was the third, time that day I regretted my remarks. The one topic I tried to avoid with Kirk was my job.

"That job," was Kirk's totally predictable response. "Why don't you get a real job?"

"It is a real job."

"With real people."

"They are real people."

"A bunch of weirdos in skirts." It wasn't that Kirk had anything against love and brotherhood and communes. It was just that he's geared to action, and the people in the artists' colony where I had my pot booth moved too slowly for him.

The real problem with my job, though, was what it did to my hands.

"Worse than hairy legs," was his pronouncement on rough hands.

"Sorry. I'll shave them," I joked the first time the subject surfaced. He didn't laugh.

In Kirk's opinion, rough hands were the most unfeminine thing in the whole world. He couldn't help it. It was his job. Also, he grew up with a mother who, even yet, is another Zsa Zsa. It was our first date, although he later denied this, that he instructed me in the lost art of nail buffing, using as his example his mother's hours of work in polishing hers to a high gloss.

Kirk had finished his meat and was sitting, elbows on table, chin on knuckles. He gave a small, soft, contented burp and looked at me. I hid my hands in my lap. But I was supposed to be eating my salad. I put them back on the table. Kirk's eyes were blue spotlights. I put them back in my lap.

Two pronged fingers jabbed out from beneath Kirk's

chin, a habit that even then was starting to make me flinch. "Where are those gloves I bought you?" he said.

~

"Oh, you are a genius." Dr. Ptyszk tried to hide his distaste. "You've done it again. Have you been walking around," he accused, "with your mouth open?"

"No . . . ," I said. "At least, I don't think. . . ." I looked up into his face and caught his chiselled profile just as it was turning away to talk to the wall.

"Have you become one of those health food nuts?" he sneered.

"No. . . ."

"Dried roots, stuff like that?"

"Just what they sell at Safeway." I tried to think.

"You don't remember swallowing a seed?"

A moment before, I would have sworn an emphatic No. But as soon as he asked the question, I couldn't be sure.

Dr. Ptyszk swung and raised his trusty flashlight. "Open!" he commanded and my mouth snapped to attention. In a replay of seven years earlier, his powerful torso pressed me down into the chair designed to hold me in place while he performed his examination, his light searching my throat for clues. When he was finished, he sat back on his stool. The creases in his heavy (might I say "craggy"?) forehead deepened.

As my heart palpitated at that combination of commanding head and white coat, he came to his conclusion. "I'm sure," he said.

"You are?" I gasped.

"Old roots reactivated by some irritant," he pronounced. "Think!" he demanded, and I broke out in a cold sweat. "Have you been swallowing the wrong way?"

Any words I might have said were stuck firmly in my throat by the cement of sheer panic.

"In any case," he said, "we'll get those little devils this time."

"You mean. . . ."

"Another round of 4-D. Cleared it up before, no reason why it shouldn't clear it up again. You had no negative reaction?"

"No. . . . Except, remember, I had to take that neutralizer. In the end."

"Oh, yes. . . ." He picked up my file from the top of the cabinet.

"Because of the caustic effects of the 4-D. Not that it bothered me," I hastened to add, afraid he would withdraw the cure. "It was my husband."

"Husband?"

"Who persisted. He said he couldn't live with me. He said I was a changed person. With that 4-D Killer in my system."

"It's supposed to know where to attack. Specific growths. Nothing else."

"It started with the wine."

"That explains it. You can't mix alcohol. . . ."

"Apparently, according to Kirk, if you don't choose the right wine you're on your way to hell in a handbasket."

"I don't see. . . ."

"Kirk always chooses the dinner wine," I plunged on. "He would never trust me. And he's right," I hastened to add.

"Something terrible happened." Now that my tongue was unhinged, it wouldn't stop flapping. "Kirk had to pick up the president of his company and his wife at the airport. The plan was for him to take them to their hotel and then come home for a couple of hours and then pick them up again and bring them to our house for dinner. But, Harry, that's the president, Harry insisted on drinks in the hotel bar and Kirk couldn't refuse and the drinks lasted well into the dinner hour but, finally, the three of them arrived about eight, all well launched I might add, but I didn't mind; in fact, I was glad to see Kirk loosened up a bit, but then he forgot about the wine so I just grabbed some bottles from the rack and it was some sort of German white."

"German white is quite respectable," Dr. Ptyszk offered.

"Not with filet mignon," I whispered. "According to Kirk, anyway." I raised my voice. "After Harry and Mabel, that's Harry's wife, left in the cab, the first thing he, Kirk, said was what kind of wine was that to serve with red meat. I said, what did it matter, they seemed to have an uproarious time. I said they wouldn't have known if I'd served horse piss."

"Perhaps that was . . . ," Dr. Ptyszk got in, but I had to continue.

"If I would have stopped there, it would have been okay. But I said some other things, including, I think, although by then I'd had quite a bit of wine too, because all during dinner I'd seen how Kirk was upset even though he didn't want to show it in front of our guests, but I was so upset about him being upset that I just kept downing this wine. But, I remember the words 'pompous, priggish prick'. Because it felt so good getting those plosives off my chest, my engorged, dripping, smelly chest, I might add, as I was just then nursing

Darryl and all that wine within a few hours released the sap like you wouldn't believe."

"All married couples have these little spats," Dr. Ptyszk offered.

"It wasn't the actual spat that bothered me so much." I tried to be clear. "But the way, when I opened my mouth, I didn't know what would come out. I had no control. . . ." I heard my voice rise. Afraid of what Kirk called hysterics, I brought it down. "So then," I said, "you gave me that neutralizer."

"And it worked?"

"Oh yes. Things cleared up just fine. And then, for the past five years things have been . . . wonderful. Well, I've been so busy, what with the Well Baby Clinic and three A.M. feedings and total exhaustion and I try to do a little of my pots on the side."

"Pots?"

"What Kirk calls my little hobby. I *do* find it very relaxing somehow, mucking about with that wet clay."

Suddenly it became alarmingly quiet in the examining room. Dr. Ptyszk was consulting or pretending to consult my file. But the strange thing was the look on his face, one of absolute aversion. What had I confessed to? Being a female mud wrestler all slimy and primal?

The voice when it came was strictly business. "You've had two pregnancies?"

"Yes." I clipped my tone and resisted an impulse to elaborate. I'd show him that two could play the professional game.

"That was your mistake," he told me.

"Mistake?"

"The relapse. I wondered. I didn't think it could be my treatment.   Pregnancy lowers the body's defence mechanisms."

"It does?"

"The body is concentrating on nurturing the foetus. Gives forces, viruses, a chance to attack. However, what's done is done. No use crying over spilled milk. No problems with the births?"

"No. Except, a little . . . something really minor." I sunk low in my chair. "The youngest, Mikie . . . toilet training," I whispered.

"I meant with the deliveries."

"Oh no, they simply popped out."

Dr. Ptyszk made a mark on my file and snapped it shut.

"I couldn't believe how easy it was," my mouth went on. "That part of it. No, the problems came later. Although, really, it's nothing. I know that, part of me knows it, the other part. It's just so . . . oh, it will all work out in the wash, I'm sure," I smiled with what I hoped was confidence.

And when it was out in the open, it did seem insignificant. I couldn't imagine why I got so uptight about it. It was true, that kid simply would not toilet train. He could be so full of it his cheeks could be puffed out. He'd get up off his potty, toddle down the sidewalk with his little wagon and return ten minutes later with a full load.

I knew it had become a battle of wills. I knew I should just ignore it. And I was able to, for awhile, but then I'd have a bad day when I'd feel like I couldn't face one more shitty diaper. I'd break down, have a tantrum, only reinforcing his control over me, which of course he very well knew, the little bastard.

I clamped my hand over my mouth right then and there. Dr. Ptyszk would be shocked.

But the good doctor hadn't been reading my thoughts after all. Rather, he was busily charting his cure.

~

"Don't tell me," said Kirk, "we have to put up with that again."

"I'm sorry," I said, flipping my sprouts in time to Muzak's "Two Ton Tessie from Tennessee."

"Just make sure this time you get that neutralizer right away." He swirled and sniffed his brandy.

"Except," I interrupted before he got his hopes up. "He can't give that to me at the beginning. He says the 4-D has to start doing its job first. Otherwise, it won't work."

"So, there'll be a period. . . ."

"Only a few weeks. . . ."

"Well," said Kirk, sipping and savouring, "at least I'll be away. . . ."

"Away?"

I waited a moment for his taste buds to complete their analysis of initial response, intermediate assessment and end result. "The Los Angeles conference," he said. "Apparent stresses, stress drops, and amplitude ratios of earthquakes preceding and following the 1975 Hawaii Ms equals seven point two main shock."

I was struck dumb.

"My paper," he announced.

"This is the first I've heard of it."

"I told you."

"When?"

"The other night."

"You couldn't have told me."

"You never remember anything I tell you."

"I would have remembered that."

"It was in the bathroom. You were bathing Mikie."

"What a time to tell me."

"It was the only time I had."

Chalk one up for him. What with my kindergarten committee and Block Watch and Kirk's Committee for the Study of Evidence of Large Magnitude Earthquakes with Very Long Recurrence Intervals, Basin and Range Province of Southeastern Arizona, and his Committee for the Study of Body-Wave Analysis Regarding Rupture Complexity of a Moderate-Sized mb 6.0 Earthquake, the only time we saw each other was sometimes Saturday night and then other people were always around.

"Mother will be here," Kirk was reassuring me, "if you need anything."

"Great."

"Just be careful," said Kirk. "With Mother. After all, a person can be understanding only up to a point."

"I apologized."

"She accepted. All I'm saying is, learn from experience to keep your mouth shut when you're on that Killer."

"You don't understand."

"What's there to understand? You just don't go around calling harmless old ladies blue-rinse bitches."

"It just came out." I winced, remembering so well that terrible scene—Kirk's mother shouting "that's a lie!" and me apologizing for calling her a bitch and her saying "I've never had a blue rinse in my life."

"I was totally wrong," I confessed.

"Guard your speech, that's all I'm saying. Show some control."

"She gets the birch blonde," I said out loud to myself, words I had often thought. It felt so good, saying those words, that I repeated them. Louder.

Kirk raised his head and looked at me across the white tablecloth, through the forest of crystal. Maybe it was the brandy, but he was giving me the same attention he would igneous. My heart did a flipflop and I grew all warm and squishy. Then came the familiar flow of anxiety. I both wanted and didn't want him to discover the truth that I was sedimentary.

His look honed down to my plate. "What's wrong with your salad?" he said.

"Nothing." I forked something into my mouth.

"If you'd eat some real food instead of compost."

"I like salads," I defended. No sooner were the words out than I realized what a liar I was. I hated salads. I was up to here with salads. What I really wanted was, no, not one of Kirk's bloody steaks, what I wanted was a Dairy Queen Blizzard, cool and soothing on my throat. What I wanted was chocolate chip, double cream, vanilla ice-cream pie. I would even settle for a Peanut Buster Parfait. But, unfortunately, I was born with a body built for comfort rather than speed, and anything remotely resembling what I would call real food went straight to my bottom like balloon ballast, settling me even more firmly onto the earth with its unfortunate gravitational pull.

Why oh why did I have to fall for a man with a delicate taste in women? Lots of men out there must like the robust

Rubens type erupting through the tops of their blouses, oozing through their seams and gussets.

I pulled myself back to reality. Mind control, I told myself. You love salads. I forced myself to clean up every speck. I was considering raising my plate and licking up the dressing when Kirk's voice shot across the table. "What's wrong with your hands?"

"Nothing."

"You've been into your pots again." His lip curled.

"Just occasionally." I folded my hands into my armpits.

"What you need," said Kirk, "is something to keep you busy."

"I *am* busy."

"I mean a challenge."

"You don't think the kids are a challenge?"

"It would do you good to get out with people."

"What do you call my preschool swim co-ordination? And my integration of inner-city lunch services for the underprivileged?"

"I mean something where you're using your mind—your degree."

"I *am* using my mind," I said, and was immediately ashamed at the feeble tone of my voice.

"Well," he said in his washing-his-hands-of-the-whole-affair-if-you-insist-on-being-miserable voice.

"And by the way," he said, "where's that dress I bought you?"

"I'm saving it," I said.

"What for?"

"A special occasion."

~

"Another relapse, is it?" Ptyszk seemed truly offended.

"You're the doctor, you tell me," I felt like saying but kept my mouth shut.

"I'm not surprised," he went on. This time we were poised either side the smooth expanse of his desk. "I know you insist on breathing," he gave me one of his sternest looks, "through your mouth."

What could I say? What he said was true. But I did it in my sleep when I didn't know what I was doing. Or when I was awake, in times of stress, like when I was putting on a dinner party for twelve people and trying not to fuck up, as Kirk would say. It was like when the kids were small and I was bathing them, trying to hold on to those eel-like bodies so their heads wouldn't slip under. There I'd be, kneeling on the bathroom floor, crouched over the tub, without support for the weight I held in my hands, breathing, trying to breathe, through my mouth. I tried to control this very bad habit. I did control it, when I had myself under control. What more could I do? What more could anyone do?

My file was lying sprawled shamelessly open on Ptyszk's immaculate desk. He seemed to be reading. "It was a bit of a beast to get rid of last time. Six years ago, no, seven."

"The seven-year itch," I tried to be jovial.

"What?"

"Nothing," I turned serious. "It *was* stubborn. And the antidote for it, the neutralizer, I mean, didn't seem to work as quickly. It was touch and go for awhile there. Kirk was a saint to put up with me."

Ptyszk was absorbed in his reading material. I wondered

what incriminating evidence it might contain. The toilet training? I now realized how wildly over-reactive I had been. After all, everything had worked out fine. Once I realized that Mikie was challenging my self-image of perfect mother and worthwhile human being, I was able to become more perfect by not letting myself get upset. So then I won. After that, he had no choice but to toilet train himself.

The black leather skirt incident? But it was so recent; it couldn't be in my file yet.

"Black leather?" came the voice of Ptyszk and I realized I had spoken out loud.

"It was nothing," I said. "At least, not really . . . only, well, . . . it has this slit up to here. Like, it's embarrassing."

"Black leather has . . . certain attractions." The voice sounded strangely soft.

"The thing is," I explained, "he caught me unaware. Kirk, I mean. I didn't expect him for another two days. A man comes home, he said, tired and hungry, from two weeks in the Santa Rita Fault Zone and what does he find? His wife in granny flannels with grease all over her face. So then I said if he wouldn't come home when he's not supposed to, he wouldn't have to know the horrible truth about me. But it was all so stupid because I was quite willing, at first, to wipe off the cream and put on something frilly, but then when he acted so horrible there was no way. Instead, I marched back to where he was sitting on the bed taking off his shoes, shoved my face into his and screamed, "You think that was grease! *This* is grease!"

Ptyszk, it appeared, was shocked into silence.

"So, then," I said, "he slept in the guest-room."

What could Ptyszk say? Apparently, nothing.

I thought a moment. I shuddered. "How could I be so immature?" I murmured, but there was no answer. "The next day," I said stirring, "Kirk came home with this package, gift-wrapped, from this very expensive leather shoppe. There it was, the skirt, complete with black net stockings and spike heels. It's just . . . ," I tried to explain, "I'm not the black leather type. It's just. . . ." I felt the need to go on, "My closet is full of clothes he, Kirk, has bought me over the years. All of them, each and every one of them, the wrong size and style. There I am," I sighed, "with all these cute little things made for a midget. And no room to hang my own."

It was then I realized that Ptyszk hadn't spoken for several minutes. I looked up. Across the shadowy desk his eyes had a yellowish glow.

"Are you game?" he said, his voice thrumming.

"Uhhh. . . ." I said.

"To try something different?" he asked.

My breath stopped.

"Let's get serious," he sat up straighter and prepared to leap across the desk onto me.

Wanting both to flee and to stay, I half-stood. "Serious?" I croaked.

"Go for the knife."

$\sim$

I didn't bother telling Kirk. By now, the whole thing was yesterday's news. Besides, after sixteen years of marriage, our territorial lines were firmly established. My job was to cope with the daily routine, to keep life running smoothly and not bother him with details.

I honestly didn't mind. Kirk's job was important. He was going to save millions of people from being swallowed by the earth. Sometimes he talked as though the earth were the enemy. But I knew he didn't feel like that at all. The earth was something he had to get under control for the good of all concerned, including its own.

"When shall we schedule you?" Ptyszk had asked.

I had to explain. "I volunteer at the school library Tuesday mornings, the rehabilitation swimming Thursday mornings. Then there's Block Watch Wednesday afternoons which I'm trying to get out of, after all I've been at it ten years now, but you know how it is, they can't get anyone else, and I'm the president. . . ."

Ptyszk stirred impatiently in his chair.

I started checking things off on my fingers. "There's soccer Mondays after school, basketball Thursdays, piano. . . ."

Ptyszk closed my file.

"Let's make it Tuesday noon," I said quickly. "Tuesday evenings is my pot class. Not that I've done anything with my pots for ages, but I thought if I took a class, you know, it would get me going again, force me . . . but I really don't have time for this course anyway . . . it was dumb to enroll. Yes, Tuesday would be all right, as long as I'm out by noon Wednesday."

"No problem," said Ptyszk. "Of course, you won't be able to speak. A bit like laryngitis for a few days, but you won't be sick, just a little whoozy from the anaesthetic."

Kirk would be away, so I made arrangements for the boys to sleep over at the neighbour's. On the appointed day, I packed my bag and off I went. The next morning early, I found myself flat on my back, strapped to a bed, delivered into the waiting arms, or more accurately, eyes, of Ptyszk. I'd been shot through the hip with something which obliterated feeling but heightened perception, so that the operating theatre was brought into painfully sharp focus. And there, with the gleaming white and glaring chrome, preparing to attack my throat, was a whole team of surgeons and assistants, not the least of whom was Ptyszk. In the blue, shapeless gown floating above me, I recognized his formidable presence and, above a face mask, the icy shaft of his gaze.

"Ptyszky," I said with genuine pleasure mixed with relief.

Was it my imagination or did a gleam of recognition cross that shaft? And what was it the voice said, sounding as it did, like a record on slow speed?

"A Ptyszkit, a Ptaszket," were my last words before going under.

～

That was when I at last became perfect. I could put on a dinner party for Kirk's colleagues like you wouldn't believe. I could juggle ten committees and be president, or at least secretary, of every one of them. The boys were top of their classes, top of their teams, top of their fitness test charts. Clockwork was my name. House Beautiful was my game. Doris Day in the early sixties reruns had nothing on me.

I even lost thirty pounds and felt almost comfortable in black leather. I found those gloves of long ago in the bottom of my drawer. They fit my new, sleek, smooth hands. I dug out the birthday dress. I told myself that its crisp lines better suited my lifestyle. Long skirts and loose sandals force a person to move with a certain slowness or your knees get tangled in the folds and your feet lose your shoes. This is especially dangerous when you're driving on the freeway and you go to hit the brake pedal and your shoe stays on the gas. Long hair, too, is impractical. It gets mixed up in all sorts of things and vice versa. I used to find bits of clay stuck in my hair, although that would no longer be a problem since I didn't do pots anymore. I didn't mind. I had already put pots down as one of those hobbies of one's youth, like romance.

In the way life has of being actively opposed to perfection, it started again. Again, I realized the scratchy, throaty feelings in the middle of the night, those times when you wake up and don't know where you are or who you are and it takes you a moment to stake yourself.

I didn't go to Ptyszk right away. I couldn't bear the thought of disappointing him. But one day I knew I had to.

"You've done it this time," he said. "You've waited too long."

"I kept hoping," I said, "it would go away on its own."

"You should know better," he scolded.

"I couldn't face it," I said, recalling the day it hit me in the face. That was the day I saw myself walking towards me in the shopping centre. There I was, zipping along in my new clothes, getting the twenty things on my list done in time to pick up Darryl at the university because his car was in for a clutch job, and Mike from band practice so he could get to a basketball game, and then home to dress and downtown to the Palliser where Kirk's company was hosting a hospitality hour for delegates to the annual meeting of Canadian geophysicists. I happened to look up and there, smack in front of me, was this woman I recognized but couldn't quite place.

I thought, my God, has she ever gotten older. Of course it turned out to be myself.

I walked right up to that mirror on the pillar and stared. I couldn't believe my eyes. It wasn't the aging so much as the sight of those curly-sproingy things growing out of the top of my head.

I had to go and sit down. I had to cool the fire that was raging in my throat. Luckily, there was an empty booth at the Dairy Queen. I discovered my mouth ordering a Reese's Pieces Blizzard. When it came, I ate mechanically, staring straight ahead. I ordered another. I had just taken the first spoonful when I realized I couldn't go on like this. I had to return to Ptyszk, fast.

"What do you expect me to do," Ptyszk asked almost wearily, "when you've let it go this far?"

"Make it better," I said, resisting the urge to plead, *kiss it better, make it go away.*

"Your throat is a mess," he pronounced. "An aberration. All that scar tissue."

"I'm sorry," I said.

"If you would only relax," he said, sticking his flashlight once more between my teeth.

When he was finished, he regarded me gravely. "All we can do," he said, "is keep trying."

I was low, very low. I stood, drooping and defeated, at the receptionist's desk. She was on the telephone booking me into the hospital. As though to confirm my mental darkness, a shadow darted at the corner of my eye. I turned my head to catch it and saw a man between examining rooms. He was short, squat, and his hair, what he had of it, was grey. He looked in my direction and, for an instant, our eyes met. His showed no sign of recognition. Maybe, even if he hadn't already been thinking about the next throat in what must have been for him an unending line of throats crying for attention, he would not have known me with my mouth closed. The only way I knew him was the white coat.

In a state of shock, I turned my back on the reception desk and on Ptyszk. Forever. And then, how can I explain it? In that moment of turning the miracle happened. I felt a feathery tickle in my throat. I didn't panic. I went home slowly. With the help of mirrors, I was able to detect just the tips of wings busily going about their business, building a nest.

~

"I've been meaning to tell you," said Kirk, not unkindly. "You're growing a moustache."

"I know," I said, attacking my broccoli casserole. "And my skin is like bark and my voice sounds like a crow. So what else is new?"

"These things happen," said Kirk. "Me, I've got these long hairs growing from my nose."

"I've noticed," I said.

"I've been clipping them," Kirk said.

"Good for you." The creamy sauce made my throat feel silky smooth.

"Do you ever stop to think," said Kirk, "that it's going to get worse?"

"Couldn't care less," was my answer.

"There are hair removal clinics," suggested Kirk.

"I like my moustache," I said. "I like the three hairs growing out of the mole on my chin."

"I wasn't going to mention them," said Kirk.

"I've earned them all," I said. "I wouldn't dream of destroying them."

"How about the boys?" said Kirk.

"How about them?" said I.

"They'll be home for spring break."

"I was going to buy a special hat," I admitted. "One that comes down close around my ears. One that hides my face. But then I said to hell with it."

Truth to tell, I did worry a bit about the boys. I knew how they would look at me, expecting perfection and seeing the little branches springing out either side my ears, the rings of growth settling around my midsection.

"They'll grow up," I reassured Kirk. "Time is on our side."

"I suppose you're right," he said. "Just wait until *their* hair starts growing every damn place except where they want it."

I flicked the last broccoli tree into my mouth and looked across the table. "You haven't even started your casserole," I accused. "What's wrong?"

"Nothing." Kirk picked up his fork. "It's very good."

Poor Kirk. He can't eat all that meat anymore because of the cholesterol. As for me, I don't even miss ice cream. Since I've been doing my pots full time and even selling a bit on the side and have my own change jingling in my pocket, I'm not even tempted. That's because these days my throat feels swell with all that exciting activity in there, my little feathery family.

I know I shouldn't have, but remembering my salad days, I took pity on Kirk. After all, he's a man who all his adult life has been studying surface rupture events over which he has no control but thinks he has. "Want me to help you?" I suggested, looking across the red tablecloth, through the stubs of candles sputtering in old wine bottles.

That's another thing, I've convinced Kirk that our favourite café is one near the collective where I have my booth. You can't see anything in there, including the grease spots on the tablecloths but as Kirk says, "this way we don't notice each other's wrinkles."

Kirk, with a look of relief, pushed his dish into the centre of the table. As though orchestrated, in time, if not always in tune, we bent to it and dug in.

≈

Cecelia Frey *lives and writes in Calgary. Her publications include the novel* Breakaway *(1974), a runner-up in the New Alberta Novelist competition;* the least you can do is sing *(1982); and* The Nefertiti Look *(1987), which won the Writers Guild of Alberta Short Fiction Award. Her newest collection of short fiction is* The Love Song of Romeo Paquette *(1990).* "The Tastee Freeze Man" *was published in* Prairie Fire, *Autumn 1990.*

Men, Boys, Girls, Women

MARY WALTERS RISKIN

Anne has driven more than twelve hundred kilometres to get to the coast and beyond. She has swerved around sheep which wandered onto the highway near Cranbrook and she's left strips of rubber in Creston, where she narrowly missed a cyclist. Near Trail she hurtled down the side of a mountain in the fog, pursued by a semi-trailer which had lost its brakes. Still, it hasn't occurred to her to worry about the car until this moment.

She is leaning against the trunk of a fir tree on the heights of Bluff Park, watching the Vancouver ferry start into Active Pass and waiting for the bellow of its horn. It has begun to drizzle, and she's moved against the tree for shelter. Although she is dressed for walking, she has not prepared for rain.

She's thinking how different the ferry looks from above— no more significant than a boat in a bathtub—than it does from a passenger's perspective. Inside that vast, shuddering vessel, she's wandered from the aluminum and glass and Arborite of the cafeteria past the souvenir and news stand, through wide-windowed rooms with rows and rows of upholstered seats, past card tables and video games and the snack shop, up to the salt-streaked window at the bow. Then, she has the sense that it is the landscape which is moving. The ferry is fixed and permanent. The water and the islands are the drifters.

It was like that in the car as they moved toward the coast. The station wagon was a piece of home, their juice cans and empty chip bags strewn across its floor mats, suitcases and shoulder bags where they'd thrown them in the back. They could put their hands on their possessions in an instant, could stop and change into an entirely different set of clothes as familiar as the ones already on their backs. Surrounded by their books, their magazines, they became settlers of a kind. What of the mountains, the villages and parks? The bridges and railroad tracks, the cliffs and channels? Those were the novelties, gone within the moment. Those things moved past the windows of their little stockpile, reeled themselves out alongside their familiar place.

After twelve years, the blue station wagon is as familiar as a car can get. Every spring and winter and the few times when it's broken down, she's taken it to the service station near where she lived when she was married.

The owner there does not embarrass her about her lack of knowledge about cars. He explains carefully what needs to be done and why, and she reads his work orders with attention before she signs them. He is a small soft man of nearly sixty years, no taller than her shoulder, his hair white and his nails ridged with black. She advises him about RRSPs and mutual funds, and they are satisfied with their respective areas of expertise.

For the weekend, she has left the car and the children in Victoria with her mother and her father. She's come over to

Galiano for some solitude, after months of work and children, and after the long drive.

She begins the five-kilometre walk back to L'Auberge, her bed and breakfast. She stops at the bottom of the hill at the edge of the park to watch a water plane land near the ferry dock, and then she starts down the highway. She keeps close to the edge of the pavement for the shelter of the trees. It is raining harder now.

When they arrived from the ferry at her parents' home, her mother gathered all three of them, in the driveway, into a hug. Anne looked over at her father, and found him a little thinner than he used to be, but not much changed from the last time she had seen him. He was walking around her car and examining its rust spots.

Eddie broke from the women and went to stand beside his grandfather. He was now taller than Anne's father, and beginning to fill out. He, too, studied the rust that was eating away the lower body of the station wagon. "My dad's just got a new Toyota," he said.

"Toyota's a good car," Anne's father replied.

Later that night, when Jess and Eddie were asleep, he came into the kitchen. "Let me lend you money for a car," he said.

There was a pause while Anne's mother looked at Anne, then at Anne's father, her face expressionless, her breath held, her hand still over Anne's where she'd just been patting it and saying again how glad she was that they had come.

The pause was not one in which Anne made up her mind. There was no question of what she'd say. She was remembering that this was the way he did things. She put him back into context in that pause, remembering other things he'd offered in the years since her divorce: a lawn mower, lift-out windows, a gas barbecue, new roofing. And then she shook her head.

She felt her mother's hand squeeze hers.

"Thanks anyway," she said to her father, who'd already shrugged and gone to pour the water for his pills.

"Any time you need it," he said. "It wouldn't put me short."

"I know."

Her mother said, "She'll get a car when she wants to, Neil. Anne is doing fine."

When she gets back to the inn, she changes into dry clothes and goes downstairs for dinner. She is shown to a table for two near the window, and she sits so that her back is to the other tables in the dining room. There was a time when she felt uncomfortable at the way her aloneness called attention to her in dining rooms and restaurants. People avoided looking at her, as though she had a strawberry birth mark on her face or had forgotten to wear a blouse. But she's learning not to worry about what other people think, and tonight she's feeling peaceful after the walk. She's looking forward to bouillabaisse and sole, and to the warmth of wine.

But she finds herself looking through the rain on the window at the cars in the small parking lot. Gleaming from the light at the top of a pole near the inn, they all look new and reliable. As though the confines of the island have compressed them, most of them are small, much smaller than her own old, ship-like, rust-eaten vehicle. Hers, she decides, is the kind of car that stalls for no apparent reason in intersections and on highways. And passers-by think, what did she expect?

~

"You had a lot of rain," her mother says when she gets back. "It's too bad." Her mother is pleased with herself for giving Anne a break, and she doesn't want to think that her rest has been spoiled in any way.

"It was fine," Anne assures her. "The weather didn't matter."

Her parents have taken her children everywhere while she's been gone. They've been to Sealand, the Wax Museum, the Empress Hotel for tea. They have saved the Butchart Gardens for Anne's return and for an improvement in the weather. When it comes, Anne wants to drive them out in her car: it's been sitting by the curb since she arrived and she's been thinking about it almost constantly since Galiano. The more she thinks about it, the less familiar and reliable it seems.

But her parents won't hear of it, so she squeezes into the back seat of the Datsun between her son and daughter, both of them nearly the size of adults, and as they drive the crossroads and by-ways of Brentwood, she listens to the steady hum of the engine of her father's car.

In the gardens, Eddie and his grandfather are soon far ahead of the women. After a few minutes, Jess runs to catch up with them. Anne's mother takes her time, admiring the flowers and naming them for Anne.

"Jennie Butchart's husband moved her all the way out here from Ontario, did you know? He needed limestone for his cement, and this was the place to get it. But she's the one who built the gardens, not him."

"A hobby. Something to keep her mind off being home-sick."

"Oh, no," Anne's mother says. "She made the place hers, didn't she? In spite of him. Renovated the island to suit her taste. Built the gardens right over his limestone quarries. He was finished with them by then, but still." She smiles. "He tore up the ground; she restored it. Made it more beautiful than it had been before."

Anne's mother looks for such subtle acts of independence. Her acceptance of Anne's divorce and her conviction that Anne can make it on her own have numbered among her own small gestures of rebellion.

"If you had been making the decision," Anne asks her, "would you have moved out here?"

Her mother stops on the path to think about it. "I don't know," she says after a minute. She looks up at Anne with her clear blue eyes. "If I'd been making the decision, I'd have been a different person, wouldn't I?" She shrugs. "We planned all our lives to move out here when he retired. It became inevitable."

They walk along a little farther. The gift shop is ahead. Eddie, Jess and their grandfather are sitting on a bench, not talking to one another.

Anne's mother suddenly laughs. "Maybe you were just asking if I'm happy here." As though to answer this, she walks ahead and tells Jess and Eddie she'll buy them ice cream cones.

≈

Three days before Anne needs to be back at the office, they catch the ferry to Vancouver. As they are parting, Anne's father says to Eddie, "You're a young man now. You look after them."

Eddie answers, straightening, "Don't worry, Sir. I'll make sure we get home safe."

"And so will I," adds Jess, a little miffed.

But they shed maturity and politeness as the ferry leaves the Swartz Bay terminal, pestering Anne for change for snacks and video games and magazines and wanting to know how long the trip will take. They'd rather fly, they tell her, than spend three days in the car.

As the ferry churns its way through Active Pass, Anne, momentarily alone, looks up at the bluffs where she stood in the rain, and thinks about the station wagon on the car deck under them. Given an excuse that her children would buy (a meeting or a death) she would abandon the car in an instant.

But she's been telling them for months that the journey is as important as the destination. It was the lesson she had in mind when she planned this trip, late nights in her living room, maps and brochures spread out around her after the children were in bed. The trip had expanded with her daring. Not only would she drive to the coast, she would take unusual routes, see places she'd never seen. At Quesnel on the way back, they would make a half-day side trip just to see the gold rush ghost town, Barkerville. She'd create a series of experiences they would not forget, memories they'd share long after they'd moved off into their separate lives.

On the freeways that take them out of Vancouver, she listens to the sounds the car makes, memorizing, monitoring. She should have paid attention before now. In the back seat, Eddie is pestering Jess, and Jess is fighting back. Anne wants to listen to the car, and she threatens to pull to the side of the road if they aren't silent. By the time they reach Hope, the car is a tight container of their irritation.

At a service station, she tells the attendant to check the oil, the brake fluid, the spark plugs, the power steering fluid, anything he can think of, and then immediately grows irritated with him, too. He's not much older than Eddie. What does he know? He is summer help, young and inexperienced.

"And check the tires," she snaps at him.

He looks up in surprise.

She can take the Coquihalla out of here, cut nearly a day from the drive. She can join the companionship of the cavalcade of vans and motorhomes and cars going through the Rogers Pass to Calgary.

Instead, she drives north with her teeth clenched. She doesn't want to stop to let them eat, or run, or go to the bathroom. She is irritated when she needs to stop for gas. She wants to keep on driving, all day, all night, until she gets to Edmonton. She believes that a car, this car, this alien vehicle, is more likely to continue moving once it's started than if she allows it to grow cold. When they stop at dinner time, her jaw and her shoulders ache from the way her teeth have been clamped together.

There's a pool at the motel and the kids are in it before they've even unpacked the car. Anne looks at the bags in the back of the station wagon, and takes out only the one with the scotch in it. She pours herself a drink and sits in the motel room, the door opened onto the grass, onto the shout and splash of pool.

She will learn more about the landscape they've passed through from Jess's photographs than she will from memory. All day she's kept her eyes on the road, her ears on the engine. She slapped away Jess's hand when she tried to turn on the radio.

Despite her weariness, she cannot sleep. When Jess, in the bed with her, finally grows still and Eddie at last stops tossing, she gets up and pulls on her jeans and a sweatshirt. She slips out of the front door and gets into the car, turns on the ignition and listens to the steady running of the engine. She looks at the mountains in the distance and at the moon rising over them. This town offers their last access to the major highway going east.

So what, she asks herself, if I make it home without a problem? I'm not having a good time. I am doing this to prove I can, and not because I want to.

But still she must press on. After Cache Creek the road is emptier and, aside from the truckers, much of the traffic is local. Tired, today Anne stops at any excuse, closing her eyes as she rests on park benches and the kids run and swing and eat. Stopping is preferable to moving now; towns make her feel secure after the exposure of the highway.

The semis which pass her on the highway travel such enormous distances, she thinks. Qualified mechanics must check them all the time. She remembers the semi-trailer near Trail, so close against her car that she could have read the writing on it if she hadn't been so frightened. She'd steered down the twisting roadway, praying for a run-off or the entrance to a park, but for miles and miles there had been nothing but the shoulder, too narrow and gravelled to pull onto, to pull away from the huge beast with its hot breath bearing down behind her.

She begins to wonder whether the driver did that on purpose, to scare her, to amuse himself. She feels violated and vulnerable.

At Quesnel, she goes straight past the turnoff to

Barkerville. If Eddie and Jess remember the side trip she had planned, they say nothing. She is losing her nerve, and she knows it.

"I wish we hadn't come," Eddie says when she snaps at him again. "This has been the worst holiday of my life."

They are driving up a long hill through Prince George and she is watching signs.

Anne takes a deep breath. "We'll probably never get another chance . . . ."

"Who cares," says Eddie. "Who the fuck cares."

~

When at last they turn onto Highway 16, the road which is also wired down at Jasper and then again at Edmonton, Anne begins to feel a little better. The terrain is bleak and rugged but the nearly deserted road is wide and smooth, and she rapidly puts miles and miles behind them. The hills are becoming larger, becoming mountains in a grey and distant haze, as the moon climbs up into the dusk. She points out ravens, and a coyote standing in the trees. She begins to whistle. Eddie and Jess are quiet, tired of the car and mistrustful of her sudden cheer. Then, as they start up a long incline, the engine hesitates.

"Don't say a word," Anne warns.

"We didn't," Jess says.

"I told you to be quiet."

Heart pounding, she's gripped the steering wheel tightly, her back ramrod straight and touching the seat only at the bottom of her spine. Near the top of the slope, the engine hesitates again, making the whole car shudder. And then again.

That was closer to the second than the second was to the first, she thinks. Though her mind seems blank, she realizes she's timing them, like labour pains. She knows about labour pains, knows about mortgages and T-bills, knows about eating alone in restaurants. She knows nothing about cars.

"Something's wrong," Eddie says flatly from the back.

"Clever," Jess says.

Anne tells them to shut up, shut up, shut up so she can listen. In fact, she doesn't want to listen, doesn't want to hear. Doesn't want to be alone out here on the darkening highway with a car that doesn't work. And she is alone, she knows it. She is the one who must make the decisions that will take them out of the bush, away from these mountains, home. Jess and Eddie's concerns are small, disproportionate to hers and to reality: they suppose she will take care of them.

She starts down the hill, and she can see in the moonlight other hills and others after that. They pass a sign which says, "McBride—80 km." It lists places after, Dunster, Tete Jaune Cache, but nothing before. The car hesitates again. The only way to keep her hands from shaking is to keep them on the wheel.

For long minutes, the car continues to run, hesitating on a basis too irregular for her to interpret it. Just when she thinks the problem's gone, it comes again. A pickup truck goes by. She wishes there were a way to flag a driver down, but she doesn't want to stop. Her car has shown itself at last, turned against her, trapping her inside it.

But that is stupid, she tells herself. It is just a car. Things fit into other things and make it run. She cards her memory for times when it has behaved like this, to put a diagnosis to these symptoms, but can remember none. It runs strongly between its hesitations. The gas gauge is at the half-way mark.

"I have to pee," Jess says.

They have been keeping low, more wary of her tension than the problems of the car: neither has said a word in several minutes. Grateful, Anne takes a breath.

"You'll have to wait," she says.

"How long?"

"Until we stop," she says. She does not say, "McBride."

The next hesitation is more than that. Anne pumps the gas but it does no good. The car is slowing. She pulls onto the shoulder of the deserted highway, ready to pull out again if the engine catches, steadies. It doesn't.

Losing power, the car slows on the shoulder. The engine dies. They roll to a stop, Anne still pumping the gas pedal, getting no response. When the car has come to a stop she turns the key. The engine makes a ripping, grinding sound. She turns the car off, and the lights, and puts on the four-way flashers.

"I need to pee," Jess says again.

Anne wants to cry. Instead she says, "Get out and do it, then."

"It's dark. There are bears out there."

"And bats," says Eddie.

Anne is certain they are right.

"You go with her," Anne says to Eddie.

"I don't want him to come with me. I want you to come with me." Jess is petulant, using a baby voice. You are my mother, that voice says. Protect me. Save me and look after me.

They go together, Eddie wandering a little distance off and turning his back to them. Jess goes to the bottom of the ditch and squats. Anne stands beside her, a box of Kleenex in her hand. It is hard to be a female in the bush. Anne realizes she needs to go too, then pushes away the thought. She's in charge. She cannot crouch. She looks up at the car while she waits for her children. She cannot crouch, or cry, or appear to sweat.

This is such a silent, empty place. A dark and empty place. A cloud has covered the moon and the highway is edged with dark stains of trees and she can see shapes of mountains in the distance. Nothing moves. Aside from the flashers on her car, which mock her with their illusion of safe passage, there is no light.

Now lights appear, on the horizon, high up: a truck. Anne runs stumbling up the slope and stands in front of her car, lit by the flashers, waving. The semi-trailer whizzes past, not slowing. In a minute, it's disappeared. Another zooms past in the opposite direction.

"I hate truckers," Anne says as they get back into the car.

"We going to sit here all night?" Eddie asks from the back seat.

"We may." She is reduced to that, to sitting.

Jess and Eddie begin to argue about who ate the last of the crackers. Anne wants to hit them, wants to be a kid and hit them both and let someone bigger, older, save them all.

If she'd told her mother about that trucker who'd amused himself by riding down the mountain on her tail, her mother would have offered the incident shape and meaning and made it into story. Her mother would have said that Anne had brought them safely down, despite the threat, that her capable driving and her calm had brought them through it.

Anne had hurtled down that mountain, mindless with

fear, and only luck had kept them alive. If the car had hesitated there, it would have been the end. But her mother would have seen what was nothing more than instinct as an act of courage and independence.

If her mother were here right now, Anne would tell her that Jenny Butchart's gardens were not a political statement. She would tell her that her stories were illusions made of nothing more than smoke, blown away in an instant.

Now in her rear view mirror she sees headlights, approaching more slowly, much more slowly than the last ones. A truck pulls slowly off the highway, a huge Mack cab which draws a trailer after it, headlights beaming hard into their car. It stops, with a sigh of brakes, so close behind them Anne can see the insects smashed against its grill. Her heart begins to pound.

Leaving his lights on, the engine running, a man in blue jeans and a camouflage vest jumps down from the cab.

"Lock your doors," Anne says, hearing her voice sound thin.

"Why?" says Jess, surprised.

"Just do it."

The man comes to her window and she rolls it down an inch.

"Problem?" he asks. He is heavily built, muscular, tall and blond. Mid- to late-twenties. Women, she thinks, are notches on his belt.

"The car," she says. "Won't go." She gropes for words that will make her sound less helpless. Finds none. "It isn't out of gas."

"You want to try it?"

"We'll be all right," she says.

But she does try it, she has no choice, and the car starts immediately and runs steadily for a moment before it falters. Stalls.

He asks her to try again. This time it won't turn over. He tells her to pop the hood, his voice commanding, taking charge. She does. He walks around to the front. He raises the hood. Through the space between the hood and the car, she can see him lifting caps from wells. She hates him. She hates sitting here.

Before she realizes what he's doing, Eddie is out of the car and around the front, standing beside the truck driver. She calls to him to come back, but he ignores her.

The man goes back to the truck and returns with a plastic jug. He pours its contents into one of the wells in the engine. He talks to Eddie and Eddie talks back to him. Annie cannot hear their words. She hates sitting while they stand.

After a few minutes, he calls to her to try the car again. She does. The car hesitates, then starts. It keeps running, steadily. The man throws the plastic jug into the ditch, slams down the hood and comes back to her window. Eddie comes with him. "What did you do?" she asks.

He shrugs. "Windshield fluid. Noticed you were low."

"That doesn't affect the engine."

"No. Kills time."

Eddie says, "He thinks it was dirt in the gas line."

The man nods. "Can't trust the gas, some of these places. I'll follow you to town."

"Can I ride with him?" Eddie asks.

"No," Anne says sharply. "You get in."

The trucker chucks Eddie on the shoulder and starts away.

He does follow her into McBride, his lights too close behind her. Anne is tense until they reach the edge of town. As she pulls into a service station, the trucker flashes his lights and zooms past, down the highway toward Edmonton. She stops the car at the doors to the service bay and puts her hands up to her face.

Eddie gets out and talks to the attendant. The two stand looking at the car, deep in conversation. Anne thinks that it is magic that Eddie is learning tonight, the incantations that make cars go. She will never know them.

~

When the bags and suitcases are in the motel room and Eddie and Jess have disappeared to find the pool, Anne phones Victoria.

Her father is surprised to hear her voice. "Everything all right?" he asks.

"Sure. We're in McBride."

"How is the motel?"

"It's fine."

"We've stayed there. Not fancy, but it's clean. And safe." He clears his throat. "Trip going okay?"

"Of course."

She can't tell her father what has happened. He'll want to buy her a new car. He'll want to speak to Eddie. Later, he'll tell her mother that if Anne were married, these things wouldn't happen. It's her mother she wants to talk to. But secure in the knowledge that Anne is at the wheel and getting them all safely home, her mother has gone out to a neighbour's to play bridge.

Anne lies down on one of the beds after she's hung up the phone, and closes her eyes. After a while, she is able to imagine her car back on the highway, its engine dead, in the middle of the dark, in the middle of the bush. She sees it as if she were on a cliff above, she can see the highway for miles in each direction and this car, this blue station wagon, is the only vehicle on it. Its yellow flashers blink and blink.

Three people are inside the car, a woman and two children. The engine of the car is dead, and the woman must find a way to get the children home.

Slowly, now, and very carefully, Anne begins to build this story on her own.

∾

Mary Walters Riskin is a freelance writer and editor who lives in Edmonton. Her first novel, The Woman Upstairs, *was published in 1986 and won the Writers Guild of Alberta Award for Best Novel. Her short fiction has been published in* The Malahat Review, Chatelaine, Dandelion, Grain, Prism International, *and in two anthologies of short fiction,* Alberta Bound *(1986) and* Alberta ReBound *(1990).*

The Redheaded Woman with the Black Black Heart

BIRK SPROXTON

A gash of white crackles across the top edge of the photo, breaking the white border. Framed by this (broken) border and oblivious to the white gash above their heads, three Mounties grin their glossy smiles. They are young these three, and they wear flat tin riot helmets. They cradle Lee-Enfield rifles in their fingertips. You can feel their confidence. All three stand between the gleaming rails, their feet spread to shoulder width, chests forward, rifle butts on the gravel. Their smiles make small white slashes against a backdrop of interlacing black and grey. Their smiles, as smiles do, tell a tale. Their smiles tell a tale of glorious pursuit, of stern justice and the heart of a woman.

Since their eyes are open, we know that these three men have shaken off the cobwebs of sleep. They have dressed themselves for action: sucked up the leather belt a notch, polished their brass buttons, cocked helmets at a rakish angle. Hefted revolvers, shrugged them into the holsters. You can smell the leather.

They puff out their chests, three jolly policemen gloating at their own good fortune. The police force has been called in to quell a strike, and they have been singled out to hunt down a lone striker. They are on a woman hunt. They are after Mickey. Their brown serge uniforms glow crimson in the light of their pleasure.

Maebelle "Mickey" Marlowe. She's the one to be arrested, the only one, though she wasn't alone that day. Mickey sang and laughed with the other women. She sang and laughed when the scabs tried to walk up the staircase. She laughed when Mathilda stroked yellow chalk down a scab's back. She laughed when the Big Weird Sister slammed a rotten tomato into a scab's ear and nose, seeds and red pulp and fresh garden smell spilling down her wrists. Mickey laughed when the Middle Weird Sister hoisted her knee directly between the big toes and up (wahh) to the crotch of a writhing scab. The women laughed together when the Small Weird Sister raked sharp fingernails down a scabby back, tore off a shirt and snapped suspenders with a fleshy twang. Their laughter drowned out the sound of popping buttons and shredding underwear. No, Mickey wasn't alone on the stairs that day. She and the others raised their voices as one: "We'll hang yellow scabbies from a rotten apple tree," they sang. Elbow to breast to backside, they all sang and laughed together: "Did you ever see a scab voting . . . ?"

And now these smiling men have orders to arrest only her. Mickey, the ringleader, the blackhearted villain, fingered by the Law.

The corporal, he's in the centre of this photo, has heard stories about Mickey. He has talked with Mickey, he listened to her big speech from the flat car. You've seen that photo, too. Mickey stands on the flat car and leans forward, haranguing or seducing the crowd. She holds her left hand up to her tam, to her dark red hair. We don't see her face, but our corporal knows what she looks like. He knows, too, the slick phrases that try to capture her in words.

"A looker, she is, but red right through. Red as the curls on her head. Red red red, right down to her underwear."

"Her voice could charm the socks off a horse."

"Underwear? She doesn't bother with underwear, that girl. Lets her bum blow in the breeze."

The corporal has his own story to tell. He fingers his moustache as he talks.

"One morning the CO—yes our man Brown, your Commanding Officer—he saw her sitting alone in the Bluebird so he walks over to her table, saying hello to everybody in the place, you know the way he is, he walks over thinking he might have coffee with her. He says, 'And you, Miss Mickey, do you need a boyfriend?'

"Mickey doesn't answer. She takes her time. She stirs milk into her coffee. Then she stops stirring, and gives him a look.

"'And you, Sergeant Preston, do you need a dog?'"

The smiling Mounties set out in the drizzling rain. They bang on doors. They ask for Mickey.

Some people say she lives on North Avenue: "One of those red light places." Others say she lives down Sipple Hill. "In the middle of Sipple Hill, that big white house. She has a tiny basement room, a closet really. Only space enough for a small bed and two copies of *The Communist Manifesto*."

Some people laugh. "You'll never find her. She lives underground, in the mine."

Or they say, "She lives with those Scandihoovians on Ross Lake Island. Trolls guard the bridge. You'll never get over, unless you have a big billy goat. Are you a billy goat, or just gruff?"

"She lives with the Tooth Fairy and Peter Pan."

"Mickey? Easy to find her. Listen for her singing."

The next morning, Monday, the corporal faces the mirror and straightens his tie. Behind him, the other officers lace their boots. A song flits and tugs at his ear, "Did you ever see a scab voting...?" He wants to laugh but adjusts his face into a policeman's frown. The wrinkle makes a dark pencil line between his eyes.

He frowns again when he learns that Mickey was seen on the street. Yesterday, Sunday, she pranced down Main Street as brazen as could be, red hair and all. Not only that, she accosted someone, an upright citizen, who, the story goes, was on his way to church. According to the upright man, Mickey offered to relieve him of his shirt, his favourite blue plaid shirt.

"We want it for our collection."

She said.

He alleges.

~

Tuesday. The search and the rain continue.

The officers knock on Early Wakeham's door.

Over the steady patter of rain on the wooden stoop, a door creaks open, a typical radio door creak.

Early welcomes his gentlemen callers.

"Yes, and here you are and what do you be wanting with me on this sweet night, my fine feathered friends." He can see the corporal's hat drooping with water, but Early stands in the doorway, blocking it. He shapes a ring of smoke in his mouth. Early narrows his eyes.

"We want to talk to her," the corporal says. "The woman who made the Big Speech." (You can hear the capital letters in his voice.) "That Mickey Woman."

The townspeople say this visit brought out something in Early they hadn't seen before. The townspeople knew Early as the sort of man who would cheat his mother and refuse credit to his sister. Early always looked after Number One, he said, and Number One is spelled with two words: Early Wakeham. They all knew that. But in this case Early showed something different—Early took Mickey's part. He wouldn't let that young woman be pushed around by cops. No siree.

So Early lets the cops stand in the rain, while he, Early, proposes that they, the Mounties and the bosses, should all take the primrose way to the everlasting bonfire. Early proposes that the Mounties and their bosses should have, for the betterment of their health, flying intercourse with a rolling doughnut. He proposes that they should get back on the train and pull their dinky little chains all the way home to Regina, or to Winnipeg, or to Ottawa. They could row across the effing Atlantic to England where they would find hundreds of lard-assed crooks to hassle. Starting with the King.

And then Early closes the door.

His head back, showing teeth, laughing.

No one laughs when the Mounties reach strike headquarters. Over the click of snooker balls, the corporal starts to ask his questions, the usual litany.

"Is Mickey Marlowe here?"

The Big Weird Sister wiggles her plaid shirt as she banks a red ball to the side pocket.

"Mickey Marlowe is not here."

The red ball rattles off the rail and knocks the pink into the corner.

"Have you seen her?"

The Small Weird Sister (also dressed in plaid) has been keeping score. She plants the pink ball on its spot. The Middle Sister moves forward to shoot. She tugs at the plaid kerchief around her neck, then slams a red into the corner. The cue ball draws back for a straight-in shot on the black. Middle Sister lines up the shot, extending her fingers as a bridge.

"I have not seen her."

The black ball hits both sides of the pocket and scoots down the table, the cue ball glides into the pocket, dead centre. Middle mutters *damn*, almost under her breath.

"Do you know where she lives?"

The Small Weird Sister fishes out the cue ball and walks over to the corporal. He has a touch of dried blood on his chin; he nicked himself this morning. (You can't see this blood in the photo, a tiny sliver of crimson slanting across his chin.) Small holds the cue ball in front of the Mountie's face and spins it between her fingers.

"Mickey lives in her blood and her bones, like any woman. And don't you forget it, young man," she slams the cue ball on the table, "don't you dare forget it."

Her plaid partners tattoo their cues on the floor. Big then Middle, Big then Middle.

≈

Tuesday passes into Wednesday.

In the assay office, Mounties with revolvers on their hips

shuffle papers into file folders. They have set up a temporary jail. They twirl stubby little pencils between their fingers. They are waiting for customers, inmates, prisoners, perpetrators, blackhearted villains, dastardly criminals, wicked folk.

Meanwhile the snapshot officers walk. Released from the frozen stillness of the photograph, the officers roll their fingers into fists and knock on doors. They plow through mud and muskeg. Up and down hills and rocks and stairs. Their smiles disappear. The crimson sheen fades from their brown serge. They have no luck at all.

~

Until Thursday afternoon, when Nick, the corporal with the tiny shaving scar on his chin, knocks on Mickey's door, or finds her nested in a tree, or catches her arm as she walks along the street, or calls her back from Kingdom Come.

"Yoo hooo. Yooo hoooooo. We know who you are. We've come to get you. We'll make you blue. "

One time my friend Tom got arrested. He was painting the town red. He staggered out of a beer parlour and tilted his way over to the police cruiser. "I bet you're afraid to arrest me," he said. Tom adjusted the side mirror on the car so he could admire his own cock-eyed grin, his green plaid shirt. The cop was not afraid. Tom was released in the morning but not before he tried to coax his fellow guests to join him in a riot, all the time sawing fiercely on the cell bars with his fingernail file.

Mickey played the temptress and dangled herself in front of their noses. "Aha, here I am," she said. "Do I get a rise out of you, Nick? Book any good reds lately? Do you dare arrest me? You are an armed man. Here's my hand, you wanna hold my hand? Did you ever see a scab voting?"

Corporal Nick lists the charges. Assault, and intimidation. Opening thy trap. You can hear the tut-tut in his voice. Unlawful assembly and tumultuously disturbing the peace. He aims the adverb at her, as if she should raise her hands in surrender. Too-mult-choo-us-lee. And we got you red-handed. This is a red-letter day.

For her part, Mickey throws words at him, pointed missiles.

Who are you?

Do you have identification?

Show me your badge, Big Boy.

Who is your commanding officer, Nickaloo?

Do you have paper with you? An itsy-bitsy pencil?

I think you are teasing me, Nickie. You have no evidence for such charges. How do you know I was there?

You're only pretending to be a police officer. You're too young and pretty to be a Mountie.

Your shirt is a dream, Nick-ups dear. (She fingers his collar.) *I want it for my collection.*

You want to climb the smokestack with me?

The Mounties lead Mickey through the picket lines to the big steel gate. She is surrounded by serge coats and rifles. Tin helmets and billy clubs. Someone rattles the massive lock, a chain rings its way through the steel mesh.

"Mickey Mickey Mickey," the crowd calls out.

Three women cloaked in plaid sing into the smoking barrel. "Double rubble trouble," they say between giggles. "We'll bake you a cake, we'll bake a file in the cake. A woman needs iron in her diet. We'll bake a cake. They can't keep a good woman locked up. "

Painted on the door in black letters: *Assay Office*. A typewriter clacks away in the reception area. Hunched over their papers, Mounties make notes with stubby little pencils. They scribble, they scribble. At last they have caught a wicked person, a suspect, a perpetrator. A blackhearted villain.

Mickey is quiet. They usher her into an inner office, close the door, and turn the lock. They open the filing cabinet, roll out the red tape. They will test her mettle. They want to shut her up in their files, to write her into a sentence as long as they can make it. Paint the blackhearted villain with their red red tape.

Mickey bangs on the door and asks for coffee. Later, she wants a refill. She bangs a third time and demands to use the lavatory.

She parks there, powdering her nose, she spends her pennies, every red cent, until the men rap rap rap.

"You homesteading in there? Hey, woman, you fall in and drown? Do you need a rope?"

She doesn't answer.

They pace the floor. They squirm and twist their torsos into strange contortions, jig and jig and jig across the room, knees together.

Corporal Nick starts to see red. He lifts the phone, cupped hand clenched between his legs.

~

JULY 6. Friday. *The Northern Mail* carries a brief report. "Eight men and one woman arrested Thursday were taken today to

The Pas for incarceration there over the weekend owing to the lack of jail accommodations." The newspaper identifies the woman as "Miss Nettie Kukarik, alias Peggy Marlowe, alias 'Mickey' Maebelle Marlowe, 23, Austrian, Winnipeg, Secretary of the Canadian Labor Defence League." All these persons jammed into a single young body.

∼

The next photo is an action shot. This time there are no smiles aimed at the camera, no chests puffed out. No posing. This time the blobs of grey and black take the shape of men and women, all of them moving. They are walking north along the railroad tracks. You can count the policemen—at least twelve, perhaps thirteen, bustle into the frame. Seven cluster right around a woman, whom I take to be Mickey, alias Nettie, alias Peggy, alias Maebelle. Seven men try to keep her from breaking out and assuming other identities. They crowd around and squish her into a single person, a single blob of grey dots, black at the very heart. She wears the same dark coat she wore in the flat car photo. One of those seven Mounties must be her friend, Old Scarface himself, Corporal Nick. The cut on his chin will have healed by now. No doubt he hopes Mickey doesn't break loose.

There are no rifles in this photo, Lee-Enfields or otherwise, but the Mounties carry billy clubs (no *billets-doux* these) to deliver their messages. They have themselves decked out in felt hats, instead of helmets. Mickey has raised her left hand to her black tam; she covers her flaming red hair. If you look closely you find only one person without a hat. Is it a man with long hair, or a woman in pants? A female officer?

Perhaps she accompanies the prisoner to the Ladies' room.

The photo deserves a title. Something like "The Mounties Get Their Woman," or "Maebelle Escorted by Beaus." I wonder if that's a smile on Mickey's face. Can you see it? That small crackling sliver of white—is that her smile?

~

Birk Sproxton *teaches Canadian literature and creative writing in the Writing and Publishing Programme at Red Deer College. His books include* Headframe: *(1985),* The Hockey Fan Came Riding *(1990), and* Trace: Prairie Writers on Writing *(1986). He is a contributing editor to* NeWest Review, *and a director of the NeWest Institute for Western Canadian Studies. His novel,* Mabel Maebelle, Outlaw, *seeks a publisher; he is currently writing a fictional treatment of Manitoba prospector Kate Rice.*

Scalps

SUZETTE MAYR

*As shown by its importance in witch-charms and in the
mutual exchange of talismans between lovers, hair was
usually viewed as the repository of at least part of the soul.*
        —Barbara G. Walker
                The Woman's Encyclopedia
                        of Myths and Secrets

The closed blinds block out the early morning sunlight, but
it's still too warm in here. This room smells of sleeping,
sweaty, angry body. I twine a clump of my hair around the
index finger of my left hand and pull. It is easy to lose myself
this way. Like flicking a switch. Twine my hair around a
finger and my head flushes vacuum clean, ready for new
thoughts. Robert hates it when I do this. He calls it my bimbo
look and says it makes my hair look stupid.

Robert. The man I am going to marry.

Yesterday when I spoke to him on the phone, my insides
were glossy, mirrored bubbles ready to sail into his arms.
Yesterday I knew who he was and it mattered to me that he
was on the other side of the country—he is my husband-to-be,
the father of the child I want to have some day soon. But today

he is someone else. I am thinking I should have the locks on the front door changed. But change sounds like hope and I am all alone while he is with someone else. Touching her the way he is only supposed to touch his wife. Fucking her.

I don't have proof, tangible proof, the kind you can hold in your hand and squeeze for ripeness, measure with a ruler. But I dreamed she was here, tucked into his mouth with her hair flowing out between his I-love-you lips. I dreamed it long and straight and yellow, a cascade of hair poking out where his tongue should have been, a thick curtain between us while he kissed and licked my sweat. I smelled her perfumed shampoo, mingled with his suddenly alien smell of unwashed Robert hair, of semen.

My own hair forms wild tumbleweeds when I clean it from my comb. I struggle to brush it after a shower and strands gather and curl into hard, black, frizzy little balls and nest in corners under the bathroom sink, behind the stove in the kitchen, between the cushions on the sofa. First thing in the morning, it rises like hairy flames from my head and the broken ends scatter all over my pillow. I brush it down and tame it with water and hair-spray, and gather it up in a small, tight bun at the back of my head. Or I braid it so hard and smooth it's a black, rippled skin covering my skull.

Robert doesn't like my hair no matter how I style it—the colour and texture are not like the hair of the women he normally looks at. Their hair is soft and falls in tendrils down the backs of their necks, along their cheeks, across their foreheads. I have tried tendrils, I have burnt my scalp with chemical straighteners and scarred myself with hot irons and pins, but my hair remains my own. Even for love it won't do what he wants. When we make love he rarely touches it.

Making love. Is that what he does? He probably likes to run her tendrils through his mouth, between his lips, drape them over his face. Maybe he washes her hair, spreads his fingers under her head and massages her soapy scalp, then slowly rinses her with cool, clean water. He is meticulous but gentle when he combs it, untangles the hairs around her face. They lie down together, he spreads the strands over his body like a fan, and he purposely tangles his penis in its sweep.

I twine a clump first on one side, then a clump on the other. I want my fingers to know every strand. I want to flick myself on with every switch. I need new thoughts. I would like new, unpolluted skin. There is still outraged sweat in my armpits and one of my breasts has slipped out from under the cloth of my night-dress. Unaroused, the nipple is soft and dark brown—a pudding dropped from a cone-shaped mould. Her nipples are pink. A pink woman to go with her yellow hair and that flowery shampoo.

The small of my back and the crack between my buttocks are still slippery with dream sweat. There is no leftover pain from my dream; I was only surprised that yellow hair travelled over my body in places only Robert has been. But who knows what Robert told her about me. My hair is rough and short and black and it takes time and patience to comb. He has never really touched it; he doesn't even look at it except to point out how unruly it is and how nice it could be if I got it straightened more efficiently. He has always been disappointed with my hair. I wonder why he is with me.

Robert. His own body ages before its time—the beginning of a pot belly, a rapidly receding hairline and a bald patch starting at the back of his head. The skin revealed by the disappearing hair is a dull ping-pong-ball white, greasy and smooth. He is practically my husband, and it doesn't matter that he is going bald, that he will be as bald and paunchy as his father and his mother's father by age forty. Up until last night, what he looked like didn't matter.

I remove my heart with my free hand from below the uncovered breast, from beneath the cotton of my dress, and lay it on the night table. It stops beating almost immediately and the red and purple fade into a dull grey. Body parts are easier to remove than thoughts. Flick on a switch.

It's someone he works with. Or someone from his fitness club. I should care more, but there are shampoo suds instead of blood in my veins. And I am hot, this room is hot and thick with my odour. If I were pregnant I would rip out my stomach, my polluted and unloved flesh with my bare hands, dig out a steaming hole with my nails and throw it, legs and arms and cord, at his face. Would he want a baby who looked like me, had hair like mine?

I twine some more hair, this time near the top of my skull.

I pull until it hurts. I pull until I am drawing blood. The phone rings, once, twice, over and over again. I know it's Robert, giving me my long-distance, good morning kiss like he promised he would.

"You gonna be awake when I call?"

"Of course, if you want me to. I'll set the alarm."

"No. Forget the alarm. You stay asleep. I want to wake you up with a great big, sloppy telephone kiss."

His dry lips and sloppy, wet tongue. His mouth is big enough to swallow half my face if he opens it wide enough. He's never learned how to kiss, he swallows instead of kissing—digests my skin with his saliva and then eats it. The last ring echoes. I should have answered it. A telephone kiss from the man I'm going to marry. I take my fingers from my hair, look over at the night table, at my drying heart; I'll have to put that someplace safe.

The numbers on the digital clock show I'm going to be late for work. I roll over and snuggle my face into his pillow, the blankets and sheets twisted tightly around my waist and legs. His smell. Strands of hair caught in the fabric of the pillow case—I pull them out one by one and lay them across my tongue. Close my lips on them. His fingertips scorch— my hair a bright black bonfire.

⌒

Suzette Mayr *recently received her M.A. in English at the University of Alberta in Edmonton, and she now lives and works in Calgary. She has written one chapbook,* Zebra Talk *(1991). Her work has been included in* West Coast Line, Open Letter, blue buffalo, Secrets from the Orange Couch, *and* Vox. *She is currently part of the editorial collective for* absinthe *magazine.* "Scalps" *first appeared in* Vox.

Earth Moving

NORM SACUTA

My mother's obsession with our topsoil began shortly after an earth mover uncovered a skeleton on Duggan hill, scooping up the skull in its middle chamber and scattering a trail of bones across the black earth like clumps of frozen cream. The movers had been wearing down the only noticeable geography in South Edmonton for over a month, making it as flat as the surrounding prairie, and whenever I watched them from our back kitchen window they looked like giant yellow and turquoise salamanders, bellies dragging a wet trail behind where dirt had been scraped away. Once they were full they lumbered towards the house, the men waving in the small windows above the churning tires as if to warn me they were about to drive right through the living room, then veering off to the left to pass through an empty double lot next door. Sometimes my mother would be at the sink as I knelt on the counter beside her to watch the machine's approach. Her family plates, brought in the move from Ontario, would rattle on the wall beside the sink, and she'd shift her eyes up from the dish water, lift a damp sponge and silence them, only to repeat the same routine a few minutes later.

But the skeleton·brought an end to earth moving for

several days, as the police and forensics experts poked around what remained of the grave. Kyle and I, just out of school for the summer, peddled our Mustangs back to the hill through the houseless maze of paved crescents and streets that began where our back alley ended. His house and mine were the only two completely finished on our crescent, and our route back to the grave—brilliant asphalt layered through brown clay—was watched anxiously by my mother. She was still watching when I returned for lunch, exactly where she'd been when I left at ten, pretending to scrub a pot or dish, her gaze moving from black to black across the middle sidewalk that split our newly seeded yard in half and led back to wooden posts that would anchor a fence, separating us from the prairie permanently. She quizzed me about what the men on the hill were doing. Had more bones been found? Had I touched the soil? When I told her the hill had been roped off with yellow tape, and we weren't allowed in, she still followed me to the washroom and watched me scrub before providing a Velveeta sandwich.

"There's something there, Joseph," she said one lunch hour and turned from the kitchen window to face me. She looked embarrassed, as if she'd stumbled across someone undressing.

"What is?"

"There's something in the middle. On the left side of the yard. I wasn't sure this morning, but I am now. Will you go look?"

I left my sandwich and jumped on the counter beside her, my hand accidentally slipping into the dishwater. She was pointing, her hand shaking slightly so it was difficult to see a precise location. The dirt had begun to sprout grass, and a thin

green film was covering most of the yard. Finally I saw it—
a small, perversely white knob sticking out of the soil a few
yards in from the alley. My father had fixed surveyor sticks
along the middle sidewalk and alley, running kite string
between them, warning visitors to keep off. But with no one
else living in the crescent I knew the string was meant for me
and Kyle.

"Don't worry," my mother said. "I'll explain to your
father about his precious lawn."

It wasn't my father I feared, really—at worst he'd lecture
my mother for letting me on the lawn. Then they'd fight at
the dinner table, in the logical and on-topic manner they had,
always asking for the point, choosing words as if filling in a
crossword puzzle. I learned to like arguing by watching my
parents.

It was Kyle I worried about, once the screen door slapped
shut behind me, and I stood in silence and growing embarrassment just below my mother's window view. I heard the flap
of bedsheets three lots over, and knew Kyle's grey eyes were
on me as he sat at the picnic table behind his house. When I
looked over he'd moved away from the table to get a better
view, and was even smaller than usual beside a waving blue
square, one hand clasping a corner, the other holding a can of
Cragmont root beer. His mother moved between the lines of
laundry, shadowy and silent as always, a yellow kerchiefed
head above the clothesline, her stockinged feet shuffling
along the cement below the sheets.

"Joseph, honey, what's happening?" my mother called
through the open window.

Kyle had an annoying habit of being always nearby when
I did things for my mother. He rarely said much as he

watched. I hated his silences, especially since he was only seven and a year behind me in school, and it always seemed like he was withholding information, refusing to tell what he really knew about girls and bikes. Now, he looked almost disinterested, the same way an adult looked reading the paper, but I knew he was loading ammunition for later. As I stood there watching the white lump glow on the topsoil, my mother's worried voice carrying across the foundations between our place and his, I wondered why I remained friends with him at all.

I followed our sidewalk back almost to the alley, then tried to step, toe first, over the kite string and onto the yard. My runner left a deep hole so I switched to walking flat-footed, a slow movement like tai-chi, crushing the green shadow back into the earth. The white clump grew more shiny and artificial the closer I came to it, and I knew it was plastic—the severed bottom half of a detergent bottle pressed into the soil, raising more questions about how it came to be in our yard than any bone could have. I waved it at my mother, who smiled, and then looked at Kyle as I tossed it into the alley with authority. He was still staring at me, his mother ignored as she stooped beside him to pick up the empty pop can.

~

"I'm phoning the sod layers," my mother said once my father sat down for dinner. He was about to twist a poppy-seed role in half.

"For chrissake, Carol, it was a piece of plastic. Joey, you said it was plastic?"

I nodded.

"I don't care. I'm tired of waiting for it to come up. And you never water it anyway. How do you expect grass to grow if you never water it?"

"Grass has never needed water to grow in its life. It's a damn weed. And I heard today anyway. That skeleton is a couple of hundred years old—probably some Indian who froze in a blizzard. Rick heard about it this afternoon. They're sending over a group of people from the anthropology department at the university to look around."

I could hear disappointment in my father's voice. For the last week he and Kyle's father had been speculating on the body, arguing murder scenarios while sipping beer in the back alley. My father wanted to believe it was murder. Violence confirmed that Edmonton was becoming something bigger than the absence my mother's relatives said she was moving to. I imagined him smiling as he phoned Toronto, telling them that his hometown was capable of terrible things too.

My mother continued to keep eye contact; they always did during arguments, as if on the verge of kissing.

"And besides," said my father, "they sterilize the soil before they sell it. It's against the law not to."

"How do you know that for sure, Jason? And it's stupid anyway. It's a racket. They strip it away and then make you buy it back once the house is built."

"They don't do it any different in Ontario. Just because they did it fifty years ago in Toronto doesn't mean they did it any different. Ontario is full of goddamn shysters."

It was a word she liked, I suppose, because I saw her smile and go back to her pasta. I was hoping to see some sign of the argument continuing, one or the other moving lips as they ate, forming ideas before throwing them across the table; but an early equilibrium had occurred. My father also started to smile.

"If we're going to order sod," he said, "let me talk to Rick and we'll order together. It'll save money."

"Ask him tonight, after dinner. And I want to be there when you do. The man is a bullshitter. He'll rip you off."

They both looked at me after this last statement, but I'd turned to my spaghetti, twirling it so quickly it started to unravel the other way.

"Don't worry," I said without looking up from my plate, "He'd like being called that."

~

Kyle's father, Rick, was a geologist and a lapsed Fundamentalist. That's what I heard him say to my father the week we moved in. He'd left a farm south of Drumheller when he was sixteen, after a fight with his parents over the religion of some girl he'd been dating, and boarded at an Anglican boys' school in Edmonton until he was old enough to qualify for a room at the U of A dormitory. He'd married Kyle's mother, that girl of Catholic faith, the day after he turned nineteen. My father told my mother that Rick was exactly what Alberta needed—men who marry and cancel religion out, to save the province from the Bible-toting screwballs who'd been in power for forty years.

He was a short man, with thinly slit eyes that looked oriental because he was always squinting through one or the other, as if a bright light were in his face. But when he laughed you could see his Welsh features come together—his eyes went wide and round, a sudden shock of blue within dark skin, and the stocky frame would flex like a rugby player's as he leaned back in the air. He always wore cotton turtlenecks, even in summer, so his skin seemed right there, something I could smell and feel moving beneath the surface when he rassled with us. He usually greeted me by gently squeezing the back of my neck between his thumb and index finger, and pretending to lift me off the ground.

Kyle and I were on the front porch of my house, watching his dad and mine walk the sidewalk around the front yard. My father squatted, fingering the soil, talking about the dry summer and the burning crops you could see just a quarter mile away if you stood on our roof. Rick had his arms crossed, pushing the toe of his runner into the soil.

"How much is this gonna cost me?" he asked, kicking a little dirt across my father's hands. They were dry and cracked from being doused with oil and washed with solvents, and he brushed the dirt away, smiling, checking his nails. He was always checking his nails.

"Forty, maybe fifty dollars for the whole yard, if we lay it ourselves."

"I've got no time for that," he said. "So you figure, what? Double that for having someone lay it for us?"

"Well, yeah, but," my father smiled again as he looked up, "if you're going to hire someone, then just pay for it all and I'll lay it on both yards."

"Christ, you're cheap."

My father grimaced and nodded towards Kyle and me.

"Your dad's a cheap-skate, Joey," Rick called over.

"And you're a bullshitter," I called back just as my mother came out the front door, and rested her hand lightly on top of my head—as if I were balancing a book of manners.

"Joseph Wynnyk," she said, "what did you say?"

Her hand stayed, weighty like a priest's, but when Rick began to laugh and his arms unfolded to move to his knees, I knew no apology my mother might make me say would carry any weight. She sifted her hand through my hair, reaching over to do the same to Kyle, as if touching us both was a way to ignore the laughter. I saw Kyle's head jerk sideways, a sudden panic, then he slid forward—down a step—and beyond her reach. She seemed confused, then rested both hands on my shoulders, her authority usurped, waiting for Rick to stop.

"He swore," she said to him, finally. "You shouldn't laugh."

"That's all right, I swore first didn't I?"

I nodded and looked up at my mother. She was staring at Rick, but he never even glanced back at her, his runner burrowing into the dirt while he smiled.

"So it's settled, then," my father said, in a voice loud enough that my mother was informed of the decision, "you buy it, and I'll roll it out."

"I'll phone in the morning," he said, and finally looked up at the steps, "Let's go kid, it's late. 'Bye, Joey. Nice to see you, Missus."

≈

That night I dreamed about Rick, his hands under my arms, lifting me up, higher and higher, until it seemed we both were rising off the ground. I flew, his hands still under me, circling the neighbourhood as cement foundations and scattered lumber passed below, looking like a tornado had hit. We began coming down, quickly, and I panicked, struggling to breathe as the black earth, rich and damp, met my descent. But after a few seconds, the darkness became the heavy cotton of Rick's turtleneck, and I could feel his arms again encircling me, muscle beneath fabric, his body warm, as the dream shifted to his house. I was laughing, tossed on the couch as Kyle jumped him from behind.

I woke with the bedsheets twisted into a knot between my pajama legs—a firm surface to tighten my legs around. The sun was rising, a little after five in the morning, and the usual croak of frogs from Duggan slough was missing, replaced by a faint hum, like a mosquito caught against a window screen—regular, irritated, but distant. I sat up, listening, the hum becoming more mechanical the closer I leaned to the open window by my bed.

A small pop, almost like a lock snapping shut, made the buzz stop for a moment, then it shuddered back to its routine. I rested in bed, listening, then couldn't hear it anymore when the shower began in my parent's room. My father had to be out, inspecting drill-sites in the Pembina oilfield west of Edmonton, before seven-thirty. When I heard him finally in the kitchen, banging cupboard doors, I went to ask what was buzzing and popping, regularly now like distant gunshots. A water pump was running in some farmer's field, he said without much thought. My father knew his pumps.

At nine-thirty a flatbed truck, driven by an old Italian and his son, stopped in front of our house with several dozen snail-shaped curls of grass. My mother stood on the front sidewalk, directing where they should place the rolled sod. It wasn't long after they moved the truck up three lots that the older man was back, knocking on our door.

"I'm sorry, Lady," he said, scratching his eyebrow with his flannel glove, "but the lady next door won't tell us nothing. She just keeps asking us to come back when her husband's home."

"Weird," my mother said, and pulled off her socks to walk barefoot to Kyle's house, "but I'm not surprised. Her husband's never had an intelligent conversation with a woman in his life, so the fact you're talking to her is probably seen as some kind of religious miracle."

The man laughed and followed her down the sidewalk; my mother seemed pleased, and kept talking to him, pulling off her apron after it flew up against her arms when an earth mover passed through the lots between houses. They sheltered their eyes as the dust reached them, and barely noticed Kyle pass on his Mustang, a metal pail slung over one handlebar and banging rhythmically as he peddled towards our front steps. He made a running dismount from his bike and slipped the pail off in one motion, letting the bike fall against the sod. The pail seemed uneasy in his hand, wobbling.

"What you got?" I asked.

Kyle limped up to the steps and swung the bucket around so it thudded onto the first stair. He didn't look at the contents, but watched me, kicking the side of the metal so it gave a watery ring. I leaned over from where I was sitting and looked inside.

The black water was moving, like gelatin, as if blades were churning at the bottom of the pail. I'd never seen water so dark, moving unnaturally. Kyle reached in with his hands and scooped out a palm full of tadpoles—there were so many, barely a few drops of water spilled from his hands. The pail was more a cargo hold than an aquarium.

"Wow! Where'd you get them?"

"Duggan Slough. You gotta see it! There's millions of them!"

Kyle slid a dozen or so tadpoles back and forth between hands; one fell on the steps and I picked it up, its tail curling a comma in my hand from right to left. It had no legs, but others in Kyle's hands had, the back limbs like two sides of an unfinished triangle framing a shrinking tail. These ones were bigger, with frog-like eyes that blinked translucent lids.

"Kyle," my mother said, suddenly standing beside us and looking down as he ran his hand through the thick water, "there must be hundreds in there! They need more water than that."

"They can breathe air already," he said, stirring the pail more violently, "I saw their mouths opening and closing."

"Still, they need water to stay wet. They need to eat. You should take them back to where you got them."

Kyle shrugged, and I wondered if my mother felt the same way I did when he used that movement with me. I never had an argument with Kyle, although I wanted to fight like my parents. When I challenged him he shrugged, the way I'd seen his father shrug at his mom, then look away as if he didn't care what I thought of him. It was the worst kind of omission, not to be considered wrong but, rather, not to be thought about.

"Can we go back to the slough," I asked, "and get some more water? We'll let some of them go."

Kyle was already back at his bike, looping the pail over the handlebars. My mother nodded, and I ran to get my bike from the backyard, grabbing a plastic pail from the basement.

～

We crossed Thirty-seventh Avenue, following the maze of suburban pavement that ran parallel to Eleventh Street and to the east of Duggan Hill. It was coffee-break, and workmen were seated all along Thirty-eighth Avenue, their legs dangling through the skeletons of unfinished first floors. They waved as we rode, until the shells of the houses were distant. The city had gone ahead of itself, raising light standards and fire hydrants a year ahead of time. When we hit Thirtieth Avenue the pavement ended abruptly, and turned into a dirt road that was marked for a hundred yards by wooden surveyor sticks with strips of neon orange attached to them. We pedalled past these, kicking many of them over as we did, and arrived at a point where the prairie returned out of scraped clay, and the road became two narrow tire-treads through grass.

We discarded our bikes when the road became so bumpy it made Kyle's pail shake, and we lost some tadpoles in the dirt. We'd gone far enough from numbered streets that it didn't seem we were in Edmonton. The sounds of vehicles and carpentry had faded, and once we hid our bikes behind some wild rose bushes I noticed that the pump I'd heard that morning was now very close, irregularly rhythmic. To the west, about fifty yards, was a small hill where I could see the tops of fir trees sloping down the far side. Kyle limped towards it with his pail, refusing my offer to help carry it.

From the top of the hill, the pump looked like a small tractor mired in the mud on the shore of slough, drawing silt and water deep from the centre and pumping it several hundred yards away through a long, canvas pipe. It backfired suddenly, like a cannon over the heads of ducks paddling nearby, but they didn't notice, familiar with the event.

"Over here, by the tallest tree," Kyle said, beginning to trot down the hill to the water, "that's where they're all going."

As I followed, the ground became soft and spongy; there was the rotting smell of algae and pond scum hardening in the sun, and a more acidic scent of mosquito insecticide. The fir trees, which had once been right beside the slough, were now a few yards back from a twenty-foot bowl of water. The ridges on the slough bottom had risen as the water fell, enclosing a circle of water separate from the rest. It looked like a tidal pool, except that the tide was permanently gone. A fast evaporation had begun.

Kyle let the pail rest on the edge of the pool and sat on the soaking ground to remove his runners and socks.

"What are you doing?" I asked.

"You can't catch anything from the edge, stupid. They'll all move to the side you're not on."

"But you've already got lots."

Kyle knocked the side of his pail.

"These ones aren't moving like they used to," he said, "I want some new ones."

I unlaced my own shoes and stepped on the former slough bottom, squeezing brown water up between my toes. Kyle was already in water up to his knees, and by the time I caught up he had tipped the metal pail sideways, the tadpoles pouring out slowly in clumps, then rushing like spilt coal into the shallow water. A few swam away quickly, but most kept up the same tired quivering in piles on the slough bottom. We both stepped over them and went for deeper water.

The black bottom was moving; as Kyle's foot lifted high in the water the slough shook forward, making clear a space for his foot to land. The pool was alive with tadpoles; in the deepest part they were unavoidable and each step I took trapped squirming beneath my feet. Surface water rippled out from our moving knees while below the tadpoles moved away from us without direction, a blind need to escape. It must have been fear which drove them to this pool to begin with, when the beat of the pump began to make the water vibrate. Now the slough bottom itself had become a bucket.

Kyle struck once at the water, like a heron, then lifted his pail; it was thick with movement, and I added more water to his bucket with my own. When I tried to capture mine, the pail entered the water at a difficult angle and sound broke like a belly-flop. I drew my pail up and saw I had no more than five or six tadpoles. My second attempt had a more razor-like entry into the water, and the pail had several dozen small shadows darting in its bottom.

Back on the hill, we both pulled our runners on and stuffed our socks in our pockets. The pump backfired, then continued its regular rhythm.

"I wonder where the water's being pumped to," I asked.

Kyle shrugged. "Another field, maybe."

"Want to go see?"

We left our buckets in the shade of one of the pine trees and walked around the slough, following the canvas pipe through a field of hay, as dry as a horse's mane, towards a small gully. There, the end of the hose emptied down a sharp slope to a storm sewer, and up the gully we could see the bar-crossed mouth of a tunnel that ran back towards the city.

We helped each other into the cement gully, then walked

towards the sewer, the silted water from the pump trickling towards the opening. Two of the metal bars had been bent outwards, away from the darkness as if something had run against the incline and burst out to reach sunlight. Looking into the sewer was like looking out from a camp-fire into the forest; something could be there, in the darkness, watching me outlined in light.

"I'll bet you could go all the way to the river under-ground," Kyle said.

"I'll bet it's cold in there," I said, "caves are always cold."

"It's not a cave, stupid, it's a sewer."

"I know, stupid."

"Why don't you go in, then?"

"Why don't you?

"You won't because your mom would be mad."

"I would too."

"My dad says your mom never shuts up. My dad says you're going to be a sissy because your mom won't shut up and do like she's supposed to."

"I am not."

"You are, my dad says."

"Your dad does not."

"Does so."

I stood there, looking into the darkness, and felt my face turn red. Rick would never say those things about me. He wouldn't.

"If I go in, will you tell your dad?"

Kyle shrugged.

"You have to tell him."

I took a step into the tunnel, bending under the spread bars, hoping Kyle would follow. He didn't. I took three more steps and turned around so I could face the light, walking backwards in carefully placed steps.

"Just don't take off," I called, "stay there."

Kyle stood in the centre of the circle of light ahead of me, his hand above his eyes as he squinted into the sewer. Ten steps into the tunnel. Twenty. The circle of light ahead of me, as I backed up, became smaller. Kyle seemed to be a criminal caught in a spotlight, his shape a black outline. I stopped walking after thirty steps backward.

"Are you there?" Kyle called. "Why have you stopped?"

I saw my breath cloud his dark outline and was amazed how cold it had become so near the entrance. The cement around me was damp and slippery despite the lack of rain.

"Hey!" Kyle shouted, angry, "Where are you? Are you there? Hello?"

I turned from him and faced the darkness, listening as his shouts echoed ahead of me towards the river. The blackness was absolute, as if immersed in a cloud of tadpoles. I liked this absence, my back to the light. I could imagine a world without Kyle, in the darkness, his father anguished over the loss, the shape of Rick in my arms as I offered comfort. The darkness offering comfort.

Kyle's voice came again, echoing, panicky, out of control.

"Joe! Joey!"

I shrugged in the darkness. He'd never needed me before. I kept quiet.

"Joe!!"

When I finally turned and began to run back towards the light, I knew he could only hear something approach. He stood in the spotlight, shaking, perhaps wondering if this was the thing which had bent the bars outward. He was out of the spotlight before I reached the bars, bolting up the side of the gully and back towards our Mustangs. I pedalled home, behind him fifty yards, calling, trying to catch up. He'd taken his pail with him and spots of water marked the new asphalt along thirtieth avenue. As the sounds of machines returned, I realized I wouldn't be able to catch him before he reached Thirty-seventh Avenue, and coasted home, curving my Mustang from side to side on the street.

~

That night my father unrolled the sod on both yards, and my mother let the sprinkler run overnight so the roots would have a decent start. It was the only lawn-watering my father would ever willingly allow. My bucket of tadpoles was moved from the basement to outside the front door, and droplets of water from the sprinkler ran across the pail's surface. I rested in bed, listening to the drops hit the lawn and the distant gunshots by Duggan slough. Kyle's house was silent, as it always was after nine-thirty. I hadn't seen him again that day.

My mother checked in on me before she went to bed, standing in the light of the hallway the way Kyle had stood in the sewer's opening. She listened for my regular breathing, but heard none.

"Are you still awake?" she whispered.

"Yeah."

The bedroom door opened wider so my face must have been visible; her's was still an outline, eclipsed by the hallway light.

"What's up?

"I have to tell you something."

"Oh?"

"I—I went in a tunnel today."

"You did?"

"Over by the slough."

"The storm sewer?"

I nodded and she stood by the door, not moving.

"Was Kyle with you?"

I nodded. She thought for a moment, then said:

"There's two new families moving into the crescent. I don't want you to play so much with Kyle anymore. Okay?"

It seemed to me a punishment I could live with.

$\sim$

That night I dreamt again of Rick, his warm arms wrapped around me as we backed into the tunnel, the air turning cold. Somehow, I could reach forward, and I bent the metal bars back into straight rows, ones that Kyle pulled at frantically to get apart so he could run into the tunnel after us. I was laughing, pulled into the darkness of Rick's body. I could see Kyle's mother in the circle of receding light, her head kerchiefed, her hand slowly waving after us.

And as I slept, the black shadows within the pail stopped breathing as the tadpoles suffocated—the water's surface soon a smooth mirror of starlight. Nearby, in evaporating pools, the earth seemed to move in waves beneath the water, like it had moved beneath graders until the bones had been found.

Norm Sacuta's short stories have appeared in Edmonton and Calgary magazines and in Grain. He is also a playwright and poet whose work has been published in several periodicals, most recently Matrix, NeWest Review, and Dandelion. In 1989, Ismay, his full-length play about the man who built the Titanic, won the Alberta Culture Playwriting Competition, Discovery Category. He is currently pursuing a D.Phil. in American Literature and Sexual Dissidence at the University of Sussex in England.

Rose

BONNIE BISHOP

My cigarette burns red in the dark.

The cat at my feet can't understand why I won't go to bed, why I sit in this chair by my bedroom window night after night. This morning my gums bled when I was brushing my teeth and my skin is clam cold and won't absorb make-up; my body wants sleep too. My friends are beginning to question the dark circles beneath my eyes and knit their brows when I gaze off in the middle of conversation. I tell them it's the flu. It is none of their business that I'm not sleeping at night, but after five nights I too sometimes worry for myself. But then I put it down to the fatigue of my body because, after all, hadn't I thought of the plan before the sleepless nights, when I must have known for sure that I was sane? All I am is the dog, passant. No froth coming from my mouth yet.

Besides, in some ways, this has been good for me. Like an errant Christian on the brink of death repenting all his sins I too have been admitting to all the mistakes I've made, or at least those that I can remember, those that haven't let me forget. Like laughing at Harriet Whitworth's period in grade five. She came to her circle of friends, all of us standing in the school yard with our skipping ropes wound tight in our hands, excited and feeling wonderful because she had started menstruating and wanted us to share in the blossoming. She must have been one of the lucky few whose mother told the truth. I know for a fact she didn't have older brothers to mock her. Yet all she got from us were jeers and insults. We made her as embarrassed and ashamed of the stuff that flowed between her legs as we were. But that's the past—just knowing I haven't forgotten eases my conscience a bit. After all, maybe no one, not even Harriet Whitworth, remembers. After all.

Tonight the trespasses that haunt me are more recent. Somewhere out there in the black night is a daughter, sitting in a bar hating me. She is sitting in a bar being beautiful down to the bone, too truthful because of too much drink. I can see her smoothing her long red hair like I used to when I was younger. She is sitting in a bar where three years ago a young woman was picked up by a man and dragged out to the country and murdered. Dragged out into the prairie fields where she fought for her life in the silent emptiness. They found pieces of his skin beneath her nails.

I give the spray can a shake and its tiny marble makes a hollow rattling sound. I like the sound because I am the one making it and it reassures me that I have control.

Mostly she tells me all the things I did wrong. Every week I hear how I've failed as a mother, that she's the one who's always been the mother. Afterward I can never remember all the things she shouts at me just like I can never remember, when we're fighting, all the good I've tried to do for her. I just know the essence of my love is there and is as real as the essence of her hate. And so we scream at each other and she leaves and I phone her friends and drive my car around the city looking for her, feeling her confusion, feeling her young life desperate for clarity, wishing for just one wish to fall true into a place called centre. Her friends tell me that tonight she's looking for it in the bar.

I bought this can of spray paint the morning after I saw him. It has my name on it—Rose. And it says shake well before using so I hope I have the clarity of thought to do this. But just in case I don't, every so often I give it a shake to keep the paint fluid and thin. I like to think of the tiny bead and how it stays silver and pure even in the murk of all that red.

When I called the police they searched the area of my neighbourhood before coming over but found nothing. I showed them this bedroom window where he had been watching me. I didn't hang a curtain because it faces the house next to me and the passage is narrow and dark and I always thought it was safe and private, do you see? Did you see his face? No. Do you know how tall he is? No. Was his hair dark or light? No. All I saw was his outline standing close to my window and at such an angle that I knew he'd been there before.

I can tell the police think I am handling the incident very well. Mostly I am quiet and as helpful as possible, showing them where he stood and knowing, at least, the size of his head. But there's not much they can do. And these kinds of things happen all the time and it could have been much worse. And he's probably harmless. But they are concerned, and ask me if I live alone and I tell them I am widowed, which in a sense is true. I tell them all about my first husband dead within the first year of our marriage of a heart attack. The younger policeman is very kind and offers to hang up a sheet. I know he is thinking of his own mother and her helplessness and how he would hate for something like this to happen to her. I think I am handling it very well too. When they leave I thank them and promise that I will put up a curtain in this window.

What I didn't tell them was what happened thirty years ago. Waking up in the middle of the night to the sudden weight of someone in a leather jacket upon me, pulling my hair and saying shut-up, shut-up or I'll kill you. Grabbing me by the back of the head and forcing me to sit up so that he could take my nightgown off. She was sick with bronchitis and she woke up crying and racked with painful cough and he let me go into her room and quiet her, but he stood at my back, my hair wound tightly in his fist all the while. I felt around in the darkness of her crib and found her bottle and gave it to her. I saw her eyes round, serious, she refused her bottle but lay quiet. He took me back to my bedroom and this is what I remember the most. His fingers, almost light, upon me. Like some kind of apology looking for my forgiveness or acceptance, and then she started to cry again, and he simply left. I phoned a man who loved me and he came and took us away to his place.

We were married a month later. He told me that he would protect me and never let anything happen to me again. And I believed him. Believed that he believed it. But he couldn't see into the future the way I could, and he couldn't have understood that he wasn't the one who saved me. When I tell people I was married for five years they see it as a short time and joke that I'm almost a virgin. What they don't see is that it took me five long years before I could bring myself to sleep alone again.

When she was ten I brought her the Kotex. I know all about it, she told me. Who told her all these things? Who told her about the blood, and babies, and men? Take those things away and get me some Tampax, is what she told me. What else does she know? Who told her?

After the police left I did hang a blanket over the window. But then I couldn't see out. How will I know if he's out there standing beside my window? He's probably not dangerous but how am I supposed to know that? Did he touch me? No he didn't lift a finger. What did he do? He looked at me. He looked at me in a private moment buttoning my pyjama top over my breasts. He was watching me when I thought I was alone. He reached in through my window and grabbed my hair, the hair that I cut off so many years ago, and he forced my head back and stripped me of sanctum.

The cat has moved to the bed; tired of waiting for me, it curls foetal on my favourite pillow. I lean toward the screened window and feel a breeze that helps clear any regard for sleep from my head.

If anyone can hang curtains properly, it's her. She's good at that sort of thing. I'm not. She's good at hanging curtains, pounding nails, reading maps; we never get lost when she drives even if we're in a city we've never been before, she always knows exactly where to go, always finds the place we are looking for. When I bought her the doll house for her ninth birthday it was she who read the instructions on how to put it together. She understands everything, it seems. Oh I know the reason she fights with me is her way of leaving, her way of saying she's not coming home tonight and not to expect a phone call. I know that I need her more than she needs me. It's not an unfamiliar guilt and I know she shares it too. She's sitting somewhere in a bar hating me for needing her life.

Despite all these nights of waiting for his arrival, when the moment comes I am not prepared. His face rises sudden and meets mine. Our faces are so close it is as though we are about to perform some kind of grotesque kiss. He is not prepared for my presence either. He looks the same way I must have looked to him five nights ago. Caught, frightened, and utterly, utterly dismayed.

Somewhere out there in the black night is a man red, red with anger and blinded by humiliation.

And I didn't lift a finger.

~

Bonnie Bishop is a freelance writer and the assistant director of the Book Publishers Association of Alberta. Her poetry has appeared in many periodicals, including The Malahat Review, Grain *and* Dandelion; *her collection,* Elaborate Beasts, *was published in 1988. Her fiction has appeared in* Event *and* Prairie Fire. *She is currently working on a collection of short stories.*

Wire Act

MARTIN SHERMAN

*"Laadies and Gentlemen . . . Circus Internationale proudly
presents . . . the first family of funambulation . . . from
Genoa, Italy . . . The Caspiris!"*

The Johnny Jones Quintet plays a light Vivaldi air. Two
young men and two young women emerge in black sequined
skin-tight bodysuits. They are unmistakably brothers and
sisters, with the same high foreheads and beautiful long faces,
the fine chiselled features and thin-lipped dazzling white
smiles softened in the women's faces only by their make-up.
The spotlight illuminates and reflects off their thick coils of
black hair sprayed with black glitter.

They emerge from behind the curtain holding aloft an old
man in a straight-backed chair. The chair is a large aluminum
cube frame topped by a square aluminum back. The old man
stares fixedly ahead, displaying only his strikingly perfect
profile to all but the far end of the arena. His posture parallels
the rigid angles of the chair. He sits upon the broad expanse
of the chair like a child-emperor, dispelling the absurdity of
his oversized throne with the regal gravity of propriety.

He is certainly too old to be their father. Grandfather,
then. His hair, unglittered, is grey and short; his costume is

a simple unsequinned white bodysuit. His mouth is tightly set. He might be a mannequin, a ceramic saint on parade, a testament to their heritage.

They move down the hippodrome track, the chair held delicately on their shoulders, in a waltzing dance step of remarkable lightness, as though only the weight of the chair keeps them in contact with the ground. Into Ring One they sweep, swirling to a spot in front of the dangling rope ladder, swinging the chair down from their shoulders with sure and steady hands.

The old man sees the rope ladder before him and suddenly comes to life. He seems to fly from the chair onto the ladder and is near the top in moments. One grandson, one granddaughter, then the other grandson, follow him up the ladder. He stops and, in a unanimous gesture, all four climbers lean back toward the ground, releasing the ladder with one hand. The remaining granddaughter hoists the chair to her sister, who swings it heavily up to one brother, then the next. The old man looks drained by the effort of his climb. He reaches down stiffly and lifts the metal chair with obvious effort, lays it against the rope ladder, pushes it upward, struggling with each step, until it clatters onto the platform. He finishes the climb and lurches onto the platform, hunched in a fight for his breath.

One by one, his grandchildren ascend to the platform as the ringmaster announces:

"Gino Caspiri, at seventy-five, is the world's oldest living wirewalker. With his brother, Emilio, he performed in twenty-three circuses, in every continent, before eighteen crowned heads of state, electrifying audiences for more than half-a-century. He has passed on his knowledge and expe-

rience to his four grandchildren Carmelo, Antonio, Angelina, and Maria-Giuseppe. Ladies and Gentlemen, the Caspiris!"

His grandchildren surround him and bow deeply one by one as their names are pronounced—the old man barely dips his head to accept the applause. He stares out across the wire.

Carmelo turns to the rear of the platform, snaps open the latches that hold one of the balancing poles. He slides behind it and lifts it free, hefting the pole, proffering it to the old man. Gino glances back, shakes his head, and turns again to the wire.

He is absolutely motionless. The audience can feel that, one by one, then row by row, section by section, they are winking out of existence before him. His body convulses for one moment and grows rigid again. The old man's face is suddenly softened. It is not fear—fear departed with that shudder. He is gathering something from within. Not courage. Look at the slow and gradual slump of his body. The line of his lowered shoulders hints at a profound gloom. He is gathering despair.

Gino steps slowly out onto the wire, like a swimmer testing the ocean's temperature. His right foot rests lightly on the wire, his left firmly planted on the platform. He closes his eyes and leans forward slowly, shifting his weight onto the wire.

He opens his eyes and raises his left foot from the platform, slides it forward. The wire shakes, his legs shiver with the pulse of the cable, absorbing it, dissolving the motion into the muscles of his legs. Hunched over, he shuffles in agonizingly slow, unsteady steps, his outstretched arms flapping erratically. He appears brittle, a dried leaf of a man as he totters forward on the wire. Where is the strength that shot him up the ladder? Each flat-footed step is strained with effort, laden with despondency. Energy drains from him into the steel cable fibres of the wire which now appears to come alive, quivering with malevolent power. Gino staggers on, seemingly drawn forward by the wire itself.

Somehow he has reached the centre of the wire. He lifts his head tentatively, brings his hands to his chest and stretches them wide in a feeble salute. The applause of the crowd seems to carry a plea. Get him off this wire. How can we stand to watch the walk back?

Then he is tilting, his arms waving useless ridiculous circles, angled like an airplane banking out of control. His left foot leaves the wire, his aged left leg shaking in the air, fighting for counterbalance. Screams from the ground. Suddenly his leg straightens, toes pointed, he tosses back his head and in a single motion he draws his hands into his chest, sweeps his leg down above the wire. Gino spins a quick half-turn, snaps out his arms.

The rigid slash of his mouth suddenly lengthens, opens into a wide flash of teeth, smiling savage and triumphant.

Gino turns again, this time his arms and legs sweeping wide. He stops again, perfectly motionless, not a hint of the fight for balance, as though the trembling cable is a wide expanse of dance stage. He walks, this time, in the proud glide of a matador to the far platform. He steps to safety, turns and nods across the wire at his grandchildren who applaud him wildly. To the crowd's applause he raises a single finger of acknowledgment. Again he steps on the wire, rolling his feet down, touching toe, sole, then heel. He ambles out like a Sunday stroller, casually checks an imaginary watch and stares down at his wrist as though amazed at the hour. Gino lifts his head in sudden panic then begins to run across the wire, his feet splayed out duck-like, the wire bounding with the pounding of his feet. The Johnny Jones Quintet snaps into a manic silent-movie theme. The crowd laughs and slaps their hands together in time to the music, to the timing of the old man's flapping feet. His grandchildren reach out to grab him, hug him, then turn to present him to the crowd.

It's their turn now and they move out gracefully onto the wire, skimming its surface, brilliantly light and aware of their own splendour.

The wire hums with their motions: Angelina jumping rope; Maria-Giuseppe's back walkover; Antonio's handstand, exquisitely prolonged before toppling and swirling beneath the wire, rising again and again in giant swings; Angelina stepping from Carmelo's knee, twisting and swinging up to his shoulders, the slow and delicate release of their fingers, straightening, stiffening, Carmelo's hands leaving her ankles, their arms triumphantly outstretched in double salute; the dual juggling, club-passing of Antonio and Maria-Giuseppe, the house lights dimming, the spotlights darkly filtered purple as the torch-clubs whirl and flicker between them.

At the platform, Gino watches only the wire. Seeing the way it moves and defines the space it severs.

He has lived on this steel slash for fifty-six years. Stood before it on platforms, on cliff edges, on the parapets of skyscrapers, churches, risen up from the ground upon it, blindfolded, at impossible angles, carved a dance of air over millions of upturned circus-going faces, over drunken throngs of Mardi Gras revellers, over cars and trucks careening through the streets of Rome, over lakes and rivers and the spray of waterfalls, over the shimmering, flashing neon of a nighttime

Las Vegas so luminous that the sky was washed grey above him, walked through the joyous scents of cotton-candy and tent-canvas, through poisonous, smoke-stained air, through the familiar silent grassy air of the meadow behind his home, in the roar of a wind so thick and liquid that it splattered swallows against canyon walls, between his brother upon one platform and his wife, Sophia, on the other, between his son and daughter, between his grandchildren who now dance before him, between one emptiness and another.

They have deserted me, he thinks. Sophia and Gina, mother and daughter, disappearing in the midnight dawn of Vegas. His son, Giacomo, shattered and physically healed, now useless with doubt. Gino can hardly stand to see him, to witness the evidence of his inability to correct with training the twisted chromosomes of Sophia's uncertainty. When they were younger, Gino would press his grandchildren close, bury his face in the napes of their necks and inhale, breathing in the scents of balsam and lilac talcum, searching for an uncertain vinegary scent of fear.

They have all fallen away, some crushed to the ground by the wind or time or fear. Some dead, some crippled, some who have locked themselves to the ground. He remembers them only as ghosts now, in the familiar shapes they moulded in the wire: the delicate shivering curvature of the line beneath Sophia; the elongated W of his children's weight; the sudden precise concavity of Emilio in the Dive of Death, touching down from the leap over the kneeling Gino; the protuberance he himself defined half-somersaulted mid-air in a salto; the final convexity twenty years ago in Monaco that was the last air sculpture of Emilio. Gino fought for his life in the muscles of his legs, absorbing and dispelling the surge of steel cable that Emilio left, whispering, "He got what he deserved." Summing up in those words all the respect and disdain he felt for his brother, all the truth he knew.

"Carmelo Caspiri will now attempt one of the most difficult and dangerous acts in circus history. Fifty years ago, his grand-uncle, Emilio, first performed the Dive of Death—leaping over his grandfather, Gino, onto the wire. Half a century later, Carmelo Caspiri will attempt to surpass him. While his brother and sisters crouch on the wire, Carmelo will attempt to leap over all three. In order for Carmelo to complete this trick he needs intense concentration. Ladies and Gentlemen, Circus Internationale asks for your cooperation in giving the Caspiris complete silence as they attempt this trick. Thank you."

Antonio, Angelina, and Maria-Giuseppe have already moved to the centre of the wire, to where the wire is tightened and guyed down by the *cavaletti* cables. They kneel, almost eliminating the centre of gravity, then straddle the wire, Antonio's hands along the wire, Angelina's hands upon his back and Maria-Giuseppe's hands upon her sister's forearms. Their legs are straddled, allowing their feet to press against the stability of the *cavaletti*. Maria-Giuseppe nods, grunts, "Hup." Carmelo begin his approach.

Gino awaits the Dive of Death, his eyes on the position Antonio has assumed along the wire. The trick is not simply in clearing the bodies, not in landing the jump on the wire nor even in Carmelo's regaining his balance. Success lies in surviving the wire's rebound. This was always the hidden secret. Emilio's landing, his battle for balance, always drew the applause but it was Gino who, unheralded, absorbed the shock of the cable, his body rippling, smothering the force that would have whipped them both into space.

He does not see the quickening approach of Carmelo, hears only peripherally the communal intake of breath from the crowd. He watches the press of Antonio's fingers remembering the overlay grip, the roll of wrist, the light embrace of forearm to cable. The wire dips slightly as Carmelo jumps; ripples when he sails over Maria-Giuseppe, as if held aloft by the indrawn breath, the witness of the crowd; arcs up as Carmelo whispers over Angelina; ripple meets arc as Carmelo's feet trace the sloping undulating form of Antonio, the ripple of Antonio's back dipping under his brother's feet. The wire shivers, trembles, convulses. Antonio, Angelina, and Maria-Giuseppe become one being who caresses the wire, soothes its spasms, assimilates and metabolizes the convulsion, feels the paroxysm subside. The wire bows, surrenders itself to Carmelo's feet as he lands, in truth, alights, the delicate press of his feet upon the wire, like a physician's hand, seeks its vital signs, searches for intimations of his brother and sisters in the wire's pulse. There! They feel each other, feel the wind of a communal breath released beneath them, feel the song of the cable become an exultant chorus of wire and flesh.

Quiet.

Applause thunders around them, reflects off the walls, rebounds from the domed ceiling but does no touch them at all. On the wire, the rest of world has evaporated.

Maria-Giuseppe, Angelina, and Antonio unfold themselves, rise, and step along the wire to the far platform, followed by Carmelo. The arena again erupts with applause. The young Caspiris turn to salute the crowd.

And look! The crazy old man applauds them, too. He claps his hands in great underhand flaps like a seal, grabs the large metal chair, tilting it upside down. He raises his head to the arena ceiling, bringing the top of the chairback to his forehead, balancing it easily. He resumes his seal clap as he steps onto the wire, his grandchildren, and then the crowd, taking up the beat. At the centre of the wire, Gino flips his head down, catches the chair with a flourish, and braces it before him on the wire. There's a chuckle from the audience as he wipes imaginary sweat from his brow, and in a single motion, half-turns and seats himself, spread-eagled on the wide expanse of the chair, his arms and legs finding his balance. One by one, his grandchildren approach the chair from the rear. First Carmelo, then Antonio, Maria-Giuseppe, and Angelina. Carmelo at the chairback clasps left arm to left arm with Gino, circles his left leg onto the seat of the chair between his grandfather's thighs, grunts "Hup!" and swings himself around and onto the chair facing his approaching brother, Gino counterbalancing heavily to the right. Antonio clasps, circles, grunts, and mirrors his brother. Gino fights the shifting weights, guides the chair to stillness. Maria-Giuseppe at the chairback, her left foot on the chair's seat behind her grandfather, clasps Carmelo's right hand, mounts to the chairback, facing Carmelo. Gino leans right, against the added weight to the left. Angelina follows, stands leg to leg beside her sister, facing Antonio, their inner arms across one another's back. "Hup!" they lift their inner legs as one, Maria-Giuseppe to Carmelo's left shoulder, Angelina to Antonio's right. Each brother snakes an arm around the leg upon his shoulder. "Hup!" they lean their bodies forward, shifting weight from chairback to shoulder. "Hup!" back legs raised in tandem. "Hup!" their arms spread in salute.

    "THE CASPIRIS..............!"

Through the sustained applause, Gino guides them quickly through the dismount, knowing the audience will never reward the dangers involved.

He sits alone upon the chair. His grandchildren already have begun their descent down the rope ladder. He casually rises and stands upon the seat. Gino raises his right leg out to the side. The chair teeters for a moment and then stills beneath him. In the ring below, the grandchildren gather then back away from one another, heads tilted up, stretching a hand net between them. Suddenly Gino snaps down his right leg, kicking the chair out from under him. He drops to the wire and lands as though weightless. The wire does not even appear to bend as the chair careens through the air, tumbles down and into the net. Gino slowly dips into a low bow, his right leg sliding back upon the wire.

At the first spatter of applause, Gino smiles in acknowledgement, casually tilts to the left, and drops. So quickly and casually is this done that there is not even time for the audience to react before they see him gliding toward the floor. Gliding! He has slid himself upon the *cavaletti* that anchors down the wire. But he slides with such force that it appears he will nonetheless smash headfirst into the ground. Then his hands clamp down upon the wire and as he stops, swings himself free and touches down gently into the arms of his grandchildren.

Again he seats himself in the chair. Again they raise his throne aloft on their shoulders, moving in light dance steps to the reprise of Vivaldi. As they reach the back curtain, the grandchildren wave and smile at the crowd. Gino stares blankly ahead, once again rigid.

The curtain sweeps shut behind them. They lower the

chair to the ground. The old man remains seated. Maria-Giuseppe extends a hand to her grandfather and he starts at the motion, slaps her hand away, then rises. Stares at the floor. He sees, to his horror, a network of lines radiating out from his feet, infinite filaments of possibility. Maria-Giuseppe alone remains with him.

Clowns dash past him holding giant props. Someone yells, "Here!" directing a line of advancing wardrobe boxes. A dozen elephants, trunk to tail, lumber along the edge of the entranceway. A guttural shout in German and they turn to face their trainer. Showgirls quickstep, tugging at their costumes.

Maria-Giuseppe takes the old man's arm. "Come, Grandpapa. I'll dress you for Finale."

Gino remains rooted, jerking his head toward each new motion and then back to the floor, searching for the wires upon which they walk, gazing in wonder at the way they move, with certainty, without guidelines and without fear through the sea of the world that engulfs him.

～

Martin Sherman is a former Ringling Bros. Circus clown who was once arrested for clowning in Chicago. His work has appeared in numerous Canadian and U.S. magazines includ-ing The Antioch Review, Canadian Fiction Magazine, The Quarterly, Mississippi Review, The Fiddlehead, *and* Grain. *His collection of short stories,* Elephant Hook and Other Stories, *appeared in 1993. He lives in Calgary with his wife and three children.* "Wire Act" *was first published in* Canadian Fiction Magazine, *no. 80.*

Tilting

HIROMI GOTO

Oba-chan was the first to come out of the terminal gates, pushed by a bearded Canadian Airlines man in a navy blue sweater. Her bamboo walking stick pointing straight up and down like an exclamation mark. The navy blue sweater man all brisk brisk and a quick fake smile hidden by his facial hair.

"Oba-chan," I said, "You don't look too tired," and tried to hug her as best I could around her walking stick, the cool metal arms of the wheelchair. Kunio held up Kenji below his armpits, dangling the child in front of Oba-chan so that she could give him a kiss, but he squirmed away from her face.

"He just got up from his nap, so he's a little grumpy," I said, excusing him. Oba-chan smiled wanly. Kunio juggled Kenji on to his left arm and bent down to give Oba-chan a quick peck.

"I'll just take her down to the luggage terminal," the navy blue sweater man said, and swung Oba-chan around us, pushed her briskly down the hall.

Kunio and I watched him stride stride his back straight and Oba-chan's bamboo walking stick pointing straight up and down. Swallowed by the elevator. Dad walked up from the helicopter game he had spent six dollars of quarters on and asked, "Where's your Mom?"

"She hasn't come out yet," I said.

"Do you have any more quarters?"

Kunio jostled Kenji from his left arm to his right and stuck his hand in his jeans' pocket. Made a fist and pulled it out. He opened his fingers and there was a dirty piece of unchewed gum, a toothpick, six pennies, a dime and three quarters. Dad picked the quarters from his palm, "Thanks," went back to the helicopter. We watched him lift his leg to straddle the seat of the helicopter. Slip two quarters into the slot and grip the joystick. He jerked and pushed the joystick, his body weaving and jolting with the movement of the machine. Computerized sounds of missiles being launched and bombs dropped. Someone tapped me on my shoulder and I jumped around. Mom's face all red and puffed and standing so close that her panting breath stirred my bangs.

"You're face is swollen. You look tired," I said.

"I'm exhausted! My head is spinning!"

"Something smells like takuwan," I said, "Your hand luggage smells like takuwan."

"Don't tell me about it! Some takuwan opened up in my hand luggage somewhere over Japan and it's been like that the whole flight home. All the way from Tokyo to Korea to Vancouver to Calgary, the thing was smelling up the inside of the plane and not a thing I could do. Your father's sister gave it to me."

"Oh, no," I said. Kunio leaned over and gave Mom a peck on the cheek and said, "Welcome home."

Mom beamed then turned to Kenji. "Give me a kiss." Kenji leaned and gave her an open-mouthed slobber press and she wiped it off with her fingers and looked pleased.

"Where's your father?" Mom asked.

"He's on that helicopter," I said, pointing. We all turned and watched him jerking around on the seat of the game, dropping bombs and firing missiles in complete absorption.

Kenji started squirming and wriggling and yelling, "Aiyai! Aiyai! Aaaiiyaaiiiii!" Kunio let him down and he ran away, laughing, towards the escalators. Kunio chased after him.

"The smell was just awful. And that was that. There wasn't a thing I could do and now everyone will go away thinking, 'It's true. Oriental people. They smell funny.'"

"You shouldn't say Oriental, Mom. You should say Asian."

"Asian, Oriental, it doesn't change the way takuwan smells," she said. "Where's your grandmother?"

"The Canadian Airlines man took her down to the luggage area."

"That man!" Mom said, "I don't know what his rush rush is all about. I've been chasing him ever since I got off that plane and me with all this hand luggage to carry."

"Here," I said, "Let me take that for you. God! It weighs a ton! What do you have in there anyways?"

"I told you. Oh, my head is spinning."

"Kunio!" I yelled. He was at the other end of the terminal, standing in front of the toy shop with Kenji on his shoulders, watching a teddy bear on a tightrope gliding back and forth on an unicycle. "Kunio, come help with the luggage!"

"Osamu!" Mom yelled, "Osamu, get off that helicopter and help!" Dad jostled the joystick a few more times, dropped a few more bombs, then flung both hands into the air. Dad and Kunio reached us at the same time.

"I think that Kenji might have pooped," Dad said.

"It's not Kenji," I said. "Some takuwan exploded in Mom's hand luggage."

"Oh," Dad said. He turned to Kenji and said, "Sorry."

Kunio picked up two of Mom's bags and Dad took the other. I took Kenji's hand and we walked towards the escalator, Mom panting behind us softly muttering, "My head is spinning. The ground is heaving beneath my feet." I lifted Kenji up with his hands above his head when we reached the bottom of the escalator so he wouldn't stumble, and let him go. He ran toward the luggage conveyor belt. The navy blue sweater was still standing behind Oba-chan's chair, making a smile face behind his beard. He helped her out of the chair and sat her on the plastic-covered bench amidst piles of luggage and travel-stinky people. Oba-chan nodded her thanks to him and he lipped a smile again and stride stride away.

"I wonder if we should have given him a tip," Mom said.

"It's not like he's a bellhop," I said. "It's not like Oba-chan is luggage."

"I know!" Mom said. "I'm just saying that it might have been a nice gesture."

"Why don't you sit down?" I asked.

"I will," she said. "I'll sit down right now and never get up again."

"Where's Kenji?" Dad asked.

We looked up and around and he was at the other end of the terminal, pushing a luggage cart as fast as he could, people dodging him and looking angrily around for parents to attach him to.

"I'll get him," Kunio said, and jogged after him. There

was a general surge toward the luggage belt and bags started spewing from the chute.

"Oh," Mom said, "Here it comes." And went to stand right in front so she would be in the best position to grab. Dad rocked back and forth, heel to toes, and crossed his arms. I sat down beside Oba-chan on the bench.

"How was your trip?" I asked. "How was Masao-ojichan?"

"The hospital was very small and there were six beds to a room. There was one window but it was quite small and it faced the east so there wasn't much sunlight and the only sound to be heard was of old people in discomfort. The nurses were very young and it made one feel that much older, that much sicker. There were patients with head problems there so sometimes people would wander in and start talking to you like they were continuing a conversation until a young girl in a white uniform rushed in and bowed and apologized and led them away. Masao-chan was all curled in upon himself when we first went to see him and I thought he looked like a peanut and I was afraid to touch him because his surface was brittle. Masao-chan, I said, Masao-chan, we've come. And he opened his eyes and looked up at me and I don't know what he saw with his eyes but it must have been something nice because he smiled and went back to sleep. We sat in the room with those sick men, your Mom and I, and we rubbed his legs and arms with a warm cloth and wiped his face and wriggled his toes and fingers and washed his hair. The nurse brought us some hot ocha and we sipped it loudly so it would sound like home and we ate some oranges. He didn't wake up so we went to your Mom's cousin's house and they made us a great feast but we were too tired to eat so we talked and took a bath and went to sleep. We ate the leftover food in the morning and took the bus to the hospital again and when we went into Masao-chan's room, he was already awake and so surprised to see us! Oné-san! he said, Oné-san! And he couldn't say anything else because he was crying and we were crying too."

I looked up. Heard Kenji crying. He was sitting on the floor and holding his knees. Kunio was crouched beside him, talking softly.

"You're here, he said, you came. Yes, I said, we were here yesterday but you were tired and you didn't see us. I saw you, he said, I just didn't know it was you. I tucked the blankets more warmly around his body and he reached up to touch my hand and hold it. His hand was cold. You're like ice, I said, and rubbed, rubbed his hands between mine. He smiled. And you too, Miya-chan, and you too. Your Mom leaned over his bed and hugged him Canada style and he was quite surprised but pleased, you could tell, then your Mom took his icy feet and rubbed and rubbed them 'til they were red and all cozy warm. Have you seen my wife yet? he asked. Kimiko is not well. She was taking care of me too much and she weakened her own body. Her back is no good. She can't move very well. We haven't seen her yet, I said. We talked to her on the phone and she's coming to your daughter's house this afternoon. Ten years is too long since I saw you both."

"Osamu!" Mom called, "Osamu, help me with this luggage." Dad walked over to where she was sliding suitcases from the conveyor belt. Plunking them on the ground beside her. He lifted two with his back, rather than his knees, and winced. Mom stared up the chute, willing her bags to come out more quickly.

"Kimiko-chan had aged. There is nothing else you could

say. Ten years is a lot if you are seventy to begin with and my brother's illness had made her stoop well into ninety. We thought he was going to die, she said, her voice was wobbling, holding my hands both, I was getting ready for his funeral. Don't say that, I said, it's not so. Yes, she said, but it is better now that you and Miya-chan are both here. It is better. And she sat down on a chair and smiled her special smile. And it felt good, to be there with my brother and his wife and Miya-chan, no matter what the reason for being there was. We were together. That was what was most important."

I wasn't looking at Oba-chan, just watching people pass in front of me and letting her words flow over my body. She was stroking her one hand, then the other, and I could feel her nodding now and then from the corner of my face. I could hear Kenji laughing somewhere and it made me warm.

"I couldn't stay with Masao-chan every day at the hospital. It would be too much for me. So I went to Masao and Kimiko-chan's house and she was with me there. Kimiko-chan and I, two old women drinking green tea and eating oranges and trying to keep each other healthy as best we could. We talked a lot of old things, but we talked of new things too. And Miya-chan, she went to the hospital every day from her cousin's house because it was closer. She went every day and changed his sheets and washed his body and made him tea and talked and talked and massaged his skinny legs and arms and washed his face, his hair. She didn't go to meet her friends for coffee or drinks and she didn't go shopping or sightseeing. She stayed with Masao-ojichan and took care of his body. And he got stronger. He got stronger and he could sit up and eat some porridge. He started walking to the washroom and asking for books to read."

Kenji came to stand between my knees, his head tilted back and looking up at my face. He reached down with his hand and tugged his pants at the crotch.

"I have to change Kenji's diaper," I said, touched Oba-chan on her shoulder. I picked up my oversize purse and walked with Kenji to the washroom.

"It was a shame. I hadn't seen Masao-chan for ten years and when I finally went, I couldn't even visit with him. Five times only I saw him even though we were there for three weeks. I had much to talk about, but my body was too weak to sit at a hospital all day. And all I could do was know that he was a lot closer to me than before, and talk to Kimiko-chan and where did all the time go? Three weeks pass like spit if you are wishing it otherwise. And I thought about staying. I did. But what would I do? An old woman with two other old people and Miya-chan couldn't stay. No, Miya-chan a grand-mother already, so hard to believe and her home is not Japan any longer. No, I cannot stay and my daughter, I saw how her face changed when we landed in Calgary. The edges around her eyes disappeared and I knew that she was at a place called home. And I was home with her. Masao-chan at home now too and Kimiko-chan's back is a little better and I can rest easy for a while now and enjoy my great-grandson. And when he talks, when he can talk to me, I will listen."

When Kenji and I got back, Kunio was eating a soft ice cream cone and Dad was sitting on the bench next to Oba-chan. Mom was at the next bench over, digging through her luggage and looking at this and that. Kenji ran over to Kunio and said, "Up-poo! Up-poo!" Kunio lifted him up onto his lap and they took turns licking the ice-cream. I went to where Mom was sorting through her luggage.

"What are you doing?"

"I'm looking for your gifts."

"Why don't you look when you go home? There's no need to do all that now. Look, we just came because we're glad that you're home safely."

"I want to give them to you now," she said, looking in this bag, that bag, removing a box, a couple of boxes, a small bag.

"These are for Kenji!" she said happily, holding up two pairs of shoes.

"Oh, that's great!" I said, "His feet are growing so quickly, I can't afford to keep up with them."

"That's what I thought," she said, and held the shoes beside Kenji's feet. They were at least three sizes too big.

"That's all right," Kunio said, "He can wear them when he's older."

Mom went back to her parcels and handed Kunio a litre carton of expensive sake, and a box of specialty ramen noddles. He glowed with pleasure. "Thank you," he said, "Thank you very much. These must have been heavy."

Mom went back to her bags and handed me a box of hot Korean salted pollock roe. My mouth watered.

Dad got in on it and said, "Here's some pickles. Take some pickles."

"Not the one that exploded, please." I said.

Mom still looked for more. "I know I'm forgetting something," she said, bending back down to her luggage again.

"It can wait," Dad said, and she finally looked up. She lifted both her hands to her face and smacked her cheeks.

"I gained a lot of weight, didn't I?"

"Oh!" I said, "I thought your face was just swollen from retaining water and being tired after the long flight."

"It was the fish," she said, "The fish was so incredibly good."

"Most people eat fish to lose weight, Mom."

"I think it's great that you ate so much you gained weight," Kunio said.

"It was fish to die for. At least gain fifteen pounds for anyways."

"Should we go for supper somewhere? I'm feeling a bit hungry." Dad said.

"*Dad,*" I said, "I don't think Oba-chan is up to sitting through a meal. She probably wants to go home."

"Yes," Oba-chan said, "I'd like to go home and get some rest."

"OK," Dad said, raising both hands and palm outward. "I was just thinking about supper, that's all. I thought everyone might be hungry."

"We can eat some of the ramen I brought home," Mom said. "Well, I can't find it. I know I'm forgetting something, but it'll just have to wait."

"Thank you for all the gifts," Kunio said. "It must have been very heavy for you."

"Not at all," Mom said, "After all that you've done for us."

"We didn't do very much at all," I said. "We're just glad that you're home and everything."

"Well, let's go!" Mom said.

"I'll go and bring the car around," Dad said.

Kenji started his, "Uhhhhn, uhhhhn, uhhhhhhhhn!" and I looked down to his face and hands covered in soft ice-cream.

"Oh, for goodness' sake," Mom said and dug in her coat pocket for a Kleenex. She draped it over her forefinger and spat on it and wiped Kenji's face. Kenji squirming. Kunio got a luggage cart and started loading it with Mom's bags. Dad coming back. Dad and Kunio took the luggage out to the car and Mom followed, holding Kenji's hand. Oba-chan leaned on my arm and her bamboo walking stick. Dad had brought a pillow and two sleeping bags for Oba-chan so she could lie down on the way home. Mom settled her in the back seat and she got in the front.

"Thank you for coming," she said.

"We'll come and visit when you're rested up."

"Bye," said Kunio. Dad saluted and got into the car. Oba-chan was lying down so I couldn't see her, but her hand was raised above the seat and she was waving.

～

Driving, the roads icy and dust dry wind. Kenji in the back looking for buses and big trucks. The inside of the car warm now and not wanting to do anything but feeling this urge, this sense of something unsaid and wanting to fill it with I don't know what. Something tinged the edges of memory and tilting.

"I was thinking when we arrived, there was this strange feeling of my feet not quite solid on the ground, the edges of my hemisphere skewed slightly and the ground was leaning with every step I took and it was a neat sort of feeling if you're not prone to motion sickness. And I was thinking that maybe the ground was trying to tell me something. That I couldn't just land and feel right at home. That there was a period of transition or something to go through."

"Maybe you were just jet-lagged."

"No, it wasn't that because the feeling was there for the whole trip and I was over being jet-lagged by the third day. No, it was some sort of land thing and it made me think about the land and my walking on it and what it meant to me and all sorts of things. I don't know. You know what I mean?"

"No, not really."

"The whole time I was there, there was this sense of feeling I wasn't ever quite there, like I was in a contained box made of Saran Wrap and I could see out in a thinly distorted sort of way, and people could see me too, but always through some layer and sometimes I felt quite lonely and other times I felt almost nothing at all and I really can't remember all that much about the trip except for the love hotel and the earthquake."

"That earthquake was one of the biggest ones I've felt."

"It was funny, because it was after that snow blizzard in Tokyo and everyone saying we must have brought the snow with us from Canada because it almost never snows in Tokyo and never so much at once and us walking from the subway station and the snow just blasting on our faces and sticking there wet and Kenji on your back hiding his face and almost falling asleep because he was so tired, and stopping in the store to buy beer and snacks and instant ramen and onigiris and Hiroshi buying a giant chocolate bar and we all laughed. And you slipped going up the stairs to Takeshi's apartment and cut your hand and blood on the snow so brilliant, so beautiful. Nobu arriving late, after we'd drunk a lot of beer, Kenji sleeping in the next room and us eating instant ramen out of the Styrofoam containers. Remember? We took pictures and drank some more and ate the snacks and I was the first one to go asleep. And I don't remember when you came to bed, but something woke me up. It was something familiar, but its relationship to place was so strange, I woke up with a jolt and sitting upright. The room was moving beneath us and the weird sense of something I've always felt as motionless heaving like nausea. And things toppled off the TV and the bookshelves and and cupboards and I leaned over Kenji who slept through the whole thing, me leaning over him and making a tent with my arms and you sat up in your blankets and said, Big one, and I absolutely couldn't believe your factual tone of voice. Not leaning over to protect me or Kenji, just you sitting up in your futon calmly. And I could hear Hiroshi in the next room, sleeping on the floor with Takeshi and Nobu, could hear him through the paper-thin walls. Big. Big, he said, in the exact same tone of voice as you and I couldn't believe it and I started laughing."

"You sure can remember a lot of details for someone who can hardly remember the trip."

"I remember the things I remember really clearly. And that love hotel."

"Well, I don't know why you remember the love hotel. It wasn't very memorable for me. Nothing happened."

"That's why it's so memorable. *Because* nothing happened. I had all this anticipation of a love hotel experience after watching those Japanese dramas and cheap movies and hearing about them and wanting to experience this really sleazy thing. Only that wasn't the way it turned out at all. I mean I was amazed at how the whole thing was set up. Nothing could be more clinically set up to make illicit sex accessible. Kenji at your Mom's and us driving back to your parents' place after visiting your friend and all over I saw the love hotels' lights flicker flacker like Christmas at home, only there, it was for sex and I said, Let's go to a love hotel. And you said, Do you really want to? and I said, Yeah, it would be neat and I want to see what it's like inside.

"So you pulled into the next one, and I was a little disappointed because it wasn't a theme one. Like it didn't have a castle front or it wasn't shaped like a spaceship like others I'd seen, but we were pressed for time so I didn't say anything and you pulled into the underground parking and into an empty stall, not that there were many left, and you showed me how you pulled the gate behind your car so people couldn't see your licence plate or recognize your vehicle and I was amazed at the thought put into the arrangement. And we went into the lobby and there was no desk, no manager, no people, nothing. Only this great lighted panel on the wall with photographs of each room so you could pick the one of your choice, like a giant pop machine, only the ones that were lighted up were unoccupied, and there were only three rooms left to choose from so I picked the room I liked the best and pressed the button and the keys came out of the slot. I was so pleased that I laughed. So we went into the elevator to our floor, six, and we went to our room and never passed a single soul. No sounds, no moans, no nothing and it's like we were the only people in a city of millions.

"And went into our room, but no sleaze here, either. It looked like a nice hotel room with an extra big bathroom and bathrobes on the bed and everything.

"So we decided we should get our money's worth and we took a bath and washed each other and me feeling not exactly erotic or sleazy and you not either and we decided we might watch a porn so we phoned the porn man with our selection from the binder of choices and he switched it on from somewhere and the porn came on, but everyone's privates were blurred out so I kept doing this thing of trying to see around the circle of blur but of course I couldn't. So we decided we should hurry and have sex because you pay for the room by the minute and not days so us lying on a bed for the first time since arriving in Japan and touching and kissing stroke and stroke and no, nothing. And touch and lick and kiss and touch and touch and no, nothing. And you all sheepish and me cranky not because you couldn't, but because I wouldn't want to even if you could and us putting our clothes back on and phoning the porn man and telling him to send us the bill. And after a few seconds, there's this *Shhhhhhhhh*-WOP. And this cannister came sucking through this piping with our bill in it. So you paid your money and put it in the canister and back into the piping. I couldn't believe it. Do you want to keep a towel or the bathrobe or something? you asked, and I said, Naw, it's OK. So we left the room and went back to the car, never seeing a single soul, and drove back to your parents."

"Funny, how you remember things like that," he said.

"Yeah, me too."

"What brought this on anyways?"

"I don't know. Something like that, anyways."

"Do you feel better now?"

"Yes. Thank you."

Hiromi Goto was born in Chiba-ken, Japan, but immigrated to Canada with her family in 1969. She grew up in British Columbia and southern Alberta. She is on the editorial collective of absinthe *literary magazine and is currently working on a novel that will be published in the spring of 1994 in NeWest Press' Nunatak fiction series.*

The Poisoning

CATHIE TRIGUEIRO

They'd found the dog on the highway near Airdrie. He was standing in the middle of the fast lane, frozen in fear, panting so hard they'd thought he'd been hit. Before Jess could protest, Karl pulled over and swooped the dog into the car. She watched in the side mirror as Karl bent to the dog and would never forget how his hair hung over his long forehead, or how her surprise reflected in his eyes and changed them into shiny crescent moons as he laughed, straining to open the car door with one hand and to hold the dog with the other. His shoulders looked so broad, picking up a big dog like that. That was the moment she'd loved him most.

On the dog's collar was stapled a note. Jess tore it open. The dog jumped all over the back seat, licking newborn Sarah, then sat with his dog-tooth grin, looking out the window. The note said, "When you find this dog run over, know I left him on the highway because he was" and here was a hole where the staple had torn through "good."

At first she thought the note had said killed because he was good, but then saw a little piece of the n, and realized it said "no good." A shiver like a cold hand touched her nipples. Her milk let down and filled her bra, making warm wet circles on her sweater. The dog nuzzled her breast and tried to lick. She pushed him back to the back seat.

They stopped at a provincial park, Big Springs or something it was called, and while Jess nursed Sarah, Karl threw sticks into a creek. The dog bounded after them and brought them back, shaking the water out of his fur the second he was close enough to get Karl wet.

"Airhead," Karl yelled in a high voice, lifting his arms in reaction to the cold water, and since they found him near Airdrie, the name stuck.

Later she wondered in what way the dog was "no good." Was it the way he dug holes in the flower garden, the way he seemed to find her favourite plant and dig up its roots, then run with the stem in his mouth around and around the yard, grinning? Or the way he shed his fur all over the house so that everything, including Sarah's baby clothes, was covered? Or how he rushed at joggers along the Edge pathway with his teeth-baring grin, his leash dragging behind, until the joggers stood still and asked, "Does he bite?"

≈

She looked now at Airhead, lying in the sunlight of the kitchen floor, contentedly surveying her with eyes that drooped like sideways commas. He had mellowed since Sarah's babyhood and no longer chased joggers, although he still required two daily walks through Wakefield Terrace. Karl walked him every evening in the alley behind the house (after twelve or fourteen hours of working outside, Karl was too tired to go farther), and in the morning Jess and the kids walked him on the bike path along the green space of the Edge and the park around Wakefield Terrace Community Centre.

At her glance, Airhead thumped his tail against the linoleum. A wedge of shadow from the blue spruce in the backyard cut across the kitchen floor, Jess's slippers, Airhead's collar. Jess sighed, and put the kettle on. She hated having so many trees in the backyard; they let in little sunlight. As the kettle whistled, she thought of Karl's work as a roofing contractor, how he could fall. The danger was especially great in the winter, with the ice on the sharply slanted roofs of the tall, narrow houses in Wakefield Terrace. Because of the danger, he usually didn't work in the winter months, but this year, after a severe hailstorm cut a mile-wide swath through the community, damaging every roof, he couldn't afford to pass up the business. She rinsed the teapot, reminded herself that the money from the insurance companies would soon be coming in, and that in ten years of roofing, he had not fallen.

~

Jess put Sarah and Matthew in the tub for a good, long bath, while she read a novel. After several chapters the kids were goosebumped and wrinkled, so she left the book overturned on the back of the toilet and pulled some towels from the linen cupboard.

"Just five more minutes," said Sarah, teeth chattering.

"No, two, two more minutes," said Matthew, pulling a face cloth along the surface like a fish.

"Shut up, you dummy, two isn't more than five."

"Time for stories, okay," Jess stretched open a large towel, hoping it looked inviting.

Sarah didn't see the towel. "Just because you're two, doesn't mean it's more than five."

"What stories tonight?" She tipped her wrist at her watch, and set the towel on the toilet. Seven-thirty. Almost finished, she thought, draining some water from a toy teapot. Ten minutes of brushing their teeth, fifteen of stories, then if the baby cooperated and went down in his crib, she was a free woman.

The kids ignored her. She shook a water-logged sailboat. If she took out all the toys and pulled the plug, they might get out of the water without complaint. She pulled the thin chain of the plug.

Matthew stuck out his round stomach and screamed.

Jess jumped. "What, baby, what?"

She pulled him from the tub, and wrapped him in the large towel. He was so upset he lost his breath; Jess braced herself, but the cry didn't come. "It's okay," she said, "cry."

Matthew took in several gulps of air.

"Cry," she said again.

Finally he let out a cry that sounded like the long, thin whoops the gibbons at the zoo make, only three octaves higher.

"What happened, Sarah? Did you see him get hurt?"

"He's afraid he's going down the drain," said Sarah, placing one foot on the edge of the tub and jumping out. She grabbed her own towel.

Jess pulled Matthew tight against her breasts, his blonde curls soaking her t-shirt. "Oh, baby, you're too big to fit in the drain." She took a little Fisher-Price man from a boat and dropped it in the water near the drain. "See even the little man is too small to fit down the drain."

Matthew took one look at the toy man twirling down and screamed louder.

Jess felt pressure under her nipples, mounting to a burn as the nipples stood erect under her bra, until a tingle of release spread in widening concurrent ripples from the tips down the skin of her breasts. She lifted her t-shirt and unhooked the left flap of her nursing bra. Matthew stopped crying as he watched her, breathing in large stop-crying breaths. He sucked lightly, but made thick swallowing noises, a bit overwhelmed at the flow of milk, and twisted a bit of wet t-shirt between his thumb and forefinger. The stop-crying breaths became fewer and fewer. Jess kissed the curls on the top of his head, glad he still nursed even though he was over two.

Karl, in roofing overalls and baby Jamie tucked under one arm, appeared in the doorway. "What was it this time, an axe murderer or imminent nuclear holocaust?"

Jess laughed and with her free arm (the arm that wasn't holding Matthew), threw a towel at him. "There's chili on the stove."

Karl set the baby on the floor. "Already finished it off." He unwrapped the towel around Sarah and started rubbing her hair.

Sarah bent with the force of the rubbing. She pushed the towel down. "Ow, Daddy."

"Sorry." He rubbed more gently.

"Daddy, what's a hollow, a hollow cost?"

Jess raised her eyebrows at Karl, thinking, good luck.

Karl stopped towelling Sarah's hair. "That's when so many bombs are dropped the whole earth is destroyed."

"What's 'destroyed'?"

"Wrecked, ruined."

"Where do kids live then?"

"They don't." Karl's voice softened.

"Don't what?"

"Live."

Sarah squinted her eyes up at Karl. "That's not going to happen, Daddy?"

Matthew stopped nursing and squirmed from Jess's lap. "Oh come on, Karl." She turned to Sarah. "Don't worry Sarah, we don't have to worry about nuclear bombs anymore."

Karl stiffened his back and hung up towels. "Those missiles are still there. And I don't see any more stability in the world, do you?"

Jess knelt over the tub and picked up a plastic cup and pitcher and put them in a netted sack with the rest of the bathtub toys. "Things are getting better every day." She knotted the sack and hung it from the shower nozzle.

Sarah pulled her head through the ribbing of her flannel pyjamas. "Daddy, what's an axe murderer?"

"That's someone who kills people with an—" He looked up at Jess.

"Enough," said Jess, handing a length of floss to Karl. "Brush and floss, now."

She pulled the floss through Matthew's tiny molars; Karl tried to get his hands in Sarah's small mouth. He tilted his head to the side and squinted an eye. "Flossing baby teeth is a waste of time."

"Tell the dentist that," she said, without looking up. She rubbed the floss up and down between Matthew's two front teeth.

"I can't, I never take them to their check-ups."

At this she looked up. "Precisely."

He dropped his hands to his side, then threw the used floss in the bathroom garbage. "Does that dentist have children?"

"Probably not."

"Then he has no idea, not one idea, of what he's asking."

"Nobody cares how much mothers are *asked*. You take them to their check-up next time."

"And waste billable time?" Karl looked to the ceiling at the absurdity of the idea.

Jess bit her lip. If she weren't here, he would have to *waste* time. She bit harder: so taking care of children was wasting time.

Karl scrutinized her face, then rubbed his forehead as if he had a headache. She peered again into the small dark of Matthew's mouth. The dog came and lay on Jess's feet while she wiped Matthew's saliva from her hands on a towel.

After she ran the floss behind the last tiny molar, Matthew padded into the bedroom to get his diaper and jumped onto the bed with it. She took the diaper pins from her mouth and stuck them into the gauzy fabric, then held his hands while he jumped on the mattress. She caught a whiff of him, a whiff of baby shampoo and Penaten lotion and sun-bleached diapers. Karl sat on the other side of the bed and ran a comb through Sarah's hair.

"Not that way, Daddy, do it in a cool way."

Karl laughed. "What's a cool way?"

"You know. Back on this way, and front on this." Sarah pulled her damp hair back from her crown and breathed out impatiently.

Karl held the comb mid-air, genuinely puzzled. "What side?"

"Let Mommy do it."

Karl handed her the comb. Jess could tell by his silence that he was hurt. He pulled baby Jamie onto his lap.

Jess set the comb on the pillow. She stretched down Karl's collar a bit and kissed the acne-pitted skin of his neck. Her nipples released little squirts of milk.

He kissed her like he meant it. The baby squeezed between their bodies. The baby kissed Jess and then Karl. Karl's eyes smiled crescent moons at Jess and they both laughed.

"Isn't anybody going to comb my hair?" asked Sarah.

"No, nobody isn't," Karl said and threw Sarah, a little too roughly Jess thought, into the bed.

Jess climbed under the duvet with Matthew and Sarah and opened a picture book with a mouse on the cover.

Karl read Mother Goose rhymes to the baby, making sound effects like falling missiles for the cow jumping over the moon. Then Jess nursed the baby in the rocking chair while Karl carried the other two to bed. Jess could hear him say as he carried Sarah on one shoulder and Matthew on the other, "No axe murderers can get in here, because Airhead will eat them up."

She felt her nipple lengthening to the tug of the baby's mouth. His rhythmic sucks were in time to the sway of the rocking chair. They were circles closing, rings diminishing to a single point, the point of her nipple, the circle of his mouth, the centre. She rocked to the centre, until it held her too, soft circles within circles within circles.

The curtains hung soft and ethereal against the bedroom wall. Her breast had the same skin as the baby's head. His body, her body; round, soft. She thought then of what Karl had said, of axe murderers, of nuclear holocausts. She stopped rocking. A wild fear clutched at her throat, she couldn't swallow: the lack of control she had over the world, the world she was bringing children into. The baby pulled off the breast and squawked as if he could taste the bitterness of fear in her milk. She shushed and rocked him, shushed and rocked him. The circle of the baby's head matched the fullness of her breast, the skin of both the same colour, the same softness. What had evil to do with softness, she wondered. Perhaps evil was being cut off from the softness. Perhaps if mothers controlled the world, words like nuclear holocaust and axe murderer would not exist. The pauses between the baby's sucks grew longer as vague ideas formed at the back of her mind, something to do with a woman's body: the way Karl was repulsed if he saw her menstrual blood in the toilet, how he saw birthing as gross. And what Karl said about women's work being a waste of time. People cut off were miserable people. If the source was unwholesome, then all was unwholesome. A waste. The baby's sucks were so light now, they tickled. She became impatient with the tickling, so with her little finger she crooked open the suction of the baby's mouth. She lifted him to her shoulder, and patted his back, his hair and wet mouth soft in the crook of her neck.

≈

Jess curled up on the couch with her book, as Karl walked Airhead in the alleyway. The phone rang. It was Grace from the babysitting co-op, wanting her to baby-sit on Saturday night.

"Sure, we'd love to baby-sit," she said. They did love it. The whole family went, the kids playing with the other kids, and Karl and she laughing through the ruckus.

"Thank God you'll come, no one else in the co-op will sit on a Saturday night anymore, it seems. Tom and I need the break." She could hear relief in Grace's voice.

What is the problem, she always wanted to ask her friends. They found it so difficult to be content. She sat on the couch with her tea and her book, rubbing Airhead's nose and the space between his comma eyes with her foot. He curled up on top of the foot. Karl turned on the TV and sat close. She luxuriated in the warmth of Airhead on her foot, the good book, the apple-cinnamon tea. She undid the barrette on her long, blonde hair, letting it fall, and smiled at Karl, but he ignored her, afraid she might talk during his show.

Then something was different. Airhead seemed agitated, circling several times, trying to get closer to her. He lay with his abdomen against her leg, then got up and circled again, resting his neck over her foot. His neck twitched. He moved to the floor, his hot breath panting on her ankle. He seemed to sleep, but the twitching increased. She ignored it, thought maybe he was running in a dream, the way he did sometimes, rotating his paws through the air above the carpet. He twitched more against her foot, so she set the book face down on the sofa and felt the twitches with her hand. His body was pulsing erratically, his heart thumping wildly. "Something's wrong with Airhead," said Jess.

"No," said Karl, raising the volume with the remote control, "he's just dreaming."

The muscles of his head were twitching now. "No, he isn't."

The dog began clawing at Jess's ankles, his comma eyes lengthening into long squints, as if pleading, 'help me.' Red scratches bled down Jess's lower leg. The dog got up, dragging his back legs. He tried harder to walk, twitching all over, and dragged himself halfway up the stairs.

Karl sat on the couch half watching his show and half watching the dog.

"Do something," shouted Jess.

Karl jumped up and away from Jess's bleeding legs, as if he thought they might contaminate him. He looked at Jess. "Like what?"

She shot him a 'you-imbecile' with her eyes. "Like grab him before he falls down the stairs. I'll call the vet."

Karl carried the dog down the stairs, then lay him on the floor. Yet Airhead would not lie still: head and front paw twitching, he dragged himself around the room. "Lie down," Karl said, in what seemed to Jess a too severe tone of voice.

"It's all right, Airhead," she said in the most honeyed tone she could muster.

The dog lay down on her feet.

Even dying, he's eager to please, thought Jess. She called the emergency vet and described Airhead's symptoms. "Sounds like poisoning," said the vet, "bring him right in."

The dog seemed to wag his tail a bit when Karl opened the door, then half-slipped, half-walked down the porch stairs, managing to drag himself, with a push to his limp back legs from Karl, into the back seat of the car.

Jess imagined she could see Airhead's dog-toothed grin within the dark silhouette of the back seat as Karl pulled away from the curb, then slowly closed the door to the red taillights. She climbed the stairs, noticing that, for once, the grey-white nests of dog fur in the ninety-degrees of each step didn't send her rushing for the vacuum cleaner. Instead she slowly turned the combination lock on the medicine chest and daubed the red scratches with a cotton swab dipped in hydrogen peroxide. She left the lock and open bottle on the back of the toilet and paced in the hall. The movement made the peroxide tingle cold in each scratch. She stopped. "But then," she reassured herself, "with all the new medical technology, they can probably save him."

Spare no expense, she pictured Karl saying, his shoulders broad under his soft flannel shirt, as he lowered Airhead onto the vet's metal examining table. Although, really, she knew they couldn't afford any treatment for Airhead, even if the insurance companies did pay. The thought of their lack of money sent a prickle of dread over her scalp. The prickle intensified when she remembered the poison. "Where would Airhead get poison," she said, "unless someone poisoned him?" She went around the house turning on lights, all the lights. Sarah and the baby didn't wake up, even with the bedroom lights bright against their sheets, but Matthew sputtered, then cried his thin whoops. Jess was glad, because now she could nurse him. She nursed him back to sleep in her bed, when the baby cried out. She went to get him; he was still asleep, but she carried him to her bed and nursed him anyway. Then she carried Sarah in and put her beside the baby.

She watched Sarah breathing through her round quarter mouth, next to the tiny rise and fall of her brothers, and thought how Karl had carried the dog to the car when they'd rescued him on the highway. It bothered her that Karl hadn't carried Airhead to the car this time. Karl must be somehow weaker now. What had made him weaker? Perhaps she had, with all the mothering and nursing, with all the babies. The thought tumbled through her mind in a jumble of images. She tried to stand back as if looking at a painting manageable only at a distance. There Karl was in a toss of nursing babies and engorged, leaking nipples; penises squirting semen; babies blue and slimy, then pink and swaddled; the pulse of umbilical cords; the huge undulations of labour; the smaller undulations of orgasm; her on top, Karl on top; babies in their king-sized bed suckling where Karl had just sucked; the salt taste of sweat; the stick of bodies, the sticky milk. She could not extricate anything from anything. Ideas of Karl stuck to babies, to each other. She pulled the quilt over her head to block out the light she had left on, and went to sleep.

"Strychnine," said Karl when he returned hours later carrying Sarah back to her own bed.

"What?" said Jess, sitting up from a deep sleep.

"He must have got poison in the alley."

"What?"

Karl lifted Matthew. "When we were walking in the alley, I guess."

She pulled her knees to her chest. "Poison," she said with a yawn. The word cleared her mind. She waited for Karl's return from Matthew's room. A flash of shade darkened the hall as Karl switched off Matthew's light. "I never let Airhead eat anything when I walk him," she said as he came in.

Karl stared at her as he gently pulled back the covers from the baby. "So what are you saying, that I did?"

"But where would the strychnine be?"

The baby startled, flailing his arms; Karl put the covers back, turning his head to her in a slow, deliberate motion, as if reluctant to take his eyes off the baby. "In some meat?"

"You didn't let him eat any?"

"He wasn't on a leash; I didn't see him eating anything."
Karl's eyes blanked, not seeing her anymore, seeing inward.

"So when will we know if he'll be all right?"

His eyes returned to her and blinked too many times.
"He's dead, Jess. I had him put down."

The shape of the words opened in her mind slowly, like
sponge letters underwater. She tried to squeeze them shut
again, back into nothingness, gripping the bed cover in her
fists.

Seeing her, Karl blanched. "The vet said it would cost
thousands of dollars and he would probably die anyway." He
pulled the bedclothes away from the baby and quickly lifted
him to his shoulder.

"Don't take the damn baby," she yelled. "I put him in
here, because I want him here. You never think what I want."

Both the baby and Karl startled this time. Karl lowered
the baby to her, placing him lengthwise between her knees
and chest. He continued talking, not raising his voice. "The
vet said the procedures were invasive and we don't have the
money. You know that. I can't even pay the roofing crew."
His voice continued in a soothing monotone. "Airhead was
suffering. The lights in the clinic, the sound of the typewriter,
any stimulus at all sent him into convulsions."

The control in his voice infuriated her.

He stood, face hard, his mouth fidgeting at what she
might say next, and shoulders rounded-in. The shoulders
looked thin and unmuscular. Weakling, she thought. "How
could you?" she yelled louder, crying into the terrycloth nubs
of the baby's sleeper.

All night she couldn't sleep. She worried about bowls of
poison lurking for her children. About mean-spirited men

who had nothing better to do than murder innocent, happy creatures just for spite. She cried all night. At first Karl cuddled her, but toward morning he jerked his pillow off the bed and headed downstairs to the couch to sleep. Jess was glad, now she could cry as loud as she liked. The baby woke twice and watched with round eyes her noisy crying, until he crinkled his brow and cried himself. Opening the slit in her nightgown, she offered him her breast. Finally after the loss of so much liquid in milk and tears, her mouth was dry. She got up and went downstairs, through the living room with Karl on the couch; he slept with his mouth open, unguarded, a whistle breath coming from his nostrils.

She stood in front of the pantry, gulping water, noticed the flashlight on the top shelf. She pushed its red plastic switch and shone it on the coat rack by the kitchen door. Karl's parka made a shadow like a grizzly bear's hump on the back wall. She pulled the parka on over her nightgown and her own Sorel boots over her bare feet, the linings frayed and gritty under her toes, and crunched out over the snow on the deck, listening to the sound of her breath inside the hood of the parka. The snow on the ground held all the light of night; everything else, the fence, the garage, the swing set, was black and ominous, blacker than the shadows that came out from under her bed when she was a child. Yet her breath inside the hood was measured, intent; she was looking for poison; she was protecting her young. She scrutinized the sandbox with the round disk of light from the flashlight, then followed the disk to a Tonka digger truck with a long arm and jagged scoop. She thought she saw a piece of meat in the frozen dirt of the strawberry patch, but it turned out to be a plastic horse without legs. She kicked at the bottom latch of the gate, swung it open to the even sheen of the ice in the alley. There she knelt to a metallic reflection, which was, on closer inspection, a bent pie plate, when a terrific roar came around the corner. She whirled around fiercely, shining her flashlight at a single light coming toward her. The motorcycle blared past, so close it raised the hair of her neck with its wind, and stopped a few garages down, where its rider got off and opened the garage door. He turned and raised his hand toward her; she didn't know if he waved or gave her the finger. She turned off her flashlight and crossed the slippery ice to her gate, letting it slap behind her.

At breakfast Jess stirred oatmeal into boiling water, the spoon turning so slowly against the bottom of the pan that lumps formed. She tried to scoop the lumps out with the spoon, then angrily whacked the spoon against the plastic rim of the garbage, as the lumps dropped down against a used coffee filter. She was angry with the poisoner, wanted to yell at him, press charges. So, after feeding the kids and wiping spilled oatmeal off the table and from around Sarah's and Matthew's chairs (Karl had left earlier for work than usual), she wrote a notice and stuffed three sets of wriggling limbs into snowsuits, then strapped Jamie in the backpack, Sarah and Matthew in the stroller, and got two hundred copies made at the printer next to the Italian Bakery on Edmonton Trail. Next she walked up and down her street, Eighth Avenue, leaving the notes in people's mailboxes. She got yelled at twice for disregarding NO JUNK MAIL signs, and hesitated before opening a mailbox labelled WE LIKE OUR TREES IN FORESTS next to a doorway where only the storm door was closed.

"No flyers," a woman yelled out the storm door.

"It's not a flyer," said Jess.

The woman opened the glass door and stuck her head out. Her face coloured when she took in Jess and the three babies. Her hand snatched the notice from the box, and she read it aloud.

"WARNING: A family dog, our pet for four years, was poisoned during a walk with his owner. He was a *good* dog and didn't bark. We always walked with him and only in alleys where he didn't bother anyone, and we always picked up his poop in a plastic bag. He wasn't offensive to anyone, yet he was poisoned. All pet owners please be careful of your pets."

"I'm sorry," said the woman, "very sorry."

Jess started to speak, but the woman closed the storm door, then a steel-painted-white one behind it. Jess stared at the double closed doors, then pushed the stroller toward Ninth Avenue, to do another block. As she turned onto Ninth, Jess told herself she was delivering the flyers to warn other pet owners, yet she knew she really wanted to communicate with the poisoner. She wanted to make him see the error of his ways. How his bitterness, his malice had killed something that couldn't possibly have hurt him. The poison, she figured, must have been intended for dogs that were getting into the trash, or perhaps barked late at night. The thought made her tongue thick. A two-year-old might eat a piece of meat. A school-aged child might get some on his hands.

She stood on the corner and didn't know which way to go next. She saw Ellen and her girls driving past in their Ford mini-van, and realized Ellen was going to exercise class, which they both usually attended at the Wakefield pool and gym. She looked at her watch, 9:45; it was too late to get changed and make it on time. Anyway, she had all these notices to deliver.

The stroller wasn't turning properly with two kids inside, and it was hard to push balancing the pile of the notices on top of the canvas hood. The baby's weight in the backpack pulled on her neck. She was tired and the whole idea seemed futile: did she expect the poisoner to change his ways over a stupid notice? Words affected Jess strongly, like when the words on the note attached to Airhead's collar had made her milk let down, but the poisoner must not be able to read right, not words or the world or anything, or he wouldn't perceive dogs as a threat, something to be killed. She stared at the bushes along the sidewalk covered with frost, but didn't see them, pictured a man reach into his mailbox, pull out the notice, then reread it again sitting at his kitchen table, having a cigarette and a cup of coffee, his lip curling up at the corner, satisfied.

A motorcycle buzzed from the alley and startled her, it was the motorcycle guy from last night. He smirked as if he enjoyed scaring her, vrooming by in a faded brown leather jacket that looked too cold for winter. An involuntary shudder fluttered her spine. His wavy brown hair flew behind his helmet, and she shook away the shudder, and wondered what kind of fool rode a motorcycle in winter.

She crossed Edmonton Trail in a lull between cars, toward the large garbage bin, and struggled to get the stroller up over the curb, cars passing too closely behind her. Somebody honked. She glared at a truck, and the truck honked again, making her drop her notices. She bent for them without thinking, and the stroller fell backward. She bent lower to lift the stroller, as Sarah and Matthew sprawled over each other, and the baby tumbled out of the backpack onto the cement of the gutter.

In a burst of adrenalin, nipples spurting, she scooped up the baby and lifted the stroller over the curb at once. Little drops of blood raised up from the skin on the baby's nose, but other than that he seemed okay. She sat him on the sidewalk and gathered the notices. He did not cry, but looked around, mitted hand touching the pavement, completely absorbed in its texture. She adjusted Sarah and Matthew in the stroller. Then, in a white, fluttery arc, she threw the notices into the bin and pushed the stroller home. She called Grace to cancel babysitting, said she was getting sick.

Happy to be out of their snowsuits and in the warm house, the kids drew quietly on their chalkboard. Jess made a pot of herb tea and sat down to read her novel, but it no longer seemed relevant, as if it were a fairy tale, too romantic. She was surprised, because it had seemed so good just a day or two ago. At least, for once, she thought, there was sunlight. It poured through the big kitchen window, warming her slippered feet. Yet as she pulled the string to open the venetians completely, the sun went behind the blue spruce and shaded the kitchen. The shade made it hard to read and darkened the kids' chalkboard, so they started pestering her for cookies. "Damn," she said, wanting to move to a house with fewer trees.

~

Friday she woke with large welts beside her eye and thought it was hives and went to the doctor. But it turned out to be shingles. Saturday the shingles went right into her eye itself with raised red skin and little pus-filled pustules. It short-circuited her nervous system. Pain shot up her cheek, her sinuses; her cheekbone throbbed as if someone had slugged her. When she closed her eyes, white shooting stars crossed the black of her closed lids. She made Karl stay home from work and watch the kids, while she stayed locked within her bedroom.

She went back to her doctor, sat on the rattling white paper, as the doctor, her brown hair smelling like peaches, looked into Jess's eye with her tiny spotlight. The doctor stood back and chewed her lip, and looked straight at Jess. There was a silence between them, as the doctor tried to form the words, stopping to chew her lip again. Jess waited and bit her own lip. Finally the doctor dropped her eyes, twisting the spotlight in her hand. "I want you to," she said, surveying the contours of the instrument, "to wean your kids, and take this new anti-viral agent, Acyclovere."

Jess fidgeted with the large barrette in her hair. She pulled it out and let the hair fall down over her shoulder. "I can take the pain."

The doctor watched the hair fall, stroked her own short brown hair. "Can you take going blind? Because that might happen if we don't actively treat this disease. And this treatment is incompatible with breastfeeding."

Jess eyes watered and her breasts tingled in a rush of protest. "I'll take my chances. I'm not weaning."

"Well, take the prescription with you. When it gets worse you might change your mind."

She replaced the barrette in her hair, running the metal part along her scalp until it was in the right position behind her ear, and tried not to cry, tried not to let her milk let down.

"What will happen if I breastfeed on the medication?" The edge in her voice broke, as everything, tears and milk let down.

"It's like poisoning your kids, feeding them a little bit of poison." The doctor's voice was gentle.

"Then won't it poison me?"

"Adults can handle it, we're not sure what it does to kids." The doctor looked at the wet rings of Jess's breasts and shook her head. "I support breastfeeding, Jess, you know that, but not when the mother's health is in jeopardy."

Jess drove to the drugstore and bought a patch to cover up her eye, but kept the prescription in the leather pouch she wore around her waist. At home, she locked herself in her bedroom again, except when Karl brought the baby to nurse.

Karl stayed home from work and cooked lasagna and chicken and dumplings over and over. He pleaded with her to take the medication, even tried to give the baby a bottle of formula. He yelled through the door that the last two roofers on his crew had threatened to go work for another contractor, who was paying regularly and not taking time off. He yelled again that he had paid the crew out of his and Jess's own chequing account, making the overdraft reach $2,500, their limit, but the guys had climbed down the ladders and gone to work for the other company anyway. He said, "It's roofer's paydirt out there right now, Jess, and you're making me miss it."

There were other groups of roofers working right on Eighth Avenue, their boomboxes blaring from rooftops and pickup trucks as they tossed damaged shingles to the ground. The music throbbed with the pain in Jess's face. It throbbed two different tunes at once. One was an old Beatles tune,

"There are places I remember," and the other hard rock, "I'm going to get you, get you down." The second gripped her face like a vise, the lyrics addressing her personally. "I'm going to get you, put you down." "A message from the neighbourhood poisoner," she said, trying to laugh, her jaw pulsing. Karl paced in the hall with the baby, who was spitting up formula. Her eye made fireworks under her patch that seemed in time to both songs at once. She started to tell Karl to ask the roofers to turn it down, but thought better of it, put cotton balls in her ears, still feeling Karl's paces in the hall.

Finally one morning, Karl went back to work without telling her. After listening to fifteen minutes of screaming from the children, she found them alone in the kitchen, hungry.

The cereal cupboard was empty, so she fed them 7-Up and some granola bars from last summer's camping trip. Sarah and Matthew watched her with large eyes, slowly chewing their granola bars. "Thank you, Mommy," said Sarah, "this is delicious."

A wave of guilt cramped her lower abdomen like someone wringing a towel. The kitchen darkened. Jess thought she must be going blind, but after a long, long second realized the blue spruce was again shading the kitchen windows. Slipping into her Sorels, she decided once and for all to do something about the shade. In the garage, she lugged a rusty axe from behind the rakes and shovels, and carted it through the snow. She chopped at the blue spruce. Even with the shingles and all the bedrest, her arms felt strong as she swung the axe into the thud, thud parting of the wood. After several swings the blade cut through the bark; several more and it was two inches into the sharp-scented wood. Snow fell and clung to the shoulders of her nightgown and the sting of the shingles along her cheekbone. She rested, turning her face to the snow wafting down, and let it fill the itching, crusted creases of her eyelid. She opened her infected eye and didn't blink as the huge crystals landed on her iris. Then back to the chopping. Twenty, thirty more swipes of axe and she was a little past halfway through the trunk. She pushed the tree toward the house, it didn't budge. She pushed it again, thought no, not toward the house, but heard a loud swish of needles as the tree crashed against the steeply slanted roof.

When Karl got home, he accused her of murdering a tree just like the poisoner had murdered the dog. "And just so you could keep me home again, huh, Jess?" he added. Everyday, then, instead of going to work, he worked on their own roof, even though he had just repaired it after the hailstorm in September. But he could work only from one to four P.M., during nap time, because the rest of the time he had to watch the kids. The shingles spread down Jess's neck and shoulders.

Jess clung to the top of the ladder, waiting to hand Karl some number three nails and a different hammer. She lifted the patch from her shingled eye. From up here, she could see everything, the mountains, the buildings downtown, the houses along the alley, she could even see the guy who had almost hit her with his motorcycle. He was pounding his fist against his garage wall. And all of a sudden Jess realized that he was the one who had poisoned her dog. Once Airhead had run into his garage when he was working on an engine and barked at him. The guy threw a wrench at Airhead and swore at her. "Christ," he had said.

Jess set the bag of nails and hammer on a spot of the roof where Karl had already removed the shingles. Carefully she descended the ladder, rung by rung. At the bottom she replaced the patch over her eye, then clunked down the frozen alley in her untied Sorels and into the garage of the motorcycle guy.

He had his back to her, his long hair looking wavy and clean under the hanging fluorescent tube of the garage, as his head lay nestled on a pile of rags on the workbench. He lifted his head and turned when she came clunking in. "Christ," he said. He looked at the scabby pus below her patch with undisguised disgust. "Christ," he said again. "What happened to you?"

She ignored him. "Did you poison my dog?"

"Your dog?" he said. "You have a dog?"

"He's dead. You did it. You were the only one who didn't like him, and you knew we always walked in the alleyway."

"Christ," he said and tore the rags off the workbench.

She thought he was looking for the wrench to throw at her. She backed up.

"You did do it, didn't you?" She backed up more, shielding her face with her hands.

"Stop that," he said, as he grabbed her wrist and pulled her toward the workbench. "I'm not going to hit you," he started to say, as she flung her arm back and socked him in the eye.

He twisted his fist against his eye like a crying little boy. The fluorescent lighting silhouetted him, the workbench, the fender of the motorcycle, with a bluish cast; the world seemed tinged differently now that she had run into a stranger's garage and smacked him in the eye. It had become a realm of tingling knuckles in the weird light, where she didn't know what to say, a realm that nothing in her life had prepared her for. She stood on tiptoe, watching to see what he would do next, rubbing the backside of her fingers. He pulled back another rag from the workbench, the remnants of a blanket. There was a dead dog. A Doberman.

"Poisoned," he said, his eye still watering.

"I'm sorry," said Jess, the strangeness of the situation and of the blue light filling her with so much awe, she didn't feel sorry or anything else.

"So some dog hater is trying to kill off the dogs of the neighbourhood," he said and stroked the Doberman's ear.

"And is succeeding," she said, starting to laugh. Then she laughed so hard she couldn't stop.

The motorcycle guy, too, bent with laughter. They patted each other's back to stop the laughing, but each bent in turn and laughed harder, until she nearly choked from swallowing the wrong way. Then he pulled out a white-labelled pint of rum from behind some open cans of motor oil, and offered her a swig.

"Damn," he said, taking a couple of swigs himself, "that felt good." They passed the bottle back and forth. Then he opened the large garage door from the inside, and pulled out two stools. Sitting on the stools, they looked out at the sunlight in the alleyway and drank rum. Water dripped everywhere from the melting snow, reflecting light and movement.

"Chinook," they both said at the same time, nodding to confirm each other.

He held his hand in the air close to her face. "Christ," he said.

She swallowed another sweet burn of rum. "Shingles," she said. She passed the bottle to him. "The doctor said I have to wean my babies to take this drug. So I won't go blind."

"So wean them."

"I can't." She wanted him to know how important breastfeeding was. "I don't know how to take care of them without nursing."

Hearing emotion in her voice, he looked at her closely. "Then stop for a while, while you're taking the drug."

She looked out at the water dripping from the garage eaves troughs. "My milk would dry up."

"Couldn't you rent a breast pump and pump out the milk, while you're on the drug? I read about it somewhere, *Maclean's*, I think; you can rent electric breast pumps. At least back East, you can. Maybe you could here, too."

She slipped off the stool and grabbed the sleeve of his shirt. Tears filled her eyes and set off shingle fireworks under her patch. "I could, I could do that."

The motorcycle guy looked down at her hugging his arm and stood up. He stroked her hair then kissed her, pushing her back against the workbench. As his tongue touched the tip of her front teeth, she felt the Doberman's paws on her back.

She might have had sex with him right there, except he was worried that the shingles were catching. She went home and told Karl she was feeling better.

Karl whistled as he climbed the ladder. She held it until she realized she was going to vomit. She threw up the rum all over the melting snow on the deck. And she thought how she had kissed the motorcycle guy and how the Doberman's paw had touched her back. And for the second time in weeks, she laughed.

From the top of the ladder, Karl looked at her warily. "Maybe you'd better go lie down. And no one's watching the kids."

"Well, which do I do? Lie down or watch the kids?"

"Can't you do both?"

"Could you do both?"

"No, but you know me."

She squinted away from him. The chinook arch capped the city with a grey rainbow.

He looked down from the ladder. "Jess?"

The motorcycle guy appeared at the back gate. When he saw Karl on the ladder, he came and held it. "I was just telling your old lady," he pointed to Jess, "goddamn those shingles are ugly, that my dog was poisoned too, and it's about time we did something."

Karl looked surprised and came down the ladder. "Like what?"

Jess went inside the house. Matthew and Sarah were sitting on the floor next to the baby's infant seat, painting him with food colours. Multicolour splotches were all over his sleeper, big splashes of colour all over the surrounding floor, and little footprints back and forth to the cupboard.

"Christ," she said, wondering if she'd ever said "Christ" before in her life, "what are you doing?" She snatched up the baby, getting her sweatshirt stained. Then set him on the floor, peeled the clothes off Matthew and Sarah, and put all three of them in the bath. Her shingles throbbed again, burning and itching at the same time. It was funny, she thought, how pain bothered you more sitting down than if you were active. The baby toppled over in the bath and got a mouth full of water. She wrapped him in a towel and nursed him, smiling to herself, she *would* get an electric breast pump, and keep up the milk supply until the shingles went away.

She looked down out of the bathroom window into the

yard. Karl and the motorcycle guy were talking while Karl hosed the vomit off the deck.

She diapered and dressed the baby, dried and dressed Matthew and Sarah, put them all down for their naps. Then slowly and methodically cleaned up the food colouring. She could tell from all the thumping above that Karl and the guy were up on the roof together.

She changed into a t-shirt and jeans from the dirty clothes hamper and shouted up to Karl that she was going to the drugstore, then walked to Edmonton Trail to get the breast pump and prescriptions. When she got home she placed the cold plastic cup coiled to the machine against her nipple. The suction pulled the nipple into the tube, then deeper into the tube, until the nipple spurted. When the spurts stopped on that breast, she switched to the other. She pumped out nearly a cup and a half of milk, watching out the windows through the kitchen venetians. Karl and the motorcycle guy came up the stairs, then stood on the deck drinking rum. She wondered if Karl would get drunk.

She took the Acyclovere and a double dose of pain killer, undressed, and fell asleep on the bed. She heard a rolling across the roof and a scream.

Half-dazed she ran outside in her robe. Karl lay on a patch of melting snow groaning, the motorcycle guy standing over him. He clutched at his leg.

"His leg?" said Jess.

"Ankle, I think," said the biker, clearing his throat. "I slipped off the roof and landed on his ankle."

"What were you doing on the roof in the first place?" She tossed her hair away from him, angry.

"He wants me to work for him."

"And you fell two floors? Are you all right?"

Karl sat up. "That's right, ask him how he is. Never mind me. I'm last on the list around here, even after the neighbourhood biker." He turned to the guy. "No offence, man."

The guy gave Karl a 'bro' handshake.

Jess had never heard Karl use the word 'man' before or do a bro handshake; she giggled.

"Michael, my name is Michael," said the guy, shaking the handshake again, "but my friends call me Molson."

"Nice to meet you, Molson," Karl said, shaking his hand with more warmth.

"Are you all right, Karl?" said Jess, feeling left out.

"You know I'm not," he said, shading his eyes against her. Then taking his hand away from his eyes he turned to Molson. "You know," he said, "a kiss is just a kiss."

Jess giggled again, then stopped, afraid of what Molson might have told Karl, but Karl and Molson ignored her, both interested in what Karl was trying to say.

"I mean you kissing her, that's understandable."

"It is?" said Jess.

"I mean both of you losing your dogs and drinking rum, a kiss doesn't bother me that much, but what gets me is how she puts every kid in the house in our bed, so there's no room for me."

Molson helped Karl stand up. Jess stretched down Karl's collar and stood on tiptoe, kissing his scarred skin. Karl, standing on one foot, almost fell over, but pushed her away.

Molson reached out his hand to steady Karl. "It's good for kids to sleep with their folks. I read about it in *Harper's* or was that *Atlantic!*" He scratched his chin. "You know, in

China, there isn't any SIDS. That's because babies sleep with their folks."

Jess smiled at Molson. He moved away from her to the deck steps and sat down. "Christ," he said, "those shingles, there's little bumps of pus in your eye."

She sat down next to him, pulling the belt on her robe tighter, wishing she'd put on her patch. "They're only temporary."

He shrugged.

To Jess the shrug meant, 'I didn't know you were married.'

She said aloud, "But you saw me with the kids."

"What?" he said, tilting his head as if puzzled, then showing he caught the gist of her words with a glint in his eye. "I may have seen you, but I never saw you."

"Women with kids are invisible, I guess."

"I guess," he said, shrugging again.

"But you told me about the breast pump."

"When someone comes yelling into your garage, you don't piece things together too well. I never thought you were married."

Karl watched them, grimacing as he touched the tip of his boot to the snow for balance. "I'll tell you what," he said, as Molson stood up and pushed a wooden lawn chair over to him, after clearing it of snow. "I'll tell you what kids sleeping with their mother is." Karl lowered himself so wobblingly into the lawn chair, Jess thought it might fall over. "It's Freudian, that's what it is." Karl lowered himself more as Molson held the chair. He clutched at his boot, scrunching up his face in pain. "Christ," said Karl.

Jess got up and touched Karl on the knee. Molson crouched before him. "You mean it's incestuous," said Molson, loosening Karl's laces. "Better leave the boot on for now."

"You and I think alike," said Karl, in a too loud voice that was edged with pain, "it's incestuous."

"I don't think that, you do."

"Do, what?"

"Think that it's incestuous," said Jess, feeling her mouth twist with impatience, "you never told me before."

"I never knew before."

"You're jealous of the kids."

"No," he said, grimacing again. "Yes."

"But they're your kids too."

"Are they?"

"You better sober up before you go to the doctor," Jess said, worried Molson would think her promiscuous. She thought she'd better make some coffee.

"Maybe biologically," he said looking at Molson, "Maybe they're mine."

She backed up, turned to the house, a flush creeping up her upper chest.

"Okay, I'll grant you that much, biologically they're probably mine." As she got nearer the house, his voice got louder, "but in what other way are they mine, I ask you, Jess?"

She went into the house and made coffee. Maybe things between her and Karl weren't as good as she thought, maybe even before Airhead died they weren't that good. Maybe the poisoner wasn't the only one reading things wrong.

"Cream and sugar?" she yelled out the door, realizing they were out of cream. The cup and a half of breast milk was sitting on the counter.

"Just cream, thanks."

She poured the breast milk in all three of their coffees.

~

Cathie Dunklee-Trigueiro is an immigrant from the States. She has a B.A. in English and has worked, among other things, as a school teacher, a cocktail waitress, and as a phone counsellor for Post-Partum Support Service. A single mother of three small boys, she wants her writing to become a voice for what she considers the most voiceless minority: mothers of young children. She has been fiction editor of Vox magazine, taught intermediate creative writing at the Alexandra Centre, and led numerous writing workshops for schools. This is the fifth story she has published.

Soap Bubbles

MATHEW ZACHARIAH

Precisely 5:33, according to the Seiko watch he had forgotten to take off when he went to bed. He hadn't slept well. And the morning did not offer any promise of a new beginning to Thomas. And those two boys he saw yesterday, they haunted him. He could blame the heat of May in New Delhi for his unhappiness. Heat that makes you see people and things as though through a slightly unfocused lens; heat that wilts your spirit. Fifteen years in Canada had changed the way his body responded to the furnace that northern India becomes in the summer. Much more than his body had changed. After yesterday, he was very sure of that. Thoughts pounded his brain like heavy monsoon rain pellets against a window pane. He wished it would rain and knew it wouldn't for several more weeks.

Was his experience really like Padman's? When they were together in college a long time ago, Thomas and Padman had little trouble keeping in touch with each other's deepest feelings. Yesterday was different. They seemed to talk past each other. The most important matters, Thomas didn't discuss at all. The bitter aftertaste was still with him.

He had gone to Calgary for higher studies in English

literature and become an immigrant; was doing quite well in his business of importing Indian fabrics for Canadian wholesalers. Padman, after passing his law degree examination with distinction, had landed a job with the Government of India's Ministry of Trade and Commerce. Over the years, they had lost touch. That is, until yesterday, when he met in an Old Delhi bazaar another friend from his college days. Amidst the din of trucks, cars, three-wheeled motor scooters and multicoloured crowds of people moving into and out of buildings and around vehicles, Thomas learned about Padman's current status. He had risen to the position of Assistant Deputy Minister for Commonwealth Trade. It would be very nice to renew his friendship with the Assistant Deputy Minister.

Rather than phone his old friend, he would make a surprise visit, in keeping with the pranks they had played on each other in college. In the summer months, large numbers of Indian civil servants take "casual leave" on any pretext to avoid sitting in stifling office buildings. So Thomas was able to reach Padman's office without any difficulty. He quietly opened the door and said in an exaggeratedly humble accent: "I would be most grateful for getting an unscheduled appointment to see you sir, on a very important matter."

Padman was staring vacantly at a file when he heard the door open. He was about to say he was busy when the face at the door stopped him. He looked hard at the mischievous smile of his visitor, jumped up and rushed to meet Thomas's outstretched arms. "Thomacha, where did you descend from?"

"Just arrived from Canada. How are you?"

More questions and answers. Rush of words about how

each looked. In college, they were both of slight builds. Hostel food, in a city far away from their respective home-towns, had kept them thin. Padman was the sportsman who used his six-foot height to great advantage in basketball. Thomas was the intellectual. Now, Padman looked pale, unhealthy: like a man who had lost too much weight in too short a time. He still had a full head of hair but it was streaked with grey. His once bright eyes were dull. His rumpled clothes added to the appearance of disorder. Thomas's new white Arrow shirt, off-white pants and tan shoes shone in that dimly lit room. His grey hair had receded, which made his large square face look even larger. Regular visits to a fitness centre in the past one year had made him look younger than his years. Although shorter than Padman, he looked taller that afternoon.

They tried to tell each other about fifteen years in as many minutes. Then the inevitable questions about family came after they sat on either side of Padman's large desk covered with a thin layer of dust, probably from the most recent dust storm.

"Thoma, is it true you married a white woman?"

"Yes. . . . yes, what you had heard is true. And how about your family? I heard you got married. How many children do you have?"

Padman's face had become as sad as dusk in a wintry Indian village.

"Yes, I am married, Thomacha, but I have no children now. Shamu, my only son, died recently. That was seventy-three days ago."

"Padma, what happened?"

Padman began his account as if he had no emotion; as if

it was a tape-recorded message about his son's death. It was a barely coherent narrative, with a thousand flashbacks on flashbacks, detours, detail.

On that Friday afternoon, Shamu had participated in the school's soccer practice and, as usual, crossed the street near his school in Daryaganj. He was exceptionally skillful in negotiating the difficult obstacle course that is Old Delhi's road traffic. But that day, he did not see the truck which knocked him down and rolled over his chest. Before losing consciousness, he had whispered Padman's phone number to one of the men who had crowded around him. Padman, after asking a colleague to get his wife Mohini, rushed to the hospital. He called his son's name several times before Shamu opened his eyes. Padman repeated the last conversation between him and his son. He was no detached narrator now. He spoke slowly, in a whisper.

"Appa, take me home please, Appa."

"Yes, son, we will go home as soon as the doctor has seen you."

"No Appa, I want to go home now. So many strange people."

"The doctors will make you well, son."

"Stay with me Appa." Shamu had closed his eyes.

"I will not leave you ever again, son."

Padman's eyes were now full.

"Soon Mohini arrived. Her first words were: 'Mone, Shamu, what did they do to you?'

"Shamu opened his eyes very slowly. With great difficulty he said: 'Amme, water.' "

Mohini asked a nurse for water. The nurse replied that as the doctors wanted to operate on Shamu soon, she couldn't give him any water. "Then why aren't they here?" Mohini had asked. The nurse had replied that the overworked doctors were attending to other equally desperate cases. Shamu's eyes opened a little. He closed them again. His whole body shuddered and he died at the precise moment when a doctor entered the room.

"How old was he, Padma?"

"Ten. We celebrated his last birthday only sixteen days before he died." Padman used his handkerchief matter-of-factly to wipe his tears.

Thomas remembered that he had walked to the large window almost opaque with dust. Through it, Thomas could see the busy traffic on the road below and the open space around India Gate far away. On the sill stood a pot with a dried stem and curled up leaves, remains of a plant that had died a long time ago. His eyes searched as far west as he could. Without looking at Padman, he said: "I think I know something about the sadness you feel, Padma."

"Did someone close to you die recently?" Padman's question was still a whisper.

"No."

"Then how can you even begin to know, Thoma?"

How permanent are our conversational patterns! In their youngers days, Padman loved to contradict Thomas during their long conversations. "How can you even begin to know women (or Karl Marx or defensive tactics in basketball)?" used to be the way Padman would start a devastating argument. Then Thomas would get very irritated. Padman was blunt in his conversations, Thomas remembered, but you could depend on him in need. Thomas hadn't wanted to engage Padman in a conversational duel. He just looked at his friend, who got up slowly and came to the window. Padman began his monologue again.

"Mohini had suggested just that day that I might go to Shamu's school to watch him play soccer. Earlier in the week, he complained to her that I didn't appreciate him as a sportsman. I had asked him several times to completely give up sports."

"Why, Padma?"

"Thomacha, sportsmanship doesn't get you a good job in this country. Only very high marks do. Now, whenever I hear Mohini weep quietly, I wonder: would the accident have happened if I had taken her suggestion. . . . if only Shamu and I had come home together!"

Thomas thought of things he had done and had not done, of his own thoughtlessness and preoccupations, of how he had neglected and hurt. But he did not interrupt Padman.

"Thoma, we have kept Shamu's clothes and books in his room as he used to keep it. We don't go in there very much. But we have to, sometimes. It is so hard to look at them."

Padman stopped and looked far away for several seconds. Thomas desperately wondered how he could console his friend. In the good old days, Padman would be depressed for days if he got low marks on a test. Thomas had literally to drag him out to the movies, or sports to cheer him up. What could he possibly do now? Padman now continued, as if he were addressing an open air meeting outside that large window through which they could see trees begging for relief from the heat.

"Shamu usually bought the daily provisions. I gave him the money in the morning and he would buy them on his way back from school. A couple of years ago, he somehow lost the money in school. It happened only once. But I scolded him as if he had committed a terrible crime. I want to take back those words, Thoma, but it is too late."

Yes, thought Thomas, you would do it. Padman could not easily tolerate mistakes in himself or others. Thomas had read somewhere that a sorrow shared is a sorrow halved. If only, he thought, he could share with Padman his own sorrow. And Thomas found his half-formulated sentences terribly wanting.

"Padma, didn't they convict the driver?"

Padman looked quietly at his friend.

"You have been away too long, Thoma. You have forgotten how things work over here. The lorry owner's insurance company came to see me. They said the police had decided not to prosecute the driver. They offered me five thousand rupees if I promised not to take him to court. Five thousand rupees for my son. I told them to go away. But you, my Canadian friend, wouldn't understand that now, would you?"

The dig didn't even register with Thomas then, as it did this morning. Perhaps Padman himself didn't consciously intend a slight. But yesterday, in that big bleak office, Thomas was preoccupied with an overpowering wish to break though the wall of separation, to reach out, to touch, to reassure.

In college, Padman had appreciated Thomas's intellectual arguments. One would be timely now.

"Padma, I find the idea of reincarnation very reassuring. We will be born again, it says. Yes, we do suffer but the possibility of attaining tranquility also exists. For you, me, Mohini, Shamu."

How paradoxical, Thomas now thought, was his Hindu friend's response.

"That Brahmin trick to keep the rest of us in our place doesn't comfort me now, Thoma."

Then Padman continued, without any attempt to engage Thomas's misplaced philosophical thrust.

"Last year, Shamu had asked me to buy him a pair of Adidas sneakers. Do you know how expensive those things are over here? So I told him that Indian Bata shoes were good enough. If Shamu walks into this room now, I would somehow get him ten pairs of Adidas sneakers."

Thomas cut in. "Believe me, I know you feel and suffer, Padma. I too, have lain awake night after night feeling guilt and remorse, fighting nightmares and wanting to undo things. I, too, have wished I had the power to go back in time. But it can't be done, Padma. So I have had to seek and find a new idea of reincarnation. Not after physical death, but after other kinds of death. The memory is much more fresh than when you reappear after a physical death, I suppose. You might get another chance to try."

Padman was puzzled.

"Didn't you say no one close to you died?"

"Yes, but in some ways, that only made the pain more poignant, the confusion harder to bear."

"What do you mean, Thoma?"

"I am talking about the death of a relationship. My wife and I were divorced three years ago after ten years of marriage."

Padman's face revealed his confusions. There was compassion there also. It asked a lot of questions. Can't you go and see her? Can't you pick up the phone and talk to her? Can't you patch things up again? She is still living, isn't she?

Thomas could see in his friend's face those questions. He

had asked the same questions. He had understood, even then partly, only when he had experienced it. Now how could he explain divorce as a form of death to his friend who had never left India? To someone who takes for granted that marriage is a lifelong matter. Whose relatives and friends seldom separate, hardly ever divorce?

Then Padman said slowly, in a measured voice: "So, you've become a true Westerner, Thomacha. You marry, you divorce, you remarry. How is that like the death of my son?"

Thomas didn't know how to answer, where to begin. He didn't even bother to mention that no other person was involved in the breakup of this marriage; that he was not involved with any woman now. It occurred to him then that most people—whether in Canada or in India—try to resolve for themselves life's great puzzles with a little knowledge, a little less wisdom, a lot of ignorance and a lot more prejudice.

"It will take too long to explain, Padma. Even then, I don't know if it will make any sense. Maybe some other time."

They embraced, tentatively, with tenderness. Something was missing in that embrace. Thomas walked fast, out of the office, through the labyrinthine corridors of the building, and across the street to the taxi stand.

That was when he saw the boys. Two skinny fellows in rags sitting in the dust at the foot of a tree. They were making soap bubbles from a dented, soot-lined aluminum pan. The rainbow coloured bubbles stayed in the air for but a moment before Delhi's heat burst them. Thomas stared at the boys. The boys returned the stare, then slowly bared their teeth.

Even this morning, Thomas couldn't decide whether they had smiled or jeered.

~

Mathew Zachariah was born in the state of Kerala in India but has made Calgary his home since 1967. Writing short stories and poetry is his avocation since his vocation as a professor at The University of Calgary keeps him busy. His short stories, poems, and essays have appeared in publications in Canada, the United States, and India. "Soap Bubbles" initially appeared in The Toronto South Asian Review, vol. VII, no. 1 (1988).

Splitting Hares

MARILYN BACHMANN

The summer of 1965 was the year we got our new neighbours.

A procession of relatives predicted we were going to feel crowded having people where there never used to be any. You're going to miss your privacy, they warned my mother. The kids won't be able to run wild anymore.

Lord, don't I know it, my mother would reply, wringing her hands. Things will never be the same. They're not even Irish, she'd add. They're Dutch.

This revelation was invariably greeted by a stunned silence. Dutch, they would repeat, . . . that's different. What are they like then, any idea?

My mother, who had made discreet inquiries as she called it, would take a deep breath, speak in a rush. Their name is Epping, she'd explain, they came over on an ocean liner in '63. They've been renting in Prescott ever since, one of those run-down apartments on Water Street.

The father's a carpenter, my mother would continue, after she had inhaled. There are two children, a boy and a girl. The boy looks just like his father and they've let the girl's hair grow so long that it reaches her knees—can you imagine? What a chore it must be to brush that out every morning, but with only two children—yes, they claim they're Catholic—I guess the Mrs. has extra time on her hands.

I was ten years old and every time my mother mentioned the girl's hair, it stirred a fierce jealousy in me. My own hair was as short as my brothers' and no amount of begging or pleading would bring the necessary permission to grow it out. Long hair is just a nuisance, my mother insisted, it tangles, and worse, it clogs up the drains. Uncle Gerry's a plumber, I would point out, but my mother said it didn't matter, she'd still have to pay him.

For weeks, Mr. Epping worked on his house alone, pouring the concrete of the basement walls, building the framing. A small creek ran between our two properties, and I would stand on my side of the stream and watch him, though I took a pickle jar along to make it look like I was hunting tadpoles. Unlike my father, Mr. Epping toiled with his shirt off, and you could see the shine of sweat on his back. No sense of propriety, my sister sniffed, but I thought taking your shirt off if you got too hot was a practical thing to do. I also liked the fact that he drank beer with the sandwiches he brought for lunch. It was like he had never heard of Coke.

They're not going to have a garden, my father said one night between bites of his dinner. We all stopped eating, looked at him in shock, it was so rare that he said anything. It's too late in the season, he continued, they've missed the planting.

We all looked at each other, wondering how to respond. Finally my brother nodded, said that was right, they had missed the planting, and my father went back to his soup.

Actually, it was something I hadn't considered. We always had a splendid garden. When my father wasn't reading the newspaper, he was out hoeing, weeding and tilling the soil. Every year he produced enough to fill our basement, Uncle Tom's cellar, and a parish member's besides. I couldn't imagine what summer would be like without fresh strawberries or carrots pulled up from the ground. Thinking about how deprived the Eppings would be, I began to feel a little more forgiving about the hair.

They moved in for good at the end of June. I watched from the bank of the creek. All their possessions fit into the back of a pick-up so the unloading didn't take long. That got me so curious, I just walked over. Where are your tables, I asked, your chesterfields? What are you going to sit on? Mr. Epping laughed. I'm going to make them all new, he declared, one piece at a time. That made sense, I realized, he had built the entire house, so I took the opportunity to introduce myself. I'm Patty Byrne, I said.

Mrs. Epping was a smiling woman whose hair curled naturally so she didn't have a tight, frizzy hairdo like all the rest of the Toni mothers. She had been shot in the Big War, I found out later, and she had a long, dimpled scar that ran down the length of her thigh, but she wasn't ashamed of it and she still wore shorts. I liked her immediately, and she welcomed me with a big smile. I'm so happy Maryanna will have someone to play with, she told me, now she won't miss her old friends so much.

Maryanna was very shy—a trait I wasn't too familiar with. She never volunteered any conversation, she only answered questions until I was just about out of them. She had black patent leather shoes that stayed shiny just by wiping them, and she took tap dancing lessons from an older woman in Prescott, who, unbelievably, had fat legs that jiggled when she taught. Maryanna wore checkered pants and she tied ribbons on the ends of her braids, a different coloured one every day. She laughed when I asked her if she wore wooden shoes. Too bad, I said, disappointed, your father could have made them.

Mrs. Epping was always asking me about the way things worked—did the well ever run dry, did the septic tank ever overflow, where was the closest public beach where you didn't have to pay? Did the St. Lawrence freeze in the winter time or did those huge ships go up and down all year long?

I answered as best I could until one day I asked her why they had moved to Canada if they didn't know anything about it. Well, she replied, a faraway look in her eyes, there is no land in Holland.

So where do people live then, I asked, in boats? No, on the canals, she said. No wonder you came here, I replied. You must have been wet all the time.

Mrs. Epping laughed, fussed my hair. Here it is better, she agreed. Here there is room to breathe. We can have some animals, a dog perhaps, we can give the children a good start in life. A dog, I asked, you're getting a dog? What kind of dog? I couldn't believe it, Maryanna could have long hair and a dog too. My father hated dogs, he said they dug up his plants. When are you getting it, I asked? Soon, she said, next week.

In the meantime, Mr. Epping built a large circular pen of woven wire. He put a plywood roof on top and used some left-over cement to make a floor. It was the best dog house I could imagine and I admired him all the more. Then he built some smaller cages on stilts and two small wooden bird houses that were exact replicas of the house, chimneys and all. He let Maryanna and I paint them both, though later I noticed he went back and redid the trim.

The animals all arrived together, a German shepherd, two rabbits, a cat and a green budgie bird. They came in the same blue truck that had delivered the furniture. I was disappointed in the dog. I would have liked a puppy with fewer teeth, but Mr. Epping said shepherds made good guard dogs.

Bit ahead of himself worrying, my mother said. They've got nothing to take.

That's what I thought too. The Epping's TV was small and secondhand with a picture that the boy, Eric, described as grey and white instead of black and white. They had an old RCA portable radio that sat on the cabinet in the living room when everybody else in the world owned a hi-fi and turntable. The dog's for protection, Maryanna explained. We needed a guard dog in Rotterdam and my mother wants to have one here too. Rotterdam, I repeated, persuaded by the ugliness of the name, no wonder you needed a dog.

The summer days flew by. It didn't take long for us to establish a routine. I would eat breakfast at eight, usually cold cereal like Corn Flakes or Cheerios with a half teaspoon of sugar on the top. Then I'd put on my runners and head next door.

The dog's name was Piet—pronounced Pete—and he eventually stopped barking whenever I walked up the drive. Instead, he'd wag his tail and do this excited trot and escort me to the back door. Just make sure you stay in your own yard, I'd tell him, or my father will shoot you with the pellet gun. Just because he can't hit the blackbirds doesn't mean he can't hit you.

Maryanna would be waiting for me in pressed pants, her shoes wiped clean from the day before. Eric would be there too, debating if he was going to spend the day playing with two girls again. But he always did. My brothers never invited him anywhere; he was too young, they said.

Before we could leave the house, we had to look after the animals. The indoor pets, the cat and the bird, were Maryanna's responsibility. The cat was easy—just make sure she had fresh water and a bowl of dry food. The bird took more time. Every day the paper in the bottom of the cage had to be changed and the plastic liner wiped clean.

While she was doing this, Eric would go outside and scrape the rabbits' cage, a rather messy job because there were now eight of them. However, the round droppings rolled conveniently along the floor of the hutch and out the side chute and I used to think how much faster it would be to clean my grandfather's barn if cows and pigs could poop in circles too.

When the hutch was clean, Eric would lay down a new bed of hay, feed them fresh grass or clover and maybe some leftovers from dinner the night before. After I realized what they ate, I would sneak over a few carrots, and once a whole turnip. The fewer turnips I had to eat, the better.

I got the best job. I fed the dog. Mrs. Epping joked about it, and said the dog wasn't going to know who owned him, but I don't think he was ever confused: I saw how much more he got at night.

After the chores, we were free to go. That summer I showed Maryanna and Eric all the spots worth knowing about. We walked through the cornfields to Jason's pond where you could go skating in the winter and we rode our bikes back to the swamp that my brothers called the Moore's moor. I showed them the tree house in Bell's wood that the Champagne boys had built before they grew up and became cops. It wasn't safe anymore but it still looked impressive, ten feet off the ground.

And when the days got really hot, Mrs. Epping would drive us all to the Johnstown beach to spend the day, a thermal jug of grape Freshie packed in the back seat.

I spent so much time with the neighbours that my mother began to feel guilty. Here, she would say, bring them a basket of cucumbers, a quart of strawberries. Tell them there'll be tomatoes in a couple of weeks. I took the baskets gladly, for Mrs. Epping was always generous in her thanks and would give me pieces of salted licorice in return for the gifts. I never told my mother about this exchange, knowing how she reacted to the word sugar. She didn't like cavities any more than she liked long hair.

The tomatoes ripened all at once. One day they were olive green and the next they were orange. By the middle of August they were all the colour of valentines.

My mother canned and my aunt canned and Uncle Tom said if he had to look at another tomato he'd pass away. So my mother looked down the road and said, I'll bet the Eppings would appreciate these. Every day, sometimes twice a day, I would carry a big wooden basket of tomatoes next door. So many, Mrs. Epping would say, her face alight. The gardens in Holland were so small, you kept all you could grow. How can we ever repay you?

And she'd give me more of the salted licorice.

You sure you wouldn't like a couple of cabbages, I asked, thinking how I hated coleslaw. We got lots of those too. Oh,

I'll make sauerkraut, she laughed. Bring them over. And I did. With a few ears of corn thrown in for good measure.

It was the happiest summer I could remember. One night, around seven, and after supper, we all sat on the verandah trying to cool off. My father was smoking a cigarette, and blowing one perfect smoke ring after another, the air was so calm. I was watching them float upward, expanding to the size of doughnuts, not paying attention to anything else, when my mother pointed down the road. Isn't that the Eppings? she asked my father, which annoyed me, seeing how I was the one over there every day and could identify them better than he.

I think it is, my father replied uncertainly.

I knew he couldn't see that far without his glasses. Yes, it's the Eppings, I said loudly.

Wonder what they want? my mother mused. Wonder if they're in trouble of some sort?

They don't look worried, my father commented, revealing they were now in his range, but they're carrying something pretty heavy.

We all stared at the shopping bag that Mr. Epping was carrying so low to the ground it almost swept the gravel.

Maybe I should put the kettle on, my mother said hesitantly, but she didn't move.

Hello, Mr. Epping called out, his accent heavy, Nice night.

My father nodded, chuckled. If you like it hot, he said.

Mr. Epping came closer, thrust the bag at my father. For you, he said, We wanted to give something back.

My father looked surprised, took the bag. What's in it? he asked.

Take a look, Mr. Epping urged, a childish grin on his face. And see.

My father parted the opening of the bag, looked into its depths. Craning over his shoulder my mother looked down with him. A look of distress crossed her face and froze there. Seeing it, all of us kids crowded around and looked in the bag too.

There were four sinewy bodies the color of worms wrapped up in plastic. Even skinned, I knew right away what they were. Mitz, I thought mournfully, Vincent.

You like rabbit? Mr. Epping asked hopefully. Rabbit stew?

My mother smiled weakly. Never had it, have we Bob?

My father looked decidedly reminiscent. I think I had it once, years ago. During the Depression. He reached for his cigarettes.

That's half our crop, Mr. Epping continued, unaware of the effect he was having. We thought it only right.

You couldn't help but be touched by the man's good intentions. Thank you, my mother said.

You can barbecue them if you want, Mrs. Epping advised happily. Canadians like to barbecue.

You've got that part right, my father acknowledged, Canadians do like to barbecue.

Mr. Epping gave an enthusiastic nod. Well, see you, he invited, drop over sometime.

Rooted, we all watched as, arm in arm, they returned home.

I didn't take them any more vegetables after that. My mother wouldn't let me.

And the next year of course, Eppings grew their own.

~

***Marilyn Bachmann** attended the State University College of New York at Buffalo, the University of Oregon (Eugene), and The University of Calgary where she earned a BA in English in 1986. Writing has always been an interest of hers, but she writes few short stories. At the present time, she is focusing her energies on learning to write novels of suspense.*

Horse

ROBERT HILLES

A horse pulled your weight as if it felt nothing behind it.
Sitting in your sled you must have wondered how you felt to
that horse but you never asked it never looked in its direction
once. That horse is dead now and you ride in my new car as
if it were a hearse. I want to ask you about riding behind a
horse about the new weight that your body takes on. Instead
you stop me with your eyes or with a shaking hand pointing
out the window at some mountain I have never noticed before
thinking as I do most of the time about the weight of things.
Even this car has a weight it pushes down the highway without
purpose or meaning merely sensitive to my foot on the accel-
erator.

    I have never owned a horse or paid much attention to
them when I passed them grazing in fields west of the city.
Always looking at the mountains instead or the city in the
rear-view mirror. I often wonder if you spoke to the horse or
brushed its mane at night while the same stars I see shone over
your shoulder. When it ate its oats did it think of you already
sleeping in your warm bed? Did it care how you were driven
mad by this world it knew so little about? Did it stand all night
by your bedroom window fitting between your breaths?

When I think of animals I think of cats not horses and how little I know about them, accept them around me like inept life forms. They are dangerous just like horses but I do not notice instead I feed them at the same time every day and let them crawl into my lap while I watch TV. But they are dangerous because they know already what I plan to do and they don't care.

As we near Banff I ask you about the smell of horses and you laugh and say nothing practising the silence you will use when dead. I want to be able to mystify your horse with my weight but that is not possible. Here in the mountains suddenly you have too much power and you don't want to get out of the car but would rather watch, be the tourist through tightly closed windows. Although it is nearly fifty years since that horse died you are lost without its scent ahead of you without its occasional glance back at you.

On the drive back you ask me to pull over and you get out of the car in the middle of the mountains and just listen in a way that horse must have shown you a long time ago. When I listen I hear my own heart beat or a distant car approaching. But that is not what you stopped to hear. For you there is an orchestra in the distance playing anguish and joy that I can see in your eyes but not hear. I see that the whole time I was thinking about the horse I was thinking about weight and how it would measure me by my weight. But to the horse I would be nothing more than a faint breath behind it something that occasionally pulls on the bit. Just something that has wonderful hands and uses them to pick flowers from the earth and holds them up gingerly as if they possess a knowledge that he can never have. The horse would have known that when I fell asleep I would be dreaming of flowers and not of him. It would not have waited by my window, it would have moved as far from the house as the fence would allow.

After a while you get back into the car shutting the door as if it is something you hate. I move the car back onto the highway looking for the right space between cars. You place your hands on the dash as if they are ugly things that you want to discard. It starts to rain as we near the city and for the first time all day I notice that there is a sky above me. I stop the car for the first red light of the city and for a moment I expect you to open the door and bound off. Instead you speak for the first time in an hour saying: "That wasn't my horse, you know. It was your uncle's but he wouldn't go near your uncle he hated the way he smelled I guess. One day your uncle shot him and left him to rot out in the field. I never went out there until next spring when there was nothing left except a few bones. Your uncle used to laugh all the time about how suddenly that horse fell without a sound just boom and down he went and your uncle was smiling when he turned back to the house humming a song his mother used to sing. The air empty even before it left his mouth. He didn't need the horse anyway he had a car by then didn't want to bother looking after him anymore I guess.

"Before your uncle died he spoke to me about that horse and how he would avoid your uncle whenever he came near as if he knew, for christ sake, what your uncle had planned for him. That horse always stayed out in the field until long after your uncle had gone to bed. Some nights I would hear it scraping its nose against my bedroom window snorting once in a while like it was trying to tell me something. Its ears turning back and forth listening for the sound of footsteps."

After I park the car and we go inside I want to go over to you, my father, and hold you. Instead I think about my smell and what it might make you feel, your mouth full of cold beer. We sit in the dark for a while drinking our beers and then you go up to bed listening all night, I'm sure, for something at your window. For a long time I just sit here waiting for the wind to die down. As I finally go upstairs to bed I feel my own weight for the first time.

∼

Robert Hilles *was born and raised in Kenora, Ontario, but has lived the past eighteen years in Calgary. Many of his poems have been published in literary magazines across Canada. His books include* Look the Lovely Animal Speaks *(1980),* The Surprise Element *(1982),* An Angel in the Works *(1983),* Outlasting the Landscape *(1989),* Finding the Lights On *(1991), and* A Breath at a Time *(1992). A new book of his poetry,* Cantos From a Small Room, *will appear later this year. A book of prose,* Raising of Voices, *is also forthcoming. He currently teaches computer programming at the DeVRY Institute of Technology.* "Horse" *first appeared in* Writ.

Jhoomri's Window

ANITA RAU BADAMI

Today Jhoomri is wearing her Meena Kumari tragedy-queen earrings. When she wears those earrings, even Amma cannot scold her for coming to work at ten o'clock instead of eight in the morning. If she does, Jhoomri will pounce fiercely on her words and spit them back like hard marbles, "Why am I late? Why am I late? My life is one big thorn that's why." On such days, Jhoomri can get away with flicking the broom across the floors without collecting any dirt. Sometimes Mother takes a chance and says, "Jhoomri there are tigers and bears growing behind the fridge, so long your broom hasn't touched that place."

Then Jhoomri throws down the broom, places her fists on her hips and says, "Look Bibi-ji, if you aren't happy with my work, tell me straight-straight. Going around the garden to pick one nimboo, I don't like that hanh!"

"Oh-ho," says my mother, "Now I am so afraid of a girl as high as my thumb that I can't even talk straight is it? Treat you like one of the family and see what happens?"

Jhoomri tosses her head, her long earrings flying gold and red.

＊

My mother always has something to do in the house. Baba
likes tea at six in the morning, as soon as he wakes up, so
Amma has to be up early too. Once when Jhoomri was
grumbling about having to be up every day of the year at six
o'clock, Amma said, "And when have I slept later than that
girl."

"True Bibi-ji, true, we are both servants are we not?"

Amma looked as if she was going to scold Jhoomri for
calling her a servant, but instead she said, "Ah Jhoomri, at
least you go out of your house every day and get paid to work."

And Jhoomri said, "Ah Bibi-ji, at least you have a posh-
pash bungala with lots of windows."

＊

Jhoomri is a strange girl. Of the sixty rupees Amma pays her
every month, she takes home only fifty.

"If I take it home, my brothers will snatch it all away to
buy bidis and daaru," she says, stuffing the notes down the
front of her blouse. She keeps her keys down her blouse too.
When I try putting ten-paise coins from Amma's change bowl
into my dress neck, they just slide down, tickling my tummy,
and clatter to the floor. Sometimes a coin gets stuck in the
elastic band of my bloomers and I let it stay there poky and
hard against my stomach, my secret. I ask Jhoomri why her
money doesn't slip down and she laughs, "Because, little
kaboothar, I have pillows in my blouse and you don't."

Amma hears this and shouts at Jhoomri for teaching me
bad things.

"Arrey Bibi-ji," says Jhoomri, scrubbing the big black pan with ash and mud, "She is also a girl na? Soon she will grow up and become like you and me. So why hide these things from her."

"No," says Amma, "She won't be like you and me. She will study hard and become a doctor."

"Okay Bibi-ji, your darling will become a doctor or an ingineer like babu-ji. But she will still be a woman one day."

~

I don't want to become anything when I grow up. I want to climb the jamoon tree like my friend Meenu, I want to stand and do soosoo like her big brother and I want to live in a house with twenty-hundred windows. I like windows and so does Jhoomri. That's why she leaves ten rupees of her money with Amma—to buy a window.

The first time she leaves money Amma says, "Why don't we go and open a bank account for you Jhoomri?"

"No, no, Bibi-ji, you keep it under your pillow or in your godrej. I don't want strange men to keep my money."

"What will you do with your savings? Buy silly earrings from Gadhbadh Jhaala?" asks Amma.

"Hah, I haven't gone to iskool, but I am not stupid Bibi-ji. I am going to buy a window with my money Bibi-ji."

I imagine Jhoomri taking money out of the pillows inside her blouse and bargaining for a window in the market. How will she carry the window home?

"Will you buy a square window or a round one, Jhoomri?" I ask, jumping up and down. No one I know has ever bought a window and I am excited.

Jhoomri taps her mouth with her fingers and nods her head so that her earrings dance in the long curls of hair she leaves loose only near her ears. "Maybe a round one with little flowers all around the edge hanh? Then every time I look out of my window, I will see a garden."

"Jhoomri, that's enough rubbish you are stuffing into the child's head. Window indeed, has anyone ever heard such foolish talk?"

"But it is true, it is true. My father is building a house Bibi-ji and I want a window of my own in it."

"Oh so now Jhoomri is going to have a palace," says Amma, looking up from the knitting she always has. We are in the verandah next to the dining room. It is cool here with its cage of morning-glory creepers. Our gardener Mungroo is clever with plants. He is the one who made our fern-house, as Amma calls it, because we keep all the potted plants in here. Only Chopra Aunty who never hears anything right tells everybody in the colony, with a sniff, that our 'fun-house' is full of caterpillars and spiders. She is jealous, says Amma, because we are the only ones in the colony with a morning-glory cage. If you sit in there, nobody can see you, total privacy, says Amma. But you can't see anything either, except our own vegetable garden.

"No Bibi-ji, it is a small house," says Jhoomri. "Two rooms, a kitchen and a ghusal-khaana. One door and two windows—one will be mine."

"What colour will your window be?" I ask.

"What do you think?" says Jhoomri.

"Make it pink," I say, "Like your dupatta with the silver dots."

"Okay my kaboothar, for you I will have a pink window," says Jhoomri, "and then. . . ."

"And then?" I ask giggling.

"And then a prince as handsome as an Ashoka tree will come and say, who lives behind this pretty pink window?" Jhoomri puffs out her chest and strokes an imaginary moustache with huge sweeping hands.

"And then?"

"And then I will look out with my Saira Bano earrings and pink dupatta with silver stars and the prince will say. . . ."

"Hai, will you be my queen," I chorus along with Jhoomri.

All her stories end like this, even the scary one about the princess who stole fire from a bhooth and ran through a dark forest holding the fire in her sari pallu. When Jhoomri is angry with me she says softly so Amma cannot hear, "Now the fire-bhooth will come out of your toy cupboard and eat you up."

Then I can't sleep at night. I don't even like switching off the light, there might be a ghost under the bed waiting to catch me by the toes. I shout for Amma or Baba to turn off the lights, but Amma shouts back, "Such a big girl, seven-seven years old. Do it yourself."

And Baba says, "Pray to God Hanuman, Sona, and you will be okay."

I've prayed and prayed but still there is a bhooth under my bed, I know it. So I build a bridge, first the little stool with a red cushion, then the black chair, then my small writing-table chair. There, now I can reach the light switch. But when it is dark, I can't see anything to find my way back to the bed. I open my eyes huge and my hands become cold. I feel like going to the bathroom, but Amma will slap me if I do it in my panties. I am a big girl now. I switch on the lights again and the ghost runs back to its hiding place under the bed. I go to sleep with the lights on. Baba always comes to check if my blanket is on.

He will turn off the lights and Amma will tell me tomorrow that I am a naughty girl wasting electricity. But that is tomorrow.

~

I tell Jhoomri about the bhooth under my bed. She marches upstairs with a broom and says, "See now I will sweep it out."

She pushes the broom into the dark corners under my bed and thumps so hard that balls of cotton dust fly out. "There, now I've killed the bhooth," she says.

"What about the one in my toy cupboard? You said there was one there."

Jhoomri flings open the cupboard and swishes her broom inside. My toys clatter out and Jhoomri dusts them hard, saying, "Chhoo-manthar-anthar-banthar, bhooth-preth chhoo-chhoo."

Her bangles go chhin-chhin and I laugh hard.

Amma comes running up the stairs, "What is all this noise?" she asks, two lines in the middle of her forehead.

"Nothing Bibi-ji, I just thought I would clean up the little one's cupboard," says Jhoomri winking at me. I cover my mouth with both hands so the giggles won't come running out.

"I see," says Amma, "And since you are in a cleaning mood, we can do the kitchen too. Dust that died ten years ago is sitting behind the shelves there."

Jhoomri makes a face as soon as Amma leaves.

"See," she says pulling my pony tail, "Your bhooth has given me extra work to do today."

I feel very bad. Poor Jhoomri, Amma always finds something for her to do. I go and tell Amma that we should give her a special present. Maybe one of our windows. We have a hundred million windows in our house.

"Amma, which window do you like best?" I ask.

"All of them," says Amma, running from here to there in the kitchen. Baba likes everything cooked a certain way. Amma has to make sure that bhindi is fried crisp, and that drumsticks are cut in one-inch pieces and tied together with a piece of string before being hung in the sambaar. I like them swimming like fish so I can grab them and suck out the crunchy seeds. Baba gets annoyed though, he thinks it is junglee to suck and chomp and make noises while eating. Amma is scared of Baba so she is always running around the house checking that everything is all right.

Now when I ask her which window she likes, she just says,"All of them."

"But which is your special, special favourite Amma?"

"I don't know you silly girl, out of the kitchen, go out," says Amma pushing me, "You'll touch something hot and then I will have that to worry about."

"But which is your favourite window," I ask from the doorway between the kitchen and the dining room. If I don't know how can I give Jhoomri the best one in the house?

"I don't like any of them," says Amma angrily, "I am the one who has to clean them every week, so much dust from so many windows."

"You don't clean them, Jhoomri does," I say.

Amma lifts her hand to slap me and I run out of the room quickly.

~

My mother is silly, first she says she likes all the windows, then she says she doesn't like any. *My* favourite is the one in the dining room. From there I can look straight into Kalpu's window. Her mother puts her in a chair every morning and she sits there all day making faces. She is a big girl but her mother has to feed her still. Amma told me she is not all right in the head and I shouldn't stare. I know Kalpu doesn't mind, she likes it when I wave and make faces back at her.

The back bedroom window is nice too. Outside is the shady place under the neem tree where Mungroo gardener sleeps in the afternoon. If I climb on a chair and lean out of the window, I can watch the way he snores, khoon-phee, khoon-phee, phrr-phrr-phrr. All the long hairs in his nose move in and out, in and out. In the afternoon Amma takes a nap, and when she is fast asleep, I pull a long piece of straw out of the broom and tickle Mungroo's nose. I have to lean far out to do this. With one hand I hold my frock down so that my panties don't show. If Amma comes in suddenly, she will get angry. One for being naughty and again for showing my panties.

"No shame," she will say, "No shame. Such a big girl, showing everything to the whole world. Rama-rama, why didn't I have a son instead of this wild monster."

Mungroo never wakes up though, only hits his nose and rubs it hard. I feel like laughing but he might get up and see me. Then he will go straight to Amma and complain, "Bibi-ji, the child doesn't even let me sleep. Whole day I am working in the sun."

That Mungroo is a chugal-kore, he tattles to Amma about everything. He told her that I was eating raw mangoes that's why my stomach was upset. Amma called me a shaitaan and told me to stay in my room all day. That is boring, I can't see anything nice from my window. Only a field. On Sundays boys play cricket there.

"Sixer!" they shout when someone hits a ball very hard. Then they run up and down in their fat pants swinging a bat and everyone else jumps and screams. Sometimes they have a match, St. Francis School against Vidhya School. The St. Francis boys wear shiny new clothes and caps and slap each other on the back when they are happy. The Vidhya School boys are more fun. They do funny dances and sing songs, "Yaaro, yaaro, ball ko maaro; sixer lagaao, team ko bachaao; yaaro, yaaro." Amma says they are goondas, the Vidhya School boys, they can't even speak English.

Lots of people in the colony come to watch these matches. Only my parents don't go because Baba thinks cricket is boring and Amma never goes anywhere without Baba. Everything in our house is decided by Baba. He decided that my name would be Sona and he never calls Amma by her name. For a long time I thought her name was Amma. But it is Malini. When I ask her why, she says I am a silly, nosy child. I ask Jhoomri and she says it is because Baba has six wives and can't remember all their names. I ask Jhoomri why my Baba has six wives, and she says it is because he is getting lots of white hair and needs six wives to pull them out. Then she quickly says, "Now don't you go and tell your mother this okay?"

∼

On cricket-match days, Jhoomri takes a different road to our house. She goes all the way around Type Six Quarters and right through the field. She dresses up like a princess in a shiny green skirt and blouse. With it she wears a red dupatta which Jhoomri says was made by a spider specially for her. She let me put it on my face so that I can see how soft it is. Jhoomri also wears ten green and ten red bangles on each hand and her special green and red earrings. She showed me a picture of film star Rekha wearing the exact same earrings.

"Why are you special-dressed today ?" I ask.

And she laughs and says, "So that all the boys will look at me and say, "Look there goes the red-dupatta waali." Then she shakes her bottom and walks up and down the room singing, "Lal dupatta waali, oh-ho-hoo," keeping a watch out for Amma at the same time.

On match days, Mungroo gardener behaves very funnily. He works only in the vegetable garden behind the kitchen where Jhoomri washes the vessels and hangs out the clothes to dry. And I have seen him, he only pretends to work like I do in Miss Massey's Moral Science class when she gives us god books to read. Mungroo sits at the cabbages, and says things to Jhoomri.

"Oh my heart is beating, beating, repeating, " he sings. I know that song, it is from the new movie which my friend said is a bad one with lots of big people things in it. Sometimes Mungroo says, "Ohey Pyaari, come with me to the sanema today." That Mungroo can't even say cinema, I've told him and told him and he says I am a little English fly, go away.

Jhoomri never answers, she sits with her back to Mungroo and washes the vessels harder and harder.

"Jhoomri," I say, "Why don't you say anything to Mungroo. Don't you like him?"

"Hai shaitaan," yells Jhoomri, frightening me, "Have I

bhoosa in my head that I should start liking a nalayak gardener?"

"Then why don't you tell him to keep quiet?"

"Because decent girls don't talk to villains like him."

"He has hair coming out of his nose Jhoomri, don't marry him."

Jhoomri giggles, "How do you know what he has in his nose?"

I tell her about my Mungroo window and she laughs till she is going to cry. "Oo ma, I think my blouse button has popped open," she says finally, wiping the laugh-water from her eyes.

"Are you going to tell Amma?" I ask, suddenly worried.

"Not if you don't tell her about your Baba's six wives," she says.

"I won't, cross my heart and hope to die," I say.

"What is all this Inglis-pinglis you are saying," says Jhoomri, "I won't tell your mother, but now I can have some fun with that Mungroo."

~

So the next time Mungroo comes close to Jhoomri and says, "Oh my golden beauty, whose thummak-thummak walk makes my heart go dhummak-dhummak."

Jhoomri spits on the ground near his feet and says, "Oh one with the hairy nose, whose smell makes me vomit."

Mungroo catches Jhoomri's arm and says, "I know the way to your house, gori, and I know your father is looking for a man to tie you to."

Jhoomri spits again, this time on Mungroo's foot. He lifts

his other hand and I scream for my mother, "Amma, Amma, Mungroo is bad, come quickly!"

Mungroo leaves Jhoomri's arm.

Amma comes running and picks me up. "What happened," she asks stroking my face, "What happened?"

"Mungroo was going to beat Jhoomri," I sob.

"She is a randi," says Mungroo making red eyes at Jhoomri.

Amma looks shocked. She drops me down hard on the ground and pushes me into the kitchen, "Run away child, go to your room and play."

She steps out into the backyard and I stay near the kitchen window. I want to see Amma scolding that bad hairy-nose.

"Okay now what is going on here?" asks Amma in a stern voice like when she sees me taking threads out of her stitching box.

"She is always teasing me, the randi," says Mungroo.

Amma holds up her hand, "Mungroo, I don't want to hear gutter language."

"Look at the way she dresses Bibi-ji," says Mungroo shaking a flat hand at Jhoomri, "Will any decent girl wear such things?"

"He thinks he is my father, telling me what to wear. Hah!" says Jhoomri throwing her head and making a face.

"If your father had any brains he wouldn't let you out of the house," says Mungroo.

"Hai-amma, now he is calling my father names, this Mungroo, half-wit son of a thieving she-ass."

"That's enough both of you," says Amma, her hands clenched together. "If I hear you Mungroo saying anything to this girl again, I'll tell Saab-ji and you won't have a job."

"It is a permanent job memsahib, saab-ji can't do anything," says Mungroo, "But you have been my mother and father, so I will listen to you."

He looks at Jhoomri, snaps his towel hard, throws it over his shoulder and walks off. He looks just like the rooster in Gopa Tailor's yard. I run out of the kitchen before Amma comes in.

≈

On Diwali Festival day, Amma gives Jhoomri a new salwar-kameez. I chose it for her, I know the colours Jhoomri likes. The salwar is red and the kameez green with red and white flowers. Amma wanted to buy a black and white one, like all her own saris. I hate Amma's saris, but she wears them because Baba says she is a married lady and should wear only quiet colours. I think that is silly. Amma looks beautiful in her red and gold sari which she wears on special days. But she listens only to Baba, he doesn't even let her plait her hair. Amma always wears a bun and no flowers in her hair. One day when she was in a good mood, she told me that as a little girl she loved wearing long strings of jasmine. I love my Baba, but I am afraid that when I grow up he will make me wear ugly clothes and no flowers.

On Diwali day, Amma also gives Jhoomri twenty rupees. "Here, you can buy earrings and bangles to match your new clothes," she says.

But Jhoomri keeps only five and gives the rest back to Amma. "Bibi-ji, keep that in your godrej-cupboard with the rest of my window money," she says. "Next month we will be putting in doors and windows and I will have just enough for my window."

Amma smiles and says, "No this is for your earrings, I will put extra twenty from my side for your window."

Jhoomri is so happy she laughs and then cries and then bends down and touches Amma's feet. As if Amma is a god or something, she is only my mother.

I want to see Jhoomri laugh again so I ask her, "Will you buy Shabana Azmi earrings Jhoomri?"

"Chee-chee," says Jhoomri, "Her earrings have no shaan, can't even see them sometimes. I am going to buy anklets for my feet."

"Enough talk now, there's lots of work to do today," says Amma. She is in a good mood. Diwali is a special day and nobody can get angry.

~

Amma wakes me up at five o'clock, before the sun has risen, and gives me an oil bath. First I make a fuss about waking up but soon I can hear all our neighbours already letting off crackers. I jump out of bed and my skin pokes out in small bubbles in the cold. After my bath, Amma gives me my new panties and petticoat to wear. I begged her for panties with lace and flowers like my friends. I hate the long bloomers she always makes me wear. I have a new frock too, but that is for the evening when all the lamps will be lit.

Today Amma opens the windows in the house, every one of them, and the doors too. She isn't worried about dust on Diwali, though afterwards Jhoomri has to clean for ten days.

"Why?" I ask Amma. I know the answer, but I like asking

anyway. It is my Diwali question. "Why do you have to leave all the doors and windows open?"

"Because, Sona," says Amma, "Today Goddess Lakshmi will be roaming around our colony going into homes to taste laddoo and burfi and jalebi. She will leave lots of happiness behind, so we can't close any doors. Who knows which one she will want to enter, no?"

"Will she go to everybody's house?"

"Yes, of course."

"Even Jhoomri's?"

"Yes, yes, so many questions from an inch-high girl."

"Even though her house has no doors or windows yet?"

"I don't know," says Amma. "Go now, go and clean out your toy cupboard. Goddess Lakshmi will run away if she sees the mess there."

"Will you wear your red sari today?"

"Yes child, yes !"

~

On Diwali day, the beggar man comes down the road earlier than usual.

"Hail, hail Goddess Durga, give, *give* to poor old Murga!" he shouts, and rattles his bowl after each word. He is a big man with long curly hair and a beard. Though he goes around the colony every Sunday, Murga stops at our house only on Diwali day. Amma gives him some money and sweets but on other days says that he is a healthy fellow and why can't he work for a living.

Murga bangs the latch on our gate and shouts again, "Jai Durga-maata, jai!"

I am playing in the front verandah and he calls to me, "O little one, go tell your mother that a hungry soul is at her gates."

I run inside quickly. He scares me. Murga looks just like the demon Raavan in my Ramayan story book. Amma tells me that story the night before Diwali. And when she comes to the part where Lakshman draws a line in front of Seetha's hut my heart starts beating fast.

"Sister Seetha," says Lakshman, "Don't step out of this line I have drawn or great evil will happen."

Then Amma turns the page and there is Raavan dressed like Murga the beggar.

"My daughter, alms for a hungry sage," he says and Seetha puts her foot out of Lakshman's line. Then Raavan turns into a demon with big teeth and drags Seetha away, laughing ha-ha-ha.

At the end of the story Amma snaps the book shut and says, "And if you don't listen to your mother, that's what will happen to you too."

"What happened to Seetha?"

"A bad person kidnapped her."

Kidnapped. Kidnapped. That is a scary word. It happens to little girls who do not listen to Amma. She told me not to eat the raisins, but I didn't listen.

"Amma, I ate all the raisins," I say. "I don't want to be kidnapped by Murga."

Amma looks at me puzzled, "What strange things you say child. Why should he kidnap you?"

"Because I didn't listen to you."

Amma just says tchuk-tchuk like a lizard and tells me not to let too much air fill my head or I will float away.

I like my mother on Diwali day, she laughs a lot and says nonsense things like Jhoomri. Maybe it is because she can wear her red sari and not worry about dust in the house. She isn't even angry with Mungroo when he asks for more baksheesh.

"Bibi-ji, what can a man do with ten rupees nowadays?" he asks when Amma hands him a new shirt and the money.

"What do you think I am? Wife of Birla millionaire?" says Amma, but she gives him another five rupees anyway.

"Do you like that shirt?" she asks.

"Yes Bibi-ji, I will keep it for my wedding day."

"What Mungroo, are you getting married?" asks Amma.

"Perhaps Bibi-ji, perhaps. I have seen the mare I want," says Mungroo laughing and I can see all his teeth orange with paan stains.

I wish Amma hadn't given him any presents for Diwali. He is a piggy man and he makes Jhoomri afraid. He wants to marry her. I know. He tells her that when Jhoomri is hanging out the clothes.

Mungroo is pulling out grass in the vegetable garden and singing a film song. I am colouring my picture-book in the morning-glory room and I can see Jhoomri shaking out the wet clothes with a snap.

"Ohey Jhoomri, do you like my song?" asks Mungroo.

"Howls like a donkey and calls it a song," says Jhoomri.

"Talk, talk all you want now," says Mungroo making small eyes in the sun, "When you are my wife all that will end."

Jhoomri drops the sheet she is about to hang out and it falls into the damp mud. Now she will have to wash it all over again.

"You dirty man," she says, "Who will marry a hairy nose like you?"

"I have a permanent job with the railways. Which father will say no to a proposal from me?" says Mungroo.

Jhoomri tosses her head, "If I tell my father what kind of a luchha you are, he won't even let your shadow cross our doorstep."

Mungroo just laughs and I can see that Jhoomri is scared.

I run to tell Amma. She will scold Mungroo and Jhoomri will smile again.

Amma is busy as usual. Baba phoned to say that he is bringing office people home for Diwali dinner. Amma does not like it when he brings people suddenly like that, but she never says anything. She only scolds me. Now when I tell her about Mungroo and Jhoomri, she catches my ear and twists it hard so water fills my eyes and nose.

"Stupid girl, poke your nose everywhere. One day it will get bitten off," she says, "I don't want to hear anymore about that gardener, and you stop listening to everything in the world, otherwise I'll tell Baba."

∼

Two weeks after Diwali, Jhoomri tells me, "Tomorrow I will take my money home, little one, tomorrow I will pay for my window."

Then she goes in and tells Amma that she will collect her money tomorrow and Amma smiles at her and says, "After you get your window, what are you going to collect money for, Jhoomri?"

And Jhoomri says, "I don't know Bibi-ji, I'll think of

something nice."

The next day Jhoomri comes in late and is wearing her Meena Kumari tragedy-queen earrings. Before Amma can say anything, she starts crying.

Amma catches her by the shoulders and shakes her hard, "Arrey, Jhoomri what is the matter with you? Today you are going to buy your window and here you look like the sky has fallen on your head."

"What will I do with a window when I am going out of the house," says Jhoomri.

"What are you talking about?"

"Bibi-ji, my marriage has been fixed up," says Jhoomri wiping her face on her kameez sleeve like I do sometimes.

"Is that something to cry about, you silly girl?" asks Amma.

"Bibi-ji, I am to be tied to that Mungroo, my father didn't even ask me if I liked him."

"But he has a good job Jhoomri, what else do you want?"

"Amma, he has a hairy nose," I say eagerly, "How can Jhoomri marry him?"

Amma acts like she did not hear me and asks Jhoomri again, "Well Jhoomri, what is wrong with Mungroo?"

A great big smile spreads across Jhoomri's face, "Bibi-ji, he has a hairy nose," she says.

Amma frowns at her, "You still behave like a child, girl, and about to get married too."

"No Bibi-ji, I am no longer a child, am I?" says Jhoomri.

Amma pats her on the shoulder and says, "Don't worry, you'll be happy, you'll learn how to be happy with Mungroo."

"Yes," says Jhoomri.

"And your window?" I ask, totally confused now. How

can Jhoomri be happy about marrying Mungroo? "Will you be getting your pink window today Jhoomri?"

"What will I do with a window now, child?" asks Jhoomri. And all of a sudden she sounds just like my mother.

~

Anita Rau Badami is a journalist educated in India. Her essays and articles have been widely published in Indian newspapers and periodicals. She has also written and published several stories for children. Since her arrival in Calgary in 1991, she has explored other kinds of fiction. "Jhoomri's Window" appeared first in The Toronto South Asian Review.

Mapping Toronto
by Darkness

MICHAEL RAWDON

Blackie tools their 1985, still jaunty, RX-7 east on the Danforth.
She whips south on Woodbine Avenue.

"She didn't ever actually puke, did she?"

No, Tyler doesn't think so. He had watched the whole
time and he is sure that she had not vomited. She had never
bent her head down, as Ross had stuck his muzzle into the
mud, and heaved.

"Putting on a display?"

How did it seem? It was evident that she was rattling the
people eating, frightening them even, but was not actually
sick. A performance too discontinuous. When people heave,
like dogs, they just keep going. In the gleam-fragmenting
Caravaggio night, Blackie turns east again along Queen and
then slows through the Beaches.

Tyler remembers the dogs vomiting at home. Every once
in a while, a dog would blast its stomach with something
rotten or poisonous. Sick, it would eat grass. Stretch its legs
forward, spread wide, and heave. He remembers his retriever,
Ross, its front legs stretched, apart, its throat and back
muscles rippling beneath the short, white hair: an old man
spewing his booze. (The noise, rasping, repetitive and deep in

the throat hacks, continuously. With each spasm of muscles, the hacking rises. Finally some white, thick vomit rushes downwards. A couple of more heaves, more deep shudders, then only some elastic strings of slaver hang along the lower jaw, bridging the teeth. On the farm the dogs would often be sick. Usually you didn't hear them, but he remembers clearly how, when he was eleven or twelve, Ross vomited in the yard. Mama, he had called, Aunt Jess, Ross is sick.)

A muggy July night, noise from the Danforth grinds behind them. They are sitting on the brick terrace at Pappas. Tyler sits with his back to the traffic, looking over the other diners. Wearing her hunter-green linen blazer from Holt's, Blackie faces him. She could see the traffic but doesn't look. She is eating lamb souvlaki with okra. There are roast potatoes, but she won't eat them. Tyler is eating a Greek salad with extra feta and black olives. He plans to spear a couple of Blackie's potatoes later. They are drinking Kourtaki retsina to ready themselves for an intense conversation. That is why Blackie has worn her special occasion blazer which, she thinks, makes her freckles look exciting. They are eating out to talk domestic relations. Blackie would like to reorganize the front room and move the bookcase into the second bedroom that Tyler uses for a study. Tyler would like to reorganize everything, including Toronto's streetcars and the Metro Council, but he likes the bookcase in the front room, just where it is. That way he can browse without leaving the stereo behind.

The first noise is harsh and continuing. Diners silence, staring. Startled, Blackie asks Tyler with her eyes to tell her what it is. At first it sounds like a two-stroke engine getting going. Low and wet, the noise natters in the distance, but ahead and to his left. It is in the street, or across at the other Greek restaurant: the deep resonance of someone vomiting. Dry heaves, Tyler thinks. But then he can hear the wet struggle for release, a steady irregular retching. He imagines the straining, convulsive passage between chyme and lips. It's a woman barfing, Blackie exclaims thinly. A dark-skinned woman in a gold jacket stands behind Blackie in the centre of the street, hawking deep in her throat. She is holding her arms apart from her body, bent towards them as if in supplication, staring. The strangling noise rises and falls, breaks off and restarts. Tyler, fascinated, wonders if he should offer to help. Blackie turns back to him.

"She's horking. Barf-a-roni."

It grossed her out, like to the max. Women were more disgusting than men when they acted like that.

Blackie finds many things repulsive. She draws her hands back quickly or slides sideways. A tomato gone soft and deliquescent, a cucumber turned liquid, its white flesh darkening to yellow, makes her squirm away. Tyler knows that he can be disgusting himself. The space between them fills with messages: slob, intellectual egotist, pig. Once Tyler might have reached out to comfort her, to touch her arm or hand. Now he just withdraws a bit, waiting for the spasm to pass, her feeling of revulsion to ebb. When they first began living together, Blackie tolerated, but despised, his favourite hobby: Tyler makes games.

Now she actively shows her disgust that a grown man can spend so much time in making games, not even games that he expects to sell. If you could buy them at the Games Emporium or at Games-A-Lot, that would be different. But Tyler only plays them alone or sometimes with friends from the Ryerson Polytechnic. He used to program computer games to play, versions of SimCity, Life, or maze games, scavenger hunts and interactive who-done-its, all in cyberspace. These days, taking a real-space path, he has been making board games. He transforms novels into games that are played with dice, using his Ventura graphics program to design the boards. The dice actualize matrices of possibilities. But Blackie hates to see fiction that she has liked, or might have liked if she had read it, turned into games. It is too cerebral. She does, truly, find it disgusting.

"Take *Lord Jim*."

When Tyler explains things his voice moves up a decibel or two, taking on a quivering whine. Blackie's spine crawls and goes stiff.

"Start with Jim in the lifeboat."

Then it would flow from there like any decision-tree. You would play Jim's forks in the road. The idea was to get him accepted back into the hierarchies of power. He could even command a ship if you played right. You could play solo, like patience, or you could play two-handed against Marlow as the representative of Victorian conformity, evading or pleasing that watchful eye. Before you started to play you would determine the characters by rolling dice for traits, out of the character-matrix, just like any role-simulation game. Tyler's Jim could be either cowardly or indecisive, depending upon the initial throw. He could be as sound as a gold sovereign or possess some infernal alloy in his metal. Marlow could be more or less morally rigid. He might even let a ship sail in the wrong sea-lane on occasion. He would be intellectually curious, more or less, but that was a trait that worked differently depending on the moral vision you gave him.

Then you would go from there. Blackie had flicked the board, all Tyler's markers and tokens crashing to the floor, wheeled out of the room, going ukk, ukk, vanishing.

The other diners are looking around. The muscular waiter, white apron, black hair, is staring across Arundel Avenue, towards the Omonia. He has plunged his hands into the pockets of his apron.

The hawking noise grows and decreases in intensity. A dark young woman in a bronze shift with an open gold lamé bolero jacket stands about fifty feet away, on Arundel by the alley. Tyler can see that she is wearing Roman sandals. She moves in a rough circle towards the tables in Pappas' terrace, and then turns away, back up Arundel. Blackie has twisted around on her chair, straining to see where the hawking is coming from. Other diners also turn and stare. The thick-set waiter with the glossy hair stands in the wide doors leading back into the restaurant, beneath the exaggerated Palladian windows, wiping his hands nervously in his apron. Across the street on the terrace at the Omonia, other diners turn, glasses and forks suspended. Conversations are interrupted. Held in collective horror, no one is eating now. The girl is very beautiful. Her mouth is open, but her lips are too dark to see. Blackie puts her fork down. Pieces of okra, still pierced on its tines, slide back into the lamb juices. Worried and tightened, her eyelids draw up into her skull. Her mouth quirks upwards on the right as her facial muscles tense.

Blackie finds many things that men do disgusting. When she sees a man blowing his nose, a forefinger pressing one nostril closed, a wad of snot snorked into a gutter with the force of a sneeze, she feels like vomiting. She tells Tyler that leaving the toilet lid up grosses her out completely. She doesn't like the way men sometimes bite their fingernails. She hates nostrils clogged with hair and boogers. She doesn't like hairy backs and bellies. Tyler is a comparatively hairless man, but it makes him nervous when Blackie finds other men repulsive merely for having hair. Once she saw an older man with hairy ears walking out Harry Rosen's on Bloor and, walking just behind him, pretended to barf on the street. Pointing. Tyler finds all these mannerisms off-putting, but he understands that sloppy behaviour can be disgusting. Perhaps, he often thinks, Blackie is right and men should trim their hairy ears and nostrils, just to make other people comfortable, not draw attention to their hairiness. Hair is primitive. Men with hairy backs remind her of apes. She could never make love to a hairy man. She thinks of them as belonging in cages. She tells Tyler that leaving things scattered about is disgusting. So is not changing his clothes more often. Jockey shorts that stink of piss gross her out maximally, so she won't, on principle, touch men's underwear. And the way he talks about things, so abstractly that other people can't follow him, makes her want to toss her cookies. Games, except to play them, some of them, rank only marginally above stinky undershorts and boogers. Long words make her think of thick, knobby turds.

(Ross stands with his front legs wide apart along the edge of mother's vegetable garden. His paws are half sunk in the spring gumbo. Bowed in concentration, his muzzle points into the mud. His back shudders rhythmically. The rasping reaches wetly through the windows. Tyler runs to the veranda to see. Oh, Mama, it's Ross, he cries. The dog shudders and hacks. Its eyes shift sideways, wander skullwards, distractedly, perhaps seeking help. Its nose points steadily into the mud. Thick cords of slaver hang from its jaw. Then a final shudder and a flowing noise, a sluice opening, displaces the raw hacking. White pulp pours from its muzzle onto the black mud. Tyler runs forward to hold Ross around the still quivering shoulders. The high, sharp stench of sour puke clogs his nostrils. Chunks, like cheese, stand out from the chalky pool. Mama, it's all right, Ross is all right. He must have been sick. Aunt Jess stands on the veranda, her wet hands closed within her apron, laughing.)

A thin, angular man wearing a blue nylon windbreaker and a red tie leans across from the next table, twisting to his left. There is an emblem over the heart that Tyler can't read. His companion, facing across the table like Blackie, is busy ignoring the disruption. He tells Tyler that the girl must be on drugs. It's probably an overdose. Must be a hooker. But Tyler doesn't think that an overdose causes vomiting. You just pass out and don't wake up. Danforth and Arundel isn't a corner where you see hookers anyway. The man insists.

"She's ODing, you can bet."

Tyler hears the twangy American accent. Border state. Blackie turns around now, still holding a piece of okra speared on her fork. Her mouth is slightly open, her full lips glistening.

"Look, she's crossing the street."

The young woman is strutting diagonally across Arundel to reach the terrace at the Omonia. Hands on hips, she bends over, gold jacket falling forwards, like puking into the sidewalk. Everyone there has stopped eating now. Tyler sees the diners in the row along the edge of the terrace covering their glasses and trying to protect their plates. The girl's hawking reaches across the street, but broken and unsteady. Consternation follows her, like a shape-shifting cloud.

"She's very beautiful."

Blackie looks back at him, amazed.

"It isn't very beautiful what she's doing now, is it?"

Tyler agrees the contrast is shocking. To see a beautiful woman retching in public is fairly intense. Blackie doesn't believe she is really throwing-up.

"She's been going at it too long."

The waiter across the street is talking to her now. She retreats, turning away, back into the street. Blackie swallows the piece of okra.

The angular American has something to say. Tyler sees the emblem on the man's jacket for the first time. It is a white embossed anchor with two hands clenched across. Beneath are the letters S.I.U.

"Don't be put off. Everybody spews once in awhile."

You had to take it in stride. Blackie looks as if she could never do that. A man had handed him a shit-covered tapeworm once. Tyler's eyebrows lift. Blackie turns to watch the girl who has crossed the street again. The man's companion groans softly to herself. He had been a first mate, and it was evidence in a case against the shipping firm.

"This stiff pulled it from his rectum. Lower than slug slime."

He had handed it over in a glass. He wanted to sue the company. Tyler is curious about details. What had he done with it?

"I reckoned he got his tapeworms eating in chop houses in Mombasa, some other trip."

But he had covered the glass with Saran Wrap and put it in the cook's freezer. It was evidence. Not very pretty though, a shit-smeared tapeworm.

The young woman is now crossing Arundel directly towards their table. The waiter at the Omonia has come out in the street to urge her on. His hands are expressive, but keep a distance. The angular man says, loudly in a stage whisper, "Better cover your plates."

Diners are staring at her as she comes closer, nervously holding their wine glasses, putting arms between the railing and their food. The young woman is now standing only a few feet away, just over Tyler's shoulder. Blackie's eyes, large and fixed, intently follow her. Now Tyler swings around to see her. Under her gold bolero jacket she has spaghetti strings holding up her bronze shift. There is gold embossing across the top of her shift, over her breasts. It looks like a fist. The angular American claims that it is a tongue. Blackie says that it is a narrow face, like a primitive sculpture. Thinking back later, Tyler agrees that it was a tongue, but now it looks like a fist. She has large hoops in her ears and clusters of bangles on her wrists, gold, or perhaps brass. Her toenails are bright red but her lips are not. The bronze shift is strained and tight, unevenly hitched up her muscular thighs. Her face is set and serious. Her black hair reaches her shoulders. The angular American, whispers, "Look at the dreadlocks." Tyler sees only curls covering the top of her forehead. When they discuss the episode later, Blackie will admit only to having seen ratty bangs. Probably she did have dreadlocks, Tyler supposes, but it had been too black on the street to see well. The serious, closed-in face, partly covered by curls or dreadlocks, shining with hatred, or perhaps only dismay, glows on Tyler. He would have liked to think his way into her mind, but the distance is very great. Without a map, he can only wander.

The girl passes their table. She hawks and pretends to

strangle. Now she stands just behind Blackie, arching her breasts. Tyler can see her sharp cheekbones and, down through the railing, the coins in her sandal straps. Her lips are still indistinct. Her teeth are square and bright. She has pushed both hands into her curly black hair, tugging, or twisting her dreadlocks. Blackie looks drawn, her freckles like smudges in the unsteady light. "Let's go," she whispers. Tyler wants to finish his salad. He wants baklava too.

The waiter at the Omonia seems to put his hand gently upon the young woman's back, pointing west along the Danforth. He may slip her some money. Taxi fare. Tyler can't see clearly as they get up from the table. Once out on the street, he looks for the woman. She has disappeared.

Blackie has turned east along Queen and they drive slowly through the Beaches. Tyler looks dreamily at the restaurants, still thinking about the dessert he has missed. No, she hadn't been ODing and she hadn't been sick, except in spirit perhaps. Blackie, feeling reflective, becomes loquacious.

"She must have hated everyone there. Hated them for being white or having too much to eat."

But she was well dressed. Loud maybe, but good clothes. Tyler doesn't like the simple answer. White. He would like to find a mental landscape in which rough country, uprolling hills, finally mountains and deep valleys, become a map. The map would show where unexplored declivities, underground streams, ice caves, thermal springs, were located. White would name a certain peak, a sheer escarpment, but not the entire range. You could climb it if you knew the paths, across ridges and crests, that led up to it. Once Tyler has a map, he can discover things that it doesn't fully show. But to make a map, you must have a starting point and a scale. You can draw the lines only from a precise spot and according to a ratio of similitude. He thinks about the beautiful dark-skinned woman. He tries to imagine her intention.

Blackie whips across Victoria Park Avenue and heads off snappily behind the Palm Beach Courts. They walk down towards the lake, turning onto the grounds of the R. C. Harris Filtration Plant. Tyler knows that she has driven here because she wants to be serious. This is one place they came to walk and be romantic with each other before they were married. Down over the huge sloping lawns, the thickset brick building looms yellowly, like a Florentine palace. The lake is calm tonight, hardly a whitecap. The glow from Rochester behind the horizon glimmers across the darkness. Down the coast, Toronto, dreamcity of towers, shines. Blackie holds his hand, palm out, tightly against her hip, as they walk. They pause on the projecting foreshore, by an ATLAS dumpster, and hug. Let us be true.

"I apologize for knocking over your game this morning. I know that games are important to you."

"You were showing disgust, like the woman at Pappas. A visible rejection of what upsets you. I accept that."

The spot begins to take shape. He can see it as an intention. It is her desire to spill over, to engulf, drown, what is other. White is a rocky peak then. But the map places it as a remote tableland, the way leads across jungles and swamps, deeper than Borneo's. Shit-smeared tapeworms rise from the thick, breathing sludge like monsters, huge and implacable. From the edge, where all the paths start, spread burning plains. And so to cross: distance in each hot grain. Blackie squeezes his hand tightly. Yes, he whispers.

Tyler imagines Dante's burning plains, the usurers and sodomites parching in the wind's fiery dryness, nothing onwards but pain. In the map that has begun to unfold within his mind, the burning plains, though surely barren, stretch out toward further dangers through indifference. Featureless people hunch over food, looking nowhere, like pale maggots. He feels the scalding air clutch him, reaching sheath-like from scalp to toes. The map, he sees now, shows exclusion, the unending nature of shutness. He feels the gorge rise in his throat, cracking.

"Tyler! You aren't listening. I said that I love you. You're a knotty-headed intellectual, but I love you. Dearly."

The cool winds from Lake Ontario make them shudder harmoniously together. God knows what goes on in his head sometimes, Blackie thinks. But she is happy with him, even though his mind is crammed with games.

∼

Michael Rawdon lives in Edmonton. He has published short fiction in Canada, Australia, New Zealand, the United States, and Europe. His most recent collection of fiction is Green Eyes, Dukes and Kings *(1985). Currently, he is writing a novel,* The Hydra's Breath, *that concerns terrorism, exile, and disgust.*

At Land

ARITHA VAN HERK

And who said it was uncomfortable in here, in this pleated space full of augury and auspice, full of the aromatic juices of a digesting whale. Dark yes, and damp, dripping from the ceiling. But uncomfortable? Far less than the cloud that I wandered through on my way to Tarshish, far less uncomfortable than the icy water that I flailed around in while I waited for that gate of teeth to open wide and swallow me whole, to save me from my inescapable fate.

But wait. I am sailing the prairie, steering this leviathan between Winnipeg and Calgary, where I will step out of its mouth between the same gated teeth onto dry land, spewed forth from a journey that has rescued me from swimming. The truth is, I cannot swim; the truth is that I have a desperate fear of water, hydrophobia, which is the same as the other hydrophobia, more commonly called rabies, and not archaic at all. And although the incidence of hydrophobia (which brings about severe thirst, a desire to drink and drink, although attempts to drink induce violent, painful spasms in the throat) is extremely rare, a disease that fewer than 0.05 per 1,000,000 of the Canadian population suffer from, the same is not true of hydrophobia, which is common at land, particularly the prairies, rather like the motion sickness that afflicts those at sea. Seasickness manifests itself through uneasiness, headache, in severe cases, distress, excessive sweating, salivation, pallor, nausea, and vomiting. The sight of food worsens the condition. At sea. Amend the same symptoms to this land, this western sea of grass, undulating in its own billow. We suffer, here in the west, from hydrophobia, the dry wallows of the cows, the thinning Battle River no bigger than a wrist, the shrivelling dugouts, offering no chance to learn the beat of arms and legs as a flotation device against liquid.

This may be an excuse for the fact that I cannot swim. I cannot swim because I cannot swim, and one follows the other as surely as an arabesque within a ballet. I drown because I drown. I once tried to drown and almost drowned, was saved, pulled from the bottom of Buffalo Lake by a classmate who was not hydrophobic, who knew the effect of stepping into one of the sudden holes in the lake's bottom. He was in love with me too, or perhaps I was in love with him, but after the rescue we were both too embarrassed to proceed with our desire. Teenagers drown more readily than most.

So call me Jonna.

Because I almost drowned, I am afraid of water, and now, although I have never taken swimming lessons, I am too afraid to take lessons in drowning prevention. But I almost drowned because I had never learned to swim, and if I had had that advantage, if I had known even the most rudimentary paddling techniques, I might have been able to turn my own drowning to advantage, and instead of being drowned by drowning, I would have resorted to a few lazy kicks, and floated on the surface of that treacherous element in that treacherous lake. But I grew up on the prairie, and learning to swim as drowning prevention was laughable. No one was going to swim in those green-algaed and murky sloughs, muddy down to the centre of the earth. No one was going to swim in the iron coffin of the cattle trough. No one was going to swim in the spring tadpoled ditches. No one was allowed to swim in the dugout. No one could imagine swimming in the Battle River—there wasn't enough river to make water. We swam ritually, once at year, at our annual outing to Buffalo Lake—a lake perfectly traced as the outline of a buffalo (that dry land animal who swam in dust, who bathed in prairie wool), which the first peoples didn't need an airplane to recognize—and that was the end of our swimming. No wonder then, that the incidence of hydrophobia is more than ten to one hundred people on the prairies. It might be considered epidemic.

By training and profession, I am a cetologist, and until last March, I worked at Sea World on the West Coast. It was a job I loved, for although I cannot swim, I splash and am splashed happily, and working with the whales was a matter of being mightily splashed and of rewarding them with fish when they jumped and dived in reasonable form. But we all know what has happened as a result of the upsurge of interest in animal welfare. Those big animals shouldn't be swimming in such small ponds, they must certainly be unhappy. Of course they were unhappy, I can vouch for that. But, apocryphal or not, Sea World was closed, and now I row my boat between wheat fields that ripple as well as any blue water, between the crisp heads of barley, between the yellow waves of canola, the mesmerizing TransCanada, which has given me as much motion sickness as any sea.

So call me Jonna.

My common-law husband's name is Glass, and he has tried many times to teach me to swim. In chlorine-suffused swimming pools, in the Sulphur Mountain Hot Springs (although there are rules against splashing), in the ice splinters of the Bow River (too shallow to be effective), even in the wave-tossed coastal waters of Australia and Hawaii, both islands we have visited. Strangely enough, hydrophobia is relatively rare on such islands; the thirsty disease is a continental one. Although our travels are good, the swimming is always unsuccessful, and Glass is a man who prides himself on success.

"Come on, Jonna," he shouts above the water's roar, trying to keep me afloat with a hand under my back. "Just kick, gently."

I kick, obedient.

"That's right, just hold your breath, you can do it."

He has a tendency to cry out his encouragements into my ear, which does not help my concentration. I cannot stand shouts or snuffles, wet tongues or water, in my ears. But I thrash, and although I try desperately to hold air in my lungs to keep my buoyancy, I sink, as surely and inexorably as a human stone. And then, drowning, need to be rescued again.

To give Glass credit, he has never stopped trying, and every visit that we make to water's unstable element requires another attempt. Although lately he has been leaving Continuing Education pamphlets around the house, advertising courses on macramé and vegetarian cooking, and yes, swimming for absolutely terrifieds.

"I am not terrified," I protest.

"But you are afraid of water."

"Not completely. Just afraid of drowning."

"Same difference, Jonna."

"No, it's not. There is a metaphysical difference."

Which is lost on Glass, who rolls his eyes, and maintains a discretionary silence. That is what I get for settling down with an Aquarius, it's a truism that they always chase after the impossible. Still, Glass is what my friends call a keeper, and I am trying to keep him, so I keep trying to swim as a behaviour modification of my own. Alas, with no success.

So what am I doing here, in the belly of all bellies, the belly of a whale. It seems impossible, a whale afloat on the prairie. But there have been boats and boat builders here before, dreaming of floods. Why should there not be a whale or two, with an abdomen, a deep interior cavity, large enough to accommodate a hydrophobic woman? Let me assure you, I am not running away from Glass and his well-meaning attempts to teach me to float. I am not running away from my own joblessness as a cetologist on the prairies. I am not running away from my own discomfiture with life, with myself, with my name, with my calling as one who brings, by her mere presence, misfortune upon others.

I am capable of drawing diagrams of ships, of drawing on a block of paper the language of shipping and sailing. If you draw the shape of a ship, which is also the shape of a fish without its tail, and if you draw an imaginary line through the centre of this ship at right angles to it, you will be able to name the cross of its directives. Anything behind the line is abaft, astern of the middle, behind the main. Anything at right angles, to right or to left, is abeam. Stick to the bow, ride with the ship into its path. This knowledge might help to prevent seasickness. Although he can swim well, Glass is prone to terrible and stomach-heaving seasickness, while I, hydrophobic me, can sail and sail. It is knowing that the deck under my feet is solid, as compared to the watery element it cleaves. Here now, in this manzanilla darkness, I reflect on my own steady stomach, and how it came to occupy this *mis en abyme*, of a belly within a belly. I appear to share this space with a stingless acalephe or jellyfish, what feels like multiple strands of rubbery dulse, and a few fightless swordfish, who bump their noses against one another and against my body with gentle inquiry. But at least I am not gasping for air in the element that comprises ninety-nine percent of the molecules in my body, but which I cannot think of as hospitable.

Glass will raise his eyebrows quizzically and ask me how I came to be in such a position.

"It wasn't a literal whale," I will answer.

"You mean it was a Cadillac."

"No, stupid. It was a whale, or at least, I've decided to call it a whale, although other people have called it a fish or a sea monster."

"You mean it was an imaginary whale."

"Oh no, it was real enough, just not literal."

"But there's no difference."

"There is a metaphysical difference."

This is when Glass throws up his hands, and goes out to the porch with a beer, where he sits and glowers at the mountains to the west until it is too dark to read them, and he resorts to what stars and constellations he can manage to pick out despite the halo of streetlights. Glass is essentially a patient man, just not quite ready for the movements I make, from land to ship to water to whale and back to land again; as if my hydrophobia were chronic.

But how do I breathe, here inside the cavity of the whale? Whether it is at sea or at land, I am still enclosed within its enclosure, airless. I discern that I am breathing—if you could call it breathing—through a kind of umbilical cord arrangement, which pulses oxygen, pure and heady, into my system. So who does the thinking here, me or the whale? Fish tale, human head, fish tail, whale womb. Philistines and Dagons, the heathen foes, the ill-behaved and ignorant, outsiders. This whale has just sailed from Jena—somehow it conveys its global journeys to me—from Jena, which was once in East Germany and is now simply in Germany, a city resurrecting itself, coughing itself up onto a claim of change and restoration (they say the German *Philister* arose from Jena's 1693 fight between students and townsmen, famous for its bloodshed, when an academic preacher proclaimed that the Philistine townspeople were upon the university). There now, in Jena, the square is being resurrected to its former state, and although the tower of the university cannot be dismantled, it looks forlorn in its modernity, a Babel to the ancient city that it rears above. But the *Wende* does not solve its own solution, and the east of Germany crouches in the belly of the west sourly, a source of heartburn. Through the Berlin Wall, *ein Loch in der Mauer*, the whale sailed, stately, imperial, a mother, *die Wende*. Straight through the skies between Europe and North America, over Hudson's Bay, to splash down in Lake Winnipeg ready to incubate me. And I sympathize with them, Philistines and outsiders, not workers in the arrogant industry of culture, but base, materialistic, craving thanks. They too drown, and by drowning are swallowed.

But these philosophies come to me through the umbilical cord of the whale cruising me gently across the short-grass prairie that is disappearing so quickly, heir to the ruthlessness of cattle. I can hear the coyotes, the chirp of gophers, the rustle of wheat, even here within these walls of blubber. Far away is the wail of a train whistle in the night, and sometimes there is the quick strike of lightning and its rotund accompaniment by thunder. In the womb, all sound is magnified, enlarged, so although I rest in darkness, here in my three-day retreat, I can hear the world we pass through as clearly as if I were walking on dry ground.

Three provinces, three days, from Winnipeg to Calgary. The giantess who carries me ignores the artificial division of this landscape into political pieces. But three days is a comfortable gait to travel, and that we manage about one province per day seems right, a gentle but nevertheless steady pace, slower than an automobile but faster than a bicycle. Glass doesn't like to move this slowly. When we travel to Ontario—Guelph, Ontario—(which is where he was born and where his parents and his two sisters and his one brother still live), we drive straight through, a marathon of pavement that seems to unroll in front of the car like a grey carpet, so that by the time we get there, we are seeing the stripes at the side of the road in our sleep. Like swimming, Glass believes in persistence, in arriving before they expect us to.

And yes, he has a right to ask. Why am I here, inside a version of sea monster, very gentle really, rocking while I lick the sedulous veins of the gooseberries that I find to eat, while I dream the travels of this cetaceous creature. I am here because I bailed out, refused to cooperate, tried to say no, took a roundabout way. This, Glass would say, is typical of me, an evader, a shadow boxer.

"Avoidance is an art," I assert.

"Avoidance is avoidance," he insists. "Better just say no and be done with it."

"But people always think that they're doing me such a big favour by asking me something that saying no is a real slap in the face."

"All they ever ask you for is advice."

"Yes, and then, after I've spent six hours giving it, they decide that they'll ignore what I say."

"Well, they're not paying you for it."

"Yeah, and they don't say thank you either."

Glass gets impatient. "Put up a wall. Say no."

That's a good one. Put up a wall.

I should explain. When I lost my job at Sea World, I became a free agent, self-employed you might say. My talents as a trained cetologist are few enough, but I know the trace of habit, of instinct, of bandinage. And I can work on presentation quite well, those first three seconds when people make up their minds about the candidate, the applicant, the aspirant. I bill myself as an advisor for small problems. How to negotiate the treacherous shoals of a shrinking office. How to get ahead without jealousy. How to look insouciant when you are going in for the kill. How to look enigmatic afterwards. It's much the same as Sea World. I don't mind getting splashed, as long as I'm not in the water. But my business is faltering because I am too generous. I offer too much, prove myself willing to talk to people on the phone, to let that monster interrupt my life at any given moment. And of course, then you get taken for granted. And *nobody* ever says thank you.

So when this contract comes up, this call, to go to Vancouver and to fix some debacle there, I get up and answer the phone, but I hem and haw, think about the mess, and then, perversely, decide I will go to Winnipeg, the opposite direction, where I invent another, albeit smaller, job. Tarshish by Winnipeg, a small community on the shores of Lake Winnipeg, that inland sea, and not so far from Jaffa either. You can only get there by boat, those still old-fashioned and deep-bellied tubs that ply the lake, so I bought a ticket and boarded, went below deck and exhausted by all this avoidance, fell soundly asleep on one of the benches, just stretched out and slept. I was tired. Glass has been waking me up to look at the stars; the meteor showers are exquisite these days, as if portending some extraordinary occurrence.

Even while I slept, I could feel it getting rough, that old boat pitching and groaning as if it would creak apart, and around me my fellow passengers—miners and geologists mostly—unable to control their retching, swallowing and swallowing and swallowing, and finally running to the one small toilet on this bark, but I slept, one of those deep hard sleeps that leave a person loggish and completely relaxed, ready for anything.

Half-awake, I heard people actually calling on god. Praying aloud. I thought that when a ship goes down, the band keeps playing and the captain puts on a white dress uniform, but no, instead, every crew member and every passenger was calling on god, or God, or *God*, or *GOD*, or GOD, Christian or Muslim or Jew, Protestant or Catholic, in the innumerable languages that one is apt to find on the shores of Lake Winnipeg. I should have realized it was bad when they starting throwing the cargo overboard, sacks of Canada Post mail, boxes of fresh bananas, at last even machine parts that they were taking to Tarshish for the oil rigs. I was still dozing, groggy, registering the confusion, but not quite sure it was real rather than metaphysical. Until the captain—and he was wearing greasy khaki, not white duck with gold piping—came below and bellowed at all of us. I know his type, they blame every misfortune on someone else, sure that they are in the clear, have done everything they can.

"OK, OK, what's going on? Who's the Jonah here?"

I swung my legs to the pitching floor, or the deck below deck, sat up and rubbed my eyes with my knuckles. Nobody answered him, their faces staring back green, and ready to lurch again.

"Who are you people? Why are we having a bloody hurricane when the weather forecast said clear and sunny skies, no wind? What does this mean?"

I didn't want to tell him that I was avoiding things, shirking responsibility again, so I shrugged and played innocent.

"And why aren't you seasick?" He was shouting directly at me now. "Or at least praying a little?"

"I'm avoiding god."

He is only disgusted. "Well, get up and gamble with the rest of the crew. We need all hands on deck."

On the forecastle the crew were bent against the gale-force winds, their shirts clinging to muscled backs that under other circumstances I might have appreciated (I'm not *that* faithful to Glass).

"Superstitious bastard," they muttered to me. "He thinks you're the cause of this, doesn't like taking women across the lake."

Sure enough, I was the only woman on board boat. I hadn't noticed before then, but I knew I could be in trouble with a zealot captain and a bunch of tough guys who had been throwing up in front of me. I could only pull a dog-eared deck of cards from my pocket and try to tell them to relax, that a good round of poker would do the trick, let the boat drift, and we'd get through the storm.

Bad advice. The storm grew cyclonic. They decided to cast lots instead, to pull straws or toothpicks, and to pinpoint the problem that way. And I came up with the short straw, the losing winner, the only finger.

"It's you," stormed the captain. "Damn these new fangled ways, they should never let women on board. And I should have known, recession be damned, to change my crew every year. Now we're paying for it."

"Well," I could hardly protest my gender, "why don't you just throw me overboard then?" It seemed to me an outrageous enough proposal, one that he would surely reject out of hand, his transport license revoked, his ship impounded, his reputation ruined, CBC cameras waiting on the dock. But no such luck.

"Good idea."

But the crew were not so careless.

"Who are you?" they asked. "Where do you come from? Why are you here? What is your occupation?"

Who can excuse avoidance? I had to tell them the truth, that I was afraid, that I was mad, that I was tired of getting called up in the middle of the night and told to go and fix some insoluble problem, that Vancouver didn't need me to tell them to repent. That I was trying to build a wall.

The looks on their faces would have turned a pillow to stone. They stumbled back from me, aghast, their lips trembled, and their eyes filled with horror.

"Why didn't you go where you were supposed to? This is the wrong time to build walls," one of them mourned. "What can we do for you, that will stop this storm?"

He was in tears, poor fellow, a nice man I could see, a father, maybe even a husband. And the gale was growing worse, the waves piling up on top of one another as if they were solid and not liquid, the foam lashed to a seething brown. You could say it was close to a hurricane, that storm, close enough to scare me too, because I knew, and how I knew this I don't know, that the only thing that would stop the tempest would be my landlocked and absolutely hydrophobic body immersed in the pitiless waters of Lake Winnipeg.

"Throw me in."

They were silent, standing as still as was possible with the wind howling at their bodies and tearing the very hair from their skins.

"Lift me up, like a sacrifice, and cast me into the water. It's my fault, I'm sure."

But they wouldn't have that, they were horrified at the thought, decided that they would head for shore, try to get to dry land. I could have told them that it would be useless, the elements were after me, even while they strained at their tasks, fighting to turn the ship around. The hurricane only grew stronger, more insistent, now a deep call coming out of the throat of the wind.

To give them credit, they were torn with misery.

"We don't want to dump her overboard," they protested to the captain. "She hasn't done anything. We don't want to die for her soul."

"Pitch her," he said.

I was standing right there. I could have thrown myself on

their mercy, I could have begged for a delay. But that captain made me so mad that I wanted to see him suffer, I wanted him up on unseamanship charges, I wanted him to lose his stripes, even if I had to drown to do it.

"Yes," I said. "Throw me in."

I'm no martyr, just aware of my endless culpability. My crazy guilt comes to me out of decades of being wrong, all the time wrong, too mouthy, too dissatisfied, full of curses and imprecations, eager with demands, which all come back to haunt me, end up on my own head.

"Too much personality," says Glass. "Put a lid on it, stay cool."

"I can't stand the distance," I groan. "Why does everybody have to be so colourless, so damnably homogenized?"

"Welcome to the nineties," he says. He can afford to be careless, he never has to lay himself on the line, play dirty or dumb; he can put his eye to the telescope lens and be instantly lost, pass through troposphere, stratosphere, and mesosphere in a blink.

That was why I liked Sea World; everyone was looking at the whales, not at me, the trainer who clicked her tongue, held the bucket, doled out the fish as reward. But I never expected to become the very thing that I had once so pleasingly distributed, a quick bite for a whale's wide mouth.

They lifted me up, like a sacrifice, and they threw me into the water, that uncertain element that I cannot tread, that raging sky that had come down to meet its own horizon. I drowned, and suddenly the storm was still, grew quiet from its rage, lay peaceful under a scud of quickly clearing clouds. I drowned. The water came up to meet me and I slid into a sea's compass, its depth penetrating to my soul. The weeds wrapped around my head, I went down to the roots of mountains, the earth shut her gates. And yes, my life passed before my eyes, I remembered every detail of love or anger, every glance, every quiet touch, every word spoken. I drowned.

And that is why I am here, inside the belly of this whale, the whale waiting when my poised and plummeting body hit the roiling surface of the water, that followed my descent. Don't worry, I went under, I got my ears and nose and mouth full of that foul liquid, enough so that I coughed and spat my way down this whale's esophagus. But it was there, mouth open, ready to swallow, as if I were a morsel of krill, as if I were a baby. It snapped me up from the bottom and swallowed me whole. And now we voyage across the prairies, a slow swim, me hydrophobic worse than ever, now that I have drowned twice, inside the swimming animal's safe warmth, and I could almost believe the illustrations in the children's Bible that I used to see, of Jonah sitting in front of a fire, toasting his stockinged feet and having a mug of tea while he waits for the whale to land.

I am supposed to pray and lament, to pay for my evasions with the proper *mea culpas*. I am having trouble with that, but my host doesn't seem to be concerned, fins her way across the land as easily as she does the sea, and does not expect too much weeping and blubbering. Indeed, it does no good to moan and whimper in here, to argue that I will keep my contracts, pay my dues, my fare, make sacrifices, no longer spare myself the rod. I will be faithful to Glass; I will learn the names of all the constellations, even those visible from Australia, the Southern Cross and its neighbours. I will no longer drown. For the truth is, I am content, saved from swimming, warm, dark, no one to call to me, and no one to listen to my own calling. The story is that I have only three days here, but I don't mind, it seems forever, a long long time, and I know that the whale won't manage to make it to Vancouver at this speed, and I am likely to be vomited out between her rows of teeth onto the dry land of the foreland thrust sheets, those grey-green foothills, at Calgary. My home, with Glass expecting that I'll have tales of Tarshish to regale him with. In this womb, this hot and yonic vessel, I am perfectly content to voyage across the prairies, enjoying the sights as I have never been able to with Glass, speeding through in his Mustang, eager to hit Ontario and the Shield so that he knows he is getting somewhere.

And when I get to Calgary, will I then fly to Vancouver, that Nineveh I avoided? Will I cry in its ear? I don't think Vancouver has that much to repent of, besides closing Sea World and getting me fired, besides the cost of housing, and the way that the drivers dodge one another, besides the interminable Lion's Gate Bridge. It's no more sinful than any other city, just Vancouver as it's always been, and the truth is, we are jealous, sitting in our prairie cities, despite our cleaner air, our cheaper rents and cheaper gas, we really want to live in Vancouver, and that is the cause of our wish to impose reforms, to get them into sackcloth and ashes. It can repent without me, and, expert at fasting and deprivation, at turning from one illusion to the next, it will, certainly. Vancouver is always spared destruction, recession, bankruptcy. They miss the bitterness the rest of us drink, here on the prairie, waiting for the weather to improve, for the crops to flourish, for the water to rise.

And when they do, repent that is, get spared again, I am determined I will sulk. All that work, all that drowning and drowning and being swallowed and burped up again, I will be furious, once again my advice ignored, no thanks, no payment, just a casual, "Well, I've changed my mind." This damnable compassion, this damnable kindness, such bitter justice for my evasions, all my out of the way travellings. Once again, I'll wish I had drowned, I'll go out on Nose Hill and sit myself under a *sukkah*, drown in the desert of prairie, blister in the hot August sun until my skin peels like a grape. Despite Glass' coaxing, despite him coming out to visit me with cans of cold Labatt's, despite him saying, as he will say, "Is it a good thing for you to be hurt so deeply? Chill out, Jonna."

"Why should I? This is why I lit out for Tarshish. I drowned for this, and all for nothing."

And Glass, poor fellow, will zigzag down the hill again and wish that I were back at Sea World. He will phone the zoo and ask if there's an opening, could I take care of the beaver and muskrats, any water mammals needing trainers?

So call me Jonna.

It's true, from the top of Nose Hill you can see Vancouver, on a crystal prairie day you can see to the other side of the Rockies.

And over me a castor-oil plant will grow, over me a gourd will grow, over me a sage bush so spicy and green will flourish, a cooling shadow that will turn me from bitterness, and from my repeated and never satisfied dissatisfaction. I will begin to feel happy, my mood will lift with the moon over the Rockies, I will begin to enjoy myself. And when the gourd gets worms I will suffer for it, and when the castor-oil plant is attacked I will cry for it, and when the sage bush withers, I will mourn. And again I will wish to drown, to die for lack of shade and respite. The wind will rise, a desert east wind that blows grains of sand against my raw skin. The sun will grow fierce, more brilliantly strong minute by minute, and I will again pray for death to come and fetch me from this new drowning.

And then her voice will say, "Can it be a good thing that you hurt so deeply? Can it be a good thing that the sage bush wilts into dryness through your anger?"

At first I will not answer.

And then, falling into a daze, wishing that I were finally drowned, I will cry out, "It would be a good thing to be dead."

To which her question will repeat itself. "Can it be a good thing that you are hurt so deeply, and only by your own compassion?"

"It is a good thing to be hurt deeply, until I am dead like the sage bush, which is more like me than I am like myself, dry, prickly, tough, an aromatic survivor of the prairie. Unforgiving, a gatherer of wool, a happy weed, an herb, a spice for fowl, hard-working, unappreciated, endlessly used."

She will chuckle then, the same low sound as the grumbles of the whale around me. "You care for this sage bush, the sudden child of night and yet in one night gone. That is compassion, and you, Jonna, are cursed to drown in it. Go home, sleep well, and do not question sage bushes or whales again."

And that will be it; I'll go home and Glass will be happy to see me, will offer me a rye and ginger on the back porch, will rub my neck. And once it gets dark, he will point out Cetus, which is visible from both hemispheres, the great fish of the abyss swallowing its own heaven, mother to those who drown and those who swim.

But for now, here in the belly of my new mother, inside a fish body that cradles me on this voyage across a country, I am content. Mother of Samuramat, Derceto wombs me on this drowning journey, from which I will alight, onto a stony ground, a dry land. They say my story was written by a woman, to ironize prophecy and its male conventions. They say this is a cautionary tale against literalness. They say this is an outsider's parable of exile. They even say that Jonah was a man, and the whale a monster. They say a Jonah brings misfortune upon his companions. They say that those of us who are impatient and evasive, who seek a gratitude impossible to find, cannot discern between our right hand and our left. Woe to us who seek to pour oil upon waters brewed into a gale. Woe to those of us who seek to please rather than appal. Woe to those of us who, in this world, court not disaster.

But here within my hot, dark, matrix, my dolphin's *delphos*, my leviathan's source, submarine, subterranean, I am at last, drowning, at land.

∼

Aritha van Herk *was born and raised in Alberta. She is the author of three novels,* Judith *(1978),* The Tent Peg *(1981),* No Fixed Address *(1986), and the geografictione,* Places Far From Ellesmere *(1990). In* Visible Ink *(1991) and* A Frozen Tongue *(1992) are collections of ficto-criticism. Her fiction, essays, and ficto-criticism have been published world-wide, and her work has been translated into ten languages. She is a professor of English at The University of Calgary.*

The Missing You

ADELE MEGANN

Irene crunches her last corner of toast and rubs it into a spot of marmalade on her plate. Marmalade sandwiches were Henry's idea. "For lunch?" said Irene, laughing, when he made the suggestion. She couldn't remember ever in her life eating a marmalade sandwich, but the idea made her feel nostalgic. "Is that what you ate on the farm for lunch?" she asked Henry, but she was in the kitchen before he could reply. "You're going to have it toasted, aren't you?"

"No. Thank you."

"But it's *white*!"

Henry said nothing, so she poked her head into the living room, to see if he was nodding.

"What?" he said.

"Nothing."

Henry is finished eating, and has wheeled off to his room when Tom comes in. "Did he have jam in his sandwich, too? No wonder he's getting so heavy," says Tom. They sit at one end of the living room table, he at the head, she at his side. They conference when their shifts overlap. The narrow rectangle of furniture easily accommodates ten places, and an extra leaf is stored downstairs. Fake grains of wood slip under the side of Irene's fist. No relief.

"Once won't hurt."

"*You* have to be able to transfer him."

The thought of helping Henry from his wheelchair to the toilet seat makes Irene's arm muscles tremble. He's started to lose strength in his left arm too, and the effort leaves her more breathless each day. She's tired of Cathy sighing "And to think last year he could walk," because she's never seen him walk. After showers, Irene hides in Liz's washroom, sits on the edge of the bath, crammed between the hand rail and the wall, massaging her arms. Pretending wears them both out. He pretends to be alone in the shower, but there she is, standing next to the rubber chair with the hole in the seat, soaping up a cloth that she hands to him, so he can "take care of himself" with the one hand that works.

"That's my problem, isn't it?" she replies.

"It is indeed," says Tom. "I hope you're going to get the grocery shopping done this afternoon."

"I will. What do you have scheduled?"

"I've got a case conference at Liz's workshop," answers Tom. "She's been crying wolf again."

"You mean about that staff she says touched her breasts? I noticed that written up in her day book."

"They're getting pretty annoyed. He's the third guy she's accused. They're afraid this one's going to quit. He's a good worker, and this is very embarrassing for him."

"Maybe he did it." Irene knows this is not true. Someone touched Liz's breasts, she's sure, more than one someone maybe, but that was a long time ago, in the Centre. Long and short-term memories are all the same for Liz. Sometimes she comes home hot with the indignity of having her braids pulled, and wants her tormentor punished, NOW. Maybe it's been twenty years since her hair has been long enough for braids. So does that make her memory good or bad, wonders Irene?

"Come on, Irene. There were three other people there. And she got all the facts wrong. Including his name."

"She always gets names wrong." Maybe it's just that people are interchangeable, thinks Irene, even across years.

"Especially if she's known someone less than five years. Who would want to touch her breasts, anyway? She's built like a refrigerator. And she smells. When are you going to convince her to use soap?"

Henry rolls back into the room. He's seen the Zippi-bus, early this time, from his bedroom window. Irene's glad Donny is driving today; Henry is picky with Zippi-bus drivers. "Rough," he says about almost half of them. "Too. Ffffriendly," he says about almost the other half. "I may have. No hips left. To break," he tells the impatient ones. "I sstill have. A neck." He hardly flinches when Donny zips him cleanly over the threshold, down the ramp from the house, over the sidewalk, up the ramp to the back of the van. How does he do that? thinks Irene. She heaves three times just to shift Henry over the threshold. But besides being better built for it, Donny's had unique experience—he used to be a prison guard. "Same principle," he explained once. "Get a body from A to B without their knowing it. Firm but gentle, firm but gentle. Less swearing in this job, and more thank you's."

Irene tries not to bid Henry adieu too cheerfully, but Henry's physio appointment will give her the time to do the grocery shopping. Besides, after a morning with him, she's bored. Is it his age? she wonders. His memories she doesn't want? Her head throbs from remembering things she never knew, when Henry had relatives, parents and siblings even, lived in a three-bedroom house, helped in the garden. If it were just the slowness, and lack of conversation, why does she catch herself wishing Joey were the one retired and home during the day?

She
Hair. Black.
Me. Hand. Up. Up. Hair. Hers. Her hair.
Joe-eee.
She. Eyes. Mouth. Smile.
Look. You remember your birthday dinner.
Pictures. Birthday. Me.
Who's in the picture? Is Tom in the picture?
Eyes. Hers.
Show me Tom.
Tom. Picture.
Where's Tom?
Picture.
Show me.
Picture.
Point to him for me.
Finger. Point.
Point.
Finger. Up.
Point.
Up. Up.
Almost.
Up. Picture.

That's right. You're absolutely right. That's Tom. Good for you.

Eyes. Her.

~

When Tom leaves, Irene stacks plates on the counter because the dishwasher is full of clean dishes and she doesn't have time to empty it. That's a great example for our put-the-dishes-in-the-dishwasher program, she thinks. After she and Cathy spent a good part of the morning designing a behavioural program to beguile the residents into doing just that. "Let's program some people!" Irene said, almost gleefully, as they sat down to it.

"It's not like we have a choice." Cathy glared. Better drop that crack, thought Irene. Tom wants a proposal ready by Thursday. When Tom first brought up the need for a program to get the residents to clean up their own dishes, Cathy laughed and remarked that the dishes get clean eventually. She must have thought he was asking their opinion. They all froze as Tom's gaze fixed Cathy, until Irene objected, ("how silly") as usual. That's what Cathy wants, Irene knows, someone else to do her objecting for her.

"So what do we use for reinforcers, check marks, or do we need to up the ante—McDonald's, pop?" asked Cathy, as she sketched out a chart.

"How about 'thank you'? You know, like most human beings find sufficient?"

Cathy giggled. At least she hasn't completely lost her sense of humour, thought Irene. She knew that morning routine had not gone well for Cathy. Henry had woken at 3:00

A.M. with leg pains, Marcel rose at 4:30 to do his laundry, and Liz was almost late for work because she insisted on wearing her cheese-sauce stained burgundy blouse. The workshop complains when her clothes are stained, which can be any time after fifteen minutes of wear, and Cathy spent three-quarters of an hour persuading her out of one blouse and into another. When Irene arrived at nine, crumby plates and milky bowls remained piled on the counter and table. "Did you make out an incident report?" she asked after hearing the whole story. "Jumpins," said Cathy, "Isn't she in enough trouble? Hitting Sarah, bossing Marcel around, stealing at work."

Irene pulls open the door to let the dishes air dry. "Let down the drawbridge!" she bellows to the empty house, and contemplates the dripping racks. "How do I fill thee?" she warbles, "Let me count the ways." Who knew filling a dishwasher was so complex a task? Plates dovetailed, spoons up, glasses upside-down, cups on top, garbage that left-over toast first, please.

Irene thinks about how people who pride themselves on being casual always say to helpful dinner guests, "Just throw them in any which way." They have never said: No, the milk carton doesn't go in, so that's where the jam jar lid is, any particular reason why you want to wash those Cheerios? SEE that fork—it's going to stab me next time I open the door.

Nor have they ever had to devise dishwasher-door-opening-strategies. Henry's not strong enough to open it himself. Marcel would be happy to do it for Henry all the time, but Tom says that's not fair to Henry, it threatens his independence. Whoever helps him needs recompense. Equity. What then, extra points, check marks, smiley face stickers, to the volunteers? (Sarah will take the plate from under his mouth because *she's* finished.) And how to give Joey the courage to open the dishwasher. Afraid the door will fall on him.

~

Joey. He treads carefully through life, observes Irene, he studies the spoons before putting them into the drawer, contemplates the Velcro on his tiny runners before fastening them, considers his hands, turns them over and over, before heading off to bed as instructed. Trying to remember where's he seen those palms and fingers before? Audio cassettes, socks, photographs, shoelaces, sea shells, sorted and placed as gently as words in a poem. Irene speculates that he's never seen a bedroom in a regular house, with only three or four, or even as few as two bedrooms. The effort of remembering a room he's never entered slows his hand, as it negotiates his space, creating; is this what a real bedroom looks like? the small hand asks, as it weighs a glass bell for several full minutes before deciding where to set it down. He is editing, thinks Irene, those must be sentences he marks with such deliberation across his room, through his body, over his face. Read carefully, says the round smiling face; each word is precious, but fragile. My single gesture, pondered over, planned, rehearsed in mind, gingerly offered, is worth more than your talk, talk, talk, Irene imagines him saying to her.

"Don't a lot of Downs having trouble talking?" Irene asked at one of her first case conferences. I know nothing about this, she thought. I have no training for this. I am making it up as I go along.

"Sometimes their tongues are too big," said Tom, glancing at Irene over the top of some papers. "Like Sarah. That's why you can't understand her. But not Joey. He has no physical impediment."

"So what's wrong then?"

"He's never spoken." He sighed, laid his papers down. "We don't know much about his childhood." He took the papers up again.

Hardly any time after that, it seemed to Irene, Cathy came to her. "We need a strategy to keep Marcel in bed until 6:30. What do you think we should do?"

Irene was aghast. "You know better than I do, Cathy. You've been here two years. You've taken courses and workshops and. . . ."

Cathy waved her objections away. As of now, thought Irene. As of now, I don't know nothing about this.

She again pursued the matter of Joey's silence with Tom. "He must have gotten speech therapy in school."

"I don't know," said Tom. "We don't have school files, we just have residential files. It probably would be noted. Come on, Irene, aren't you underpaid and overworked enough? And I don't think we should be discussing this in front of him."

"He knows he doesn't talk. Don't ya, kid?" Irene laughed as Joey turned his head toward her. Straight hair stuck up from his forehead. His right eye twitched away. Eventually, he grinned.

She. Look.
Who's in this picture, Joey?
Me. Picture. Me.

Hummmm. What a nice smile. Can you point to the person in the picture?

Point. Finger.

Is the person in the picture in this room? Can you point to that person?

Finger. Up. Up. Up. Chin. Me.

That's right. It's you. That's a picture of you.

She. Smile. Me.

~

Newest staff does the shopping. It's a kind of trial, Irene decides. After six months of shopping, you've either quit or been promoted. When she finally knows what aisles to find rice and macaroni and toilet paper and tuna, she won't need to know.

Irene hooks her fingers around the bars at the front of the large cart and pulls it behind her so she doesn't have to look at the cart. Before this job, her idea of major shopping was yanking around a clangy little cart at Cornucopia Natural Foods. She manoeuvres a corner, and takes a deep breath before plunging into the next aisle, thirty-six-roll packs of toilet paper towering over her. So many bums to wipe, so many toilets to clog up. The Association wanted her to go to MegaStore, but she had to leave fifteen minutes into her first expedition, shaking because the other end of the building seemed so far away. When security tried to stop her from going out the "in" door, she vowed never to return. "It's a friggin' wholesale warehouse," she hissed at Tom that day she had to explain why there were no fresh groceries. "There's no food for *people* there."

"Families shop there all the time," he said lightly, "I hope you can make some supper out of what's around." The association agreed to let her go to Food Acre (an improvement, Irene felt, only in being more like a barn than an airplane hanger), if she could keep within budget. She now appreciates regular supermarkets, can picture herself in that commercial with the friendly butcher in the store where they pack your bags.

Blue packages pile up behind her. Blue tins, boxes, pouches, jars—blue with yellow lettering. She grimaces as she tosses six boxes of sugarless strawberry gelatin, the metallic taste of sweetener already behind her teeth. ("We're all watching our weight," says Tom.) They actually ask for it: "When are we having Jell-O again, the red kind?" In the following aisle, she spots her next weapon in the convince-Liz-to-use-soap battle. Bubble bath. Four dollars for a litre bottle. Cheap enough, even if she uses a cup a bath. Strawberry? No, she might eat it. Bubble gum isn't age-appropriate. Lavender? Too matronly. Rose. Perfect. Bubbles to your chin, like a real lady, "Bubbles, bubbles to stroke your refrigerator breasts," hums Irene. Who needs check marks when you can have a bath like a lady on TV?

She. Stand. Glass. Outside. Look. Outside.
She. Forehead. Glass. Breathe. Fuzzy. Glass.
She. Arms. Hold Elbows.
She. Breathe. Big Breathe.
She. Going. Away.
Going Away

≈

Joey's first to come home. She wonders what he did today—put pencils in boxes, seeds in packages, plastic forks in plastic bags? His workshop closes at 3:00 P.M. Probably so the staff can spend two hours writing behavioural programs, muses Irene. "Did you have a good day at work?" "A smile might tell me maybe you had a good day, but can you sign 'yes'?" Maybe they were stapling. He likes stapling. "Sign more clearly, Joey." "Well, I guess that is a 'yes.'" A fist. A fist is "yes." Whose idea was that? The fist is supposed to nod, but Joey's never does. He signs in whispers.

Joey shuffles into the living room. He walks almost sideways. Forty-five degrees, pulling one leg behind him. There's nothing wrong with the leg. That's just how he walks. He crouches in front of the stereo, his eye twitching from button to button. Finally, he picks one. The radio. A country tune twangs into the room. Joey's body curls up, he binds his arms across his chest. Eyebrows crowd into his eyes, lips purse out, head rolls onto his chest. Stony, except his chin darts to the side and one eye catches Irene's. "That frown would turn a gargoyle green with jealousy," she says. Another dart. "So Henry's a country boy. Don't hold it against him." She fiddles with the dial. Top forty bursts into the air. Joey unfolds, grinning, stands before the radio, beating his right thigh in rhythm. The day enters its next phase, thinks Irene. Up goes the sound level.

> She. Music. Me.
> She. Laugh. Hands. Clap.
> She. Hand. Leg. Clap.
> Me. Hand. Leg. Clap.
> She. Hand. Leg. Clap.

Me. Hand. Leg. Clap.
She. Music. Me. Laugh. Clap.
We. Music.
We.

~

Then Henry, home from physio. God, I hope he went to the
bathroom, thinks Irene. Where there's male staff. Here we go,
thinks Irene, hop on the merry-go-round. Now Liz. Who'd
you malign today, kiddo? "Have I got a surprise for you!"
How exciting can you make bubble bath sound? "Thank you,
Reen. You're my friend. My best friend. I love you, and I'm
keeping you!" Someone's in a good mood. Must have been
vacuuming day. Marcel. "Lady drive bus. Lady!" Imagine
that, Irene doesn't say aloud. And what am I when I'm
chauffeuring you? "Can you bring in the rest of the groceries
from the van?" Lines crack Marcel's face as his fist pounds the
counter. "Me carry. Me carry groceries." Before Tom sees
you with the keys, please. "Into the bathtub, Liz. Now."
Sarah. Licking her fingers. Cola moustache. Must have
tossed the crumpled chip bag on the lawn. Every morning,
they send her off with a frozen cheese sandwich, and no
money. Every afternoon, she returns with a bag of chips and
a soft drink. Who needs the mysteries of the universe? We
have Sarah. ("Can't you find out?" says Tom. "One of these
days," shrugs Irene, "I'll tail her home. I'll schedule it in. Real
soon.") Liz's conversation with herself in the bathtub echoes
loudly, but unintelligibly, into the kitchen. Reminds Irene of
those whale albums that were big in the seventies. "Joey, how
many cups of tea have you had?" He's sitting at the dining

room table now. His feet don't reach the floor, but Irene can see them keeping time as they dangle. A grin cracks his face in two. Why talk? Liz, tidal waving in the bathtub, tosses her words against the unresponsive walls. "Don't forget the salt!" is all Irene can make out clearly.

Irene digs the econo-pack of pork chops out of the freezer, and tries to imagine a person who looks like a refrigerator. The fridge is brown, like Liz (or walnut, if you're a fridge) who Irene thinks is Cree or Métis (the files don't know), although as far as Liz knows, she sprouted from the cellar at the Centre. But the fridge is vigorously rectangular, and if Liz lacks anything, it's symmetry. She wears industrial strength bras, bigger than Irene ever knew existed or thought necessary, but Liz's breasts stretch thinly down to her stomach without them. A sight Tom has never seen. One of her shoulders is at least a fistful shorter than the other, so one breast sags even lower than the other. Her left hand is permanently curled up towards her elbow, that arm unused except to steady the paper she crayons, or tuck a vacuum hose under her arm. Still, thinks Irene, as she recalls Liz showering in the wave pool locker room, in the stall with the wooden seat, there is a certain dignity in the naked body unencumbered by ill-fitting clothes. Refrigerator is not the first image to come to Irene's mind.

Tom scurries into the kitchen. "Where's Liz's day book?"

"There were no problems today." Irene arranges pork chops into the pan. "She did a good job at vacuuming." One for everyone, she counts, except two for Tom, who is watching our weight. "Did you just come from her workshop?" Irene can't make out the words of Liz's bath-time conversation with herself, but she is eavesdropping on the tone. Is she talking out anxiety? Or thrilled with bubble bath?

"Yes."

"Why didn't you give Liz a ride home?" Two cylinders of mushroom soup from blue and yellow cans glop into the pan. She doesn't have time for anything else, and they all like tinned soup, complain that Irene's home-made sauces taste funny.

Tom stops, a page of the day book held upright between his thumb and forefinger. "Liz is supposed to take the Zippi-bus. That's her routine."

She mushes the soup over the pork chops. "You just drove here from there." Lighten up, sweetie. It's just a little irony.

"She takes the Zippi-bus every day. I don't want to disrupt her routine."

"If she was your sister, you'd damn well disrupt her routine."

"Watch your language," he whispers hoarsely.

"You're the one who tells visitors that we're just like a family."

"How does that justify swearing?" he says as he leaves.

Potatoes. Where's the peeler? (A long time ago, Tom said, "You aren't going to peel them? They deserve peeled potatoes, just like normal people.") Damn the peeler. I'm normal, thinks Irene. I eat them with the skin on. I'll just poke out the eyes.

She. Potatoes. Rub. Rub. Rub.
Me. Potatoes. Cut.
Knife. Drawer.
Drawer. Pull.

Knife. Up.

You want to chop up the potatoes, Joey? It's Liz' evening to help, but she's otherwise engaged. Forever blowing bubbles. No, use that knife.

Knife. Potato. Push. Pieces.

Sorry I've already opened the tins. Next time.

Knife. Potato. Push. Pieces.

She. Potato. Rub. Rub. Rub.

Knife. Potato. Push. Pieces.

She. Mad. Potato. Poke. Poke.

Knife. Potato. Push. Pieces.

Thanks, Joey. That's enough potatoes.

She. Going.

~

Tom returns Liz's day book to the shelf over the counter. Irene palms up the fat she trimmed off the pork chops and drops it in the garbage can.

"How did the meeting go?" Irene asks. Liz is still splashing and chatting away. Irene reminds herself to tease her ("So who was in there with you?").

"I'm supposed to talk to her, explain why this finger-pointing is serious. They're going to take away her coffee privileges for a week. Then see if she gets the message."

"You can't withhold coffee from someone just like that. Coffee's a drug."

"So she's better off without it. Irene, you say the strangest things. Why did you buy yellow napkins?"

"They're for Sarah's birthday. I'm going to put them on the red table cloth. Cathy is making her a Flames cake." Now what's wrong? We need another vegetable.

"Don't you think it's a little extravagant to buy a whole package of paper napkins for one meal?"

"No." Three half-empty blue and yellow bags of vegetables wait in the freezer to be selected.

"Irene, I'm house manager here, and I'm responsible for the budget. . . ."

"And I'm responsible for the kitchen and you can damned well get out of it, I'm busy and you're in my way." Peas. A lovely contrast to the beige tones of mushroom soup and pork chops.

"Don't talk to me like that. Can't you be professional, for once?"

Irene shuts the freezer with both hands. The bag of peas crashes to the floor. "Fuck away!"

"You are totally irration—"

"Now!" The bag wasn't tied and the peas, frozen peas with individual icy sheens, bounce around the kitchen floor in a chorus of pings. Tom spins away as Irene stoops to restrain the errant vegetables. Her foot meets the bag, and releases more peas from their plastic prison.

Sarah runs into the room, "Hoh! Hoh! Hoh!"

"OK, kid, rub it in."

Sarah gets down on her knees, and starts collecting peas, one by one, as Irene watches, kneeling. She's sure that each pea she tries to corral would just roll off under her finger, set off more avalanches. After every three or so peas she gathers, Sarah turns to Irene, hissing giggles. Her little eyes, magnified by thick round glasses, crinkle into her chubby white face.

"For crissake. It was an accident. You've never had one, I'm sure. Miss."

"Goh. Goh. Goh. Goh." Sarah jabs a sharp finger Irene's way. How effectively people who sign can point, notes Irene. I can almost feel that finger tip on my chest bone.

Look at this one, Joey. Who do you see here?
She. Picture.
Is the person in this picture in the room? Can you point to that person?
She. Eyes. Me.
Who is it, Joey? Who's in the picture?
She. Eyes. Me.
Show me, Joey. Point.
She. Eyes. Me.
Who is it? Use your finger.
"Whhhew."
Oh God, Joey. Yes. It's me.

≈

Adele Megann is a Newfoundlander who moved to Calgary in 1985. Educated in Montreal, Indiana, and Calgary, she currently works as a reference assistant. Her short fiction has appeared in blue buffalo *and* Secrets from the Orange Couch.

On a Platter

CATERINA EDWARDS

Fulvia was not one for waxing nostalgic. "I'm not the type," she told Anne. "You know that about me by now." Which was why it was so startling to find herself caught—in the middle of their ladies lunch at The Happy Garden, in the middle of *Moo Shui* pork and pancakes and tea—caught and locked in memory, as the words "this takes me back . . ." slipped from her mouth. And she paused. She apologized. "Not me," she told Anne.

She hated it when Nino launched, as he did too often, into a paean of the glories of Italian ice cream or coffee, mothers or cheese graters: Italian anything when he was in his remember/remember mood. "Sure," she'd say. "Tell me another one." Or, borrowing one of their daughter Barbara's phrases, "Give me a break." "Your memory's faulty," marshalling facts to deflate his nostalgia balloon.

Fulvia was not one even for remembering. Her childhood was closed off, walled up, thousands of miles and twenty years away. Barbara was so used to listening to her father— the tale of the cowpattie, the fall into the lagoon, an entire volume of legends—that lately she was asking for her mother's stories. And each time Fulvia was stuck; she could call up no equivalent. And what she could have called up—what she knew lurked behind those stone walls topped with broken glass—couldn't be spoken of. Couldn't, shouldn't. Just the thought of remembering made a jagged shard twist in her chest.

"They can't be all bad," Barbara said. "Don't you remember anything happy?"

"I must have forgotten," Fulvia said. "But have I told you about how your father and I met? Or about the time you smeared diaper cream all over the furniture? Never mind the long ago and far away."

Never mind. Fulvia's memories tended to be rare and involuntary, physiological responses beyond her control. (Never *from* the mind, never *in* the mind. Or not for long.) Sensations rather than scenes. Sensations of sun, light, heat, dark, enclosure, shame that she associated with her childhood, with Sicily.

Long ago and far away. I am lucky, Fulvia thought. I see nothing, I meet no one to remind me. Nino's crazy to want to move back. Just look at Anne, who'd been born and spent nearly all her life in Edmonton; it seemed as if whenever they were out together they ran into someone from her past. They had barely sat down at their table when a bearded man, Eddie Bauer parka and moon boots, stopped on his way to the door. "Anne, long time . . . ," he'd said. From his smile and Anne's, Fulvia presumed he was another old boyfriend. He was introduced as "a friend from way back." Let the back stay back and the past, past, Fulvia thought. Nino must have known she wouldn't agree to go back. Why was he so insistent? So self-righteous?

For better or for worse, he reminded her, only slightly

tongue in cheek, you swore. And she had sworn, dressed in white lace with orange blossoms in her hair, she had sworn, but here in a clean, bare Canadian church, not there, not encased in the baroque excess of St. Agatha's.

Here. The restaurant was cheery with year-round Christmas decorations, shiny balls and silvery garlands, noisy with patrons flushed by the February snow and ice outside and the steamy warmth inside. Anne and Fulvia's table was squeezed into the middle of a throughway. Waitresses, arms laden with plates, bustled by.

Anne and Fulvia had been having lunch together for years, from the time they both worked at a dress shop. Since then their lives had gone in different directions: Fulvia at home with the infant Barbara during the years when Anne was most career-driven, now Fulvia had her boutique, and Anne was tied down by three year old twins. Still, despite their differences, which were not just situational, their friendship survived. Mostly because of Anne, it survived: she was the one who cultivated and tended, the one who phoned.

And Fulvia was almost always happy to hear from her. Although there had been a stretch early on, after Anne had been a dental hygienist for a year, when Anne's view of humanity became so dark ("people lie" she would repeat over and over again, "you can't trust anyone"), that Fulvia had avoided her. Luckily, Anne came to understand what her job was doing to her. She returned to university, saving herself from permanent pessimism and those around her from conversational ennui.

Now Anne and Fulvia talked about all sorts of things: the minutiae of their lives, motherhood, bargains, weight loss, whatever issue was flavour of the month. Today, since Fulvia had been called in by her gynecologist because (as he explained it) "there's a spot on your mammogram that falls into the grey area," they were exchanging medical stories. "I asked her to check my thyroid," Anne was saying, "but she kept insisting I was suffering from depression."

"You should have filed a complaint," Fulvia said. "I would have."

"I have no doubt about that. . . . Try these, Fulvia. They're delicious." The platters of food exhaled foreign but comforting smells: ginger and soy and lemon grass. And when Fulvia took a bite, the flavours were distinct, sharp and salty.

"I don't trust doctors," Fulvia said.

Anne smiled affectionately. "You don't trust—period."

"Don't let Nino hear you. He's always looking for ammunition."

"He accuses you . . . ?" Anne said.

"Of all kinds of things when he's in that mood." Fulvia noticed that Anne's blue eyes, behind her goldrimmed glasses, were alert, focused. Anne loved any kind of emotional revelation. "How do you *really* feel about that?" was one of her habitual questions.

"This sounds serious."

"Not at all," Fulvia said, keeping her voice light. "Well, he's always had his moods. We've discussed that before."

"But this is something different? Something worse?"

"It's this recession. He insists the company's on the edge of bankruptcy."

"Oh no."

"I went over the books. And it isn't in danger. Not really. A few changes. That's all that's needed."

"You've always had such a good head for business. He should let you run things. He must realize that."

"Umm. Give up the boutique for construction? I don't think so."

"Of course not—just help him out a bit."

"Let's have dessert," Fulvia said. "I feel like stuffing myself today. They must have something disgustingly sweet."

"I crave sugar when I'm tense too," Anne said. "Are you *very* upset about the mammogram? Well, of course, you are. Who wouldn't be? You can sit there, as impassive as ever. . . but inside. . . ."

Fulvia lifted one shoulder in the smallest of shrugs. "I'm going to get a second opinion. Probably a third. Before and, if necessary, after the biopsy. So I can choose the best course of action."

Fulvia had intended to stay calm with Nino, to discuss things rationally. Instead, faced with his intransigence, she found herself shouting. "You don't make a decision about moving back and then expect me to go along with it. You don't choose for me. No one does."

For better or for worse, he had said. Here or there.

Gently, insidiously, last night's dream came back to her, like a white-gauze curtain, separating her from the bustle of the restaurant. She was alone in church, her old church, white marble carved into confusion, a riot, a jungle of leaves, garlands, cherubs, saints: the plenty of earth and heaven. St. Agatha's, gold-daubed statues, a glowing, gory painting, a wall of hand-written pleas and testimonials, blurred snap-shots and silver amulets, hundreds of them: hands, arms, legs, eyes. Currying favour. But not her. She was alone. Before the altar. And she would not bend her head. She refused, and her refusal was hard and sharp against the shifting sickness set off by that unchecked excess.

A dream? A memory? She struggled to push away the gauze curtain and focus clearly on Anne and the platters of food. That was there and then, she reassured herself. Long ago and far away. Not just a few years and thousands of miles lay between Alcamo and Edmonton. The gap was one of centuries. It could not be bridged. Time was not reversible. Nino was wrong-headed. No plane could take them back. It was impossible

"Earth to Fulvia, come on, try one," Anne was saying, "You insisted on ordering these. You haven't been listening, have you? Don't apologize. I'd be in a worse state than you. I remember when I got a positive PAP smear. It turned out to be nothing, a yeast infection, but for three months. . . ."

Fulvia bit into the bun and the sweet, elusive flavour teasing her tongue caught her (was there no escape today) caught her and she remembered—Sicily. Though it took a moment before she actually identified the taste, before she understood what had been recalled. "This takes me back," she found herself saying. "*Zuccata*, these preserves the cook used to make. Boiled summer squash and jasmine water. Heavenly." She paused.

"The cook?" Anne said. "I never imagined you with a cook. It's not my image of you at all."

"We rarely made desserts at home. They were bought. Mostly from the local convent. Only on special occasions, thank goodness. You can't imagine, Anne, how amazing, how subtle they were. The triumph of gluttony they've been called. Those nuns must have poured all their blocked sensual appetites into their culinary creations. *Minni di virgini*, the base was a pastry crust of almond flour, then layers of *zuccata* alternating with sponge cake and custard, topped with almond paste, and on top of the mound—you see they're called Virgin's breasts—a red cherry."

"You got them from the convent?"

"They're named for St. Agatha, a much beloved Sicilian saint, to commemorate her mutilation and martyrdom. Each convent had their own version, their own triumph. Sicilian sweets are the best in the world. Nothing comes close." Fulvia pushed away the dish with the remains of the bun. "I'm sorry."

"Why? It's fascinating."

"Ah yes, you told me you started in anthropology—ritual foods among the primitives."

Anne looked startled, perhaps even hurt. "Don't be silly. Honestly, Fulvia, sometimes—"

"I am sorry. I just caught myself off guard. I hate that. All this remembrance of things past—I'm not the type. You know that about me by now."

"What's the harm? It does good. Lets your friends understand who you are. I mean, I had this view of your childhood which I now see was all wrong."

"Ah, the cook."

"Was it just her? Did you have other servants?"

"Inside and out."

"Your family had money then."

"No end of it."

"And you. . . ."

"I withstood temptation. I got out. I left it behind." Did Anne guess? Her cheeks and eyes were glowing with curiosity. What's the harm, she'd said. And, of course, it was the fashion, using one's past, like décolleté or a miniskirt: look at me, pay attention, childhood trauma as titillating accessory, a spike-heeled shoe or a white lace bustier. "It wasn't easy." Fulvia could go no further. She could not brush away the jagged shards. She could never knock down the wall. If she tried to flaunt those stones, if she fashioned them into a folkloristic necklace, they would break her neck or, worse, her daughter's neck, so long and straight and slender.

Nino had let himself be tempted. He wanted to go back.

"I'm free here," she said to him for the thousandth time. "There I'd be shut in. Trapped."

"You only think of yourself," Nino repeated yet again. "For me, it's a way out."

Fulvia waved to the waiter for the bill. "Look at the time. I'll be late for the appointment if I don't get moving."

Anne nodded. "This has been good. Let's not wait so long next time. We could go out to dinner. Have more time to talk."

"I'll have to see," Fulvia said, buttoning up her coat. "I'm not sure. " She pushed open the inner door and then the iced outer one. Anne was right behind her, still chatting. Fulvia took a deep breath of the cold, clean air.

"Next week," Anne was saying, "I have to finish that presentation but by, say, Friday. . . ."

Fulvia pulled back her coat sleeve to check her watch. As she noted the time, she saw the date: Febuary ninth. The feast of St. Agatha. So that was it. There was nothing sinister, nothing psychic about her sudden memories.

"You're a hard woman," Nino had said. "You only think of yourself. You don't consider me. Always. Part of you has always been untouchable."

"Don't put *me* in the wrong. What's right is right."

"See, little-Miss-Purity. This is the real world, Fulvia. Not black, not white—grey."

All these years of marriage and he still didn't understand. It was not grey; it was either/or. And she had chosen here, she had chosen white. (Lace, jasmine, snow.)

"Call me as soon as you get the results of the biopsy," Anne said, as they stood by Fulvia's Taurus. "I'm sure it will be all right."

Suddenly, Fulvia was afraid. She saw again the murky painting in her old church, the painting of St. Agatha carrying the platter with her sacrificial breasts. She saw the wall of offerings, the riot of metal amulets. She was not inviolable. And she knew only too well what would be required of her.

~

Caterina Edwards has published one novel, The Lion's Mouth *(1982), a play,* HomeGround, *and many short stories in literary magazines and anthologies. Her latest book is* Whiter Shade of Pale/Becoming Emma *(1992), two novellas; a collection of stories is scheduled for appearance in 1994. She lives in Edmonton with her husband Marco and two daughters.*

Balancing Act

SARAH MURPHY

WARNING: PROCEED WITH CAUTION
(instructions to hold the tightrope artist)

Proceed with caution. It will not be easy here. With the darkness of the shadows and the brilliance of the lights it will be hard not to get mixed up. Do your feet tread the wire do your hands hold the railing do you feel the evenness of your steps do you feel the movement of the wire do you feel the stickiness of your fingers do you feel the cold stillness of the railing. It will be hard not to get mixed up it will be hard to know.

Proceed with caution. Balance is for a lifetime. It will be hard not to get mixed up. Anything can happen here. It will be hard to know. Where you are. What holds you up. You will learn the art of silence. High on the wire. High among the crowd.

Proceed with caution. Balance is for a lifetime. You must bear some responsibility. You must not look down.

WARNING: BALANCE IS FOR A LIFETIME

I
THE TIGHTROPE ARTIST'S LAMENT

She's convinced it's her own fault, really. That's the truth. No matter what she says. All of it. She blames herself for all of it. The bad things that keep happening to her. She doesn't know why. But she thinks it's because she's curious. Even at the kindergarten they said she asked too many questions. About everything. So she started to fight instead.

Getting her to do things used to be easy. Like taking candy from a baby. Or giving it in her case. She'd take anything she was offered. And she'd go anywhere you asked. She wanted everything. Hugs or kisses or answers to questions. Or even that play among the tangled sheets. With its kisses inside her mouth. Its hands along her body. When she was so easy to trap.

Now she doesn't want to be curious anymore. She's just scared. Scared all the time. Mostly scared except when she's angry. That's why I came to help her. Because they keep trapping her anyway. She doesn't know how to tell them to stop. To tell them it makes her feel bad. Maybe she's afraid they will go away altogether, the way her father did. Maybe she thinks that would be worse. Even if I'm here.

It's not so scary when she can talk to someone. When she has someone to play with. Who can take her mind off what's happening. We have our own kind of play. And a wonderful language. We whisper in it together. We have long conversations. And we write in it too. She's a good writer now. She makes beautiful titles for her pictures.

I can't help wishing she felt better, though. She says she used to. That her body felt good. That it didn't itch all over right under the skin, and that she enjoyed taking her clothes off. She says it felt good to have baths with her brother, and for someone to come and wash her. Even peeing in the tub felt good.

They both did that. And farted. So they could watch the bubbles. Though he did it more. Peeing out of his pee-nis, she used to say. Then one day she took his legs and whipped them up over his head while he was doing it and he peed in his face, and she ran away. All the way down the stairs laughing, while he peed over the banister after her. But she says that was fun. And that there was no harm in it.

It's not like that now. Even with her brother. I don't know what happened. Now she fights more than she runs and jumps. And she doesn't want anyone to bathe her. Or to touch her. And she doesn't like hugs and kisses unless she's really upset. And sometimes not even then. She just huddles in the back of her closet, and we talk. She's afraid they would notice something if they came too close. Then everyone would know what the ones who trap her know. Maybe then they would all make her do bad things. So she's ashamed of everything. You should have seen her the time she got ringworm. She was sure she got it because she was bad. How bad I am, how bad I am, she whimpered to me. Then she told her mother she hadn't scratched any place, she hadn't touched them. There are no more, Mom, I haven't touched myself she said. She wanted to save herself the examination, especially inside her underwear. When she would close her eyes and whisper to me. Completely still. Like she was saying a prayer. Just the way she is when the bad things happen.

She waited days before she told anyone, looking and looking in the mirror downstairs for hours, concentrating on the first one on her cheek, a red spot that she watched grow bigger and bigger. Until it became a ring. Then she tore at it. Because she knew they would see it then. And she was sure that circle on her face had come just to show the world what was wrong with her. That it was a secret brand that only the bad received. That everyone could read. And by then she had them all over. From all that scratching to make the first one go away. So she didn't even want to go out until they were gone.

Then when she got the sore inside her mouth, way back on her gum, she didn't tell anyone at all. She knew she didn't have to. She knew they couldn't see. And she didn't even care how bad it tasted. Or that it always felt so squishy when I touched it, as she let its liquid ooze out into her mouth. She thought she deserved that. Bad tastes for bad girls who do bad things.

She's the same way about going to the doctor. She always calls me to come help her when she goes. It's one of the times I get to go outside. When she points out the grass by the edge of the sidewalk, or the caterpillars. And I tell her how lovely they are. Sometimes we even sit down and rest. And I sing a little song in her ear. Or recite a poem. Help her play pattycake. The last time she lagged behind and got her new shoe caught in the mud. She tried to look down into the pit where they're starting to build a new apartment building, while I balanced on the edge. Anything is better than thinking about the needle. Or even worse, the moment when the doctor will look down there, opening that place between her legs, to see if there's any white stuff, or any stains on her underwear.

It usually goes okay if she doesn't scream. Or moan and groan and throw herself around so that they have to hold her down. Or carry her while she yowls and kicks. That usually doesn't happen until she gets to the doctor's office. When she goes completely out of control. I just hope they don't take her back to that other doctor. The one who makes her play with blocks. And asks all those questions. To try to get me to come out. As long as they don't do that.

I think she needs me too much to ever let that happen. Though I'm not always so sure. I help her a lot when the bad things happen. It doesn't matter who else is there. Her brother and his friends, or the boys down the block, or her uncle, or the men downstairs. I can even talk to her when she's scared at night, or when she plays with her dolls, though it's harder for me when she starts talking about her body. About how it all proves how bad she is. Sometimes I just want to tell her to shut up.

Because even the shots prove that. It doesn't matter that everyone else gets them too. Even her brother does. Though she gets more. These are blood tests, they say. To see if you are all right yet. But that scares her worse. It's in my blood, she howls. Deep inside where they'll never get it out. She forgets that she was sick for a long time, and that she's gotten better.

Or how much fun it was to play on her bed, by ourselves, when no one else was around to bother her. Even if the medicine did make her dizzy. And me lose my balance. She thinks that the tests mean she will start to rot soon too. Just like my gum, she says. Just like those things I see at night. The ones you make me look at. And that's true, too.

Sometimes I do torment her. Sometimes I even agree that anyone who thinks she's so bad deserves to have bad things happen. That's what her brother's friend tells her.

When you're bad you're bad. And everything else follows naturally. Except that he thinks he's bad, too. And the only bad thing that's happened to him is those glasses he has to wear. He's blind without them. The rest of them he just does. But I guess that makes you bad too. It's funny that way.

Mostly I just do the things she asks me to. That are just like the things they do with her. The ones she wants them to do with me now. Like getting down under her mother's bed where we can see the old springs all covered with dust, while she plays with herself down between her legs the way they ask her to. Only when she does it herself she still tries to make herself feel good. She doesn't pretend she isn't there.

Sometimes it does feel good for a while. Until her whole body seems to itch and hurt again and she wants to explode and tear at herself, and she imagines those things. The ones I torment her with later. Like seeing her body painted the way her mother's was after that operation, all red from belly button to halfway down her legs, when she watched her from the bed. Then she imagines herself pinched and prodded. While lots of people touch her. All dressed in white like doctors sometimes. Or she remembers the old cigarette butt being stuck up there between her legs.

Once she had me imagine she was being cut up, that the springs were twisting around her and trapping her and poking into her and opening her up and making her part of the bed. Only that went out of control. And it really scared her. Like the rotting sometimes does. When she really starts to scream. Then she thinks I do it on purpose. The way they do. That I enjoy seeing her like that.

She thinks it proves there's more wrong with me than there is with her. I don't think I believe that. Even if I don't remember being a baby the way she does. You know where babies come from but you don't know where you come from, she chants at me. But I still don't believe what she says. It's not true. That I just arrived one day. Just because she called me in that language we both speak. Or that I wasn't anywhere at all before I was here. I think she got me instead of the little sister her mother got rid of when she had that operation. I think I come from a circus. She found me in a circus. And brought me home. I think I was the tightrope walker.

She used to love to go to the circus with her father. I don't think I ever met him. Maybe I saw him at the circus once, but that's all. When they would sit way high up in the last rows. At the same level as the trapeze or those women who spin around on ropes by their teeth. Or the highest high wire acrobat. And she would laugh and clap. And insist on being bought one of those thin plastic Kewpie dolls. Then she would go home and draw. All those women balanced in high and difficult places. And write underneath them, in letters just like the ones we use. In a language just like the one we speak.

That's why I think that's where I'm from. I must have been a baby tightrope walker. I must not remember. The way there are so many things that she does not remember. There must be things I forget too. Like being a baby. Or having wonderful soft pillows, or towel rides along the floor. Or the circus. All those bright colours. And how I looked down onto the crowd.

I help her learn it all sometimes, though. Maybe that's why I was chosen to come here. To teach her those things. Because the tightrope act always was her favourite. So I help her do it. Even if we don't have a rope we have a fence in the backyard. Made of wire with metal tubing along the top. We can pretend the tubing is a rope. And I can help her balance. Walking along with her hands held out from her sides.

She does well most of the time. Even if there was the one time she fell. That was very bad. I started to think about one of those awful times and she noticed and she stopped paying attention and she fell. Just like that. And hit the concrete with her mouth.

She knocked out a tooth. That was the bad part. She said it was my fault. You see, you're the one, she said. You're the bad one. And she shut me up in the dark. Until I had to send her those awful visions again. They were perfect for when they gave her that gas and she saw all those colours. When they tried to put the tooth back in. Visions to make her remember how much she needs me.

It worked. She took me out of the dark so we could play together. And whisper in the closet. Only they made her think I was even badder. See the things you do, she said. See. I wasn't like this before you came along.

So now she makes me do all the bad things by myself. Circus people are good at that, she says. Standing around without any clothes. Or being touched all over. Circus people are good at that. They're pro-mis-cu-ous. And she writes it in the language we speak together. Though she never draws the bad things or says them out loud. I'll make you come out, if you mention any of it she says.

Then she tells me it's all my fault. That's her favourite thing now. It's all your fault, she says. Then she tells me that she can make me come out if she wants. But that's just to scare me. And it doesn't anyway. That's not what I'm scared of. Not really. I just tell her that to reassure her when we go to that doctor. Don't make me come out. I'll never come out, I say. But it's really like Br'er Rabbit saying Don't throw me in the briar patch.

I like it when I get to come out. As long as I don't have to talk to the others. When I can rest up in the corners of rooms. On lampshades or dusty chandeliers. I can try my balance on the mouldings, or slide down the wires the pictures hang from. And land on my feet with a bow. While I hardly notice what's going on around me. I just concentrate on my work. I'm good at all that. I'm a tightrope walker for sure. I know that now.

But it doesn't make me like the bad things. It doesn't even make me like to watch them. And they're not my fault. I didn't make her feel the way she does. And I don't make her scratch at herself or tear at her hair. Even try making cuts in her skin with knives. Little cuts where the ringworms were. I don't do that. And even if I helped her under the bed it was still her suggestion. She said she needed it. I prefer to climb trees. Or to walk on the fence.

She even threatens me about that now. Soon I'm going to be able to do it all by myself, she says. Then I won't need you. You can just keep doing all those bad things you like so much all by *yourself*, she says. You by yourself and me by myself, she sings.

And even when I say I don't want to, she just says, Shhhh, and goes back to hurting her dolls. And secretly doing to them the bad things she pretends not to remember. The ones she now says are all my fault. That's what really frightens me. That if she doesn't need me anymore she'll just shut me up in the dark except to do those bad things. And that's all I'll get to do. Bad things all by myself.

She seems to be able to do that. To keep me in here. Where there's no light at all. But I can't do it to her. All I can do is send her those visions. Or whisper in her mind. And then she blames it all on me. See how bad you are she says. Even as she tears at her body. Or her dolls. See how bad.

Sometimes I think I really was a baby once. Sometimes I think I'm the one who went to the circus and had those baths. Sometimes I think that. Sometimes I think she's lying to me. She can't ever have liked that body she mistreats so much. That she's so ashamed of. But she just laughs. No, no, she says. This is your picture she says. And she shows it to me on a piece of yellow paper. Here on the tightrope, with the umbrella. A little girl balanced on one foot. And she laughs. And we talk about the circus. And we're both happy.

Then suddenly she says, But I'm going to make you go away. And she takes a black crayon. And she rubs it all over my picture. Holding it in her closed fist. And then she tells me she's going to shut me in the dark. For a long long time, she says. Because of all those bad things I do. People who do bad things get shut in jail she says. They get punished. They go where they can't tell their awful stories to anyone. And she laughs. And she presses harder with the crayon. Harder and harder. Sometimes I go away then. Sometimes she doesn't even have to tell me to.

She's almost as good at reading and at writing as she is on the fence now. I used to help her with that too. But the last time they made her go see the doctor with the blocks she wouldn't even let me do that. She wants to write in that other language now. The one the doctor can read. To show off. It makes the doctor smile at her. And she wouldn't even let me play with the blocks.

I told her I wouldn't come out, no matter how many trick questions they asked. That's the point you know. You have to be careful with the questions. That you might answer, Oh yes when I was in the circus. Or, When they put a cigarette butt up there, or something. Instead of how much you like your brother, and your mother's new boy-friend. You might say he's better than the last one who kicked her head open. So that you could see all the way into her brain. To what she was thinking. That kind of thing.

I know she doesn't have to worry about me, even if I remember more about the bad things by now than she does. She doesn't have to shut me up to stop me from telling. Because I'm smart. I'll never come out. Not to where they can see me. And I'll never open my mouth. Even if I did perch up in the doctor's bun. And walked, balancing, along the tight wires of her hair. They never even knew I was there.

But she's different now. She's the one who's changed. She's determined to get into that special school. Determined to get all the answers right so they accept her. She even tries to stop fighting. To smile more. She thinks that if they do, it will be safe to be curious again. And maybe she won't have to do any more bad things. Or send me to do them.

You won't get to do what you like to do most, she says. Maybe you'll get to stay in the dark instead, she says. Maybe I'll meet other little girls, she says. Girls that aren't like you, she says. Who don't like bad things, she says.

I won't be able to let you meet them, you know. They'd think you were dirty. A dirty pro-mis-cu-ous circus person. So you'll have to stay shut up. Shut up, shut up shut up. Now it's your turn to shut up, to be shut up, shut up shut up, she says. And she giggles. And then she relents for a moment and takes me for a walk. And we talk to the ants and the ladybugs. And last week there was a praying mantis who spoke our language.

Sometimes when she's nice like that I still try to explain. To make her understand how unfair she is. That she can't just shut me up after all I've done for her. I start off quite casual. As if I was speaking about the weather. I didn't make you feel this way, you know, I try to whisper. I didn't do it. I didn't feel ashamed of getting ringworm from petting a cat, I say. And I didn't want you to feel that way either, I add, to help make it better.

But she just pretends she doesn't hear. And she sings a little song. Rot in Hell, if you tell, something like that. Something I didn't teach her. And then when I try to scream over the noise, she just sticks her fingers in her ears.

I do wish she would listen. Really, I do. She should remember who did this to her. She should. Who made her feel this way. Which one of them it was. And when. Who started it. She should try as hard as she can.

Because I don't want to have to be the one who is scared all the time now. Or to think I'm bad. I want to go to the country when she goes with that special school. I want to see the cows and the goats. And climb the trees and play on the swings. I want to show all those other little girls how well she can balance, walking on the fences for miles.

Please, remember, I scream at her. I didn't do it. You know that. It's not fair. I don't want to be trapped. No, please. I don't. Forever in the dark.

Go away, she replies. Some day I won't remember you at all.

WARNING: BALANCE IS FOR A LIFETIME
(instructions to hold the tightrope artist)

Proceed with caution. Balance is for a lifetime. You will bear some responsibility. It will be hard to know. It will be hard not to get mixed up. Do you hold the Kewpie doll do you hold the umbrella can you feel your hands where are your feet.

Proceed with caution. You will bear some responsibility. Everything will happen here. Far below the ponies will circle the ring the bareback riders will perform somersaults the clowns will be shot from cannons the lion tamer will put her head in the lion's mouth the magician will saw his assistant in half he will forget to put her back together.

Proceed with caution. Balance is for a lifetime. The tightrope walker will not notice. The tightrope walker will notice only the wire. You will be the tightrope walker. You must stare into space. You will hold the tightrope walker. You must bear some responsibility. You will learn the art of silence.

Proceed with caution. Balance is for a lifetime. You must not look down.

WARNING: IT WILL NOT BE EASY HERE

II
THE TIGHTROPE ARTIST'S REVENGE

She's grown so old now. That's what I don't like. I never expected this. Not ever. Not from someone who used to say that she would never stop climbing trees. No matter what happened. Or how many bad things she had to do. That was one thing she would never stop: she would always climb trees. And now I discover she's given up everything. She hardly ever moves quickly. She just sits around thinking. Thinking and thinking. I can hardly believe it. That this is what adults are like.

It hasn't been as bad as I thought. Even if I haven't been around too many places since the bad things finally stopped happening. By then the dark seemed a comfort. Though I don't know what happens there. Sometimes I think I play. With blocks or with crayons. Even with the old pictures she used to make, the ones from the circus. Sometimes I think I dream, beautiful coloured dreams. But I don't really know. Sometimes I don't remember myself at all.

There are some periods of brightness. When the light filters in with visions of places I can balance. As precious as the porcelain dolls in the windows of stores we could never afford. As soft or as fierce as the stuffed animals in F.A.O. Schwarz. The ones we would make stories about, times we could laugh and rest. The only problem is she never talks to me about those places, not the way she once did.

She does call me sometimes. Though I don't think she does that on purpose, not anymore. She's too much like Wendy in Peter Pan. So grown up and dignified. She refuses to remember where the border crossings are located, even if it's not "on until morning," and never has been. For us, on until morning was just a way to get through the bad things.

So even when she wants me to play with her, she doesn't know how to ask. She hardly remembers our special language at all. She must do something without thinking to make things change. It's like waking up after the gas, all bright colours, and suddenly I find myself there talking to her. Telling her things. What I think, or what she should do. I don't know how she understands me, but those times she seems to. She screams too, calling out to me, but even then, I don't think she hears herself.

I always come. Just the way I always did. Because it usually happens when she remembers the bad things. That's happening more and more with the new doctor she's going to. This one doesn't make her play with blocks. With him she just sits and talks: that's what adults do. They make up stories with pictures in their minds as bright as books. That's the only fun part of getting to know them. Their bodies are useless.

The only thing she does with any grace at all is ski. The mountains where she goes are beautiful, and the movement almost as pretty as the trapeze artists. Only she hardly does that at all. She calls it being responsible. She has work to do, she says, talking to herself. A family of her own to take care of. I just call it being tired.

The blocks were much more fun than this droning on and on. I told her how much I hate the new doctor but she doesn't seem to care. I know she heard me. I just know it. It was a very short statement. Very clear. I hate that man I said. And she flinched. So I know she's just pretending she didn't. She's just the same as always that way. Though she doesn't stick her fingers in her ears.

But she's gotten used to this. Process, she calls it. This process. It must be what they taught her at that special school. To enjoy building block towers with her words. And then looking at them from all sides. Before knocking them down. Without moving a muscle, except in her mouth. They both seem to enjoy that.

The difference is that he knows what he's doing. He's better at this than the rest of them. He knows just what to ask, while she doesn't even think she's saying anything. Maybe she's grown stupid as well as clumsy. Or maybe she doesn't remember. How dangerous talking can be. How ashamed she would be if it all came out.

I remember. I remember very well. How hard she worked at keeping it all inside. It's just harder for me to remind her now. To give her a clear picture of what that was like. The way it's difficult for her to recognize me.

So I just listen to them talk. To the way they go on and on. It's boring. Even if I'm starting to pick up a lot of new words. And to talk the way she does. At least a little. Maybe that means I'm starting to grow up. I'm not sure I want that.

There is one thing I've noticed that's better than all the things I could do before. More powerful even than the visions I used to send her. Something amazing. Though I didn't invent it. She did. So it's her fault. Her problem. Not mine.

I don't even think she knows she did it. What it meant to tell me to go away. Go away you dirty pro-mis-cu-ous circus person, she said. And that put me in charge of the memories. They're mine now. And she's never even guessed what it means.

Listen closely, it's a secret. It means: I can tell her anything. Anything I want.

She'll have to believe what I say. She won't know how not to. Or when. Her body still remembers something that makes her want to tear at it. To take razor blades or knives, the little ones with the sharpest blades, and cut herself up, or at least leave marks. She still wants signs along her arms and legs of the shame she can't help feeling. Even if she can't remember where it comes from. Any more than she can remember carving those same signs into her dolls. But it lets her know something happened. Something she should maybe leave alone.

Right there at the edge of memory, beyond the small tiny bad things she can recall when she tries. That kiss inside her mouth, that time with the cigarette butt, the hands on her body that just didn't quite seem right, or the way she sat naked on the chair.

And I can tell her more. Things that will seem right. Things her body can feel. Things she made me do. I can make an image of looking directly at that place between a man's legs. Before I had to put her mouth there. And then the smell will come back. Not just of that thing but of the room, the pantry with its old wood and its old copper sink. That dripped until the sink turned green and the smell of copper was always in the room. She will remember that, and her nostrils will flare, and it will all become real. All of it except me.

But she will know that it's true. Just as she won't know where she is for a moment. Her head will feel light the way it did when they gave her those drugs, and she will shake her head and shake it, but the image won't go away. Not until she says, Oh God there's more, I didn't know there was more. And then after that I can tell her whatever I want.

That she was so-do-mized or forced to admin-is-ter oral

sex. She loves those big words now. They use them a lot in that doctor's office. Big words that you can balance on, like the edge of a razor blade, that stop you from feeling the cut of what really happened. I can watch her trying to do that. String the wire between the blocks in her mind. She makes her voice very flat. Very smooth. It doesn't go up and down the way mine does. But she always falls off anyway. Because she loses track. The way she did when she fell off the fence. Then she starts to whimper. And rock back and forth.

I never did that. It didn't matter how bad it got. Even when I walked along the picture frames as I felt that man's hands, her mother's boy-friend, the one who kicked her mother's head in, reaching up under her nightgown and playing with her. Maybe even attempting to rape her. I could say that too.

That's not a big word, it's a little one. I didn't have to learn that word from the doctor. It doesn't protect you from anything. I learned it from her brother's friend. A long time ago. Not that he ever did it, he just talked about it a lot. And looked at me. Maybe I'll tell her that too. Or that her mother was sleeping next to that man. Too drunk to know.

She really hated him. Sometimes lying in her bed at night, she can smell him. Only she doesn't know where it comes from. The smell or the hate. If it's what he did to her in the kitchen or on the bed or just the fact that one day he took her for a haircut in her blue jeans and they cut her hair, in a crew cut just like a boy's. She remembers that clearly. It was another mark of shame. Something that set her apart. That and her torn pants. It made her different from the other pretty little girls. Maybe she did want to be a boy too. Maybe that's part of the shame. And fighting so much. Maybe she wanted to grow one of those things between her legs that got to be boss of the bad things. That made you feel big instead of cut up. At least that's what she thought.

Sometimes she would pretend to be a boy when she tormented her dolls. Or with her brother and his friend. She would be a boy like them and it was just me who was the girl who got to do bad things. Dirty, dirty, dirty. Shame, shame, shame, she would say then. Because it was all my fault.

But she knew she was shameful too. Wanting what she could never have. She fought really hard then. Beating people up. She was good at that. Then she would tell me about lace dresses. And she would dress me in them, in our minds.

She still does that sometimes when she has sex. Both the lace dresses and the pretending she's a boy. She doesn't think about what it means. Only that it's fun. A fantasy she says. She only pretends she's herself when she makes love. There's a difference. I've learned that recently too.

I could tell her about her uncle, if I wanted. The one with the smile like the wolf in *Little Red Riding Hood.* Or about all the roomers who lived upstairs from time to time, and all the others who drank downstairs again and again. Like walking through a field of grabbing hands. There's all of them and so many of them, that even I get confused. I can't always tell the difference between what's real and what she made me imagine, there under the bed.

I think I might even hint that her father was just as bad as the rest. It won't matter that I never knew him. For all I know that's why. Maybe he's the one who started it all. It's really hard to tell. That's the part I could never get hold of either. But if I do that, it should throw her badly. He could be a skull with rotting hands screaming, No. Don't look. Not at me. No. I don't want you to remember. Maybe that would make her stop.

I shouldn't have to tell her what a bad idea all this looking is. She should already know. If not from before, then from right now. She knows what happens when she goes to see her friends, the ones who are so much like the nice girls she wanted to meet at that school. She sometimes shows them her journal. That's what she calls it now, instead of a diary. I liked the diary better, it was bound in blue leather and had a little gold key.

Not that the lock made her feel safe. Even years after she stopped talking to me, she would still only write about the bad things in our special code. The one she can't decipher anymore. And then she would pretend they hadn't happened at all. Dear Diary and that special pen she saved for talking about the boys she had met, with their sweaty palms, in junior high.

Only now she's trying to write it all out, trying to get all the details into this plain old notebook that she carries everywhere. The pages are already stained and dog-eared as she opens it again and again trying to find the textures of the things she doesn't know. She works at it painstakingly. Day after day. Pressing her pen hard into the page. The way she did when she covered me up with black crayon. She doesn't seem to know bad things aren't hidden there. Under the surface of the page.

She always shows it to one of those friends when she's done. Look what I've discovered, she says, pointing to the blue scribbled words. Look at how I'm putting this together. And she talks about how she plans to type it up, maybe she'll even publish it, maybe that will help make it all real. Maybe then she can come to terms with it. That's what she says.

Her friend remains silent for a minute. This is what always happens. Then she shakes her head. This is very private, she says. Very difficult. Only it sounds like Shsh. The way I always remember her saying, Shsh. A pained expression on her face.

But her friend smiles then. It's a quiet smile. Sweet. Pitying. Not like the new doctor, but like the old one with the blocks. Who always looked at her and said, That's good dear. You're obviously very bright. Then told her to be different. The way her mother's friends did. Or her aunt.

If you keep doing these things, saying these things, you'll worry your mother, they would say. She has enough to worry about, don't you think. She's not very well, you know. That's what they called the drinking. And you have enough things to do. Good things. Wonderful things. You can be a good little girl. I know you can. You don't have to do bad things to get attention. And she would shiver. Even if they didn't mean the same kinds of bad things.

That's what her friend does. First she says, This is wonderful. You're obviously onto something here. Then she tells her she has to be careful. This friend understands. But her *other* friends might not. They might be worried. Or worse. She might give them cause to worry about *her*. And it's almost like the friend is pointing.

After that the friend calls that writing dangerous. Dangerous material. You should stop forcing yourself to look at it, she says. Maybe you're not ready, you don't know what might happen as a result. It's too potent. Maybe you'll just find it all too much. And I do want you to stay with us, you know.

And then the friend pats her hand. I don't want you to, well, you know, to break down.

Or sometimes she talks differently. Or maybe that's another one. Who says, There's a lot of this stuff around. Everyone's doing it. And she doesn't mean bad things. She means writing about bad things. You're so original. Do original work. You should take on something else. You'd think women were nothing but victims. It might make it hard for people to take your other work seriously, for them to hear the other *important* things you have to say.

I think the only good place to be when bad things happen is far away. I think that's what they're saying. It's certainly what I learned. That's why I liked the picture frames so much. And the mouldings. They were always good places to be. Up so very high.

So maybe bad things are good as long as they stay on the page. Someone else's page. Where they can never come too close. Or make you dirty too. When you read about far away bad things it's en-light-en-ing. If you listen carefully, you get to understand. And feel sorry. When you do bad things, it's hard to believe there isn't something wrong with you. No one has to listen to you then. They just feel sorry.

I think that's the way it goes. Maybe I haven't grown up enough to understand the trick yet. Like I don't know where the rabbits come from that the magician pulls from the hats. Maybe I'm missing something.

At least they don't treat the far away bad things they read about the way her brother's friend did those magazines with pictures of bad things he always brought over. He rubbed them with his fingers. And let his face get red. They just roll that word around in their mouths as they turn the pages. Even her pages. They love that word.

This is very en-light-en-ing, BUT, they say. The longest word is the but.

It's when she hears that but that she starts to hear what she used to tell me. It's like the word gets longer and longer until she hears, You ought to be ashamed. You ought to be ashamed. YOU OUGHT TO BE ASHAMED. Over and over. And she doesn't hear en-light-en-ing either. She hears pro-mis-cu-ous.

It's funny what happens then. Since she can't put her fingers in her ears, grown-ups don't do that, she kind of goes away from them. And her whole world turns grey. Except for the blue words on the white page. So it's not like me going into the light, but like her coming into the dark with me.

I'm sure that if she knew I was here she would get even by shouting. And chanting her little chants. Go to Hell if you tell, things like that. She would probably call me a dirty pro-mis-cu-ous circus person again, and say I wrote all those words there when she wasn't looking, even if I don't know how to write that language. I'm only just learning to speak it well. To sound grown up.

Only she thinks she's all alone and she has to take it all on herself, just the way she did when I first met her. When she felt so ashamed. When she was so sure it was her own fault. That's the way she is now. Trying to call that doctor and looking at all the knives she has in her kitchen and lining up the pills in her medicine cabinet. Before she goes into her closet and tears the clothes off the rack, and retreats to the very back, and pulls them on top of her, and sits in there, her head pillowed on her arms, and screams and beats her head against the wall while she cries and cries.

I spend that time with her. The way I did when I first came from the circus. I know I could laugh at her if I wanted to. See what you've done, I could say. See how stupid you are. See what those nice girls *really* think of you. You were right all along.

Shame, shame, shame, I could chant. Dirty, dirty, dirty. But I don't. I'm better than that.

And besides, it's then she's willing to listen to me. Or at least to try. Though mostly she just hears a vague babbling no matter how hard she tries. That's why I usually just cry with her and send her images. I don't try for memories then. I do pretty pictures full of light. The kinds she finds in her dreams. The kinds I find in mine. That have made me like her so much, the times I've gotten to see her, even with everything else she's done, all these years. The kind that remind me of the things we shared. The fence and the dolls and the pictures of the circus and the tightrope. The way I still love it when she skis. That's why I send her visions of the mountains.

Beautiful in blue and white, mostly blue and white, the long views from way up at the top. But in green too, green and brown, and full of air and silence: the spaces that I love. I think that will take her mind off her shame, off all her difficulties. Just like it did when I asked her to watch me climbing along the edges of the mouldings. Or the way her friends tell her to get into something different, to take her mind off her problems.

It doesn't work very well. Not that she isn't comforted. Not that she doesn't finally fall asleep exhausted watching the mountains far below. It's that she won't stop.

She won't even believe me about that doctor. She thinks she's found a noble cause. Made more noble by her friends' dislike. She thinks their disapproval will purify her. Like a trial by fire. If she can just bear it long enough to find out. She carries those words around with her. To Find Out. Like a standard a knight could carry. Curiosity is her motto. The way they taught her at that school.

She thinks her life is one of their puzzles, the kind she always loved to solve, the kind that brought her so much praise. She thinks it's just a matter of getting all the pieces in the right order. That everyone will praise her when she does. Even her friends will praise her. And recognize what she's done. Returning healed from her quest. They won't believe she's dirty and shameful anymore. She won't believe it herself.

Maybe I could have agreed with her once. Maybe I even wanted her to do that. The problem is I don't think she'll find out anything I don't already know. I just think she'll find me. And if you ask me, that's what this process is all about. Finding me. Blaming me. Doing it all again.

Not just letting me out, pushing me out. Letting that doctor insert a long fishing line down her throat. To pull me out wriggling so they can look at me all over. And I don't want anyone to do that anymore. Look at me like that. I'm tired of men doing that to me. I had enough of that a long time ago. I prefer the dark to being poked and prodded the way her brother's friends did, or that man, or all the others.

Even the way her mother did to her that time she got the ringworm. Or those people who thought they were helping. When she had to get her mother, drunk and singing. Off the subway. Making you stand there. With a smile on your face.

Besides, I'm probably ugly now. She's probably right about that. You can't do the things I've done, live the way I've lived, and not be ugly. Maybe I'm all covered in sores the way she was, only worse, because maybe they're cut and bleeding. Maybe I look the way she made me imagine her that time under the bed. Maybe my face is all contorted, and my body too, the springs twisting in and out. Or maybe it's all rotted away just like those images I used to send her. Just a stiff rotted twig, or skinny like an insect. Maybe I'd be able to do even less with it than she can.

I might not be able to balance on the furniture the way I used to, or in the doctor's hair, to make her laugh. If she laughed now, it would be to make me feel bad. I know that. Maybe she would even crush me like I really was a bug, before I could say anything. Just to hear my body pop, the way her brother and his friends liked to do with the big black beetles that got into the house.

I can't let her do that, can't you see. I just can't let it happen.

That's why I've decided I'll finally teach her a lesson. It's my turn now. I know I have the power. I've never even been able to shut her in the dark, but there's something I can do. I know that now. And I'm better than she is. I won't just do it for me. I'll make us both safe. That's what she really wants anyway. It's what she's always wanted. Not adventure. Not beautiful circus tricks: safety.

Sometimes that doctor takes her places when she goes to see him. Places inside her head. Visualizations he calls them. Guided visualizations. He's the guide. He takes her in and out of her old house. Things like that. But he's never taken her where she really wants to go. That's what I'll do.

He's asked her to try to recover the child she was. To go back to that. To enter that place, and to get her. He thinks it will make her whole. If she walks along a path and through a forest and out into an open space, where she can find herself playing. Only she never imagines it terrible the way it was, full of cold and shame and that awful sense of rotting. It's always that place in the country she went with that school, with its swings and its fences.

She sees herself as an up-set child, a vic-tim-ized child, a sorry child, a vi-olated child. She brings out all the big words for this one, going through them again and again, like those prayers her aunt used to say with those beads she carried. Because only one thing is important. And she's got to get it right.

She's got to make sure that child is dirty only on the outside. That the child she sees will be a child anyone would want to have, one you would just have to clean up a bit, to make her ready for the nicest girl to play with. The kind of child she convinced those little girls at that special school she really was: a lovely un-der-pri-vi-leged child. She chanted that too, once she heard the word. I'm un-der-pri-vi-leged, I'm not pro-mis-cu-ous, she used to say.

Such a bright and curious child would know it wasn't her fault if bad things happened to her. She would sigh a lot. And wait to be rescued. By nice people. Like the friends she has now. Or the person she likes to think she is.

That child wouldn't torment her body or her dolls. Not the one she built so long ago for the doctor with the blocks, the one she keeps building again and again with the blocks in her mind, even for this doctor now. The one she wants to see all crying and lonely inside that enclosure. Waiting for her. As if that prissy child hadn't had a companion all these years. Who knows better.

One time she's going to try to find that child. Maybe when she's alone, driving along a mountain road, or in city traffic, or walking in the park. Or maybe she'll just be sitting in her favourite attic room, doing what she does so much now, just thinking and thinking. When suddenly without hardly noticing it, she will start down that path again. Only when she sees the enclosure it's not that child she constructed like an erector set, it's not the one who pretended she never knew me, no: I'm the one who's going to be there. Me, the dirty pro-mis-cu-ous circus person, the one she let do all the bad things. I'm the one who will be playing there.

And I won't be crying. I'll be singing. And as she comes closer she'll be happy to see me. Because I won't be ugly. For the last time it will be my world and I will still be the tightrope walker and I will take a wide bow my arms held out beside me and I will hop up with my umbrella onto the very top of the fence that encloses me, something that erector set child would never be able to do, and I will balance there and I will walk. And the sun will glint off the spangles in my costume and it will shine all the colours of the rainbow and before she can even think to stop or call that other doctor she will climb up too and she will follow me with her clumsy adult body. And I will finally lead her along the fence the way I wanted to do so long ago.

Only it won't be the fence at that country place anymore. It will soon be a fence, and then a tightrope, not in the circus but in the mountains. Stretched from peak to peak so that we will be surrounded by sunlight. While below us there will stretch the forest and the river that leads far far away to the ocean. And her gaze will follow it, until it disappears into the mountains along the horizon. Her eyes fixed along the distant peaks as she will keep walking and walking, one foot in front of the other. Until there will come a moment just as we reach the top of the peak where the high wire ends on a small metal platform, a moment when I will turn and face her.

And maybe in that moment she will remember me, and maybe she will remember it all, and maybe then we will both know the whole story. But it won't matter whether she does or not because she will never write it in her journal. We will keep our little secret no matter what it is, because in that moment she will look down. And she will suddenly be afraid, and she will start to whimper, and she will remember that she is an adult, suddenly caught like a child in a world she doesn't understand, whose balance is not what it once was. And maybe she will even feel the front of her mouth, all that bridge work where her tooth was knocked out. And she will start to rock back and forth, and pretty soon she will fall.

But I'm not cruel, I told you that.

No matter how many bad things I've done or she's made me do, I would never let her fall alone. I will not laugh at her, or chant, clum-sy grown-up, clum-sy grown-up. I will jump forward from the place where I stand, perfectly balanced, my umbrella held high, and I will grab hold of her. And hugging each other tight we will fall, fall and fall, toward that river where it glints. The two of us, turning around and around, so very slowly, like little cartoon characters under my umbrella. And it will be that time before when we were happy, falling and floating, spinning and laughing, like the dust motes in her father's study when she first drew my picture. Suspended together. Forever in the sunlight.

Hello, I will say, Don't you remember me?

WARNING: IT WILL NOT BE EASY HERE
(instructions to hold the tightrope walker)

Proceed with caution. Balance is for a lifetime. It will not be easy here. You will bear some responsibility. It will be hard to know. It will be hard not to get mixed up.

You must think only of your breathing. You must not think about how it will end. Such a moment does not exist. When the tightrope walker reaches the platform and the audience begins to leave, she will turn and start back. The audience will be riveted. You will suffer only a brief intake of breath. There will be no way to imagine the end. There will be no way to know who you will be then.

Your feet will press the wire. Your hands will press the railing. You must think only of your breathing. You will learn the art of silence.

Proceed with caution. Something could happen now. The nature of the equipment is unclear. The act has no end. You must not look down. There is only the fall.

WARNING: YOU WILL BEAR SOME RESPONSIBILITY

III

THE FALL

WARNING: YOU WILL BEAR SOME
RESPONSIBILITY
(A checklist for the fall)

Proceed with caution. Since no model contains the words of instruction for weaving a safety net, this will be your job. And already there is little time.

To look elsewhere has made it easier to slip. To think of the net has made it easier to fall. In solving this problem you have increased your loss of balance. That is why it will be harder to know. Harder not to get mixed up.

You must bear some responsibility. You could have let go before you were ready. Before the net was in place.

WARNING: YOU MUST UNLEARN
THE ART OF SILENCE

≈

Sarah Murphy is a translator, interpreter, teacher, visual artist, social activist, and author of fiction. Her works include The Measure of Miranda *(1987),* Comic Book Heroine *(1990), and the* Deconstruction of Wesley Smithson *(1992). Her short fiction, essays, translations, and reviews (of both art and literature) have appeared in Canada, as well as in Australia and the United Kingdom. This piece is part of an upcoming cycle of work that deals with child sexual abuse. It first appeared in* Grain, *vol. 20, no. 1.*

Dreamwoman

KRISTJANA GUNNARS

Edith Hansen did not hear the telephone ring till she had
turned the wringer on the washing machine off. Finally all the
linen was pressed and ready to be put on the line, but the
wringer ground as loudly as an airplane at times. She jumped
up the three steps into the hall where the black telephone
stood on the old mahogany table her husband Unnsteinn had
inherited. By then the phone had stopped ringing. She untied
the scarf she had bound around her hair and wiped the sweat
from her face with it. Dampness from the washroom leaked
into the hall in clouds of steam. This work took all day. First
the linen was boiled, then washed, rinsed, pressed and finally
put on the line.

Edith went into the kitchen. It was two in the afternoon
but the lights were on for it was almost dark outside. Her
daughter Alfrún sat curled up on the window sill, staring out
the window at the raging storm. She joined her daughter and
they both looked out at the fomenting ocean below their
horseshoe-shaped street. The fence around the garden clat-
tered in the wind and pieces of tar paper from the roofs of small
houses shot across the street and into the hill north of the
house, where they were caught in the small boulders. All

around the deep moaning of draughts in the house and the high-pitched howling of the wind outside filled the air with an eerie sound. Five-year-old Alfrún pressed her forehead against the glass. In the fjord below, a trawler struggled its way into harbour, leaning sideways at the push of the storm.

A thin layer of ice had formed on the puddles in the road. All the streets in the village of Kópavogur were gravel and only the highway to Reykjavík had been paved. The village lay on a peninsula between two fjords and the ocean surrounded the town on three sides. Every time Edith looked out the window she was greeted by the coldness of a choppy sea, which showed only distance and insurmountability. This fishing place was a long way from the city of Copenhagen, where she grew up and where she nurtured dreams of a musical education. Dreams that had dissipated in the steam of the washing house and the roar of the storm.

Edith and Unnsteinn's house was small and painted tomato-red against the grey drabness of surroundings consistently overcast, with dark clouds and hostile soil where no green things grew. The garden was fair in size and the grass survived the summer, but the nasturtiums Edith religiously planted along the walkway every spring struggled against the odds until the end of July, and then faded.

She brushed her daughter Alfrún's straight, yellow hair back as they leaned against the window. Her older daughter Hildur was at school in the afternoons, and after Christmas Alfrún would be as well. Edith had reconciled herself to the slavery of housewifery in a developing country, but for her daughters she expected better opportunities, fewer hardships. Hildur would be a painter, yes, for she drew so well. Alfrún would be—it was too soon to tell about her, but perhaps the singer she herself had never had a chance to become. Even though her singing teacher in the Hvidovre school had expressly commanded her to study for the opera after her primary education.

"Will you look at that ship there," Alfrún whispered, "do you think it'll sink? It's completely on its side."

Edith stroked Alfrún's hair.

"Well, if they have trouble," she replied, "you see, they're so close to land that they can all be saved."

But she reassured her daughter without conviction. Hardly a day passed this season that the radio did not carry news of some fisherman overboard on the banks, or some trawler down.

As Edith was tying the scarf back around her hair in order to go back to the washroom and finish the linen, the telephone rang again. She went into the hall and picked up the receiver. The white cat sat on the table, looking out the long window into the back yard where the empty clotheslines flurried nervously in the wind.

"Hallo," Edith sang, as it was her habit to answer the phone in a lilting accent.

"Phone call from Denmark, one moment," the operator said brusquely, "madam go ahead."

A faint voice was audible on the other end. Edith felt that something was amiss, for her family in Denmark could never afford a long distance call.

"Edith?"

She recognized her sister's gentle, drawn-out voice.

"But Grethe," Edith began, "for goodness' sake!"

It was necessary to speak loudly, for the connection was poor.

"Unfortunately I don't have very good news today," her sister Grethe called into the line strainedly. "Mother has unfortunately passed away earlier today, she had been fighting pneumonia for the last week and then finally she succumbed to it."

"What?" Edith replied in disbelief. "What are you saying?"

She had no idea her mother had been ill.

"Yes, we have written but that was only three days ago and a letter takes at least two weeks to reach you, that you know. She went to the hospital that day, but there was nothing that could be done, you see. I am very sorry to bring you such news, Edith, that you know, and I am very sorry about mother."

"But good God," Edith stammered, at a loss for words. "But good heavens." She felt a choking sensation rise in her throat.

Grethe continued to talk. "I am very sorry about it. She had it so hard the last two days, her fever was very high and she didn't really know where she was or who we were. It was very sudden."

Edith no longer heard what her sister was saying. Images of her mother piled up in her mind in a confused jumble. Her mother with golden red hair, walking between shops on a Monday. Rye bread at the baker's, pork chops at the butcher's, butter in the milk shop. Her basket hung on her arm and she stopped to talk to Fru Nielsen across the way. Her mother on the bicycle, with cucumbers in the basket on the front handlebars. Then her mother bent over her and felt the back of her neck for fever, speaking softly. Her mother, too nervous to go with her brother Kaj in the ambulance, Kaj screaming at the top of his lungs. Of course, her mother was a little heavier in her later years. The hair was matted and more brown, cut short and curled. Her mother stood by the ironing board, waiting for the iron to heat up on the stove. She lit the gas flame on the new stove, beaming with a smile at the marvels of technology.

"And the funeral will be in three or four days," Grethe was saying. "We are not sure Edith, it is all so new you know. See what you can do."

"Yes," Edith answered absently, "yes I will. But this is terrible."

"So sorry, but you will try now and I hope it will be possible. I unfortunately have to stop talking, it is so expensive you know."

Edith found herself standing by the telephone in a stupor after replacing the receiver. Tears had begun to rain down her cheeks and she felt herself beginning to sob. Her eyes fell on the yard outside the window. The air was filling with large snowflakes that were blowing back and forth in confusion. While she had been on the phone, the ground had turned white in a thin layer of snow. It would be impossible to hang up the wash outside in this weather.

Turning she noticed Alfrún leaning against the corner wall at the end of the hall, with the edge of her sweater between her lips, as she always did when she was insecure. Edith tried to brace herself. Alfrún should not see her crying, so she turned away long enough to wipe her face and then put on a strained smile for her daughter. Alfrún asked no questions, she was never one to talk, but she looked at her mother uncertainly. Edith picked her up, brushed the bangs from her forehead, and said, "Grandma has had a bit of trouble out in Denmark, but I guess it's OK now."

Alfrún kept looking silently at her face until Edith's arms wound around her and hugged her close. "The ship out there didn't sink, did it now?"

"No," her daughter whispered.

Edith put Alfrún down again and tied the scarf on her head. It was just as well to continue working, she could think while hanging up the wash. The sewing machine that took up space in the hall was shut down, the lid closed and the cast-iron frame made it look like an imposing piece of furniture. The rubber ring between the pedal and handle-wheel stood idle. Sigrídur, the seamstress who sewed for Edith, only came twice a week and would not be there until Tuesday. If only she were here now, Edith could talk to her and tell her how she felt. It seemed appropriate to Edith's fate that the day she received news of her mother's death, January 15, 1953, she was alone, without comfort, doing the weekly wash in a steam-filled basement. If only that slim figure in her long black Icelandic outfit, the thin grey braids falling down from her little cap, concentrating over the sewing machine, if only she were here today.

For the next two days Edith and Unnsteinn went over the possibilities of a quick trip to Copenhagen for Edith to attend the funeral. No matter how they turned the problem over, it seemed impossible to make reality of. The weather this season was violent, as always in January when winter was in full force. Storms tore the roofs off houses, shredded storage shacks and fences, and blew those who ventured outside on foot into walls and lampposts. It was literally not possible to gain a firm footing. Freighters were stalled in the harbour, airplanes were grounded in the Reykjavík Airport, and transportation schedules went awry. Even if an airplane did take off for Kastrup in the next day or two, Unnsteinn reasoned, it would be a dangerous flight and a long one. She would be gone for at least a month, and who would take care of the girls? It was foolish to endanger one's own life because another had died, to Unnsteinn that was compounding the problem. In the end Edith acquiesced and resigned herself to being absent from her mother's burial, but throughout the weekend she kept the issue alive by questioning her husband about alternate possibilities.

It was on the Monday that the funeral was to take place. The family was gathered for breakfast in the little kitchen, the table set with tea and oatmeal, rye bread and cheese. Hildur, the older girl, was putting together a cardboard boat, replete with mast and rigging, concentrating with her tongue in the side of her mouth and her light brown hair falling into her face. Alfrún looked on in admiration, dangling her legs. Unnsteinn ate quickly and listened to the radio intently. Edith was fastidious and buttered everyone's bread. She was sorely pained this morning and clamped her lips together in an effort to hide her disappointment at still being in Iceland, on this day of all days. Unnsteinn noticed her grief and turned the radio off. As soon as he spoke, Edith broke into tears and stopped trying to hide it from her family.

"Your mother will go down whether or not you are there," he consoled her. "She is not alive to see you and your presence would alter nothing."

Edith did not reply but dried her cheeks with the corner of her apron. When Unnsteinn went to work, he patted her cheek and left her with a kind word.

That day Edith dissipated her grief by shopping in town and seeing her friends Eva and Blix, who came in from the town of Selfoss on a political errand. The two friends treated Edith to coffee and Blix's good humour got them all laughing.

"Things don't go the way they should half the time," Blix exclaimed in her loud voice, which always made people turn and look. "I've been convinced of that for ten years and see no reason to be optimistic. That's why we have so many political parties in Selfoss; they all think like me!"

"You know what you should do," Eva, whose voice sounded as though it came from behind a box of oranges, suggested, "you should sit down and knit a sweater, and remember not to stop until the sweater is done. By that time you will be thinking no more about your mother's funeral."

It was not until that night that the full extent of Edith's guilt feelings became evident to her. She woke up several times with a sense of alarm which she was unable to account for. At two in the morning she went into the kitchen and made a cup of tea in an effort to get her mind off her mother's burial that day. Unnsteinn, who always shared his wife's troubles, joined her, and the two of them sat in silence while the wind howled over the pitch-black ocean outside and screamed caught in the window frame.

An hour later they went back to bed. Edith tried to sleep but her ominous melancholy kept her from relaxing. What if people who are dead know everything? she thought. Suppose that when you die you really awaken into a complete knowledge of everything you left behind? If that were true, her mother would know she had not been to the funeral, that her oldest daughter had sent her away without saying good bye. Eventually Edith slept, but at six on Tuesday morning she awoke out of a dream with beads of sweat on her chest and the back of her neck. She put on her robe and went into Unnsteinn's study, which was off the dining room. The old oak desk he had inherited from his father was strewn with documents on drilling and bore holes. Stones Unnsteinn had gathered from geological expeditions into the Vestmannaeyjar Islands stood on the window sill. Edith sat down at the desk and looked out at the stars. The weather had calmed somewhat and the cloud cover had blown over, revealing a heaven littered with specks of light.

Her dream was vivid in her memory. She was walking on the black sand on the southern Icelandic coast, where she had gone with Unnsteinn on a geological expedition. While the men were scanning the sands, Edith walked along the ocean. It was dark and overcast, and the ocean seemed silver in the grey afternoon. A wind was blowing off the sea and she clasped her coat tightly to keep warm. As she walked, she noticed a figure in the distance and thought it was unusual to find a traveller in this coastal desert. Coming nearer, she was surprised to see it was a woman in a long white dress. The woman wore no coat and did not seem cold, but walked smoothly towards her, as if it were the height of summer.

The two women approached each other and Edith found, to her amazement, that the woman was very young. The stranger's long red hair waved gently in the wind and her ankle-length dress was covered in lace. When they came face to face Edith discovered to her horror that she was looking at her own mother. It was not the mother she had known most of her life, with matted short hair and tired features, but rather her mother when she was very young, maybe sixteen or seventeen, and she was wearing the confirmation dress she was photographed in. How beautiful she looked, Edith thought. What had life done to her? The young woman smiled gently and placed her small hands on Edith's arm.

"I wanted to come and tell you," Edith's mother said to her, "not to worry. I know you could not come to my funeral, it was not possible to travel yesterday. But I want you to know I understand." As Edith began to shiver, she awoke.

She did not tell Unnsteinn of her dream, but let on she had slept well until eight. She saw him off on his daily hike into Reykjavík and tidied up after breakfast. Hildur was at the table putting the finishing touches on her cardboard boat and Alfrún was walking a miniature dollhouse doll around the scraps of paper discarded by the shipbuilder. During the morning Edith dusted the living room and spent a couple of hours weaving on her loom. She was earning extra income for spring by selling hand-woven scarves in the tourist shops. At noon she fed her daughters and Hildur went to school, leaving Alfrún as usual at the kitchen window, envying her fortunate elder for the distinction of a schooling career.

At two, Sigrídur, the seamstress, appeared with her constant smile and soft voice. Edith took Sigrídur's coat and shoes and showed her the linen that was to be sewn into pillow cases. Soon the sewing machine wheel was spinning and Sigrídur's foot rocked back and forth on the pedal. Alfrún dressed in her boots and sweater and went outside on some mysterious errand. The weather was good and the ice had melted off the puddles in the street.

At four-thirty Sigrídur took her usual coffee break and Edith sat down with her in the kitchen. After buttering some bread and pouring coffee for the seamstress, Edith opened her anxieties to the old woman.

"Sigrídur," Edith began, "there is something I want to talk to you about. My mother died last Friday in Denmark."

"Jesus my own," Sigrídur broke in, "but this is sad. Now I am completely taken aback. Your mother. But she was just a young woman."

"Yes," Edith agreed, "she was fifty-two. But life was hard for her."

"That is nothing," Sigrídur asserted, "fifty is nothing. My sympathies are with you, my girl."

At the old woman's heartfelt manner, Edith again broke into tears and proceeded to tell the story of her mother's sudden death and her own inability to go to the funeral. Finally Edith told her about the dream she had the night before.

"And you know," Edith concluded, "I am really frightened. I have never felt like this before."

Sigrídur put her wrinkled hand on Edith's arm and began to reassure her. "Your mother appeared to you in a dream," the seamstress said, "and told you not to worry about it. Well don't worry about it then. Believe her. She understands."

For some reason Edith found the old woman's words comforting. She could not say she agreed that her mother had actually appeared willingly in a dream, but Edith found herself far calmer than before. She washed the coffee cups and listened to the old woman's humming at the sewing, the tassel of her cap thrown behind her back so it would not catch in the machine. The sun was making an effort to break through the clouds and in places the grey outside glittered like silver. Edith stood at the window with the towel in her hands.

Out by the street she saw Alfrún kneeling by a huge puddle that rippled as the girl touched the water. On closer inspection, Edith saw that Alfrún was floating Hildur's newly made cardboard boat in the muddy brown water. The boat would soak in the water, come apart and be destroyed. Those girls would have a row when Hildur came home and found her boat demolished, and Alfrún would hide in a closet somewhere until Hildur got over it. As Edith wiped her hands, she instinctively began to sing softly to herself.

~

Kristjana Gunnars teaches English and Creative Writing at the University of Alberta. She is the author of several books of poetry, including Carnival of Longing *(1989) and* The Night Workers of Ragnarök *(1985). She has also written two cross-genre prose fictions,* The Prowler *(1989) and* The Substance of Forgetting *(1992), as well as a memoir concerning her father,* Zero Hour *(1991). Aside from editing and translating, she is at work on finding a place for the poetic voice in prose. She has published two collections of short stories:* The Axe's Edge *(1983) and* The Guest House *(1992). Her current interest is a gathering of reflections on Buddhism,* The Scent of Cedar.

Preparations

ROSEMARY NIXON

"You know something about catching shrimp?" the girl says. "Me, I catch the shrimp I want." She lifts her skirt as if to curtsy, swings it left to right.

Gordie watches the girl, dressed in a blue and white school uniform. Maybe fifteen. Her short hair clings to her scalp like all the girls' hair at Milundu school. The prefét has strict rules, Ndadia says. Will not allow the girls to grow their hair and waste study time fashioning elaborate braids.

"Eiii, Ndadia," the girl says. "You did not attend church this morning. The Citoyen Panza is angry. You will lose points in your school cahier." Ndadia snuffs. The girl looks at Gordie and laughs.

Ndadia says, "Let's fish, Gordie," and he and Gordie shed their clothes and sink to their chests in sweet cool mud. The girl too slips off her skirt. She wears nothing beneath. She turns to hang her blue skirt in the palm tree and Gordie sees her buttocks look wide and happy. The mud down the riverbank squishes.

"Eiii." The girl sinks to her chin. When she comes up her body hangs thick with mud. They all three, giggling, rub their bodies in its thickness, dig tunnels that begin to close the instant they are dug. The girl wades to the mud's edge, squats, and deftly draws up three small fish which she tosses into Gordie's pail. Then Ndadia squats and works, earnest, in happy silence. Gordie joins them, syphoning for fish and the odd shrimp.

"Enough," Ndadia says at length, looking at the sun.

"Come near, *mundele*," the girl says. Her legs are longer than Gordie's, and wider. Ndadia splashes into the river and drops to a swim. Ndadia is brave to swim alone. He believes a *nkita* lives in the water. It can steal your powers. The girl puts her hand out and touches Gordie's mud-crusted under-arm. Her hand moves down his side. They move into the palm trees' shade. The girl writes "Canada" across his chest and "groundnut" down his thigh. "Monsieur Lauber is my English teacher," she announces proudly. And slips both hands between his legs.

~

Gordie races through an overhang of trees and enters the sudden clearing of Lusekele village. The compound smells of lemons and mangoes and burnt goat hair. Ndadia squats before his house, chopping manioc with his coupe-coupe.

"*Mbote*, Ndadia."

Ndadia looks up, nods. A strip of hair has been shaved off the left side of his head. The Kunda family's monkey screeches, skitters up a tree.

"*Mbote*, Gordie."

"Caught speaking Kituba at school again, I see."

Ndadia shrugs.

Tata bends over the cooking fire in the courtyard, stirring

a red-brown mess of eucalyptus leaves and bark and roots. *Coscos* for Mama's cough.

Gordie's Mom and Dad have tried persuading Tata to hospitalize Mama at the Vanga mission. The doctors at Vanga village say she has Slims Disease. But Tata spends days cooking *coscos*, nights in the cemetery, calling on the ancestors for help.

Ndadia's small sister stands over a termite hole, grabbing termites as they fly out, ripping their wings off and popping the insects in her mouth. The monkey chatters from the baobab, turns silent, scratches his behind.

Gordie ducks inside the smoke-filled interior of the hut and hands Mama a bag of coffee beans between his palms. Tata and Mama grin widest for South African coffee and Gordie sneaks something his mom won't miss—sugar, a few eggs, a sardine can—each time he visits. Once he brought cheese, but Ndadia said they fed it to the chickens. Mama's never been in bed at noon before. Always in the fields, coughing, leaning on her hoe. Right now she should be preparing *fufu*, *saka-saka* and sardines for Sunday dinner. Her face, puckered like avocado skin, crinkles into smile.

"Gordie. Merci *mingi*." She strokes his hand with her gnarled one, her finger curling and recurling as when a person beckons. Above her head, a small green lizard slips down the wall and plops behind the bed.

Tata Kunda clucks behind them, dips his head and offers Mama the reddish mess of herbs and leaves. Mama smiles and shakes her head.

"*Mawa mingi*. She cannot eat. A spell's on her."

Gordie looks at Mama, her thin face folding in on itself. Insects sizzle in the lazy heat. She has a big sore on her jaw.

"Gordie! Hopscotch," Ndadia calls.

Five years ago, when they were only ten, when Gordie first moved to Milundu, he taught Ndadia hopscotch, and still Ndadia wants to play. By the time Gordie steps back outdoors into parched heat and startling sunshine, Ndadia has drawn the hopscotch pattern in the dust under the mango tree and waits, leaning on his stick.

"*Kiadi*. Mama is worse," Gordie says.

"She has pains in her stomach now," Ndadia says. He lands, spread-legged, throws hard his second stone.

Gordie says nothing, dusts his knees where he rests beneath the mango tree. Inside the hut Mama coughs, a hollow wracking sound. The monkey coughs once, loudly, from his tree. When Gordie looks up, the monkey is looking down at him warily, one hand cradled in the other.

"Last night Tata called Mama's clan together," Ndadia says. His voice is low and Gordie leaves the mango's shade to crouch beside him.

"They stood round Mama's bed. Tata said, 'Simbi, leave my wife alone so she can recover her health.'"

A rooster with a broken beak pecks dully in the dirt.

"But the witchdoctor says perhaps her sister Simbi's not the cause. Now we must pay another goat. Tata blessed Mama and jumped in the air three times. Everybody spit in a bowl of water and Tata bathed Mama in the water." Ndadia throws a second stone. "Yet she grows weaker."

"Do you believe in it, Mom?" Gordie says when his parents talk of *ndoki* in the village. His mother flushes and her forehead forms a horseshoe. "Of course not, Gordon. It's hocus pocus." Then she adds, "Just stay away."

At the close of this morning's final hymn, Gordie slipped

out the church door past his mother's whisper, "Chicken and yams!" Eating wasn't on his mind. Anyway he prefers Mama's *fufu* and *mbika* to his own mother's criticism of the Sunday service. Gordie left his mother standing on the church step looking windblown and scornful, one large hand against her stomach. Her mighty pregnancy empowers her: his father brings her food and pillows, Gordie brings her drinks. Ndadia's been after Gordie's mother never to look at the village cripple who shuffles along on his backside, flip-flops on his hands. He crouches Sundays by Gordie's mother's pew, waits for *makuta* coins to fall. Knows she will show compassion in public. It's a different story when schoolgirls stop by the house for a drink of fridge-cold water. His mother fixes them an icy stare and answers nothing, so that finally they back away, giggling and angry.

"If you look, the *nkita* will cause bad mischief to your baby, Madame," Ndadia says. Ndadia says the cripple is a sorcerer paying for the crimes he performed through bad ancestors, those unwise while on earth. Gordie's mom smiles with her mouth but not her eyes and tells Ndadia the hour is late and he should run home for supper. Early in the pregnancy Mama sent Gordie's mother a thick-roped bracelet to wear, to make sure the baby comes out normal. Ndadia carried it the four kilometres dangling respectfully from his fingers, but Gordie's mother laid her large hand over the bracelet and said, "Ndadia. Return it."

Tata steps from the hut squinting in sunshine, carrying a pail and basin. Maybe this afternoon Gordie and Ndadia will snapfish. Gordie's brought a joint along, hidden in his shorts.

Sleepy Sunday afternoons Ndadia and Gordie, Mama, Tata and Ndadia's seven brothers laze beneath lifaka trees and drink *mulafu*. Before Gordie goes home, Mama gives him a long-stemmed root to chew, to take the smell of palm wine away.

"*Masa*," Tata calls in the direction of Ndadia's brothers, who are passing a calabash of wine, and the monkey shrieks, swings from the tree and hightails for the hole beneath the shed.

Tata returns, sets an empty Coke bottle and a large calabash on the hard courtyard dirt beside the pail and basin. Ndadia's oldest brother grunts and calls to the next oldest, "Fetch the water." That brother shifts in the heat, takes a gulp of *mulafu* and calls, "Ndadia." And Ndadia drops his stone, and he and Gordie head for the containers. When his sister grows, Ndadia will order her, but for now her arms are too small to lift a full pail of water to her head.

Gordie places the pail within the basin and loads them on his head. Ndadia balances the Coke bottle in the wide neck of the calabash and does the same, then grabs two palm branches tied with nylon string from inside the hut. Gordie has two number sixteen fish-hooks in a small pouch in his pocket. They set out down the red dust path toward the river.

"But it *is* Simbi!" Ndadia says the minute they start out, his legs dusted gray in churning heat. Eyes sorrowful. "Simbi." The sun is so hot it hurts. "Simbi's jealous she does not have a fine husband like Tata. The ancestors told Tata last night in a dream." Sweat shines Ndadia's nose. Simbi. Mama's sister. The one unmarried woman in Lusekele. Mama's sister who lived two years in Canada where she studied at a nurse's college. Since she's returned to work at Vanga hospital, the villagers say a spirit possesses her. They know this because she cannot catch a husband. Gordie's mom says Simbi's too smart to fall for an uneducated village man, but the women only laugh.

The boys reach the river's edge and collapse in grass and dirt under the trees' dense shadow. When Gordie was kicked out of TASOK International school in Kinshasa last year for smoking dope, they sent him up country to Milundu. That principal knew punishment. Three weeks of his parents' silent grim reproach. You'd think he'd had Slims Disease. But Ndadia. He was there to meet the Cessna when Gordie landed. Ndadia took him snapfishing at the river every afternoon, Ndadia held his head when Gordie cried. When your heart is aching, turn to Jesus, Gordie's mother tells the village women. Gordie has no need for Jesus. He has Ndadia.

Somewhere, behind them, a parrot screeches. Gordie passed Grade Nine at TASOK International school, although he didn't make the honour roll, disgusting his parents once again. Ndadia dreams of going to the International school with Gordie, staying in the Baptist hostel, but his parents have no money, so in six weeks Gordie will leave Ndadia behind again and head for Kinshasa. Ndadia walks daily to Milundu school, four kilometres each way. At Milundu the teachers show up when they want to. Ndadia wrote exams last week. Zaire's out of paper so the students copied questions off the shiny blackboards. Gordie asked his mother if he couldn't give Ndadia's class some of the paper stacked in his father's office.

His mother said, "Gordie, that wouldn't solve Zaire's problems!" It would solve Ndadia's problem. "Zaire needs Jesus," Gordie's mother says. "Our Saviour can solve every problem."

The sun hangs low in the sky when Gordie and Ndadia fill the pail and basin with murky river water, and head through the sand for Ndadia's hut. The girl in the river mud last week whispered to Gordie, "I shall visit your home," and disappeared into the forest, trailing her mud-splashed clothes. The first time Gordie had a girl was last year after they expelled him. That girl also came to his house after, a Sunday evening, while his parents were in Vanga at the white's church service. She didn't come back for sex. This one won't either. She came with a basket on her arm and searched his mother's cupboards, dropping into her basket canned beans, canned tuna, a half dozen muffins, a loaf of bread, a pineapple sitting on the cupboard. His mom and dad returned early and Gordie shoved her out the back door off his bedroom, sent her tripping in darkness over the hot water bucket, bumping the ash-filled burning-barrel. He listened for a week to his mom's astonished exclamations about his eating habits.

They walk slowly now, Gordie and Ndadia, through the oiled heat, pail and basin on their heads, sharing the marijuana. Then Ndadia says, "Boma."

It's a game he started years ago. Ndadia's travelled no farther than Vanga, but he knows geography.

"Boma."

"Ships and yellow hills," says Gordie.

"Moanda."

"Mist."

"Kimpese."

"Red African tulip trees."

"Canada." The boys look at one another. It's been nine years for Gordie. Who could imagine.

"*Mawa penja*," Ndadia says, his voice stresses air, "What I long for more than life is Mama's health and a small notebook."

~

Matondo Sunday today. Thanksgiving Sunday. Zaire's yearly sacrifice to God. An upsetting day, what with the women going wild. Vera enters the church on her husband's arm, followed by Gordie. She sets her heavy body on the backless bench. Three months to go. Some of those shameless girls turn, stare at her belly. Then the first hymn begins.

> *Diansambu diadi ekangu*
> *Mu zola tukangaziananga*

Eight verses if there's one. On the second verse Pastor Pambi raises his arms and already here come the mamas dancing their garden produce, their animal offerings down the aisle. Vera's discussed this behaviour at women's prayer group. They don't need to be so suggestive with their bodies; they choose to. Stan winces in disgust but Gordie's lapping it in. The newly arrived missionary's wife says accept it, it's cultural. But then what can one expect, she's Lutheran. They don't baptize right or anything. Of course it's cultural. It's cultural and wrong. The women giggling, now laughing outright, sure their sacrifice will outdo the men's. There goes Mama Lutantu, breasts bouncing in time to her oranges and grapefruit. Look at their swaying hips, clapping at the front while the men dance. Vera would like someone to tell her what this has to do with praising God. Turning church into a circus. The baby hangs like a stone-filled apron in her lap. Cackling ducks, chickens, the village rooster, legs pinned together, quivering rabbits, a quilt of eggs, peanuts, beans, papaya, blanket the church platform. The front row worshippers clap at the goats breakfasting on the offering. What's the commotion? The village rooster. He's kicked himself free of the string that bound his legs, he's sailing through the window, and Pastor Pambi, hands undulating air, cries, "Praise for your resurrection, Lord." It's so unworshipful.

~

Six women arrive today for Vera's cooking class. Only Mama Kiamfu is absent—at the Vanga mission hospital having her seventh baby. And she barely twenty-eight years old. Her two youngest have the straight hair—a sure sign of malnutrition. So how will she feed more? And of course Mama Kunda, at death's door with Slims Disease. Vera's heels hurt. Today they're cooking with bananas. Using the oven in the back yard, for really what's the point of teaching these women to use a stove they'll never own? They come, polite and head-dipping, but Vera can see contempt behind their eyes. The new missionary's wife told Vera she overheard the women saying, "The whites have so few babies because white babies come by luck. Each time they must figure out anew how it is done. Monsieur and Madame Hutchison took fifteen years to remember." And the young wife laughed. Gordie says nothing about the baby.

"Could we come to attention please. Today I'll demonstrate banana bread and banana cake. Bananas are a good source of potassium. We'll use palm oil instead of margarine." Already they're bored and shuffling, looking round Vera's kitchen, at her tins of relief food—MCC beef, at her chunk of South African cheese, her dirndl skirt laid on the ironing board. Their eyes miss nothing.

Vera sets out the measuring cups, the bowls. The women touch the glassware and chatter in Kituba—on purpose so she cannot understand. Vera divides the group in two. In the middle of her final instructions, just as she's handing out the powdered milk, there's a "Ko-ko" at her door. Two boys from the elementary school to get their drooping basketball pumped up. As if she has nothing else to do. When Vera returns, the women have mixed all the ingredients and she can tell by looking that they haven't measured.

"How much flour did you put in?"

They nod. "Eeeh."

"But did you measure carefully?"

"Eeeeeh."

"This will not work," Vera says, "because you were too careless with the measurements. Look at the recipe—see here—*two* cups?"

The women watch Vera. She gives up, waves them outdoors to carry their two pans of slopping batter to the old cook stove under the palm tree. Mama Lutantu lights a fire beneath it. They stay out in the back yard gabbing while Vera in her silent living-room puts her aching feet up on the plastic ottoman and folds her hands over her stomach. The baby's still. They want her to offer them ice-cold water from her refrigerator, but if she does, she'll have ten more in cooking class tomorrow.

The back door opens. Vera watches the backs of Gordie's long rooster legs beneath his cut-off shorts. His bare feet slip through the living room into Stan's office. A rustling. He sticks his head out, holds a notebook and his whispered voice holds a question. "Mom?"

Vera opens her eyes.

"I suppose that's for Ndadia," she says. "Firstly, Gordon, those notebooks are for Dad's workers to purchase. Secondly, we need to teach these people to work for what they get. You can't just give your things away." She closes her eyes against his blue ones.

Forty minutes in hot bleak sunlight and the women carry two overdone soggy-in-the-centre breads into the house. While Vera slices what should have been banana bread into neat squares, Mama Latantu takes the knife, chops a rectangular section from the other's centre and offers it to Mama Luwenge, who cuts a hunky parallelogram for Mama Tumbu.

Vera closes with prayer.

~

Stan and Vera's Land Rover jolts down the rutted hill, over the creaking wooden bridge, through the thick sand up to Vanga village.

"Prepare ye, Prepare ye, Prepare ye the way of the Lord," Stan sings. "And the Saviour bears me gently, O'er the places once so rough." The baby rebels. The Land Rover stops dead at the clinic and by the time Vera has hoisted herself out, she can only see Stan's feet sticking out from under the vehicle.

"I'll need to check with Dudley if my supplies are in," Stan's voice says beneath the jeep. "I'll be back around three." Vera heaves herself, sweating, into the green-walled clinic and sits near the door. Simbi, dressed in her green nurse's uniform, is helping an old man hobble across the waiting room floor on a gangrenous foot. Vera's heel throbs. The other nurses, all men, circle wide around them.

"Madame Hutchison," Simbi says. A moment later, under thirty pairs of eyes, she shows Vera into Dr. Schappert's office.

"They stare at me because I have this baby, and at you, Simbi, because you don't," Vera says. Simbi's hair is combed into seven braided coils around her head. It's hard to believe, looking at her, that she lived in America. Stan and Vera's Evangelical Renewal Baptist Mission placed Simbi in a nursing college in Alberta. This ties them somehow. Simbi must be back over a year.

"Monsieur Hutchison and I will shortly be commencing a preaching series called 'Oh the Peace the Saviour Gives' that we'll take around to neighbouring villages. Perhaps you'll want to help." They could use Gordie's help as well, but Gordie is more interested in living like the natives than in being a personal witness. Simbi, her back to Vera, washes her hands at the sink and doesn't answer.

Vera sighs and says, "How's Mama Kunda?"

Simbi looks startled.

"She's very ill, Madame." She bends low, examining the callouses on Vera's heels.

"Simbi, my husband and I have heard ridiculous rumours." Simbi's cool fingers press into Vera's pulse. Her lips move. Counting.

"Gordie brings home a lot of silliness about the cause of Mama Kunda's illness." Vera stares at Simbi who has lifted Vera's dress and is kneading the skin of her vast stomach.

"When have you last felt movement from this baby?" Simbi asks.

"Oh heavens, not five minutes ago," Vera says. "In America no one dies of a curse. You know I believe they have a name for Mama Kunda's illness in America. What's it called?"

"Slims Disease," says Simbi, looking in Vera's ears.

"Well, yes," Vera shifts on the table. "That's the African's name for it. I guess you couldn't learn everything during the fortunate time you spent in America. Anyway, it's deadly, the disease. How old is Mama Kunda?"

"Forty-two."

"My. That's my age." Vera says. "It's not that I have anything against Mama Kunda." Simbi's long fingers begin to probe Vera's privates. "It's just—what will our workers think with Gordie running off there every day, up to goodness knows what?"

"Slide down," Simbi says. She probes some more.

"That we favour Tata Kunda's family. That's what. Now you're a smart woman, Simbi." Vera pulls down her dress, her body humming pleasantly from all that probing. "Some day you'll find a lovely educated man who appreciates your smarts . . . ."

"Why did you wait so many years to have this baby?"

How dare the woman meddle in her business. Simbi has come around the table and is looking at her. Vera speaks severely out the window where a July wind shakes leaves on the orange tree.

"Well, we chose to have one child, but the way things have turned out—God, seeing us as His worthy vessels, has now entrusted to us another."

Simbi smiles. She turns to the sink to scrub her hands. Vera stops thinking of Simbi at all. She closes her eyes, lies still and irritated, trying to bring back the humming. Why didn't Gordie just take a notebook if it's so important? He steals food for himself right from my kitchen, she thinks, but won't steal a notebook for a friend.

"Gordie always twists situations to look like our responsibility," Vera says to Simbi, but Simbi's gone.

≈

Gordie and Ndadia reach Lusekele clearing in Zaire's quick-gathering dusk. The monkey streaks towards them over the hard-packed compound dirt, leaps into Ndadia's arms, clawing his shirt. Tata Kunda, and Ndadia's brothers speed behind him.

"Grab the monkey now. Hang on to Kiki," they call. Gordie and Ndadia lunge, bump heads as the monkey skids between Ndadia's legs. Gordie catches Kiki by a paw and the monkey squeals and hoots and scratches.

"What's happening?" Gordie asks.

A brother brushes a skinned knee and says, "The monkey's stealing chicken eggs." Broken shells scatter the courtyard dirt. Tata has disappeared inside the makeshift shed. He steps out with his machete, and heads for the chopping block. Kiki screeches and tries to twist from Gordie's arms.

"Gordie. Come." Tata calls, and Gordie carries the scratching animal to the chopping block. Tata spreads Kiki's fingers against the block, lays Gordie's hand over the monkey's wrist, raises the machete. And as the small hand strains, curls against his, Gordie sees one finger is already cut off at the knuckle, the wound days old, scarred and infected.

≈

In darkness, Tata draws a cross in the compound dirt, stirs in the cemetery mud he's fetched, mixed with palm wine, and pours it all into the indent. Scooping up the mud, he disappears into the hut to rub Mama's body. The monkey has not come out in hours from the hole beneath the shed. A thin dog appears and wails, eerie and shrill. Mama sleeps. Odours arise: the smell of unwashed body, death, herbs, and *sakasaka*.

"Ndadia, she will get better," Gordie says to his friend. The small sister watches from her grass mattress on the courtyard dirt. Ndadia's black face stretches suddenly, contorts over white teeth. And Gordie leaves him.

≈

On Milundu compound, Vera, awake with discomfort from the lump of baby and the memory of Simbi's touch, reviews in her mind the song she and Stan will sing at their first outdoor Oh The Peace the Saviour Gives rally.

Only a little while,
Of walking with weary feet,
Patiently over the thorny way,
That leads to the golden street.

Somewhere a cock crows.

≈

Rosemary Nixon *writes in Calgary, Alberta. Her work has appeared in literary magazines across Canada. Her first collection of short fiction,* Mostly Country, *was published in 1991 in NeWest Press' Nunatak fiction series.*

At the Trailer Park

RICK BOWERS

I woke up on the living room couch, hungover something terrible. You know the feeling: crusty light around the eyes, a squeeze-vice on the temples, dust balls in the throat. I felt as though someone had beat me up.

Two kids were sitting cross-legged on the floor, watching me. After I had stirred and opened my eyes, the little boy got up and turned on the TV. It crashed with cartoons and toy commercials. Saturday morning. "Mommy said not to turn on the TV until you woke up," said the little girl. She crawled across the living room floor to sit beside the little boy about a foot away from the TV screen. She was much smaller. I looked at their backs, their shoulders nearly touching. Brother and sister, I guessed.

Neither of them looked around as I peeled back the sleeping bag and put on my jeans. My bare chest and shoulder had the pattern of the couch imprinted on it. It looked like a rash. I hawked once or twice, shook the baggage in my head, carried my shirt off in search of the bathroom.

"You're up," she said as I went by. Kind of startled me.

"Just barely," I answered.

She sat at the kitchen table with a mug of coffee at her

elbow. "Care for a cup?" she asked.

"Please," I said, fingering my temples.

"There's Aspirin in the medicine cabinet," she said.

Her voice sounded far away, as I had already passed by a big bedroom and was at the bathroom door. Children's clothes and wet towels were scattered all over the tiny space, and I thought about how all these house trailers are laid out: living room up front at the hitch, followed by full-size kitchen area, master bedroom, bathroom, and small bedrooms at the far end. I must've blocked up a hundred of these things. Anyway, here I was with a woman and her two kids on a Saturday morning. What was her name again? She'd told me a couple of times the night before.

My neck cracked as I splashed water on my face. I remembered how my employer insisted that I call these house trailers "mobile homes." "They're *homes*," he would emphasize, "mobile *homes*, not 'trailers'. " After a while I gave up referring to them altogether in his presence. Just did my job on the trailers and around the grounds of the park. But I couldn't help thinking that for being "mobile" homes, people did a lot of moving in and out of them. The "homes" themselves stayed pretty much immobile on their blocks, most of them weighted down with heavy tires on their roofs. Working at the trailer park, I'd seen a lot of people move in and out. Figured I should move along out of here this morning too, soon as I could.

~

"So. How are you feeling?" she asked.

I said I was all right.

She poured coffee, sighed with morning gloom, pressed down on the cover of the pot with her pointing finger. Out in the living room it sounded as though the kids were fighting each other with the furniture, and she turned her head to yell at them. Coffee spilled on the table. "Little bastards," she said between tight lips. Then she slammed the coffee pot back on the stove, charged out into the living room, shouting, "Bobby! Joanne!"

Her hips moved large under her housecoat, and her furry slippers flopped against the floor, which fairly shook with her exertions. She was tall; I noticed when she stood up. Kind of fleshy too but she carried it well. I thought back to the night before: drawing my pay at the trailer park office, stopping off at Penny's near the bus stop for a couple of beers, meeting this woman—was her name Connie? Carrie?—and now here I was. Last thing I could remember was her paying off the babysitter, and then the two of us hunkering down on the couch. Afterward, she broke the awkward silence. "You must think I'm some sort of slut," she said. We lay there in a pile on the narrow couch, breathing, dozing. Then, sometime during the night, she went to her own room.

~

I was trying to think of a strategic way to take my leave, when she sailed back into the kitchen. "God, those kids!" she exhaled in a fluster, as she extracted a cigarette from the open pack on the table. Before lighting up, she motioned toward the pack and said, "Help yourself."

I told her I had to get going.

"Relax," she said. "It's Saturday. Have another coffee."

I shrugged my shoulders in assent. She smiled. I pushed my cup across the table toward her.

She poured coffee again, dragged deeply on her cigarette. "Did you say you were a gardener?" she asked.

"I work on the grounds around the park here," I said. "Landscaping, general maintenance."

"The kids say they've seen you driving a tractor," she said.

"Probably the ride-on mower," I said.

She leaned forward, chin in cupped cigarette hand as if interested. But her large brown eyes had that morning glaze. Her blonde head nodded encouragement for me to continue, but I didn't really think we had a lot to say to each other.

"How long you been working here?" she asked.

"About three years," I said and took a long sip of coffee.

"How come I've never seen you around?"

"After working here all week, I like to get away," I answered.

"Smart boy," she said, getting up and moving toward the kitchen counter. I could hear her humming something, her back toward me. She started handling some plates and dishes.

I looked down into my coffee cup, felt kind of uncomfortable.

Three evil years working at this trailer park, I thought. Then I thought that this woman's little girl seemed to be about three years old. I didn't recognize either of her kids, but the trailer park was full of them: pre-schoolers, grade-schoolers, young high school punks. Didn't seem to me as though the trailer park was the right place for kids. Of course it was none of my affair. I cut grass, planted bushes, blocked up the occasional "home." I built the playground, with its sandbox and swings. But it was mostly the older kids who hung around there. Now and then I'd pick up a beer can or two, an empty pint, or a ragged page out of a skin magazine. A group of young devils even offered me a toke over there one evening when I had to work late. A couple of little girls were molested in that playground a month after I fixed it up. I thought again of her little girl's face first thing that morning when I woke up; thought that I could have had children the same age as hers if I'd had any industry about me. Then again, I've never really thought all that much about children.

"I work for the tightest prick in this town," she said right out of the blue, standing by the sink with a fresh cigarette between her fingers. She might have said something before that, but I missed it. "William J. C. McAlindon and Associates," she announced with a humorous snort. "The old bugger's so goddamned tight he squeaks."

"The lawyer?" I asked.

"That's him. The prick. I asked for a raise yesterday and he wouldn't give it. He said that everybody has to be prepared to tighten their belts these days." She rolled her eyes just as the toaster popped. "Can you believe it? I don't imagine that he has to do too much tightening."

She turned toward the toaster. "Probably I told you all this last night," she said, rattling utensils in the drawer before her. She kept talking as she buttered the toast: "If he *had* broken down and given me a raise, I might not have met you at Penny's," she said. "Of course, then again I might have."

"You a secretary?" I asked.

"No," she said. "I search land titles at the Registry Office, run the lawyers' messages, answer the phones, and do other things I'd rather not mention." She rolled her eyes thinking about those "things," and crushed out her cigarette. "D'you eat breakfast?" she said.

I said no.

A cry welled up from the living room and came running around the corner of the kitchen. It was the little girl. She stood beside the table hopping from foot to foot and showing her arm. She wailed something that was hard to make out through her snivelling pain. It sounded like: "Tea burned me, tea burned me," but I guess she was saying, "He hurt me, he hurt me." Her face was hot and screwed up; her bottom teeth protruded.

The mother held her, made soothing noises, shouted in the direction of the living room: "Bobby! Did you hurt your sister?" She looked at me and said, "He's all boy; a little rough sometimes." Then she said to the little girl, "Take out your dolls and play outside."

The little girl sniffled, hugged her mother's side; eyed me.

"Go outside and play now," the woman urged. "That's a good girl, that's my baby." Then she yelled, "Bobby! You look after your sister and leave her alone." The girl sniffled again as she left the kitchen, her eyes looking back at me as if I were to blame.

"Damned kids," she said after the girl had gone. Then, in a longing voice, "Oh to be single."

"You married?" I asked.

"Seems so," she said. She set her cigarette aside and levelled red jam on a slice of toast. Bringing it up to her mouth, she added, "Married I am, but I haven't seen evidence of it for three or four years now." She chewed her toast thoughtfully, seemed to be thinking back. "The bastard walked out on me and the kids just after Joanne was born. The bastard. By that point, I didn't give a damn whether he stayed or left. More coffee?"

I shook my head, no.

"All I know is that those kids need some sort of a father," she said. "Either that or a good watchdog. I shiver to think of all the creeps there are around here. No, on second thought a dog's better—most fathers are creeps in their own way. Their father sure is."

Then she looked at me right in the eyes. Seemed a peculiar sort of emphasis. "Are you a father?" she asked.

I said no, not me. Felt kind of relieved to be able to say it.

"You're lucky," she said. "Anyway, he's long gone."

I was going to ask about her husband, but thought that the topic was best left alone. I asked instead about her. "Are you and the kids doing OK?" I asked.

She shrugged. "What's to say? I wake up in the middle of the night with a strange man that my children recognize in the morning. Not much different really from my life with Robert." She selected another cigarette, smiled with a shake of her head. "God, how we fought," she said. "It beats the world."

Domestic squabbles seemed pretty ordinary around the trailer park, and I thought back over a few I had witnessed. Like the time I saw this guy with his arm in a sling, beating on a woman with his free fist. He chased her around the corner and caught her in a spot she couldn't get out of because the narrow run between the trailers was blocked off by a junked car. He really gave it to her, called her a slut and a whore. A couple of kids stood on the trailer porch, wailing.

Another time, real early in the morning, I saw a woman pounding on the door of her trailer. She was begging to be let back in, was wearing nothing but her panties and bra. She crouched down when she saw me, making herself small, hiding her face. I looked the other way. Was on my way to fix somebody's furnace, I believe. God, I hated being called out to the trailer park at odd hours. I remembered, too, that the guy who molested those two little girls the other year was also found guilty of indecent assault against the daughter of the woman he was living with. He got off by promising to attend A.A. meetings. Afterward, a petition went around the trailer park to get that woman and her daughter to move out. Seemed like a strange response to me.

"So you're going," she said, kind of accusatory like.

"I should get home," I answered.

"Got a woman waiting?"

"No."

I made like I was going to move away from the table, but she stopped me with another question. "How'd you come to be a gardener?" she said.

I told her I used to be a farmer.

"My old grandfather was a farmer," she said. She smiled. Seemed like she remembered something about him. "That was long ago and far away," she said. For a second her face looked like it must have looked when she was a little girl; then it looked hard at me again. "Tell me about your farm," she said.

I told her about the old homestead in Lot Five—the Stewart Estate—as it was called before P.E.I. joined the confederation of Canada.

She said that I sure knew my history.

I went on about how my great-great grandfather marked his *X* on a Colonial Commissioner's Deed, and about how the place had been farmed by the family for five generations, including me. Grandpa made it big in the fox business in the twenties and thirties, bought up the neighbouring farms on either side of our place: 375 acres all told—which was big by P.E.I. standards. But I stepped it off one time along the rear line, and figured the total acreage at closer to 390. Most of it was cleared, with green pasture at the road near a creek and good sandy soil reaching back up a slow grade to the woods. One of my earliest memories was hearing an owl in those woods; of Grandma covering my toes with a woollen comforter and telling me that the owl was asking if I'd said my prayers.

Dad and I incorporated when I turned twenty-one. Made me feel proud to be considered asset enough for re-financing. Our quotas went up right across the board. Together, Dad and I had a personal lawyer, a bank manager; we even hired a hand—a young fellow who had nothing to do while he waited his call-up to the army. It was a fine few years. We were milking twenty cows at one time, had a radio always going in the barn to keep the tethered bull quiet. Dad kept the books and I spent the money. When we needed something we bought it; a day or two later we'd phone the bank manager and let him know.

We had no worries. We had the good earth underneath our feet, fertile soil between our fingers. For a while I handled the milk run contract for the dairy in Summerside, but it got to be more trouble than it was worth. Seemed I was always headed somewhere but getting nothing done. Dad warned me that I'd work myself into an early grave, just as Mother had.

But I'd respond that I was patterned after him too closely to worry about the ravages of overwork. We'd both laugh about that. Funny thing how we laughed at the same line, just the two of us. Grandpa came from a big family and Dad had four sisters as well as an older brother killed overseas. I was an only child. But I never craved company.

Anyway, machinery was our biggest business expense, power bills, gas for the tractors and trucks. I owned a big white Chrysler then too. Sometimes I'd drive it back into the fields at night, steer it right out into a stand of tall timothy and floor it. The hay would part before the lights like a never-ending wave. I could go for a half mile in any direction with my eyes closed. I loved the reckless freedom of it. Then I'd stop, get out of the car near the far woods, and hear my voice echo back at me in a roar from the wooded hollow where a wall of large oaks stood. After, in the quiet, I'd consider the rows that sloped back toward the house with its one or two yellow-lit windows. Dad would be sitting up with the paper or doing figures in the account book.

We grew Elite seed that was shipped all over the world, from Guyana to New Guinea. Seemed pretty far removed from the earthy potato fields that I walked about after dark. I loved the damp green smell of those fields. I'd lean on my car and look back beyond the house to the glimmering waters of the bay across the road. Often I'd think about sailing off to some of those hot countries to see what they were really like. Maybe find myself a woman. Marlene was out of the picture then. After some more silence, I'd get back in the car, punch "Drive" on the push-button automatic and cruise slowly back to the house—a house so big for just Dad and me that we could hardly keep it heated in the winter.

I heard myself talking; shut myself up.

"Don't stop," she said. "Go on. Tell me about Marlene."

"No," I said. "Marlene and I were childhood sweet-hearts, that's all. And there's not much else to tell. Dad and I couldn't afford to keep up the place. Prices kept going down just as acreage and expenses kept going up. What came in on one hand from the government went out on the other to the bank until finally the bank took us over."

"That's banks for you," she said. "Corporate snarl all the way."

I didn't really catch what she meant, but she went on about how she often dealt with mortgages, liens, and foreclos-ures in her job at the lawyer's office. I knew the terms only too well. "It's liens and foreclosures that's got me living over here," I said.

"D'you ever go back to the Island?" she asked.

"Not much," I said.

"Where do you live? Downtown?"

I said yes—in a high-rise, downtown.

Then I got up to go. My jacket was hanging near the door, and I felt vaguely embarrassed about something, eager to get clear of the place and out of the trailer park in general. I felt as though I had said too much.

At the door she said, "You can call me anytime. I'm in the book." Her brows were pinched together with concern.

But I never said anything either way, just said goodbye.

At the bus stop, I remembered that she had borrowed fifty dollars off me the night before. But what the hell. I figured it was money that I would never see again anyway. I waited a long time for the bus, hoping all the time that her kids wouldn't see me, thinking too about what a loser I was.

I got drunk again that night. Woke up the following morning to the phone ringing off the hook. I thought it might be her. But it was the hospital in Charlottetown with word that Dad had passed away in the night. I took the first part of the next week off with pay, and went home for the funeral. That was when I worked at the trailer park.

~

Rick Bowers *was born in Prince Edward Island. He now teaches English at the University of Alberta and is the author of a book of stories entitled* The Governor of Prince Edward Island *(1986). "At the Trailer Park" appeared previously in the* University of Windsor Review *21.2 (1988).*

The Ways of Luck

WEYMAN CHAN

That afternoon the wind had risen so shamelessly that everyone strove to send their own prayers rising first. The mother, who had been told not to part her legs for me since this morning, sat frozen in her seat. She could have spoken, if disdain did not hang so remarkably in the air, the faint currents tossed off from the lashes of her eyes, blinking, her hands sliding along the edge of the table like balanced spiders.

Around the table sat the other players. How slowly they moved; she would catch the decisions of their eyes shifting like counterweights, and I would hear mother's dry sighs above the pause. "Your turn." "Hurry, it's your turn."

As always, their huge knees like wrinkled stumps around me, began shifting at the roots of their toes, pushing my breath out from all corners. I wanted to touch them, but could not. I wanted to break them, but the rules of the game interfered. Instead, I heard the heavy mah-jong tiles clatter and knock overhead, like misshapen dice fighting to present a lucky face, a lucky number. I noted closely how mother's wine-coloured slacks and tucked-in blouse rose and fell in short breaths: this time she wanted to win.

Although I was not curious, I looked up from the chipped

green paint of the wooden porch and found there was no place to go: mother's friends had deliberately sat so close into the table that their legs formed a cage whose bars nudged me on all sides.

"Poong!" the mother cried.

Now I was certain she would win. I felt the scuffling of disgust in the bare feet of two of the ladies, though the other lady, who faced west, was concentrating on the tiny world of dried mucus she palpitated in her fingers below the table.

"The east wind," the mother said, revealing three identically marked tiles from her hand. She laid the tiles down in an even line on the table. I could barely hear them touch, but I saw concentration in the tensing and untensing of her thighs. She said, "Now maybe luck will take a better turn for me."

"You're just saying that," one of the other ladies snapped.

On my behalf mother was indeed cautious. She, like the other women, knew the ways of bringing down luck. The gods were appeased by this, the sad beggar's despondency which fortune could not pity more and therefore be lured into helping. Nor I to pity, even more. I would still like to think, however, that she was not entirely sly nor prudent. Prosperity has its reasons. After all, the father had something to do with it, the kind weather had turned the world around him green. What the mother said next, in fact, bore this out: "Well, now that it's not all that bad, you'd better come and take him!"

The mother's voice carried, as always, higher than the farthest kite!—but for a moment everyone sensed confusion. Who was being spoken to?

Looking over to my right, behind the north-facing woman's tainted ankles, were bedsheets fluttering dry in the wind and sun. Luckily, a quick gust of wind lifted the whiteness up before my eyes began watering. Standing there beside a hole in the ground and pointing a bent pitchfork down at his feet, was the father. He'd just appeared, like a magician at the end of a performance after the last bedsheet illusion was performed, the one where a sleeping woman floats upward to the amazement of the audience, but must always come back down. The father—he used to be mine—had long ago performed his last trick, his last attempt to rise above the clamour of common life and be told about how far he'd come. Upon losing face with himself, his hands promptly forgot how to cook; they trembled and stamped mutely at night, at one with the tip of his spine, which rubbed against the bedsprings, robbing him of sleep. And his tobacco lungs forced him to make imaginary distinctions between the foods that would and would not make him cough. His face reddened at times with the look—hard and judgmental—that somehow life had cheated him, his right was to get back at it, and I still must have been the lucky one, summoned by incense, who would grant his condemned existence clemency. Thus, we all gaped at him: so suddenly had he appeared that everyone expected him to dissolve or to hide inside one of those holes of his own making.

He looked like a bedtime ogre. For any Oriental to wear beard and moustache on such a fine day was thought unclean, unless you were Japanese or incredibly wise. He was neither. He has never turned his back on his visions. He was wearing the family garden galoshes with the unbuckled straps dragging behind him, as if he were a child just stumbled out of winter. His hands, like two wiry horses without tooth or whinny, appeared ready to rear up against anyone standing too close. And finally, there was an anger about his face that would not go away. I saw the vanity of comprehension charge across his eyes. He looked at me and at where mother sat; now he understood that his wife was referring me to him, and he stoically stood his ground under the assertion that he was in the know about me all along.

"No!" he cried. "That's your responsibility!"

Grinning wildly, he turned on the minimal heels of his galoshes and went away. Later, as the wind picked up even more and revealed through the sheets his somber activity—digging more holes in the lawn to accommodate a variety of fruit trees which he'd propped up against the garage—I suddenly pitied him for the sacrifice involving such work. He wanted to talk. The trembling in his hands, the sweat running thin cursors down his big and small chins, was less from the exertion itself than the thought of exertion. And he had reasons for envying mother, too. She who had the counsel of friends and so had influences over other opinions; she whose leisurely business about the house afforded her the energy to be demanding, particular, crass; she who thought I could be fooled by her skill in manipulating the four winds and therefore submit to her wishes. These grievances like tears came running down the father's silent, furrowed brow.

Now mother—she was angry. There was no deception behind the hurried flurry of her spider hands, how they pounced upon the wall of mah-jong tiles when her turn came. The underside of her thumb brushed the tile, and her shopkeeper's shout surfaced immediately as she shot the tile into the centre for someone else's taking. She hated to see the sweat of other people's brows, especially when that boded a suffering that she did not intend. And with each flick of her thumb preceding the expulsion of a tile, her big toe would stub me in the ribs or at the back of my head, not far from the left ear. Meanwhile, one of the women, the one who faced south, was trying to weave a conversation around the eggs she would never buy.

"I haven't broken one open either. If I try to I shake all over, get a headache, and my whole day is ruined. Thoroughly. I wouldn't want to think of what might be inside."

"And. . . ."

"Well, it was dead. . . ."

"Suffering these days is so easy to watch."

"And you're against it?"

"No. Yes. Well, it used to give me such a sense of feeling."

"Your turn," mother interrupted.

This was the closest the four women came to quitting the game and saving face at the same time. Mother's friends could not presume to be at her house for any reason other than to play mah-jong; but mother, on the other hand, had the freedom to join her husband planting trees. The game advanced slowly and because she always won, her victory today could not even delight herself. For a moment her stomach rose and fell rapidly, as if this exact thought had struck her. How stubbornly it glowed. It seemed to say, *my labour is superior to yours*. It stopped her breathing for a full five seconds, in which time her resolve strengthened around a single question: if she were to give the game up, would she not then be admitting its weakness, its mere shadow of substance compared to her husband's work, manly, rooted in conviction and hardship, not a mere game, not a lazy diversion of a struggle within imaginary rules divorced from real life? He would not stop, he would torment her, day and night he'd say that she was everything less for what she was, while he would be everything more for what he'd become. Mother's resolve turned to stone.

She threw a hateful look at him and shouted, "I will not give up!"

The father replied with a spurt of perspiration.

I was getting tired and dopey from sitting so cramped up between the legs of four women, and nowhere to go. It was dark and hot from the smells of the women's warmed bodies; from the west-facing woman's feet rose the fragrance of ginseng oil, which she used secretly against the dime-sized wart under her second toe. Counteracting this was an earthy smell of rain-drenched worms which, sniffing carefully, I found festering at its source. For within the fleshy pocket behind mother's knee, was a spot of garden dirt that she'd ignored two days in a row and was now very proud of. It had just been a scratch before. Was her sacrifice then to be so complete, did she believe that it truly gave her the winning edge over those desperate bids by her friends?

The west-facing woman had long before dropped her wad of mucus and pretended that nothing had happened. Little did she know that the wad had not fallen between the floorboards of the porch deck, nor had it even fallen on the porch. The wind picked it up. Such a heavy, sullen grain, buffeted like fly dust and carried out of sight by the inexplicable wind, did not illuminate the mystery further. The women believed the wind incapable of bearing up such trivia in the first place.

Meanwhile a change in tempo sounded in the toppling of tiles above my head. Someone else had just shouted "Poong!"— it was not the mother this time. This time it was the north-facing woman who, wrestling down her own spirit of excitement, brought up her foot hard against my upper thighs.

"The north wind!" she cried.

I yelped but could not move for the legs of the others, whose bulging calves and sandpapery heels pinned me down at the neck, the hip, the lower joint of my thumb. I could not ask for simple mercy.

"Quiet, quiet," mother said, stubbing her toe off my left earlobe. "We'll be finished soon."

"Poong!"

I felt a good kick in the rump. It came from the west-facing woman. Above me the expected words rang: "The west wind! What luck!"

"It seems that luck is really turning the compass today," said another whose voice strained innocence.

"And you think that luck answers all prayers equally?"

Everyone at the table went quiet. The bitter voice was mother's; long after she spoke them, the words still shook above me, fearfully, for she was the kind of woman for whom victories should be quick and splendid. Only then did I realize how necessary it was, her winning.

"Silence!" she cried, and the bony edge of her foot chopped me in the mouth. "This game must not be made light of."

"No," someone said. "No one has said anything about winning, Mee. Do you really think it makes that much difference?"

"And luck has its own reasons, too."

Everyone was silent. For a while the tiles struck and collided and exchanged hands, but no one seemed the better for it. I was accustomed to hoping for a quick escape, mother winning all four winds (for in mah-jong her skill and luck were undisputed) by early afternoon and freeing me to run around in the yard. I who would pull down bedsheets and storm clouds and float objects across the room on a blue fog, unplugging the refrigerator and unbolting window bolts, until the father, catching me in the act, would scream, "You're not a ghost yet! What do I have to do to convince you!" upon which he would chase me out of doors, throwing rocks and knives at me to show how alive I was, how bearable was pain-giving when made virtuous by love. And me, scrambling around the apple trees delightedly, pretending I was a scared deer in father's back yard forest, always quick to scoff at the robins and magpies for my precariously good fortune.

Such silliness was not mine alone. It belonged as well to the friends of the mother who had lost their luck in the game; who enjoyed watching me; who clapped and threw plum seeds and orange rinds in appreciation of my glorious tricks, which they really did not fathom at all as beauty.

"Eat up!" one of them once shouted, hurling crumbs at me from an egg-yolk cookie. "Don't be like my daughter. She starves herself no end, thinking to change herself into the shape of a perfect cross. Eat up. At least boys don't know of such vanity!"—and of course I ate for them. I saw how their assurances flourished at my presence; their ripe smiles, always on the verge of exclaiming, "How wonderful to have a son whom death has forgotten! A corporeal spirit, who must be beaten to life, offered meat instead of prayers, and can be tied in one place to fulfil your every wish! What must we do to our sons to have the same dream-come-true?"

These thoughts they kept to themselves. They never betrayed their outer dispositions, mild, affable, willing to exchange recipes as quickly as they exchanged glances because the weather should have no bearing on domestic breeding.

Often they would see me right after the father's attack, how the bones of multiple fractures stabbed out of my skin, the veins and tendons stood exposed, clenching and unclenching slightly with every heartbeat, my tongue pushed down to the larynx, my face blue. The women would stand apart, a bit rigid, to show that their dignities still upheld at least a small sense of surprise; yet as soon as the healing began, they would relax any stern repose, smile benignly and then gradually comment, suggest to me with fingers pointing, which organs should be restored next. What they saw was pure aesthetic, the bruises and cuts receding in seconds, gaping wounds snapped shut like eyelids, and flailed intestines crawling back inside their gigantic slashes for another day. Not even the birds could get a nip of me. How these women marvelled, sitting on the grass under the apple trees nibbling apples, and I, prostrate on the ground, healing my wounds and smacking cookie crumbs off my lips—smiling up at them heroically.

Father, I knew, held back all interest. Wheezing heavily, as if his lungs could no longer contain the air—the smell of the horses of his hands which had torn me apart so utterly, now pounding at his sides as my fragrant remains stirred and congealed and rolled back together again without the slightest effort—he held his breath and kicked dirt up from the garden. He did this hoping that the wind would carry the dirt into the eyes of the women. That they would sneeze and become upset and turn against me, their teardrops and stray polyester sleeves dabbing at both eyes as evidence of their patience worn thin, a dutiful laugh outlasting its joke. The women may have pretended elegance, but on my behalf they were genuine.

"Your first-born," they breathed out in unison, their eyes entranced and unflinching. "What a lovable boy." Of course that was as far as praises went. The ladies never revealed more lest jealousy be suspected; besides, they had sons of their own to garner their hopes from.

The wind stirred. The sun had just banked a bit off zenith, it was hot and I sat (or curled, or lay) under the table's shadow. Wanting to see the brightness outside and only having a view of (through the north-facing woman's tainted legs) the brilliant white bedsheets, I looked in that direction.

The sheets were gone.

Above me the tile-shuffling and murmuring ceased.

"Look!" the mother shouted. Her voice rang loud and white—higher than a soaring kite—and saying this, she threw back her chair and she stood.

She stood!

Without thought my weight shifted back to my hamstrings and with both haunches springing I leapt to my freedom.

The sky's brightness blinded me. I could not look up though I knew that mother, still standing, was pointing toward something there, in the distance, perhaps fluttering upward, perhaps disappearing forever. Then, through tears and desperation, my eyes opened and I looked: I braved the blazing in my eyes.

And I saw it!

I saw the last bedsheet, a dreamy cloud flapping away like an abandoned bird. Before long the father came and threatened me with the pitchfork, while mother began kicking me back under the table. The other woman put in their kicks' worth and resumed their place at the table.

By dint of this freshly founded miracle, a kind of alliance formed around the group of women. Now and then someone would say, "Poong!—three of a kind—three bamboo sticks, three dragons, three circles—" but so far no one claimed the last wind; indeed I noticed now that the women's attention was not half as much on the game as it concerned their disbelieving certainty of what the wind had been capable of.

The mother, of course, sensed this first.

"That's the sixth bedsheet I've lost."

"Ever since . . . ," one of the ladies queried, ". . . the child . . . you mean?"

"My son, yes. Just because he never did like bedsheets . . . ."

"And they'll just go off like that?"

"Yes."

"It must be a sign of good luck."

"No: luck always comes down. It never goes up."

"He *is* the favoured one in the household."

"But the first is always supposed to be the luckiest."

"But *I* think part of the *real* reason for all this is this," said the north-facing woman, who suddenly crossed her legs. "These afternoons, they're just too long. You're never happy with how they just roll by so you keep hoping that everything will happen at once."

"That's ridiculous," mother said. Not satisfied, she said it again, louder, and added: "Everything happens bit by bit. It is part of the plan. The gods make us to die off one by one so that the separation is felt. The silence is heard, the pain is felt like a missing tooth for years so you forget to talk about it."

"If you lose one of your legs you still feel the pain of your missing toe," said the north-facing woman, attempting to prove her worth as a sympathizer. Mother ignored this. Instead, her right foot sidled over toward where her husband was still busy at the dirt holes.

"Look at him. He doesn't go to work but at least he stays home and keeps me company and these days he's even doing chores around the house. We work hard for what we get. Your turn."

"It is a hard world out there these days," replied the south-facing woman, who until now had been the only listener. "You do have a perfect house."

"Except for the sheets!" said the mother.

I was afraid that these words might be taken the wrong way. They were. All three women scratched their back heel with their big toe at the same time. They hated to be thought guilty.

The father by now had finished the holes, and thrown down his pitchfork. There were six of them and six crab apple trees which he carried in a large sack on his back all at once; then, trudging ceremoniously along an imaginary file between the holes, he reached back, hauled out a tree with each horse of a hand and plunged the roots of the trees into place, thudding the entire ground-lot and scattering mounds of soil in his path. For a week now he had been planting trees, six trees a day. Trees, trees, trees. What had been the garden plot farthest from the house was now consumed by fruitless white and pink blossoms, and these latest holes dug from the earth touched the cement walkways that bordered the house. I could not gather what the father would do tomorrow afternoon.

"Did you know when I lived in China," the south-facing woman began, "we decided to move into the city. All of our friends thought we were mad. But you know, we did it because we didn't know what to do with all that land."

"Yes, like so much of anything. All the worry about the crop, the weather, the harvest."

"Yes. Where *does* it end?"

"Well, I see *your* husband knows what to do with it all, doesn't he!" laughed the woman with the tainted ankles and feet, swivelling her whole torso around to point at the father. "I see he's run out of room."

"Aren't those trees apple?"

"You make a jam out of them."

"It's good eating I'm sure."

"Will he dig up the sidewalk next? He could get paid, you know, for doing things like that—"

"Enough!" Mother stood up once more but this time her eyes glared down, her feet poised to kick if I dared move. Addressing the ladies she roared: "We will now play for money!"

At this, everyone froze. And the wind, which until now had not acted strange, began to breeze and gust. The dirt from father's planting rose steadily, colouring the air with a greyness which hurt the eyes.

"How's that?" shouted another voice, far-off and much rougher than anything that could possibly belong to the voice of a woman. I turned toward the voice (as I am sure the others did, too) and found (surprisingly) the father, approaching the bottom stairs of the porch. In his hands was the pitchfork which he seemed too intent on using.

"Listen," he said, waving his pride at the mother. "No

one gambles with my money but me."

One of the ladies sneezed.

"Sounds like trouble, Mee," said another.

But the mother, over the wind that whistled through every ear and nostril, had only perceived the anger of her husband as an eroded whisper, quiet and unprofound. This was what she detested most about him, the self-parody he struggled, unsuccessfully, to escape from.

"Money is better invested than spent," she said to him.

"Invested in luck?" he bellowed, and the grieving dispensation of his tone warned me of his fear. One only trusted luck when firstly, nature failed; secondly, human ingenuity and suffering failed; and thirdly, all that was left were the final answers. As far as he could see he was succeeding on the grounds of human ingenuity and suffering, no one could tell him otherwise. "As far as I can see," he said, "luck's a bitch."

"He means to say he doesn't believe in it," responded one of the ladies, I could not tell who. Already the leaves and white and pink petals from the father's trees were circling about the air like thoughts too heavy for absorption by wind alone. Even the apple fragrance had thickened and fallen out of the air, leaving the nose staunched with odours of salt and sand.

Above the wind the father felt compelled to shout once again, "Luck's for the laziest bitch in town!"

This the mother heard, clearer than the spattering of shit.

"How dare you. How dare you!"

Father continued. "You can't keep him here against his will. You can't make him serve you like some old ancestor. He has to want to stay." At this the father raised his hands, embracing the garden which he would have sworn was the only paradise one should ever behold. "Behold! This is the home I make for him!"

"How dare you. How dare you!" mother shrieked, the fire of sin burning down on the father from her wide-open mouth. The father frowned. He did this whenever he felt unjustly reproved for being truthful. So, just to prove that he truly dared, the father—with the buckles of both galoshes whipping the rails behind him—leapt up the porch stairs two at a time and poised himself before the mother. Meanwhile the three seated ladies, mother's guests, could not resist haranguing the opponents. They disapproved of their attentions being so rapidly shifted from one scene to the other: first the mah-jong game, then the absurdities of husband and wife, and now the grey-coloured air and the flapping branches of the fruit trees, hazy in the distance, whose slowly twisting trunks seemed to be whistling in their own language the psalms of defloration and decay. The imagining was fearful. Through the rage of wind I heard tatters of mother's and father's exchange:

"—luck—the soul of mankind—where would we be without—"

"It is a distraction—the world is green with life—sit back down there and keep him under—"

"—how do you expect me to play when you deny me my only purpose—"

"Sit!"

Mother sat. Her buttocks bending the chair like a leaf, her legs jackknifing inward and spotting me in the forehead. Obviously the father did not want me free yet; he did not want me tearing around in his forest, as if the fact that I had legs were a threat to him and must be forgotten. Balanced against his argument was the mother's. I could see the logic of her wanting to finish the game as soon as possible, scalping a bit of money from her friends while demonstrating her luck. But surely she understood that I could not serve two masters equally.

Surprisingly, no one had yet been caught by the wind nor been blown away. I could not see farther than the four inches of mud gusting between my face and my legs, and presently I heard the rasping of mah-jong tiles overhead once again: the game had resumed.

Although I had not thought about it at the time, the greatest mystery of that afternoon was the obsessive stability of those mah-jong tiles. It must have been the sheer gravity of authority behind their profound symbols. How masterfully they tamed luck, held serendipity down into a sure pattern for all to behold and wonder at! That the game continued in this weather was impossible to believe. I heard mother's spider fingers groping in the whirlpool of dirt and sand and dust, reaching for a tile, reading it with the underside of her thumb and pitching it into the centre of the table. Then the other women would fight for this newly tossed-in tile, tangling their fingers and re-reading the old ones that had been thrown in previously. There was only one way to know which of these unseen, unplaced tiles was the newcomer.

Before long, I heard—although the wind had long since scored the insides of my ears—lines of incanted garble from each of the women. These were acrostics, truncations, mathematical patterns by which to remember the old tiles, so that as soon as their hands brushed over the new one, they would know.

Then a violent whoosh assaulted me head-on. A throbbing crash shook the porch, a smell of dry, dead apples sputtered all about me. Eventually I could make out the branches of a tree. "I'll have to start tying them down," a voice seemed to part the haze only briefly before dissolving back into grey. Soon we heard hammering, a hushed thud of stakes being pressed into ground. It continued for hours. The sharp rasp of what I heard was surely imagined. I suspected by now that the women were playing on a uniform layer of dirt that shifted and crested like desert dunes over the table surface: now and then I heard the loud slam of a tile that had managed to hit the table top itself. Soon, however, it became obvious what this was for: to indicate whose turn it was. I tried to roll over to one side so as to stretch my legs, but found that everything below the shoulders was entombed in dirt. I could not move. Out of desperation I cried for help. After about an hour the dirt had buried me up to my mouth. Only then did the face of the mother appear, upside-down from above.

"Will you be good?" she said. "Will you behave?"

I tried to nod yes at both questions, yet every effort at affirmation was subverted to a jerking lateral twitch of my head: no.

Oddly enough, the mother understood. Soon there was no more tapping of tiles. Instead, each time one of the women had finished her turn (or was about to begin), she kicked the offending mound that had grown about her feet, me; running clockwise, they jarred loose hunks of debris which by their tumbling indicated to the next woman that her turn had come. So it went on and presently my neck, then my shoulders, then my elbows and wrists, were freed.

In the distance the hammering stopped and I heard the father's imperious voice shouting, "Leave him like that!"

upon which the ladies brought him down with insults.

This time the mother got the last word: "There's still the luck in him to keep him going, although he's dead. You'll bury him over my dead body." She resumed kicking while in the greyness we heard hammering again.

Maybe it is easier to believe now that the father was right: they should have left me to my shame, its consequences. I would have liked to see father, coming up to where the mound of dirt lay like a brown scarab's egg on the porch the morning after the wind died down. With his pitchfork he'd slice deep into the mound, hoping to expose me. And he would find a body embedded in the dirt, eyes closed, safe on all accounts because real deaths alone are what he understands. My soul would have been non-existent, I would have been absorbed, cleanly and so simply gone . . . except for maybe a vapid trace. A bluish outline of my limbs, strolling or floating between the apple blossoms of the father's orchard, as placid as any private celebration of the dead may dictate. What a boon to the living, the makers of paradise on earth, if we could be so willing and disposable, everything but their memory of us disappearing without a trace.

What really happened?

This.

The women kicked me free. Except there was a price. Even when no more dirt was about me they kicked me, and then I kissed the foot of the woman whose turn it was. After her turn was up she kicked me again and I bumped my back against the table just enough so that the others knew it was time to grope for the new tile. This pattern continued. I came to realize that it would not take much to knock the whole table over, break the web of searching fingers and scatter the promise of tiles to the four winds; all I need do was stand up, fully defiant, on my two legs. Ghosts, who walk two worlds under the slightest compulsion (not to be confused with those like me who shun notoriety), would have thought of this long before. I surmised that the mother and father would interpret this as rebellion. Would they chop me to pieces, have me roll boulders, torment me by an eagle and an open wound?

These were not practical. Or maybe they foresaw that history would always turn such deeds against them.

I chose compromise. Even this was new for me. I would wait until the fourth wind, the south wind, was claimed. Either that or until someone had matched all the tiles of their hand and won. But surely the rules had already altered; they would declare the winner of the fourth wind the champion, for luck seemed to ride in the wind tiles this afternoon.

Soon the father came up to the porch.

"It's finished," he cried. "I've tied down all the trees. Now let the wind blow!"

"Poong!" a voice cried out suddenly. Following the blow to the side of my head was the admission that this voice belonged to mother. She had won the last wind, the south wind. "Isn't that wild?" she roared. "For a while I was afraid that we'd each end up with a wind and then nobody would have been the wiser. Luckily, though. . . ."

I was about to rise. I swear it. My feet were planted on the porch, both palms and the back of my head braced against the bottom of the table, any second my legs and my whole body's breadth and height would assert their power and strike upward at the lost and unbelieving. Death to all chance and coincidence; destruction to unproven possibility. Certainty was mine.

Yet, then the wind rose. Like the last tide of reason it knocked me off my feet and lifted me like paper. Instinctively I grabbed onto the table, but this did not prevent me from rising, carrying the table along with me into the sky whose conflagration drew shivers from me, thrown into its greyness as worthless flotsam.

I looked back for an instant at the retreating figures of the father, the mother, the three women. They stumbled toward the apple trees, clasped themselves fervently to their trunks and roots. By now the trees were truly small, smaller than the smallest carrot tufts, all the easier to be uprooted and trod upon and forgotten; but generosity prevented this.

Nor did I ever regret looking back again at the disappearing porch, the distraught birds, the streamer of dirt and mahjong tiles trailing under me like the tail of a kite or a slow-dissolving dragon whose significance has deserted him. Thus do I attribute the world's ignorance to the wild profusion of luck that they would never know enough about to dispute, nor I to disprove, from my silent enshrinement in this reluctantly revered summit of all places.

∾

Weyman Chan lives and works in Calgary. His short stories and poetry have appeared in NeWest Review, Vox, Many-Mouthed Birds: Contemporary Writing by Chinese Canadians, absinthe, *and* The Road Home: New Stories by Alberta Writers *(1992).*

The Mother Died

RUTH KRAHN

One theme is her goodness, how kind and gentle she was, solid as a rock, she always knew what they needed, always, always. Specific scenes: the moon from a bedroom window late at night. This would be in sickness perhaps, her cool hand on a burning forehead. Or what about the garden, that deep mysterious fragrant place, remember the size of it? *Acres!* Who did the work? She did. She is wearing a long dark dress and a white kerchief on her head as she hoes between the carrots, the peas, the beans, between the long quack grass, rows of raspberry cane. Near her squat the children, inspecting hard clumps of dirt or maybe earthworms; high in the air, the top leaves of poplar trees move lightly in the breeze.

I seem to recall putting in a few hours myself, says Uncle Jake.

They all laugh. Oh Jake, try that on someone else. It was us *girls* who did all the work. Eh, Rosa. Who picked the raspberries, Jake? Come on, tell us. Who spent all day out there anyway?

Hilling potatoes, that was my job.

Anyone for more coffee?

One thing, she never forced us to work, did she.

She made you think it would be fun. Racing to see who could fill their milk pail first, imagine falling for that.

Sometimes she was quiet, if something was bothering her.

Whereas when *he* got into one of his black moods. . . .

. . . . but that's another story. Let's not get going on that.

Always, always her gaze was pure; they all agree, she could see past the surface.

∼

What else about Grandma. Her size, the large print dresses, the aprons we could wrap ourselves in. That she was generous. One year she gave all the girls rings; mine was silver with a pale blue stone. And that she could see into your heart. Henry having punched Lydia in the chest, all of us running through the trees in a wild little pack. *You're it! No, you! I got you! I got Annie!* The scent of spruce needles, welcoming coolness. *Annie's it!* Our voices ringing in this dappled stillness, our parents far away, gathered round the dining-room table. And suddenly Grandma was there, plucking distraught hiccuping Lydia from our midst, holding her up high, wiping away the tears. Then Henry. But she knew just by looking at him that he hadn't meant to hit so hard. That was the thing about Grandma; she forgave you before you ever said a word.

∼

But getting back to *them*, something else that keeps coming up—his ferociousness. . . .

He almost—well, did someone in once. It's true, why deny it! Why deny it all the time! Let me finish!

Why make things bigger than they are? He grabbed the closest thing to him, that's all. It could have been a broom.

So he has a temper, what's new about that in this family. We're all lucky to be alive.

. . . . the time he almost lost his arm in the threshing machine? He blamed her for that, for not being faster with the bandages.

(Which she ripped from her dress, her pale sturdy peasant legs revealed, soon red with his blood.)

They were making chop, not threshing. It was on the yard. Why do you think she was there?

A real shyster in his youth. Wild-haired, smoky-eyed, a regular daredevil, look at this one! Margaret, did you see this one?

A trip to Mexico. Something about girls, what girls, *his* girls?

Now I've heard everything.

He was *young!*

They keep stressing how young. They claim not to remember anything else. Everything here is unclear. Including the year-long absence.

What?!

Locked up you mean.

What nonsense are you talking now, Abe. Him getting old age pension and you bringing that up. Look at them, all ears. Girls! Go get washed up for *faspa*. Hurry! Did you hear me?

Anyway, it's hard not to tell the difference between a broom and an axe.

~

Pension, yes, but the same youthful intensity, the arrogance and the wilfulness unsubjugated. Entering a room he brings a furious energy. All his sons are taller than he is; he towers above them on the steps reminding them of their place. Dismissed, they move meekly toward wives and children waiting in the wings. Hurry up Dad! Respect leaks away in that next generation.

With age comes a slight change in his face, a certain something unreliable there now, a small defeated shiftiness. He is suspect whereas she is saintly. Or is this gleaned from too many overheard conversations, incomplete, unreliable?

~

Our mother who didn't complain. That's what they could have put on her tombstone. The one who kept them all together even after she was gone.

Long past midnight I heard my mother's weeping.

~

He was indecent in grief, a crazed animal; the whites of his eyes glowed in the dark. A man in his prime with energy to spare and no language for his loss. Nothing had prepared him for his new role. *Widower*. It was not something he had counted on. Some of the children were still at home. They circled him stealthily, their faces pale as bones. He went to the barn like every other night and milked all fourteen cows by hand, then lunged across the yard toward the milk shed as if the pails held chicken feathers. The girls took over from there. Someone else—a neighbour, or a grown daughter—cooked the supper. It was not satisfactory; he shoved it away. He took the jumpiest horse and went riding in the back fields, the trees flaming red in the setting sun, rode till the horse was slick with sweat.

In the house he glimpsed their wedding photograph, smashed the wall beside that serene face, took a fistful of living room drapery and ripped it down in slow motion. He kicked one of her faded walked-out slippers down the stairs. He would not look at the photograph but he continued to see her infuriatingly saintly look, a Mennonite madonna without guile, as if she were in the room with him. She was the steady one, the one who took care of things. Look, her grocery list, the jar of ivy shoots. In the sewing room, a dress cut out for one of the girls, socks to be darned, overalls to patch, the same as any other day. The children wandered through all the rooms of the house sensibly picking up socks which had fallen to the floor, a ball of yarn, some paper. A large bee had got inside; they stalked it half-heartedly with a jam jar, let it out the front doors, never used. They saw the large sagging veranda as if for the first time, sat in the grey peeling rocking chairs left there all year round.

A car was coming to the yard so they went down the hill and sat by the creek, dragged willow sticks through the water, not talking.

~

My mother drove over to sit with him that first evening after Grandma died. They sat on the porch, staring out at the yard.

Those days yards weren't so fancy, my mother says. Then you could see them. Where the chickens scratched, where the dog buried its bone. There was a pile of quack grass and hollyhocks along that broken-down fence—a mess! A tangled up mess. Do you remember that yard?

After Grandma's funeral we all lined up, each separate solemn family, and had our pictures taken there on that yard, that hard gravelly place where camomile took root and where a long furrow had been worn in the ground from slop heaved out the kitchen door. Shortly after that he sold the place, except for the house and yard.

I don't know, says my mother absently. Maybe we had fewer words in those days, or was it just him. How he looked stays with me, nothing he said. Thirty-five years later and I can remember *her* voice better than his. And he just died!

I remember how the kitchen smelled, she says, how it looked with the sun coming in through the porch window early in the morning. I'd *still* know how to open the first cupboard door, how much pressure to use. Do you know what I mean? Or her china cabinet with all those things, those ornaments she collected. I can see it as plain as day in my mind. We were supposed to divide up all that stuff. But I didn't want any of it then. I was like him I guess. I didn't want reminders.

~

A hot fall day, thunderstorms predicted for later in the evening. At nine o'clock in the morning, the phone call comes that they have all been expecting; he was ninety-two, after all. Nobody expected him—even him—to last this long.

He lived on and on after her death, four more decades of him and his smouldering eyes and his mean streaks.

~

Come for supper, Dad! You've lost weight! Staying in pretty good shape, aren't you?

And to each other, Did you see his basement when you visited? A regular wine cellar down there, whole place is a fire trap if you ask me. Doctor says he has the stamina of a fifty year old.

This was when he was in his seventies. A spare spry man wearing smart dove-grey suits and crisp white shirts. Always a tie, always his shoes polished, even though his house was a pigsty. Always full of energy, although you might find him walking in his garden at ten o'clock at night feeling too low to speak.

The daughters took turns—for years—cleaning up the kitchen, scraping week-old dinner plates, pulling black charred heaps—potatoes maybe—from the oven. The sons lumbered out to the fields on the old John Deere until he sold the farm. They fixed the windmill, shipped the cattle, made the hay. But nobody stayed in the house with him. Who could stand the moods that came over him in waves, the cold brooding misery that hung around him like a cloud? They showed up after supper with plastic ice-cream pails full of cookies, took a scythe to the tall grass growing right up beside the house, gathered butts accumulating near the foot scraper.

In his eighties he married a widow from Penticton and they lived near where Ogopogo had once been sighted, waited for the moment when that long snake neck would rise up out of the waters. He had learned to garden like a man of leisure, planting and weeding and pruning, a tan Picasso-like figure trundling around a terraced garden with a trowel and a panama hat.

~

Years later my mother holds my daughter by the shoulder, turning her toward me so I can see. Just take a look at this. Look at her eyes. Who does she remind you of. I don't believe it.

His personality too, I sometimes think, when she is being remote and difficult. Thirteen and, like him, she doesn't seem to have words or, if she does, she's not using them on me. Remote, vague, uncommunicative, a look of such utter loathing will form suddenly on her delicate face that I can only watch helplessly.

One of my brother's daughters is just like her, as dark, as difficult, a formidable unforthcoming pair. Aberrations in this large family of basically ordinary uncomplicated people.

~

How do I stop this, my mother says. All morning it's as if I'm pedalling backwards.

She laughs, startled, thinking back to when her mother— his wife, my grandmother—died, years ago. My mother is running along a dirt road in this memory, a road hard with frost, past leafless trees. That's why she dislikes this season. Give me blizzards any time, she will say. She is cutting across a field, running to my father who repairs a fence, the children—me, Willy, Justine—stacking stones in an elaborate monument, as if we saw it all coming. Then the rush to the hospital, but her mother never regained consciousness, simply drifted off sometime in the middle of the night, no farewells. Holding her hand, several of them claimed to have felt some returning pressure.

Sometimes *now*, my mother says, it still feels like it didn't actually happen. As if she is playing a trick on us, but why would she want to do that.

The *not speaking*, that's the worst, she continues. She always listened and talked to us—endlessly! You know, sometimes I almost catch sight of her. It's as if she's just around the corner of the house, waiting. I can smell the weeds, there's shade, and when I look up . . . .

$\sim$

On this hot fall morning there is no yard with camomile, no windblown hollyhocks tangled in weeds. My mother has to look beyond yard, past concrete. No slop-pail refuse, no poplar trees shimmering in the wind. She looks past patio doors, past plastic lawn chairs and wrought iron railing and the two-car garage with the basketball hoop. Beyond that, more houses, more cedar, more ornamental shrubbery.

We take her car, drive slowly out of town. The gas tank shows empty. Oh it doesn't matter, she says, staring out of the window. If we run out, we'll push it to the side of the road and walk.

High in the sky a V of geese moves south. We pass the cemetery, a tractor (the guy waves), a deserted farmhouse. It is the kind of day that stays in one's memory, the still beauty of it, the clear brilliant sky, the pure air, the first leaves changing colour.

We turn into a driveway. Aunt Inga, in a white apron, is waiting for us. She and my mother embrace, both making snuffling noises. Isn't it awful? I never thought I'd feel this way, they say right away, acknowledging the loss and the pain.

More cars arrive, moving slowly—like hearses—up the long rutted driveway. Other immediate family members get out, the sons and daughters. Their spouses. One of my cousins arrives and we stand at the edge of their inner circle, his six remaining children and their spouses. Three have already died in this family, two before they were twenty years old.

Toward evening more grandchildren arrive, bringing baby strollers and diapers, soccer balls and homework, coming from jobs, from schools and universities, towns and cities. I watch my husband and kids get out of the car. My oldest son, sixteen, strolls out to the garden. What does he see, look for? I don't have a clue. He has a bookish introverted look, not unhappy. He's probably the one I should worry about, the one who has never given any trouble, or expressed the slightest dissatisfaction with anything. So, says my husband mildly, how's everything? Not bad, I answer. And in this simple exchange many things have been acknowledged. My other son, age nine, heads straight for the cement-floored barn with his skateboard. As for my daughter, she simply looks surly, like she'd like to be anywhere but here. I put my arm around her and she allows that briefly.

People have brought food—buns, bean salads, carrot cakes. Someone brought a whole tray of crab appetizers, which the kids taste and feed to the dog. A new set of lawn darts to play with, another skateboard which the adults keep tripping over.

A very pregnant daughter of Aunt Inga's phones, says she's not going to risk coming out. The women consider the significance of this, of her giving birth at this time. The smell of roast chicken drifts through the house. On a shelf, pies thaw. Coffee percolates, a fan whirls. There is music now, they have put on his favourite hymns. That's about as serious as it will get, this casual memorial service with all the family. Later—when the small children are asleep, the older ones watching TV downstairs—the adults will gather in the living room and maybe someone will attempt a few words. But nobody is much good at speeches in this family, also nervous in front of the others, who will watch and listen critically, waiting for errors, for any sign of pomposity. Some of them will fly to the funeral tomorrow or the day after, but not everyone.

Remember Mary's funeral? says Aunt Rosa. The bird that came in through the side window?

It rained right through Mom's, says my mother. It poured! The most awful day I can remember, in more ways than one. Dark?! It was as if the clouds were going to land on the church, awful.

On Mary's it rained too.

Yeah, Mary.

The dead seem to have moved in closer, wispy, maybe even comforting presences. Once Aunt Margaret spins around, says apologetically, Oh, for a minute there I thought I heard Dad's voice.

What on *earth*? says Aunt Inga, looking out of the window.

And now, past Aunt Inga's lavish roses, still in bloom, past the wind-wrecked daisies, come the horses, hitched up to the hayrack. Mark, Inga's son, is grinning, waving, steering them around to the front of the house. C'mon! he shouts as he goes past the living room window. Everyone! Get out here, we're going for a ride! He presses an imaginary horn. Some of the men are already out there, leaping on like boys, grinning, one foot up on a bale. Children running from the barn, out of the house with their mothers behind them. Reluctant aunts coming to the doorway, arms folded across their breasts, aprons already donned for the upcoming supper marathon. Leave it! yells Mark. We'll only be gone about an hour. I'll get you back in time to slice the bananas on the Jell-O.

Everyone laughs, recognizing Aunt Inga's standard Jell-O salad.

Aunt Rosa! Aunt Katie! You too, Mom! Coercing them all into coming along. Finally it looks like everyone's going, surprised aunts clambering on to the hayrack at the last minute, their faces red from the exertion. Did you turn the oven down? Over here, Rosa, here's a place for you to sit.

Horses moving neatly down the driveway, onto the road, a quarter mile north, then a right turn on to the dirt road leading west, into the hills already in shadow. *Merrily, merrily merrily, merrily*, life is but a dream! the kids sing. *White coral bells*, someone else begins, the two tunes colliding. Some of the older boys are running along behind. At one point the deep reddish glow of the setting sun appears through the trees, then because of the hills we are back in shadow.

The women are resplendent in their flowered dresses, luminous in this late light, mosquito bites on their bare legs, wearing elaborate white sandals. Someone's huge white purse sits propped against a bale. The men have removed their suit jackets, rolled up the sleeves of their Sunday shirts.

Clop, clop clop down the country road, farther into the hills. We pass a family having a campfire beside the road in what looks like a pasture, cowpies everywhere. They stare solemnly at us, as if we are a movie. They look strange too, but they fit in with the general mood of our group, recklessness and tolerance and a sense of loss.

Now they've started on hymns up at the front, the more upbeat hellfire ones first. *Work for the Night is Coming!* sung half-mockingly. But Aunt Rosa's quavery voice earnest and emotional, determined to sing, *to not give in*. A few exchanged glances among the younger ones, but then everyone is singing, even quiet Uncle Jake who ends up singing a whole song in a clear dead-on tenor voice I didn't know he possessed.

Clouds appear over the treetops; suddenly it is dark and almost eerie out here, this gang of dressed-up people on a hay ride in the modest prairie hills on a Tuesday evening somehow surreal. The two old horses clop-clop doggedly down the hilly country road. My mother is up at the front. She is standing there with two of her brothers. I see her for an instant as "sister" instead of as "mother" or "grandmother," glad she has that protection.

≈

She told me earlier that Grandpa sang when Grandma died, sat on a wide double swing he had built for the children when they were younger. He sat there, swinging slightly, one foot on the ground, humming in a low absent-minded heart-broken voice. My mother was there, sitting on the grass at his feet.

I cried all the tears he couldn't cry and then some, she said. You know what he sang? Hymns. That miserable man sang hymns, you wouldn't expect it from him, would you. I guess you do what you can.

One of my brother's kids goes up to where my mother stands, tries to pull her down on a bale. But she refuses. Never have I seen her resist a grandchild but this once she does not want to be with him, does not want to sit down and make herself available in that grandma way, the comforting flowered lap, the strong arms, her breath on his cheek.

I think about the moodiness in this family and how it was handed down, to whom. An awareness of loss and impending loss as real as anything that was happening, a thin, at times bitter, thread running along in a life.

My daughter needed me that summer; she was fragile and impossible but she still looked to me. I don't know if I really saw then the extent of what was required of me. Later on, the normal pattern: she left home, graduated from university, got married, moved away.

～

There is a letter from her in a pale green envelope on the table, also a glass vase full of lilacs sending their heady almost unbearable smell through the house. But I am trying to get used to some things. I have pulled out the oldest family album, the limp heavy one with the black matt pages. I turn around sharply. That's twice this morning that I thought I saw someone go by the window, but it's only the lilacs moving in the wind. My daughter wants me to remember names of old aunts, old female relatives. She is going to have a baby in four months and wonders, are there any good names in the family, wasn't there a great-great-aunt called Natasha?

And what about Grandma? She writes easily, lightly, perhaps feeling excited about the baby. She's lost the obituary, but didn't Grandma have an exotic second name? Lavinia? Lydia? Something quaint like that, something with an *el*.

I get over that too. I think instead, irrationally, of the frozen vegetables in the freezer that my mother did up for me last summer, vegetables I can't seem to cook.

∿

How do I stop it, my mother said.

She said, Sometimes I almost catch sight of her. It's true! At the—how would you put it—at the very edge of vision, as if she is slipping back into the trees the second I'm about to see her. Or around the corner of a house or on a path ahead of me, in the dark, just as I'm focusing. It's terrible! She was always so straightforward and ordinary, you didn't have to think about her. And now? Now I'm always wondering about her. She seems to be laughing at me, smiling from some hiding spot, refusing to be caught. I hope I don't do that to you.

∿

The smell of rain is in the air that day and far away the sky lights up briefly. We have turned back, the horses eager on the downhill homeward stretch. The hymns have changed to sad remembering ones, and the women can't resist harmonizing, the soft shy mournful altos and the odd tenor bleating through. I want to laugh, I want to cry. My daughter, seeing me get emotional, is embarrassed. She swings one leg back and forth. You're weird, she says, disgusted, stares resolutely at the fading scenery.

At the front of the hayrack, my mother stands like a captain in the wind, head up, cloudy white hair blown back, guiding us through the storm. I try hard to memorize the moment. She is holding the reins, the first born, sixty-five years old and nobody left in front of her. I watch her for a long time but she doesn't move.

After awhile, my daughter puts her arm through mine and reluctantly joins in the singing, drawn in whether she likes it or not, all of us staring down at the road skimming along at our feet.

≈

I make it up, because later on I won't be able to.

≈

Ruth Krahn *was born and resides in Edmonton. Her stories have been published in* The Fiddlehead, Grain, Dandelion, Event, Prairie Fire, *and* Prism International. *"The Mother Died" first appeared in* The New Quarterly.

Nudities

GLEN HUSER

The electric heating-fan is perhaps a bit too close to my left foot, assuring a small, relentless wave of warmth with its element incandescent and uneven, reminding me in some way of a seismograph or an electrocardiogram. Earthquake or heart murmur? My ankles are burning; my nipples are freezing, but it can be endured for five more minutes. Mind over matter. Mind over what matters. Wasn't that what Ulla said? "You take your thoughts and move away, anywhere you want, leaving your body in place like one of those possessed people in *Invasion of the Body Snatchers*. I can be with you for a day and feel that I have spent the day by myself. You make love to me and I feel that you haven't been there." Years of living together has made us aware of each other's failures, failures in accommodation. I try, especially after tears. But she is right. It is something I have always done. Not so much fantasizing, not the Walter Mitty-Billy Liar trip, but just a slipping away to a calm centre, a quiet, secluded landscape. No, landscape is not the right word. There is no sense of land, rather a kind of soothing buoyancy. Maybe cloud one, far removed from cloud nine. The hierarchy of clouds. I have made an effort, keeping my eyes open when we make love, conscious of my St. Vitus dance of sex, back and forth against her, into her, my hands anchored to her scapulas. You learn the anatomical terms. But consciousness is not the answer, not in making love. It is something we both know. To think of sex, however unsatisfactory, is a mistake. I can feel my body stirring, blood moving along canals, floodgates closing. The body has no sense of its history of failure. I think of the winter evening, wind and snow, the great effort to move from one point to another in the city with buses running off-schedule, roads drifted over. A mental cold shower.

There are eight in class tonight, despite the storm, pieces of their bodies showing from behind the rectangles of their drawing boards, the sweatered arm of Mr. Clement who came in brushing icicles from his beard, the grey, matted hair of Mrs. Dorchester, working at an easel which reveals her purple Fortrel legs, square-toed black boots. Randy and Eldridge, the two drama design students, show flashes of black leather and weathered denim, the glint of an odd metal stud or pin. Laurel and Hardy, the nurse, Janice, calls them out of their earshot. Her own Cossack boots splay out from the drawing board over which she has folded her arms, staring at me, given up on the pose, her hair, wash and wear, sphinx-like in its form, almost vibrating with static electricity.

The Japanese dentist reveals the most of himself, working in a sketchbook open on his lap, his gaze relentless. He is close enough that I can watch the progress of his drawing, his pencil moving as if it were involved in automatic writing, lead discovering the contours of a man, hip-bone softened with skin, like the edge of a violin against folds of drapery, pencil moving down the sweep of thigh, circling on the knee.

Beyond him, at easels, are the two high school art teachers, Daphne and Sylvia, thickening into middle age, their stolidity showing in bits of bulky sweater, the flash of a ring, dark slacks. They talk incessantly, both of them weary of the pose.

"Gordon," one of them says, "Let's have some action poses after this. We're all hibernating."

The lab supervisor smiles at them, an ingratiating, automatic smile, his lips in pained parentheses, his face a page of boredom. Anxious to get home, old Gordon, home to a glass of sherry, the Rubenesque Mrs. Kerrip, a fleshy cuddle, an electric blanket.

"Okay, let's grab a coffee," Gordon says. "Thank you, Joseph." He is very formal, Gordon, using the stiffness of phrases to cover my nakedness, a small kindness in a way. I massage a muscle in my leg that has gone to sleep. When it is possible to stand, I slip into my bulky turtleneck first. This is deliberate. The sight of a man, naked except for a sweater, is startling enough that it always stops the two schoolteachers' chattering for a moment. It is worth it. The one garment makes me suddenly obscene. Ulla has accused me of doing things for shock value. "Probably an insecurity," she once said in the same voice that she used for identifying the acne sprinkling my upper back. "I think this is actually a boil." She had taken to reading pocket-books of psychology to ease her through the last months of gestation, sometimes propping Karen Horney or Jean Piaget against the ledge of her stomach. "It's rather endearing. Like James Dean poking his phallic finger at the world." My jeans lie in a heap of denim wrinkles next to my sneakers. I put them on in descending order.

The group has pulled two tables together in the coffee room. I feed coins into a machine that spills thin, watery chocolate into a corrugated plastic cup. It is, at least, hot.

"Christ, this evening is a waste," says Janice, lighting a cigarette, drawing in the smoke, holding. She offers the pack to me. "Nothing is working," she exhales a laugh. "You would think I never put pencil to paper before in my entire life."

"We all have our days." The Japanese dentist smiles as if he were an advertisement for his profession. "Have you been keeping warm enough, Joseph?"

I make a so-so wavy motion with my hand. "The old place is kind of draughty. But the heater's warm."

"How's the bambino?" says Daphne, the school teacher who asked for the action poses. "Still got that cold?"

"Naw. It's gone." I'm surprised she remembered. I see Ulla bathing him as I leave. He does the cooing, giggling things that babies do in their bath, smiling at his mother. "You silly," she whispers. "Do you think you're on television? Some ad for baby shampoo?" The small, naked body shines under the kitchen light, the skin a warm, pinkish-orange against the blue wallpaper. "See you later," I call. She doesn't respond. It seems deliberate. "I should be back around ten." Does it matter?

"Some action poses will loosen us up," says Gordon, breaking a small silence that has settled over the group. "And it'll keep your blood moving, Joseph. You need to on a night like tonight." Words fall with the banality of snowflakes. The old man goes on about a television show he has seen on the Group of Seven. He has a particular enthusiasm for A. Y. Jackson. "The rhythms," he chatters. "The closest thing to a Canadian Van Gogh."

"Lend me your ear," Eldridge snorts, nudging Randy.

"What?" The old man's face is beginning to match the maroon hue of his patched sweater.

"Nothing," mutters Eldridge.

"I should say nothing." He gasps for words. "Less than nothing. What do you know? I ask you that? What do you know from anything?"

I take my hot chocolate and head back along the corridor to the labyrinth of studio rooms. I cannot bear to hear again the old man tell us of Dachau, the litany of remembrance. The break will last for another ten minutes. With the drink in my hand, I move from one drawing station to the next. Lines of conte and charcoal and Chinese ink catch my body.

I am eight different figures. Sylvia, the other high school teacher, has drawn my head and shoulders only, the hairs of my head formed individually, line upon layered line, lapping my ears, my neck, my shoulders. My eyes are dead, unfinished. It seems a waste, the rest of my body neglected. She's paid her money.

Daphne's pencil, as if making up for such parsimoniousness, has roved everywhere, but with little effect. The parts don't seem to fit. I can see her frustration. Randy and Eldridge, for trying to look like they are cut from the same mold, have very different styles. Eldridge sees the figure as Conan the Barbarian, muscles anticipated from the faintest suggestion. Randy lingers on surface detail, my mustache, my lips, the decorated almonds of my eyes floating in a blank face, the washers of my nipples afloat in the torso, the scribbled coil of my navel, my genitals a trefoil.

I am studying the old man's drawing when he returns to the studio, first back from coffee.

"Nazi punks," he mutters. "They know from nothing." When he sees me looking at his sketch, he brightens. "Good lines," he says, without modesty. "Lotsa movement." My body undulates over the page.

Mrs. Dorchester, juggling an oversize patent leather purse, a box of Smarties and a cup of soup, joins the old man and me.

"I was just saying lotsa movement in these lines, eh?"

The Smarties have slipped out of her grasp, and, moving suddenly in an attempt to catch them, the old lady slops her soup onto the sketch.

"Pepper towels," Mr. Clement hollers. "Pepper towels." I make a dash for the distributor by the sink.

"Oh, my God," Mrs. Dorchester is moaning. "How clumsy."

I stuff the paper towels into the old man's hands. He dabs at the newsprint. The roiling lines of my torso deepen and set in the stain of chicken broth.

"My God, my God." Mrs. Dorchester has set down everything to free her hands, which now grab at the paper towels. Mr. Clement's attention shifts from the sketch to warding her off. "It's OK," he protests. "Just a sketch y'know."

The others are returning.

"My God," Mrs. Dorchester laments loudly, "Would you believe I spilled soup on Mr. Clement's sketch?" She laughs suddenly, a laugh close to a cry.

"Hmmm," says Janice, the nurse. "It adds a certain something."

Mr. Clement smiles weakly and pins new paper to his drawing board.

"I'm sorry." Mrs. Dorchester has modulated her voice to a heavy whisper. She is fussing over her own sketch of me, cramped into one corner of a page of newsprint. There is no sense of form, only a sense of struggle. Abandoning the details of my body, she has taken great care with the leaves of a philodendron plant to the side of the podium.

"A disaster." The nurse gestures toward her drawing. It is obvious that she wants me to look at it, to confirm, or perhaps deny. It is a startling, almost cubistic drawing, large Picasso feet and toes, simplistic profile features of my face set in the circle of my head.

Gordon, who has followed everyone back in like a plump shepherd, comes over to us. "In-ter-esting," he says, "very interesting."

Ulla calls it the kiss-of-death word. Interesting. "Say anything," she had exploded in a drawing lab we once took together, "but for Christ's sake don't say it's interesting." The lab instructor had backed away from her fury.

Gordon rubs his hands together in some odd little pantomime of labour, or perhaps enthusiasm. "Ready, Joseph?"

I slip off the shoes, remove my jeans, pull the sweater over my head. The buzz of talking stops, creating a silence defined only by the ruminations of an old heat register, and, beyond the window, the muffled insistence of the wind seeking its way around the corners of the building. It is something that always happens, the human voice struck dumb by the sudden revelation of the human body. Was there a great silence in those camps, the ones where Mr. Clement worked, a hush along the rank and file, the figures shuffling naked to the showers, hands held awkwardly, covering the secrets of sex? A quietness before the crying? A silence before the death showers?

"Two minutes each," Gordon says.

I reach my right arm toward a point on the ceiling where water has made a pattern of small, flower-like shapes on the ivory plaster. Laurel and Hardy have just returned from coffee. I can feel a draught swirling in from the corridor in the minute before the door is closed again. My skin tightens. My genitals pull close to the warmth of the body mass. Ulla likes the cold, walks unclothed through rooms with windows open while I shiver under a quilt. She has some northern ancestry.

"No wonder the baby has a cold," I complain. "And there's snow, wet snow getting onto the books and stereo."

"So you care about some things." Her voice is softer than the snow. "The baby's fine. They don't get colds from fresh air." She doesn't close the window. I think she wonders how long I can wait until I move, the quilt wrapped around me, to close it myself. Wipe the moisture off *The Paintings of Egon Schiele* and *The Post-Impressionists* which lie flat on top of the other books, dry the speaker tops, the Plexiglas cover of the turntable.

"OK," Gordon signals a change. There is a stir of papers, a brief resurgence of talk. I go down on one knee, clasp my hands around the other. I feel Mr. Clement's gaze, unblinking, following my descent. Closing my eyes, I see the bodies collapsing, hands grasping, hear a moaning like the sound of wind. A mass of lines such as the world has never seen before, the rake of fingers against the soft mound of buttocks, a stretch of thigh, the right angle of an arm, the dark, matted pubic nest, an open mouth.

I move again, stand, twist my torso. The play of muscles will appeal to Eldridge. My back is to him but I can imagine him working feverishly to model each muscle. I kneel and lean as far back as I can, my hands flat against the wood of the podium, my head flung back so I can feel my hair along my shoulders, my larynx pressing against the taut skin of my throat. No one speaks. Is it because there is no time, or because the sudden changes offer variations on a theme of vulnerability, a vulnerability that strikes us dumb? I do not allow them the chance to ease past the humbling fact of my nakedness, shifting, reassembling.

When I move into the long pose, there is a corporate sigh, a riffling of papers, small mumbled comments. Nude reclining. I see the drawing boards move from portrait to landscape position. I lean against a mound of cushions, my legs crossed at the ankles, one arm resting on my abdomen, the other in a crevice among the cushions.

"Aah, good," says Mr. Clement. "That's a good pose. Lotsa possibilities."

"Yeah, that'll do," says Gordon. "You can keep that one until we're ready to quit."

Daphne, though, is dragging her easel across the room, its metal legs scraping against the floorboards. "You know damn well I'm a flop at foreshortened feet," she mutters.

Mrs. Dorchester pops a Smartie contemplatively into her mouth before brandishing her charcoal. "Is your picture drying off OK?" Her other hand hovers close to Mr. Clement's cardigan sleeve. "So clumsy."

"It's OK."

I close my eyes. Somewhere there is a sound of water gurgling. The same sound that the bathroom radiator makes in the flat. I see Ulla, through veils of steam, lying in the tub, her breasts floating, islands lapped against by the shore foam of soap. Her head is supported by the tiled wall. Small rivers run down the wall; small rivers run down her cheeks. "Are you there?" I think she says, "Are you there or are you only pretending?"

"What do you mean?" I remember saying that.

"What does anything mean?" The radiator clangs to life and covers the sound of her gasping. I can feel the water welling in my own eyes, blink them open quickly. Eldridge tears the paper from his board. "Fuck," he says through clenched teeth. "Fuck, fuck, fuck, fuck."

Janice rolls her eyes to the ceiling. Gordon says, "Now, now." It seems to be a time for repeated words. Mrs. Dorchester is stuffing the remaining Smarties into her mouth as if to shore the opening against escaping words of her own.

"Do you want me to keep my eyes closed, Eldridge?" My voice comes out louder than I expected.

"Naw. My drawing's just shit tonight. That's all."

I keep my eyes open, not wanting to slip back. It seems to have grown colder in the room, despite the clanging and gurgling of the radiators, the steady hum of the electric heater. Goose bumps surface along my arms, my upper legs. Mentally, I pull on my sweater, my jeans, my wool socks. Dressed, I can, in a turn of the mind, strip the class. Crinkled flesh hangs from old arms. Mrs. Dorchester. Mr. Clement. Gordon is the most exposed, sketching into a handheld notebook as he moves around the room. He is plump and almost hairless, pink buttocks, his stomach round and firm, his sex almost hidden in its small patch of sandy wool.

Janice stretches, revealing small, sensible breasts, the construction of her collar-bones, the cage of her ribs. Sylvia and Daphne present, from behind their easels, glimpses of voluptuousness. The two graces. Like a figure in a bathhouse, Mr. Hakashimi gleams, his honey-colored skin catching the hanging light. Randy and Eldridge are pasty and white except for their patches of sex. One circumcised; one uncircumcised. Roundhead and cavalier. Laurel and Hardy.

I allow them their clothing back. There is a cramp in my leg. I try to communicate this subliminally to Gordon. He does look up from his notebook, glances at his watch, nods at me.

In the dressing room, I get into my outer gear, light a cigarette, lean back in the chair, massage my leg. When I head back into the studio, Gordon is unplugging electrical cords. The easels, drawing boards, odd bits of studio furniture have been left like one of those scenes in a movie when all life is sucked up by some alien force, or suddenly struck by a nuclear disease and everything has remained at odd angles, bereft of what gave definition and meaning to its arrangement.

"Can't give you a ride tonight," Gordon apologizes. "Heading the opposite way. My wife's sister. . . ."

"No problem." I flag a good-bye.

For once the Number Sixty-Four bus is waiting. The snow, softlit by street lights, swirls against the window, like television snow. I make my own pictures. I see myself walking up the stairs to the flat, easing myself in, careful with the quiet. Ulla is on the sofa, her robe undone, suckling the baby. She is conscious of the effect: the pale, striped dressing gown, flesh pinkened, fresh from the bath, contented child.

Something by Mary Cassatt. A small smile plays on her lips before she remembers herself.

The bus turns along a downtown avenue, pauses. Three bundled figures emerge from a theatre foyer and hurry to the stop. I close my eyes, shutting out their entrance into the bus. Life is filled with too many details.

I have, already, the details of Ulla and the baby, the flat. Closing the door quietly, in case they are sleeping, I move forward in semi-darkness. There is the sound of water dripping. In the bathroom, Ulla lies on the floor. Nude on an indoor-outdoor carpet. Moss green. Red a contrasting color, looking even more vivid against its complement, roseate stains by her still wrists. I am afraid to go and look in the baby's room.

In the showers, Mr. Clement's showers, did the naked women clutching their naked children embrace the lurking exterior of horror knowing that there would never be the luxury of self-despair? Decisions being made for them. The threat, "I'll kill myself," unheard. So hush, Ulla, hush.

The snow has thickened and it is hardly possible to see beyond the window. There is a particular sound, though, to the bridge spanning the ravine and one set of lights beyond is my stop. I pull the cord and letters flicker in a plastic panel above the driver. Descent is into fully-formed drifts. There is a dance of snow like frenzied moths around a street light.

The walk-up is close to the bus stop. Just a few feet but it seems like a long way and, when I get there, definitions have been smudged. There are no front steps. I find it difficult to make out the window on the third floor that allows us to look out over the street. It is only when I have eased myself into the flat that I can tell the window is open, allowing the snow to come into the living room, covering with its fine powder the books, the box-like shapes of the stereo, the television. In the night-light, a silvery dust. *Hiroshima Mon Amour*. The first film Ulla and I ever saw together. The landscape of bare bodies, the softly-falling radioactive ash. Ulla had been mesmerized, her hands at times reaching up as if to touch the flickering radiance.

I am afraid to look in the rooms but do it automatically, as if I am checking to see if any other window has been left open. There are many things missing, which is somehow a relief. The wonders of negative space. It is only when I sit down at the kitchen table, clear as Ulla has always kept it, ready for its many functions, and light a cigarette, that I allow an acknowledgement. It comes in a funny, odd rattle deep in my throat. I am warm, too warm, even though I have not closed the window.

I see the man moving from where he sits, removing his clothing with the quick, efficient moves he has mastered as a model. I see him moving as a pale ghost, back to the door, nude descending staircase to the step, out into the cold waving sea, lotsa movement, cold moving back into warmth, curling in the snow, the blanketing snow, the covering snow.

The rattle in my throat becomes a small laugh. A cough. Emphysema mon amour.

I borrow Eldridge's words: fuck, fuck, fuck, fuck.

Last chants, I think.

Putting the cigarette at the edge of the table, I get up and close the window.

~

Glen Huser's *short stories have appeared in* Dandelion *and* Prism International. *His novel,* Grace Lake *(1990), was nominated for the W.H. Smith/Books in Canada First Novel Award and for the Writers Guild of Alberta Fiction Award. A consultant in school libraries for Edmonton Public Schools, he is the managing editor of* Magpie, *a magazine of student writing and graphics, and a co-editor of Nelson Canada's Mini-anthology Series for junior high school students.*

Betwixt and Between

JOAN CRATE

The children, each tucked under an arm, press into his warmth. "A story, Daddy," Sarah pleads, and before he can answer, Zach has slithered off the chair and snatched a book from the shelf. *Peter Pan.* It's their favourite, Khalil's as much as the children's, and the pages are pocked from his big thumbs flipping them over and over again, the children's sticky fingers snatching at magic.

"Peter Pan was a strange creature," Khalil begins, "A betwixt and between, neither one thing nor the other." I look up from the elusive buttons I'm attempting to attach to Zach's denim overalls, the needle poking through the holes of the button, getting lost in faded cloth, and see three pairs of molasses-coloured eyes glistening with anticipation.

They take after Khalil's side of the family, our children, the same dark eyes and hair, though their skin is lighter, like mine. We compromised on their names, chose ones that are acceptable in both Arabic and English, though Zach's name is really Zachariah. Still, they are Canadian children, and sometimes I wonder if they could fit into the scrambled puzzle of their father's homeland.

Khalil refuses even to consider taking them to Lebanon

to visit. "Not until the wars are all finished," he says, "and that may be never." Still, I wonder whether or not they would feel any attachment to their grandmother, their aunts, uncles, and cousins whom they resemble, but whose language they cannot understand. A family of strangers. And the physicality of the land. Would they feel at home there? Could the sky and sea unveil hidden dreams; or would it be only a foreign country, an address to send postcards from? "Today I helped Grandma dry *burghal* in the sun. Tomorrow if there are no snipers, we'll go down to the sea. I miss you."

Khalil has told us about the farm he grew up on, the almond and olive trees, pomegranates the size of two fists, figs and dates, the five kinds of apple trees, and fields carved from the side of a mountain and brimming with tomatoes and watermelons, until we could smell the swollen fruit, taste its warm juices, and feel the baked mountain soil and scorched air on our skin. We were there, or at least we imagined we were, but really, each of us was in our own familiar world. We can never totally shed the predjudices imposed on us by our birthplace. This I discovered one day when I asked Khalil how big his family's farm is.

I'm no stranger to farms. I grew up on one southeast of here, near Fleming. Every summer I take the children to visit and often Khalil drives down on the weekends to argue with my father about pesticides and taxes over a beer and one of Dad's machine-cranked cigarettes. The children love their grandparents' farm, the space—land stretching as far as the eye can see. Forever, I thought as a child. Planted with just one crop, an endless golden chorus. Dad always takes Zach and Sarah for rides through the fields on the old John Deere, points out the quarter section that their great-great-grandfather started with, tells them stories of old horses and frostbite, and how in the dirty thirties the farm was almost lost to the bank. Although they've seen it all, have heard each of Dad's stories, they find themselves again immersed in earth and words, mesmerized by the unbroken line of land, sky, and generations.

"We had the equivalent to . . . let's see . . . almost five acres," Khalil replied.

Sarah and I burst into laughter. "Almost five acres? You call that a farm?"

I push at the needle, try to coax it through the uncooperative fabric, the too small button hole, then give up and clamp my teeth around it and yank with my jaws. What the hell, it works. But Sarah has noticed. "Mo-om, that's not very safe," she admonishes, stroking the wrinkles from her corduroy pants with delicate fingers, as if it's a gown she's wearing, silk and lace.

We tease Sarah, tell her she was born into the wrong class, and she solemnly agrees. She has such an aristocratic bearing, has had since she emerged from my womb clearly disdainful, and ten days late. She stared blindly down her perfect nose at Khalil and he kissed her and called her "princess." Sarah means princess.

Of all the places we've visited only one has ever lived up to Sarah's impossible standards: Notre Dame Cathedral in Montreal. We were in the city visiting Khalil's sister, Yasmine, and she took us to the cathedral. Sarah and Zach, who was just a toddler at the time, were holding hands, but once inside the entrance, Sarah gazed up into the dome, felt the height, the distance, saw gold-leaved walls, intricately carved alters, statues of bruise-eyed saints, the holy, flowing fountains, mosaics of angels, of the serpent, of Christ stepping from death to immortality, all dyed by shades of light pouring from stained glass windows, and her hands flew into the air. "Yes," she cried, voice shrill amongst the dull murmurs of tourists, and she twirled, eyes lifted to the highest point in that ceiling, hundreds of yards through space. "Yes," more quietly, her tone approving. She sat down on the front pew and glanced contemptuously at those less full of grace shuffling by.

"As if she owned the place," Yasmine commented later as she served us tiny china cups full of sweet, thick coffee. Khalil and I had to agree. Strange what we think we have a right to. Everyone, not just Sarah.

Would she, would Zach, look pale beside the sun-brown faces of their Lebanese relatives, their clothes—fleece sweatsuits and insulated jackets—so terribly out of place, their voices too low and even their limbs, their movements, expansive, melting away in the raucous heat, the shouting, wailing, the explosions, and dazzling sunlight? Would they disappear like so many in Lebanon have done before, but their demise different, nothing to do with guns and blood, a simple dissipation into the air, a transcendence into the vast, sweeping lines of Canada, the hush of winter, their home.

Sarah, Khalil says, reminds him of his niece. Rima, her name was. She was his sister's oldest, and beautiful too. He teased her when she was young, called her "cow eyes." "But really, her eyes were heart-breaking, so large and soft." She was too young to die, just fifteen.

He kisses Sarah's forehead and her nostrils flare slightly against his scratching whiskers. She points to the picture of Wendy, Michael, and John airborne in the bedroom, their beds small countries below them, the boundaries escaped.

Rima ran off and married a man from the mountains, a Shiite Muslim, and her Christian father was incensed. "He wouldn't accept Rima's marriage, was furious, and my sister finally got fed up with his anger and moved back to my parents' house. She and her six other daughters."

I remembered then that Khalil's parents lived in a tiny cottage, three rooms, he had said before, and I tried to imagine the snarl of bodies and gossip, bed rolls, summer sweat and girls' secrets.

One uncle told Khalil that Rima's father hiked up the mountain one day to find his daughter. He wanted to tell her he forgave her for her marriage, to accept his new Shiite son-in-law into the family, and to finally make peace with his wife and six other daughters, still giggling and quarrelling in their grandparents' shack.

But Rima was shot. Her father shot her, or maybe it wasn't him. She could have been caught in crossfire between her father and her husband. Or her husband's friends. Who knows? There are too many stories, too many theories; every relative has a different one. "So which one is right?" I finally shrieked at Khalil in frustration. "Who killed Rima? What is the truth?"

He shrugged.

She was carrying a basket of pomegranates, and when she fell they splattered over the ground. At first her husband thought she had tripped, that the red stains around her were merely pomegranite juice, and he ran to her, her father ran too. I suppose that's when they stopped trying to kill each other.

When I look at the old photographs Khalil keeps in a dresser drawer: his mother and father old and bent from their years together raising children, some who are still in Lebanon, some in Canada, some dead; his six nieces standing over lumpy bags of their belongings, his sister and brother-in-law staring uneasily into the camera lens, the farm, the old donkey long since left in the hills for the wolves, I feel the weight of heat and dust, of anger and gesture impossible to understand, of overwhelming confusion, and I tuck them away under his pile of winter sweaters.

"Tick-tock, tick-tock," the children chorus joyously. Captain Hook aboard his pirate ship winces. Time is running out.

I re-thread the needle and glance towards the fingerprint-smudged window. Outside there's a chinook. Dark cloud is sliced neatly away by a blade of yellow sky and the trees blow with a west wind that tears the snow to tatters. Tomorrow a fresh snow is expected, or so the weatherman says.

I like snow, the way it insulates everything, keeps Khalil's and my pasts separate, yet pushes us together here and now, seeking the warmth of one another's bodies, drifting us into a future together. "Too many differences," my father said when I told him I was going to marry Khalil so many years ago.

"Nevah-nevah land," Zach squeals, pointing at the book. "Never-never land," Khalil repeats, trying to enunciate, though he's never been able to master the Canadian r.

Zach has his grandfather's way of watching, Khalil has said many times, the same expression. Just a few months ago we heard that the old man had disappeared. Khalil called his mother's neighbour, the one with the phone, and she ran to get his mother. It was the morning of the next day in Lebanon, the sun already beginning to bleach colour from the trees, but in Calgary it was the middle of night and the sky was stung with cold, white stars. I counted them from the bedroom window while he talked to her, his voice so familiar, so foreign, speaking words I couldn't understand. They had found no trace of his father.

The afternoon he disappeared he and his wife had finished lunch—feta, black olives, bread, tomatoes, and strong, sweet tea, she told Khalil—and then he kissed her throat the way he had done for years—and left for his daily hike up the rocky path, up into the mountains.

He didn't return. No clothing was found, not the ragged patch of a shirt on a prickly *shummuleh* bush, no shoes thrown down a ravine. No shadow torn away like Peter Pan's and left, a smoky film on the ground.

Khalil is at the part of the story where Peter begs Wendy and her brothers to stay in Never-never land and not go back to the real world where they'll grow up and grow old, develop aches in their joints, cry, and worry too much. This is the part the children don't understand, that as a child I questioned. Why didn't they remain in the ageless circle of fairy light, play at being a mother, at being a hero, battle the evil but ultimately harmless Captain Hook and win, win forever? Suddenly they're back in their bedroom at home with Nana the Newfoundland dog.

"Was it a dream, Daddy?" Sarah wants to know. She's getting older, I realize, beginning to understand the uncertainty of truth, the diverse ways it can be interpreted. Khalil and I exchange glances. He winks. Sometimes it seems as if I've always known him and we're each part of something whole. But once we watched a hostage who was released in Beirut on the news, and he said, "When I was kidnapped. . . ." Then I realized there's so much about his life I don't know. He was afraid then, and his fear seeped into the room, into me, and I was afraid too, of our pasts, the places in each other we can't enter, can't even imagine. These are our own personal stories deplete of magic, that bellow out every now and then, that will not be silent, and each language is foreign to the other, though we try. We each try to understand.

Khalil's at the end of the book now, where Mother and Father kiss Wendy and her brothers. As a kid I thought this was pretty corny. Me, the daredevil on a John Deere charging down country roads, and as a young teenager sneaking out my bedroom window and running off with forbidden friends to forbidden parties, always wanting to get away. Now I'm satisfied with this, find the foggy London air, the cozy parlour soothing after swords, ropes, and cannonballs. Even Zach and Sarah look content. Khalil closes the book.

"Want to go outside and make snowballs?" he asks the children, and they run for their coats. "You coming?"

"In a minute, after I finish Zach's pants." The thread struggles up through the last button, anchors it. I can't sew worth a damn. I'm not much of a cook either, but Khalil doesn't care. We use team work to keep house, raise our children, much to his sisters' chagrin. I'm not the responsible little mother I once thought I wanted to be. I've grown up.

I watch him through the window as I knot the thread clumsily, clip the ends away. Sarah and Zach squeal with delight as he sprays them with a handful of snow. They chase him and he falls, rolls on the ground with them, laughing, all three of them laughing. I grab my coat and head out the door.

I catch Khalil gazing up into the sky where warm chinook wind has burrowed through the cloud. There's a hole there someone could fall through—a terrible accident, one blink and they're gone. Or perhaps it's a tunnel for those who must escape a night too dark, a world too strange, one in which they no longer belong: a young torn wife, a tired old man. John, Michael or Wendy. Even Jesus.

~

Joan Crate was born in Yellowknife and has lived in places throughout British Columbia, Alberta, and Saskatchewan. Currently teaching at Red Deer College, Joan writes both fiction and poetry. She has had work published in several journals and anthologies and aired on CBC Radio. In addition, she has published a novel, Breathing Water *(1989), and a book of poetry,* Pale As Real Ladies *(1989).*

Krishna saw the universe in his mother's (father's mouth

ELIZABETH HAYNES

The body wakes. Lies, eyes closed, listening to the ceiling fan. PUnkaPUnkapUnk.

The body pushes away sheets, pushes self to edge of the bed, sits. Reaches for clothes on the floor beside, puts them (same as yesterday on. Looks to the picture above the door, festive cows and dancing girls beside a river. Lies, eyes closed, listening to the ceiling fan. PUnkaPUnkaPUnk.

At the door a tap tap

tap

Miss?

tap

Yes

Breakfast

Thank you

She waits until he's gone, then opens the door a crack, slides the tray inside.

Over lips tongue hard soft palate esophagus stomach runs the hot sweet milk of tea—like tea poured by mom after Em's finished all her steak, beets, corn, potatoes, after she's heard about starving children in Biafra, her mom bringing in the brownbetty with the orange teacozy that was accidentally left on the element, that caught on fire.

Fan pUnkapUnka air smells like dirt hot hot. When you gonna? When you gonna, Em?

When you gonna out. When you gonna out, girl, when you gonna? Can't go on forever swallowing peptobismal, lomotil, tea and dry toast and tea and rice and tea and

Elsie Marley grown so fine
Won't get up to feed the swine
Stays in bed 'til half past nine
Lazy Elsie Marley.

Sick, sick. Stupid. Forget Fodor's, forget the Michelin guide, you're here to experience, Em, those samosas that vender is selling smelling tumeric ginger have one have a few I'm sick damn I'm. . . .

Voices: shhh now, you haven't **seen** sick, honey. The Colins boy your father was up with all night, he has leukemia. You'll be fine. Fine, yeah fine, lying here with my insides falling out

Sleep. Wake. How long? Six o'clock—morning or night can't see no windows light whispers around the door   night?

The body is empty. The body is hungry. Tired of tea and toast and rice. Finished all the books. The body may, might, could, should, try a chapatti, a bit of dahl, surely it can't object? A bit of meat, of beef, would he bring it?

Cows chewing boxes, streaming/screaming rickshaws and taxis and people and bicycles, with cars honkhonk weaving around them crazy crazy, gotta cross, gotta cross Chandni Chowk, follow the people, Em, go, one rupee Mrs., one rupee, boy with no legs handrunning across, smell of fat, cries of frying street vendor, do what they do, Em. GO.

No. No meat.

Why not? The man could get it. The man with the gentle voice. Is it he she sees behind the desk when she walks cramped down the hall to the bathroom, is it he the old one standing ruler straight beside the door or the younger one middle aged, slouching chairsoft under the floating blue babe Krishna, is it him tall who watches her from under hooded eyes watches her walk trying to keep what's left of her butt from swaying?

The body curls up.

Easy to find a small place here. Even in India even in Delhi even in Govinda Inn, even in a small bare room with a fan PUnkaPUnka, easy to find a small place to curl up in easy to find.

She takes up little space.

Once, on a bus home from university, she watched a large woman fold herself up like an umbrella, pull in elbows, legs, shoulders, jam thighs into hard, cold busmetal, making room for another person.

The body makes room.

Boys in school. You always knew where they'd been— lives strewn over desks, tables.

Her father didn't take much room. He sewed people up so fast, so silent—you couldn't tell where the wound had been.

Now she's home, packing. Pack light said her mother and the *Travel Survival Kit.* Pack light—clothes for the hot in Varanassi and in Goa if she goes for Christmas, clothes for the cold in Kashmir if she goes to hike on the glaciers, to ski.

Pack light, said her mother.

Don't go, said her father.

Shut up, Em says.

Light. Lightness. The incredible lightness of—what, Em?

Stomach churning.

Eat your toast. You wanna get better? Eat!

She picks up the plate with the one cold piece on it. Runs her tongue around the sharp edges, bites down, chews. Chew, chew, chew. Stops. Waits/listens for stomach—that sharp tightening she knows will move down forcing her to walk cramped like an old man as fast as is decent to the bathroom down the hall to that small squatting space in the dark no light can't find the light and a river of water shit.

Wait. Listen. Nothing. Take another bite of toast, Em. Take another. Now drink. So it's cold, no-one ever died from drinking cold tea—lots of people die from dehydration. You wanna get out? When you gonna get out, Em? When you gonna figure out how to get that bus to Varanassi, Em? When you gonna?

Tap

Miss?

Yes?

You would like some more tea? Some soft drink? Limca? Goldspot? Thums Up? Campa?

No Thank you

Miss?

Yes

You are feeling better?

Yes

You are travelling alone?

Yes

You are travelling without a male relative?

Yes

You are not married?

Yes

Your father knows you are here?

Yes

You will be staying how long miss?

Not very

You are still sick, miss?

Not so

I will fetch a doctor

(Tired, dizzy, can't remember damn somosas damn vendor stupid girl stupid

A doctor, miss?

No Thank you

Will there be anything else, miss?

No

Thank you

Her father opening the car door, Emily sliding out, boots first, sun on snow, the snow glazed and shiny, wheeeee, on her bum in the snow. Craack, foot stomp in the ice pool, craaack, lines shoot out, her father taking a gloved hand and pulling her gently toward the shop.

Inside, Mrs. Najerski in the blue light from the sign *Mike's Meats*, *Mike's Meats*, huge behind counter, behind trays and trays of meat like flowers—blushed pink of pork, cream of chicken, purple rose of steak.

She comes from behind the counter, smell of rust and salt her bosoms falling onto Emily's face pushed between.

Hand disappears into apron pocket, emerges with sausage. Skinny girl. Eat.

Then Mr. Najerski is there, blue sign from outside flashing in *Mike's Meats Mike's Meats*, splashing over the blood on his apron.

And Emily is inching, over to the glass counter, trailing a finger along its cold ice smoothness, around, slowly, while her father arranges for Mr. Najerski to pick up a deer left by a patient, inching front, side, Mrs. Najerski's great bottom in the air as she bends to set in a tray, the door to the cold room behind ajar. Emily screws up her eyes, thinks she can see an upside down cow, horns and all, swinging from a metal hook.

The body wakes hungry hungry lights blazing in its eyes.

No. No food. Let this thing pass.

What time is it? What time? No time. Watch has stopped.

Find out, find out what's the matter.

Hungry. Food.

No!

Em flips through the medical pages of her guidebook:

Dysentery: amoebic, bacillary or chigella. A form of diarrhoea in which the stools often contain blood and mucus. May be accompanied by nausea, vomiting and fever. Lomotil or codeine may be effective in the early—

If all the world were paper,
All the sea were ink,
And the trees were bread and cheese,
What should we have to drink?

Will you just concentrate?

OK. The things in this room. In this room there is a bed, small, single, hard with two lumps, one in the middle, one near the head. On the bed are two sheets (white and thin, one small pillow, and one stiff gray blanket. The walls are white. On the north wall are black marks, some thin and long, some thick and long, about waist high. There is a brown metal chair (folding, to the east of the bed. The pack rests against this chair. There is a small built-in closet with two rusty hangers. The floor is grey concrete. There are books and clothes around the bed. One is

She closes her eyes, just for a minute, dizzy, shit, feels her forehead hot closes her eyes just for a minute a minute then she'll be OK, then she'll be strong in control know just what to do

She is in a slaughterhouse. A single blue bulb hangs from the ceiling. Cows on tethers wait their turn. There is blood on the floor. It is her job to mop it up. The cows are led to a man, a man in a white labcoat, a man wearing a white mask. The cows don't complain, don't moo or balk. Emily mops the blood around, squeezes the mop so it runs into her pail, thinks stupid cows they don't make a sound. She watches as a brown velvet cow walks softly up to the man. He takes it tenderly by the throat and, as if wiping off a bit of grass or spittle, draws the blade cleanly across the neck, drip drip, dripdripdrip, then sews it back up, lickety split

Miss?   Miss?
Oh, uh, yes?
How are you?
OK
I will tell you a small story
Alright
A story about the god Krishna
All right

The god Krishna, as a boy, he saw in his village the preparations for the worship of the rain god, Indra, and he was angry

(tired so tired

So he came to his father and said to him we, father, are not tillers of the soil, nor dealers in merchandise; we are sojourners in forests, and cows are our dieties. We who tend our herds in the forests and mountains should worship them, the mountains and our kine

I'm sorry, I can't concentrate (eyes of lead *I'm*

I will come back

Yes Please

Thank you

(Close them, yes, just for a sec

Dark in the room. The lights, she was sure she left them on, just closed her eyes for a minute, was going to read, to read her *Travel Survival Kit*, was going to find out about the Canadian embassy, was going to find out where she could go to a clinic, was going to find out about dysentery giardia typhoid cholera

"You have no idea," her father shouts, "absolutely no idea what kind of diseases you could contract."

It was a busy time, then, disease-wise.

Stampede time. The Williams Lake Stampede.

Her father offered brochures: "Experience the regal majesty of the Taj Mahal, the ancient holy city of Varanassi—deluxe two and three week tours led by highly trained and hygenic English speaking guides familiar with all local customs."

"I'm going for a year, dad."

Who turned out the lights?

They were on, the lights were on.

Who turned out the lights?

Em sits up, head spinning, damn hard to focus, lies down again. Lies, silent, in the dark, listening for that tightening of stomach   listen   nothing. Sits up, hears music, faint, a tiny tinny melody, sees   something, a man a god a gold something yellow peacock crown blue body shining and shining above the door

Sits, slowly, pushes away sheets, stands, hand on wall, staring at the blue gold man god, walks slow watching, dizzy shit, stops, eyes closeopen. Gone. Replaced by cows, river and shepherd girls.

Back. The tray. Where's the tray? The tray is gone. Did she? No she doesn't remember taking it leaving it outside— no. She didn't. Did she?

The onset of typhoid is gradual with headache and sore throat. Victim's symptoms include pea soup diarrhoea, rose spots, abdominal distension and fever. Intestinal haemorraging common. Death occuring in third week. Contagious. Treatment includes

She lets the book fall. Yes. It was Krishna, Krisha with a peacock headress, blue chest bare, lower body draped in yellow silk, playing his flute for the shepherd girls.

It was.

She sits up. Yes, she is feeling better.

Could just be the Duricef working, though. Killing the parasites, amoebas, what are they, small transparent things swimming around the perimeter of a petri dish under the microscope's all seeing eye.

She is much better.

What you need is a shower, pee-you girl you smell bad, your underarms, yeasty underpants, disgusting.

She climbs out of bed. Finds some new clothes. Snaps the bedsheets tight, tucks them in, straightens the filthy blanket. Swipes up her dirty clothes, folds them ready to leave outside the door for the man to pick up. She will leave a note. Or maybe she'll just walk down to the front desk, her clothes laid carefully on her arms like an offering, she'll walk up to the erect gray haired man reading the the *Times of India* under the floating blue babe, she'll excuse herself, say "are you the one who brings me tea?" "Oh yes," he'll say, smiling, laying down the paper. "I'm pleased you are feeling better." "Yes I'm feeling so much better thank you very much. I'll just be going down to the bus station now to get a ticket to Varanassi then I'll be off to the telephone office to call my father, tell him everything is fine. Just fine."

The sheets are wet, sweat. Hot, so hot.

Tap   tap

Yes

How are you, Miss?

OK

You haven't had food for a long time, Miss

No

I will bring you some rice

Thank you

Some dahl

No (a bit of meat, meat for strength, iron   *perhaps a bit of be*, uh lamb, *if you can*

Yes, lamb. I will tell my wife

Fine

And I shall continue with the story

Yes Please

So Krishna's father and the people of Vraja they began the worship to Mount Govardhana and to the Brahmins and the cattle. And Krishna, you know he can take many forms

He can

Yes, many forms. So he assumed the form of the mountain and began consuming quantities of food while at the same time climbing the hill with the other cowherds. And the god, Indra, he could be a very wrathful god

Yes

He sent his clouds to destroy the region. And so a frightful storm began, with claps of thunder and the pouring down of rains. The cattle shivered and the people were so afraid

Yes (feels rising of bile, groans

Miss *You are very sick*

No

Bile moving up from stomach, swallow, swallow it down, get down, get over to the edge not in the bed, shit, oh shit, stupidstupid shit

It is raining outside. Emily watches the drops race down the living room window. Her father is dressing. Putting on his big blue sweater from Alaska, yellow slicker, yellow rainpants, black boots. He is going away, to Riske Creek her mother says, a man got shot. Why mommy? For stealing cattle, sweetie. Was he hungry? Perhaps. Sister Josephine found him, my father says. Thank god. Though why anyone would steal those starving animals.... Can I go with you? He lifts her up—such a scrawny little thing, no honey you can't go. Shot? she asks. With a bullet from a gun, says her mother.

A man who has been shot has a round hole in his forehead and a dreamy smile on the face, thinks Emily.

Pushing open eyes. Her clothes and the vomit have gone.

He must have come in. Can't have, shouldn't have, she could be contagious, poisonous, dangerous like Putana, the demoness with poison breasts. And what happened to her, girl? Krishna killed her, that's what.

Stupid. Get ahold of yourself. Think. Do.

She stands shaky cold all of a sudden so cold walks to the door feeling the cramp of stomach quickening of bowels opens it bright light from the hall so bright flooding her body walks quickly down the cold brown hall to the bathroom sudden cramp and omigod hurry clutching stomach open the door squatting in the dark a river of watershit. She curls up around herself, cries and cries.

Later.

No-one around, late it must be, the man—her man?—at the desk sleeping grey head in his arms under Krishna innocent all knowing babe smiling serene from his floating lotus leaf.

Miss?

Yes

Miss, you are needing a doctor

No

Miss?

Yes

Your father knows you are here?

I don't know

I also have a daughter. Her name is Radha

That's a pretty name

How many in your family?

Just three

You would like to hear the end of my story?

Please

So Krishna he lifted up the mountain and bade the people to go under it. And the rains continued for seven days and seven nights. Finally, seeing he was outwitted by Krishna, Indra made the storm cease. Krishna restored the mountain to its former site. And Indra came down from the heavens riding his elephant, Airavata, and worshipped Krishna and purified him.

And?

And?

What happened?

They embraced each other and all was forgiven.

All was forgiven?

Yes, everything.

The mind struggling up from sleep, dreamless this time. Hot, so hot, the lazy fan PUnka, PUnka, too slow needs to be higher dammit, everything here slow as a postal clerk.

Em struggles out from under the covers, turns the fan up as high as it goes. Not very damn high. The lights are on again. There, beside her bed, is a tray a pot of cold tea a plate of congealed lamb—when?

Cholera is characterized by sudden onset diarrhoea— rice water stools—and excessive fluid loss resulting in rapid development of metabolic acidosis. Rapid progression with coma in final stage. Fifty percent fatal if untreated. Contagious

There are boys, everywhere boys pushing each other off the swings. Jostling for the four square and the tetherball.

Emily is standing still against the wall beside the girls' washroom watching. It is hot. The sun is hothot, Emily puts her hand across her eyes. A boy runs across her shadow.

Help, he screams. Help, help.

Another boy has fallen from the top of slide. Fallen or pushed. His body is twisty. Red falls out of his head.

Emily's shadow shrinks.

Then he is there. With his blue Alaskan sweater and his black bag from when he worked with the lepers in Nigeria from before she was born.

He takes out a needle. Threads it. Holds the boy's head gently in one hand. Begins sewing with the other.

Miss!

tap

MIss!

tap

MISS!

What, oh, sorry, I was sleeping—

You are needing a doctor now

I think my medicine—

Your medicine does not seem to be helping

I think it is

No, I do not think so

The third day, coming off the bus. A boy had been hit, rickshaws and cars and buses and bullock carts were stopped, people swarmed around him, a man was taking his pulse. Em pushed her way up to the front. Is there a doctor? A doctor? Em cried and a woman said yes, you go, go away, go away now. The boy was skinny, you could count every rib. Flies danced on his eyes.

A beggar girl came up to her, put two skinny fingers all she had on Em's arm, cried one rupee missus one rupee.

You could die here.

Stupid.

Fall into a coma and die.

Idiot.

Death within the week. Dehydration, delirium, too late for the man can't help you then. Does he care the man you send him away, delirious too late anyway says the doctor the doctor says foolish girl stupid tourist girl why didn't you come before why did you come at all its too late much too late.

Shut up!

OK, sleep.

Dark for sleep.

Clothes in a heap beside the tray beside the bed beside the dark

Kali

The halo the picture not the girls not the cows where's the other?

Krishna

Where are you?

She is in a white room. Her father lies on a stretcher. A tube extends from his stomach, another from his nose. This is how he stays alive, it seems. The nurses feed him thick white liquid through a tube in his stomach. She sits on a metal chair. She tells him about her Religious Studies course. Her paper is on the concept of Maya in Hindu thought. Maya, she explains, is that which stops man from seeing the world as it really is. Oh, he says. Another doctor comes in. He is wearing a white labcoat and mask. There is blood on his gown. How are you feeling, doctor, the other doctor asks. How is the diarrhoea? The shits, Em's father replies. The other doctor laughs. Now Em is feeding him cut up vegetables through the hole in his stomach. Some of the pieces fall out. Things fall apart, her father jokes. The centre cannot hold

Or maybe

Maybe this one goes on and on and she can't wake though she tries commands wake up stupid stupid it's a dream dreaming of tap tap tap, the door cracking open, miss, light, squeeze the eyes shut the doctor the shits, eh, haha doctors make the worst patients, open wide now aaah, I'm fine, really, a man in a white mask brings her more food on trays, bread, vegetables, meat, and she's cutting it up, feeding him through the hole in his stomach, eat you must eat something she pleads while Krishna watches angry may kill her tear out her bowels yes oh yes anything my cows are sacred sacred no that came later, scared and she whimpers sorry and he looks at her gently and with love and begins to play a melody strange and haunting on the flute as he walks toward the forest open now open wide you must come with me and the voice she can't see says miss, miss, you must open, I'm trying, Krishna saw the universe in his mother's mouth, father's mouth? and he didn't get punished, all was forgiven, open, if you don't open, please miss—no it was in Krishna's the universe in Krishna's mouth behind those lovely flute lips. If you don't open he will go away

(Or maybe he doesn't come at all

≈

Elizabeth Haynes' fiction and poetry has appeared in literary magazines and in the anthologies Tilted to the Plane of the World *(1987) and* Alberta ReBound *(1990). She edits fiction*

for blue buffalo *magazine, works as a speech-language pa-thologist, and travels. "Krishna saw the universe in his mother's (father's mouth"* was first published in absinthe, *vol. 5, no. 2, as "She's Perfectly Well (and she hasn't a pain."*

Entry Site

MARY HOWES

He kisses her hello & she thinks he does love me.
But still I may have damaged him.
And he just doesn't remember.
Maybe he remembers & he's just not saying.
Maybe he really hates me.

He pulls a chair across the dockboards & stretches out his hands. They're large & tanned, calloused. There's golf course dirt under the nails.

"I can't feel anything. Do it."
She touches him gingerly.
"Go on. You showed no mercy when I was a kid. Do it. You can't hurt me."
She presses the splinter towards the entry site & pushes it out.
It's so small. Smaller than the smallest eyelash.
He flutters his long ones at her.
"Amazing how something that small can hurt that much."

His hands are like his father's she realizes with a start.

She can't remember his face anymore.

Something about Tanya Tucker. "Lineman for the County."

Oh yeah. He won a Glen Campbell lookalike contest back then.

He doesn't know his hands are like his father's.

He doesn't know what I'm thinking right now.

I could scream when I think of what I'm thinking right now.

He looks like an Italian movie star.

The dark skin & hair, the black shirt, unbuttoned.

The brown bone buttons, unbuttoned.

The Ray-Bans.

He shifts his shoulders against the sun behind on the lake, leans his elbows on the picnic table.

She sucks in her breath, lies back on the chaise.

"Two thousand bucks for a blowjob," he says. "The guy must have been one helluvan oral artiste, huh? I mean if you weren't there at the time, they couldn't connect you to it, you were guaranteed a mil just to sign the insurance papers & split til it was all over & done with, Christ, it'd be tempting, huh? Live that life? The Mediterranean, the boats, the chicks, the dough, huh?" He flips the pages of *Vanity Fair*.

I should take a picture of him like this. Backlit. Outlined.

A real star. But she doesn't want to go inside for the camera.

Something might change by the time she gets back.

"I'm not going to kill you, Wendy. I'm just going to bash your fucking brains in."

He's coming at her across the dock, waggling his fingers at her in a "c'mon, c'mon" way, the killer smile in place. Sometimes he does the chicken salad sandwich bit from *Five Easy Pieces*. That's her favourite. That's her cue to laugh. It hurts, today. The sun. Her eyes.

Closed, she feels the chaise lift & roll a bit with the waves underneath the dock. He keeps on talking. Low, intimate. A sense of complicity. Urgency. Somebody else's voice. She shudders, picks up the black and white book at her feet.

I am Right/You are Wrong: From Rock Logic to Water Logic. Sometimes you give me the creeps she says under her breath.

How perception works: the brain will reconstruct the whole picture from just a part of it or a sequence can be triggered by the initial part.

Hey it's only a game, mom.
Did he say that?
She looks up.

"Hey, it's only a game, mom. Quit trying to beat me. You know I always win. I'm your nemesis."

He swivels his great head around to her, wolf eyes, slanted & leaf brown in the light from the citronella candle in the silver pail on the table. Beyond him, the black lake, something silver, too. Just a flash. And a pair of loons.

Ibex. Ibex. Use it in a sentence.

She fiddles with her tiles, stymied.

How can he be so good at this?

He doesn't even read.

The next night they play anarchy scrabble. Anything's a word.

Unchallengeable.

Thineapathy . . . obittable . . . crellow.

He craps out. He slides the tiles into the Crown Royal bag.

"It's too hard to play with no rules," he says.

"How about a swim?"

She hates anything watery, especially water. Being in it. Underneath it. Anything touching her legs. Fish, weeds, rope. She showers, never bathes. She makes soup thick as stew & milkshakes you can stand a spoon in. She wears loose skirts, no stockings. She dangles a toe in the water, flips bits of bread to the sunfish. They flash turquoise silver heads, fins. One of them nips her toe. When she screams, he laughs.

"Hey toebread," he says. "That'd be a good one for anarchy scrabble, wouldn't it? Except we're not going to play that anymore, are we? See the dots on their sides, the orange & black spot just past their eyes? Pumpkinseeds. That's what they're called. Pumpkinseeds. Get it?"

Later, when he goes into town for cream, the kid from the next cottage staggers over, a huge puffball in his arms.

"Do you want to eat it?"

Alabaster buttocks severed at the waist.
Thwack. Thwack. He smacks it with his palm.
"It feels like rubber but it's real good fried in butter."
She reaches out & touches it.
She says no thanks, I just had lunch.

There are five kinds of memory: recall, which is conscious. Then imagistic, feeling, body & acting out, which are all unconscious. You never get repressed memories back by trying to remember them. Trying to remember will only access what you already know.

He's stirring the bolognese, adding cream in a careful white stream. He's careful with his words. He doesn't look at her. She's careful not to interrupt the flow, him talking & cooking in the middle of the night.

"So," he says, "whaddya think? Is it genetic?"
"What? Insomnia?"
"If that's what you call it."
"Did you hear me?"
"Yeah, I heard you."
"I'm sorry. I didn't mean to wake you."
"So why should tonight be any different? What's going on?"
"I'm trying not to remember."
He sets the spoon down carefully on a saucer on the stove & looks at her.
"You, too, huh?" he says, shaking his head. A flash of something silver as he turns back to the stove, starts to stir the sauce in small circles.

"I don't know, mom. All summer. It's almost Labour Day. I wake up when I hear you. I know you said not to come in, not to interrupt. It's something you have to do alone. I know the rules. But it just kills me. What am I supposed to do? Lie there? Roll over & go back to sleep? I gotta do something . . . I get up and . . . ."

He dips the spoon into the sauce & lifts it to her lips.

"Careful, now," he says. "It's hot. Blow on it."

~

Mary Howes, an Edmonton writer and performance poet, has published three books of poetry: lying in bed (1981), Vanity Shades (1990), and QHS, winner of the 1990 bpNichol Memorial Chapbook Award. Howes' text and voice, with music by the nouveau jazz group, Guerilla Welfare, is available on the audiocassette Evidence I was Here. "Entry Site" is her first published short story.

Sleeping (uneasily) with Franz Kafka

RUDY WIEBE

CLOISTER:

The memory of mirror. Nothing of its size, or shape, or what must have been its inevitable baroque trim—merely the angle in it of that enormous room and window before him in the glass, as it seemed, and which followed him in through the tall door. Was it that huge nun-like space which first lured them into never closing a bathroom door? The morning light there slants upwards into long, vanishing emptiness. And Adam staring at it still thinks that Kafka is something else Karan can eventually be persuaded into forgetting.

"Would it help," he calls to her, trying in the mirror to recall all the pictures they have studied of those deep-set eyes, the long, bumpy nose, and doing so only too well—in generalities the face might be tilting forward on his own naked shoulders—"say, help if I parted my hair in the middle? Trimmed it up sort of high, sort of shaggy, like a fur cap?"

Out of sight she is still laughing at the vegetarians' fuss in the restaurant the night before. Her voice echoing such auditorium rhetoric: "Those people, they play around with their health as if it were a sickness!"

"You're quoting again," he says, very nearly bitter.

Perhaps she hasn't heard him; she is still laughing.

"How about if I prop my ears out," he calls again, louder, "like his, sort of these big scoops catching the . . . ."

"O shut up and get back here."

She was there then, her tender body then still waiting. The ancient, noisy bed too tiny in the room under ceilings that vanish upwards, somewhere in air; her slender body seemingly as forgotten there as all other possible nunnery purposes that vacant building once had. Only hidden under the close warm tent of sheets, and skin along skin, can they see each other and escape its cavernousness.

"Why do you always want me?"

"An unfortunate state of mind. For me."

"Don't you mean 'body'?"

"Not at all."

"The body is a state of mind?"

"Abso-loo-loo-lutely."

"'The applicant,'" Adam quotes in German between her breasts, "'is fluent in the German and Bohemian languages, in speech and writing, and further he commands the French, partly the English—'"

She thumps his head fiercely, "Stop it! It's hopeless, you never had a huge Freudian father to hate."

But he cannot stop quoting against her incredible skin, "'"It's a unique apparatus," said the officer to the research traveller and considered, with a certain look of wondering admiration, the to him very familiar'—ugh! that hurt!—or should one translate 'Apparat' as 'execution machine'—ugh!—"

Karan is on top of him, his arms pinioned back flat, her tense knee thrust between his legs and threatening.

"I'll kick you out," she pronounces through her perfect teeth.

"Okay—okay, but please, please—" He is trying to laugh, but sad words suddenly sing in his head: *memory is but a cruel frailty of the mind; mixing memory and desire breeds pale, lost lilies out of the dead land.* Such confused words, really. Hopeless.

$\sim$

STREET:

A microscopic image of his face shining in her black eyes. Was he that small to her, always so tiny? Tiny as an archaic keyhole they peer through in some unreadable street in the Josefstadt area of old Prague, a keyhole she found too, she is a superb research traveller. As she has quickly found the air-blackened bust with its unreadable Czech on the corner of what was once, she informs him, Karpfen and Engegasse, everything of the building torn down and rebuilt except the original entrance and even that veiled by scaffolding which might have been clamped together there since his birth in 1883, bleeding such a century of rust. No Intourist official in Wenceslas Square who could speak either English or German or French would admit knowing the least thing about that corner, that building now built over and into the baroque profusion of the St. Niklaskirche behind blue hoarding, the nine-spired towers of the Tienkirche shrouded in iron above an angle of roofs. However the youngest female guide acknowledged *sotto voce* as they all bent together around the mapped bend of the river pulling the old city together that o yes, Franz Kafka was of course born and lived his life in the ghetto of Prague, yes, right here in this curve, but it all had to be rebuilt again, *restored* after the war, All The Peoples' memorial to the horrible Nazi elimination of *all* Jews once living in Prague, one person safely dead and buried in 1924 could be no more important than any other in a rabid, genocidal destruction of an entire race, though Prague itself had not been as much bombed by the Allies as all those other defenseless European cities and of course the Grand Soviet Army had not fired one single shot more than necessary to wrest it from the last Nazi gauleiter, shooting him down in this very street, she said, pointing—what were they really looking for, exactly?

Karan says nothing as Adam bends to the keyhole; he half expects inside the bolted planks of the door an insect's legs to waver in unresisting air. Oddly, the door is at street level, though the long brick wall stretches away a metre above his head, and the gravestones seem to stick out over it to the far walls of buildings, stones shaded in brilliant sunlight by the moving branches of trees. With stones there so high—could a city be sinking even as it was torn away, leveled and re-built?—the remains of the dead must be buried at eye-level, an elevated cemetery in a city quarter dug twice out of decrepitude and bordellos? *Was the patient earth dragged away to eliminate the sweat of lust and poverty soaked into it? Where could you bury that?* But inside those ancient planks—they couldn't have been that old he thinks, the wood should be more rotten—the graveyard apparently drops to the level of the cobbled street, and an insect remaining would have been too much to expect from relentless National Committee cleaners. Gravestones only, thick as files in a cabinet. But unrifflable; unreadable. Each one thin as a graven hand carved edgewise, blundered with moss through what might be Hebrew, or German, or conceivably even Bohemian notations that continue their centuries of settling over the bodies layered in this long-suffering earth, every tiered body pulling its slab down at its own sagging angle into rot and falling slowly, surrendering nothing of its irradicable stone. Peered at from this tiny angle, and ignoring the drone of the city, the tall sunlight makes it appear a gentle, mossy garden of crusted knives.

Or had he actually been looking below the cemetery protruding above the brick wall? Had Karan somehow found and shown him the truer graves hidden below a tourist surface, the green bottomlessness of old burial? It was possible; without him she might have found anything.

"He isn't buried there, not there," a voice says behind them. Gravelly as small water in a stream bed long dry. Like her desiccated face.

"Whom do you mean?" Karan asks.

"They'll charge you five korunas to go in, but you won't find him."

"Whom do you mean?" Karan asks again in her delicate German.

"In the graveyard in Prague-Straschnitz, there's his stone." A dark round mound of a woman, her crushed face held together snugly by a cowl. "Though who knows if he has a body."

"We're interested in Franz Kafka, where he—"

"Who else?" her mouth gums words, "on this street." Laughter ripples, a small wind shivering over her. "But I wouldn't go make the effort to look. If he still has a body, it's been dug up seventy times over."

Karan steps close to her. "Dug up? Who dug him up? When?"

Adam understands each word, but cannot fathom them together. A sunlit summer street in a huge city roaring with markets and voices and cars, its historic centre designated heritage and so saved from the grotesque castings of 1980s subway tunnels. Nevertheless this apparition in sibylesque charcoal transfixing his beautiful friend between baroque building, cobbled street and an iron-studded door in a contradictory graveyard wall with uttered aphorisms. They face her together, startled, more than a little frightened.

"Heh heh, o they were such organized hunters, where was there earth enough to hide Jewish bodies, dead or not?"

"When?" Karan repeats. Her hand has lifted, she may be about to tug the next, true word out of this featureless human hiding.

"If he was ever there, and his parents lying right there too."

Karan's face slowly freezes, mouth slightly open to the icy tips of her teeth. The sunlight is so brilliant Adam understands how Hermann Kafka could once live somewhere here in a house called "To the Golden Face."

"Where? Where do they lie?"

"Straschnitz. There you'll see what they did, the few Jews that ever got rich in Prague."

"We were there, it's just... an ordinary... graveyard...."

The word Karan used was, of course, 'Friedhof'—literally 'yard of peace'—peace! The crumpled face actually crumples farther, into what must be accepted as laughter. To all appearances sympathetic; or ghoulish.

"That poor Franz! Only for seven years hid in the earth,

alone—ach and then his heavy papa lies down on him again."

Mama too. That's what the stone said: "Dr. Franz" . . .
"Hermann" . . . "Julie" . . . Franz, not Frantisek, as the river
for him was 'Moldau,' not 'Vltava'—but their quest seems so
ridiculous to Adam, suddenly: to know *all* the facts about
someone you'd have literally to relive their entire life, stu-
pidities and all, thank god this one lasted only forty-one years
and not like Goethe eighty-three. What the hell anyway did
it matter where Kafka lived, or if his body was still disintegrat-
ing somewhere? They hadn't wiped out his stories and
novels, even though his literary executor Max Brod published
the bulk of them after death in direct contradiction to Kafka's
will that they be, without exception, burned. Max Brod.
What kind of a shit friend, and executor—executioner?—was
he, huh?

"You're the shit. You never listen," Karan tells him,
striding back. "You see and hear what suits your fixed
preconceptions. And remember even less."

He should have looked through the keyhole once more.
Or let her walk away, left her and gone past the brown and
the yellow Skoda to the cut-stone building at the corner and
paid the five korunas and gone in past the inevitable girl
asleep at the entrance, her hand open for a ticket. Perhaps if
his ignorance had searched among those broken knives of
stones under the trees he could have found something he
could not now misconstrue, or forget. An entrance opening
down. A helpless beetle on its back. Lovers locked apart
forever in adjacent stone. A printer ripping back and forth,
buzzing out a bloody text between its fixed margins on
folded automatic-feed skin not yet, quite, turned into parch-
ment or paper. As she once said, with Kafka who repeated

and anticipated everything about humanity like certain writers in the Old Testament, with Kafka all horror is already possible.

≈

CLOISTER:

"I told you and told you," she tells him. "He lived his life in that Prague ghetto, Josefstadt they called it, right there within two hundred metres of where he was born. Grew up, was sent to a Hapsburg dying Empire German school, to Charles University eventually, graduated a doctor of laws, went into work recommended by his business uncles but didn't stay—his father moved the family incessantly from one house to the next—upwardly mobile!—and when he was twenty-five not one building in which he had lived remained standing, anywhere—not one. Can you retain that one simple fact?"

"Aren't you distorting? If all the buildings were gone—"

"Can you under*stand*? I'm talking about *vanishment!*"

"My parents homesteaded in Saskatchewan, I can't even find the cellar depressions."

"Jesus you're a self-important bastard."

"If you're talking vanish—"

"You can travel the world and see nothing but yourself!"

"And you're a bitch with keyhole vision! Franz bleeding Kafka, middle-class, educated, super-achiever Jewish suffering, such suffering on a permanent disability pension from the Workman's Compensation Insurance Comp—"

"You're being an ass."

"Who the hell hasn't suffered? See anybody, ask them, they'll yell it in your ear—who?"

Very quietly: "I'm talking about the writer of *The Metamorphosis*."

"Suffered, and suffered *without* full pension, *without* beautiful women in every spa and hotel in every great city of Europe more than willing to lick the goddamn sweat off your goddamn suffering brow!"

"Did you hear me?"

"Every romantic opera heroine dies of tuberculosis, lungs gloriously unclogged, singing full tilt!"

"Did you hear what I said?"

"Yes yes. And also 'The Great Wall of China' and *The Castle* and *Amerika* and *In The Penal Colony* and whatever else he scribbled and scribbled, hundreds of pages. Most of which he ordered burned."

"What do you know what Kafka ordered?"

"He wrote it, so why shouldn't he ash it?"

"Who told you?"

"His will! But Max Brod and his dear Momma decided it was worth too much—"

"You think anything he ever wrote was that simple, even his will?"

"Maybe he didn't write it—he just signed it."

"Well . . . ?"

"Well what?"

"Do you know? Did he write his own will, word for word? What it said?"

"Karan, he had a Ph. D. in law, his will—"

"And if he wrote this very personal document, his will, he meant it to be taken literally, word for dictionary word?"

"Arrrggggh," he groans, "you of course always know—everything! Your endless overload of ironic facticity. I'll tell you what I know Kafka wrote, because he published it while he was still alive! He didn't burn it—*A Country Doctor*, Munich and Leipzig, Kurt Wolff Verlag, 1919. And in it a postage stamp story—as translated by Willa and Edwin Muir in 1933, or a little later—and I quote: 'The Next Village: My grandfather used to say: "Life is astoundingly short. To me, looking back over it, life seems so foreshortened that I scarcely understand, for instance, how a young man can decide to ride over to the next village without being afraid that—not to mention accidents—even the span of a normal happy life may fall far short of the time needed for such a journey." ' "

He stops; her face is as expressionless as only unmoving perfection can be. He says, "Facts enough?"

"What happened to your favourite passage, in the first book he ever—"

"Answer my question, please."

"O yes fact, to the very comma . . ." she peers at him from under her lashes, "but I meant your first memory-work, from his very first collection, *Betrachtung, Achtzehn kurze Prosastuecke*, dedicated to Max Brod, Leipzig, Rowolt Verlag, 1913. The one sentence story, 'The Wish to be a Red Indian.'"

"I have," he declares formally, "as you well know, vowed never again to mention that one, to you abhorrent, *word* in your presence."

Yet even as he speaks he is reaching for her shoulder, which for a moment isn't there, but comes.

"You have an outstandingly selective memory."

"Never to mention it, in any form, either as 'native' or 'aboriginal' or 'Amerindian' or 'first nation' or 'indigene' or—"

"Ree-ally—'indigene'?"

"Yes," he says, dripping formality, "nor even to quote it from the writer whom you have now so conceived of in your mind as to worship. I will no longer express any wish, ever in your presence, aloud, to gallop spurless, reinless, over the smooth prairie (which is never actually smooth but then your idol, never having seen any, wouldn't know that and perhaps didn't care to try and imagine it—even the ambiguous greatness of Kafka eventually reveals that some writing "types" are always necessary) when one's 'horse's neck and head would be already gone'."

"Facts, dead on," her kiss nuzzles tongue and lips in his ear. "Correct to the semi-colon, my lovely camera-eyed lover."

And she is running ahead of him. Along the wall of that devastated nunnery, past the locked and boarded chapel doors singing,

"Come run in the woods . . . come run in the woods . . . come in the woods . . . come   come."

≈

CLOISTER TOWER:
But, very oddly, the double tower doors open when he hesitates after her, and tries them. A small, square space scattered with straw, mouse and rat leavings, with bird shit. It must be pigeons, when he looks up he sees a beak protruding here and there where the black crossbraces angle into corners. Bobbing out, and back again, single eyes, perhaps they are brooding there in the lengthening summer. A fine tight space with beams to pattern the long emptiness up and up, upward openness for an only son who at thirty-one (be accurate from

1883 to 1915) has not yet left the clutching itinerant house of his parents. High beyond the fluttering thump and scrabble of pigeons, there, where inside the dome the light dusts long beams into existence.

He can rest, and lean his hands on that light as if it were oak. The sustainable iridescence of air, a Kafkaesque quality indeed. Far below him her beautiful face—*that was memory of memory only, he was certainly too high to see*—rests on the tiny roundness of her bared shoulders. Her body dropped away, gone, and as unrecognizable as his own face upside-down.

"Come down."

Her voice climbs the off-set sections of ladders to him so cautiously, so thinly; when it reaches him she is stretched into one sweet word,

"... sweetheart. ..."

And then he desires suddenly, overwhelmingly, to climb higher than is possible, to see only the backs of the pigeons as they open and lift their dappled wings wide to escape, even momentarily. She will have to be terrified; with him.

Climbing up is always so easy. In the empty dome of the cupola he has to jump a little to clasp the empty bell-beam, and then he swings out. On air. But he can't get his feet to lift high enough over his head to catch himself up and hook, they seem too distant at the end of his sudden heavy body. Hand-width by width, the squared beam cutting his wrists, he manoeuvres himself nearer the arch of the wall, then walks his feet up until he hangs at right angles and parallel to the long column of space below. But his body will not pull up and over, onto the hewn beam. Not like he once lifted himself and walked the two-by-four rafters of houses in southern Alberta wind, or swung over scaffolding onto the slender parallel facts of strapping—the beam is straight between his straight arms, he does not look down, he will listen only to the beat of birds below him, the blotches of medieval stucco fallen away, the air now straight as a bed of needles which he lies on like prickling silence, his clenched stomach and crossed ankles and hands may hold something somewhere and feel nothing. Nothing. Like resting on the brief moment of freefall. Or possible prayer.

~

CLOISTER WOODS:

He finally catches up with her where the beech branches reach past her into space. The forested ravine is sheered away level below them by the evening sunlight, and he is gasping.

"'And there in the wood,'" she sings, dancing, "'a piggywig stood with a ring at the end, of her nose, her nose, with a ring at the end of her—'"

"Toes, her toes, come toes or come nose, we will come to blows."

"You blow or I blow?"

"We'll blow together. . . ."

"And come together. . . ."

"Can't—it won't rhyme."

"Piffle," she swirls that away with one naked arm flung over the ravine of the world, "flow together, grow together, stagger to and fro together. . . ."

The branches and their perfect leaves fly beyond her black hair against the sky, bits of light opening in his eyes like the slow elliptical movements of all-night stars. There is a jagged branch thrust under him, he knows it with a quick stab of pain and he thinks, I'll carry a scar on my ass for life. But he forgets about that then; forgets it completely at her marvellous, ineffably sensual movement.

≈

CLOISTER:
It is only visible in a mirror, bent over and backed up looking ridiculously between his legs; *and only for a few months. That wasn't where he carried a scar.*

"A new angle on yourself, my love?" she asks, suddenly there. "The pucker of your piles?"

"I don't have any."

"I know that perfectly well. I've kissed your every pain away, again and again."

"Not every pain."

"O you poor darling," she nuzzles his head into her opening lap.

"Kissing should make you feel *all* better."

And she turns the tables on him, again.

"Our kissing never will, will it."

Perhaps they were seated on the bed in that cavernous room. Or he was kneeling against her knees after she had folded herself into the stuffed chair—was there a stuffed chair?—when she said that. Actually, it must have been much later, if there was no scar. At the time she said they should find a doctor, the skin was really broken and who knew what infection lay scattered in a German forest, she was always more concerned with his bodily ailments than he. Perhaps because he had so few. If he could only be sick sometimes, he thought then, or have some small, trivial but very visible wound on his body—even a barked knuckle would help—then for a short time at least they might not have forced each other to find such extended furies. But they lurked everywhere, wherever they were, anywhere in the world together.

~

STREET:

"And his three younger sisters," the old sibyl laughs, "they were all very close, those four Kafka children, Elli who travelled with him to Hungary and at last to Mueritz on the Baltic, and good little Valli, and Ottla the youngest, she gave him his last summer cottage when he almost couldn't eat any more. Ottla he loved best, but he died in the soft arms of Dora Dymant."

"So . . .where are the three sisters buried?" he asks. So stupidly. Karan turns, stares at him in shock.

"You can look in the air," the old woman croaks. "Buried in the air, like garbage!"

"The polite word is 'Assanierung'," Karan tells him. "You knew, why did you ask?"

"I did, but . . ." he can never explain how he could have, even momentarily, forgotten the long list of women whom Kafka loved, as much or as little as he could, who within twenty years were annihilated so grotesquely one way or another. "Only Felice Bauer, whom he refused to marry, every five years, and—"

"Only refused twice."

"All the fives he had time for."

"And Dora Dymant. Dead in London, 1952. The human 'Assanierung' of Prague."

"I . . . what does that mean?"

"The word they used—architectural clearance, *cleansing* would be the present word—raze every house in Josefstadt, after 1893, and build this quick imitation Vienna. Kafka said, 'Our heart still doesn't know anything about this completed 'Assanation'. The sickly old Jewish town is much more real to us than this hygienic new city around us.'"

"God, you've memorized *every* word he scribbled, even his letters."

"At least I don't pretend they're the Deathless Word of God."

"Hell no!" Furious irrationality bursts in him. "*You* never pretend, *you* just know! Everything!"

The jumble of Friday market in the Great Ring he is striding through is so much like the imploded mess of his feelings that he could smash, throw, crash into—it doesn't matter, do something physical, violent, break something absolutely and forever irreversibly—*DO!*—when she slices him, her brilliant, perfect angling of the slipping knife, his mind just—annihilated. He has nothing but legs with feet to kick something into disintegration, long cramped arms and empty hands clamping onto something, heave it up, smash it—a heap of cobblestones thuds against his toes, the mason looking up at him calmly from his padded knees. His hammer poised for another tap on the last stone he has placed in its necessary angle of concentric curves; speaking to him some words in Czech. Could it be 'comrade'? Wearing a bruised grey leather apron. Adam discovers his arm is raised, an edged stone clutched high in his hand.

He is looking at the great clock in the City Hall Tower. Low as it is, he doubts he can hurl the cobblestone that high. Such an incredible clock of interlaced faces, built when you couldn't buy Japanese time at any stall in the market and carry it away, Emperor Franz—Franz indeed!—Josef I should be riding by with his giant white whiskers and inbred Hapsburg razored chin in medals and fourteenth-century uniform on a perfect black horse. Going nowhere.

Karan lifts the stone from him; his hand, so foolishly empty, sinks. She hands the stone to the mason, who places it in the sand at his knee and chooses a black one. He is talking to her, Czech perhaps or some dialect of it, and she nods, answers in perfect accent with the few words Adam knows she knows—"Yes," "Why?" "Thank you"—as if she understood perfectly every word the man is at length explicating. "Goodbye."

"This," she says in his ear, "is the Clock of the Apostles—all except Judas. And that," her warm arm turns him slightly, pointing across the stones circling themselves one by one for those thick hands, "that is the one Kafka house still standing. That's his 'Minuta.' You ran right to it."

How often he has dreamed since that he looked at her then; could remember the exact openness of her obsidian eyes. **You ran right to it.**

"His three sisters were born in that house, the family lived here seven years. They moved to Zeltnergasse just before his bar-mitzvah in the Zigeuner Synagogue."

"'Gypsy,' o gypsy," he muttered. "When?"

"June 13, 1896. Ten-thirty in the morning."

Saturday no doubt, and Leap Year. But he doesn't look at her watching him, *still knew exactly why he wanted to say nothing*. Lived there to age thirteen, when everything new and unknown in a life has already happened; when it is all over but the variations of relentless, grinding repetition. The building stands attached to all the others, three stories above arches and below a steep tile roof. Blank as a stupid cobblestone. The attempt to re-assemble a life out of the minutiae of accidentally retained accidents overwhelms him with futility. Especially creative genius.

"Come," she says. Kissing him with her particular softness among the rushing comrades of the Great Ring. "We'll go to Ottla's rented house in the Street of the Alchemists. It's across the river."

Where in the last years of the Great War he wrote most of the "little narratives" published in *A Country Doctor*. Little perhaps to suit his small daily routine in the little black house. Two odd windows, a chimney, a door below the immense Gothic castellated cathedral on the hill where the queens and kings of Bohemia were crowned; when they still had bodies to bury.

≈

CLOISTER TOWER:

The arches where high bells should hang are older than Gothic. He hangs beamed like a bat above the forest and the never distant clearings of German fields, bent roads, villages, the perpetual whine of Autobahn somewhere its national drone, but he is resting calmly in a great silence. He knows he cannot jump back to the beam on which he stood, impossible, and it crosses his mind, suddenly, that he would like to hear the cantor at a bar mitzvah sing the dark, strong songs of sorrow and dedication, of lament thick as human secrets. For all their endless, imaginative articulation, the words between Karan and himself, not even the very simple ones like 'go!' or 'ahh god' or 'come' ever quite found them home. Never completely. Never as they endlessly desired of them, search though they might forever deeper into their mutual and singular aloneness. *It would seem he knew even then that words would never be enough, why did they groan themselves into each others' bodies as they did, searching and momentarily on the brink but never quite finding what even they could not express to each other they sought?*

And if they couldn't express it to each other, who could there ever be to say it to? Would there be? Why must it be said? What was it? Who?

The sound of nuns comes to him on iridescent air. The tower does not open from the nave, nor out of the choir, it opens upwards to end merely within itself. Nevertheless their ancient song has been waiting for him to climb, to sway into, has been held here for him throughout the centuries of air they have already been forgotten, high and weightless into his hanging, free from every sorrow and transparent as ice, voices of women obsessed in adoration stretching so high, free, slender as silk, the spin of spiders floating without end beyond the tips of the tallest trees into sacrifice, their white wimples wrapping their throats so tightly and opening their faces like bells up into light, voices faceless, soaring together indistinguishable and pure. Song without body, there cannot be any such thing as body, it is merely memory exhausted and forgotten, a yearning upwards together solitary as points of flame.

"'History is a needle, for putting you to sleep. . . .'"

She is there very nearly beside him, reaching, reaching for him. She cannot touch him, but leaning far she does. When his feet let go the maw of space swings up from under him and his heart lurches wauggh! his hands open. But she pulls him across air and into her strong as steel.

"You ass," she breathes in his ear. "You goddamn ass."

The beam is exactly wide enough for their interspaced feet. The air, swaying, wraps them around each other, brief summer clothes, skin, bones, hair.

"'Anointed with the poison,'" he mouths on her bare shoulder into that medieval void. "'Of all *you* want to keep.'"

"You misquoted."

"So did you, I used your word."

"Nor is Cohen Kafka."

"You started it."

Up is always so easy. He climbed up and then she climbed up. Or did she climb and he climbed after? They are held by nothing but the air of their longing on a beam perhaps rotten, they enfold each other with each other's terror. But their hands, their implacable bodies find the relentless movements of love, imperceptibly she opens her thighs, imperceptibly he pulls her harder against himself. Here. Their bodies intensify, this shell of air is all that needs to hold them, is the sheet enclosing them under unseeable ceilings or stone floors, is always their own small, all-sufficient place in the unrelenting voyeuristic multiplicities of the world.

"Will you come when we fall?"

"Always."

"Why Kafka, why not Rilke?"

"A Catholic is too much old Paul, organizing everything."

"At least Catholics have The Virgin."

"True—she's more beautiful than Moses."

They sway gently like the clapper of a bell a memory too light to strike sound. Either and both of them hang on the lip of falling; the upper edge of terror on deepest ecstasy. Endless at last.

"We must now search for Rilke," Karan breathes in Adam's ear. "Their lives overlapped, they never met."

"But Rilke . . . wasn't a Jew."

She says then, "He didn't have to be."

Bending him so gently. Relentlessly.

≈

Rudy Wiebe is the author of three short story collections and seven novels. His latest books are a series of essays, Playing Dead, A Contemplation Concerning the Arctic *(1989), and* Chinook Christmas *(1992), a story to be read to children on a cold winter night. After twenty-five years he retired from teaching creative writing at the University of Alberta, Edmonton, and since 1992 he writes full time.* "Sleeping (Uneasily) with Franz Kafka" *was first published in* The Malahat Review, *Fall 1993.*

falling angels/
have this memory

CATHERINE A. SIMMONS

There is a lip. An edge. Threshold/precipice/fine line. Between the hard surface upon which I stand and   air. Air. A simple word, air. Monosyllabic simplicity a rush of the very thing spoken as it is said. Air. Say it out loud feel   air. And looking over the lip the edge the threshold, I see 7,115 feet of air. Matt black air. Matt black air thick with stars, singed by light of a quarter/rock-a-by-baby moon. Nighttime and I'm looking down. Looking into the jump target zone a ring of white light; a fairy circle.

My jumpmaster breathes out words: *Main parachute personally packed?* I nod. *Reserve parachute packed by certified parachute rigger?* I nod. Even up here where we stand in the black wind with the door removed from this Fairchild 24 I hear   air as it rushes out of her lungs   air giving me solace; air, her breath, a warm connection to something vitally human. To step over the lip is to step into   solitude an unequalled aloneness.   It is to move through darkness where lucid moments of simplicity hang as uncomplicated as clean   white   sheets. A falling star, fast white arc of thought. There is nothing complicated out there. It is. It just *is.* And

when I am out there I am   intensely   detached. And when
I am out there, I am being perfectly   selfish.

Her hands, my jumpmaster's hands, move over my body
checking harnesses/buckles/straps. Belts. She looks into the
complexity of my automatic opening device *thirty second
delay—right Angel?—opening altitude 2500 feet jumping
altitude 7115 feet.* I nod. Within the first five seconds of
jumping my body will reach a speed of more than 70 miles per
hour. During the next seven seconds my falling speed will
increase by 50 miles per hour. Then: terminal velocity. My
body slowed down and stable falling at 120 miles per hour this
for eighteen seconds eighteen seconds my mind ploughing
white through the night sky my body   blood and thinking and
womb   suspended star-like and husssshed between heaven
and

> *falling stars and angels*
> *I have this memory*
> *of guilt:*
> *twenty years ago lying*
> *with other girls*
> *on some*
>
> > *farmer's field*
> > *backs pressed to the scent of summer*
> > *fallow*
> > *faces*
> > *to the matt black*
> > *sky*
> >
> > > *to the stars*
> > > *above*

Gloves? I nod. *Helmet? Goggles? Appropriate footwear?*
I put on my helmet. My goggles. My runners are on. *Ready,
Angel, for countdown?* I look below again. At the tiny fairy
ring target zone. *Yes,* I tell my jumpmaster. *Yes.*   Thinking
how   air when you're on it is not nothing but very much
something which piles up beneath the spread and stable body:
my body over/air   my body balanced over/a huge balloon   air.

A vast and translucent balloon. *OK Angel. Prepare to exit
aircraft. Ten!*

> *falling*

I lean into the rush of blackness see   air slightly silvered
between the hard earth the moonlit marbled abstract   and me.
I reach out my

> *and as each star*
> *burned through ebony*

hand pluck light-reflecting film. This nacreous material this
Saran Wrap of the night is the beginning of my balloon. My
jumpmaster shows me how to work, enlarge it. Like pulling
taffy rolling dough. She holds my growing material to the
night, pushes down;   air piles into it and it becomes
circular. Ten seconds and

> *its husssshed*
> *white   journey*

my body not her hand will push against the starry starry. *You have to work more on this one, with your mind, Angel, rather than with your hands,* she says.

caused squeals and oohhs and oh sally

Nine! My jumpmaster lifts both hands holds one

look at that jasmine do you see

thumb down. Nine fingers.

holding hands

and sharing

this memory is one of
guilt   and I am sorry
I alone   in
the opposite sky saw

a thick furrow
of burning light
plough through the
*   harvest   sky*

Mommymommy Angelmom!   Hi Mommy one more kiss.

I look beyond my jumpmaster and know Jemma before I see her deep within the body of the aircraft. Jemma, my three year old. *What the hell!* I say. *Here,* I hand my jumpmaster my balloon material, *hold this for a moment will you?*

a laster

Jemma what are you doing here I told Daddy — but beyond Jemma stand Krystal and Fern. And of course Daddy. They smile like they're at a surprise party.

a laster for me white

*Gene! You can't do this to me, I'm jumping. I'm **night** jumping!*

slow

The girls just wanted to see you off. You know one more kiss and stuff.

I look at them at their happy faces. They think they've done something wonderful and so I drop to my knees take their clean and nightied bodies into my arms smell warm flannel of the night rather than daytime peanut butter/ bandaids. *Thank you darlings.*

> *and while it arced*
> *the earth took*
> *a breath: a deep*
> *breath in*

I look at the three of them lined up and smiling and think

how good of Gene to have bathed them my little angels. And
I think of how

> *the earth's airy rise*

he's trying so hard and of how delighted they all are

> *lifting me*

and I can't possibly be angry. *One more kiss and I'll be off.
Just sit here and be quiet and wave good bye. Good girls.*

> *to my star's reach*
> *after that the other stars were useless*
> *their final moment weak and I am*
> > *sorry   I did not squeal nor ooohh*
> > *I did not say oh sally*

And they are good girls. They sit nicely and wave. Gene
stands behind them looking proud. I smile at him, then again
at the girls and return to the removed door of the aircraft. My
jumpmaster hands me my balloon and I begin, again, to work
with it.

> *look at that jasmine do you see*
> *but kept*
> *the white arc for*
> > *myself*

Eight! she says.

> *and I am sorry mommy*
> *always said   share angel*
> *share   and be kind*
> *it's something only*
> *humans do*

Angelmom!

I look at my jumpmaster, sigh and hand her the translucent film. *Sorry*, I say.

Krystal kicked me Angelmom!

My Krystal/Fern/Jemma call me Angelmom. I want them to call me Mom, but they never do. I'm Angelmom to them and well   now that I'm used to it I think it's nice.

Krystal, I say, *stop kicking Jemma. You have to be nice, Krystal, if you want anyone to like you. You must be kind and not kick.*

Krystal crosses her arms wants to stick her tongue out at me. *There*, I say, *that's much better, we have to work at being kind you know.*

I look at Gene. *Did you bring them anything to play with?*

No, he says.

I unsnap my jumpsuit reach into inner pockets and bring

out a pack of crayons. *There must be paper here somewhere,* I say. I find some on the counter, at the sink beside the dirty dishes. I start to pull up my sleeves.

Oh leave those, says Gene, *I'll do them later. We just had a bed-time snack. Get jumping.*

It's OK, it'll just take a second. We shouldn't leave the aircraft messy when the pilot's been so kind. You really aren't meant to be here you know.

A few dishes don't amount to messy, Angel.

I know but he's doing you a favour.

Angel! Jump.

OK, I say. And blow kisses to the girls. They are colouring happily. I return to the removed door. To the 7,115 feet of   air; to what will become my balloon a huge

Seven! says my jumpmaster.

ball of air upon which I will balance. My mind assumes the stable spread position for my body: arms extended out from shoulders legs extended slightly spread. Stable. It's all about stability atop this vast   air. If I move my weight forward, I'll swoosh head first over the ball and down; tilt to the left or right and I'll slide slick in that direction. Free falling

and I have this memory

> of the scent of summer
> fallow at my back
> a sense of guilt at
> my neck I should have
> falling stars fallen angel

I want the orange the orange not the green I don't want
the green Angelmom!

> should have look at that jasmine
> do you see   share if you want
> others to like
> you

My jumpmaster takes my balloon material.
Any chance you'd work on it for me for a bit! I'll be right
back.

I'd love to she says, *but it has to be your own doing.*

> should have opened
> O   oh do look

Angelmom! Angelmom Fern won't give me the orange!

It's not very big yet I say.

> but I was
> ploughing   through
> white

No, she says, *it's not. What are you thinking—now?*
                    single
                    minded thinking

single-
minded thinking.

   Now pull/push   like I showed you.

   I pull taffy roll dough and the material spreads reflects
moonlight   and that brief moment of white   again I pull

   Angelmom! You aren't listening!

   I lift my shoulders. A shrug of apology to my jumpmaster
a motion of that's just how it is with children to myself. Inside
Fern and Jemma struggle over orange. Krystal is being good
and kind. She is working with intense concentration on a
picture. *Look how good Krystal's being,* I say to Fern and
Jemma. *Why can't you girls be good and kind like Krystal is
being. Fern!! Listen to me you must share. You must let
Jemma have a turn with the orange. You must share all the
time Fern, it's best for everyone. People like others who are
not selfish.*

   Fern hands the orange to Jemma.

   Say thankyou, Jemma, I say.

   Thankyou, says Jemma.
   You're welcome, says Fern. *Guess I'll go read a book,* she

says. I smile at my girls. Rub their heads. *That's better* I say.

They're such good girls, says my mother hands in the sink.

Mom, I say. *Leave those, I'll do them*.

Now honey, you just go and do your jump. I know what it means to you. I thought if I helped out you'd be able to get on with it. And Gene's had to go to the office he's so busy lately—

Thanks mom. But I can't leave you with these dishes— here. Move over if we both just get at them they'll be done in no time.

So I pull up my sleeves and start drying the roaster from the Christmas turkey. *Krystal*, I say, *come and help*.

Aw Angelmom! I'm colouring. It's going to be a great—

I know. But it's important to be helpful—

My jumpmaster waves her arm, catches my attention. I hand the tea towel to Krystal. *Thanks for being so kind and helping to share the load; look at your grandmother she shouldn't have to do these.*

So when do I get to finish my picture?

Later honey now there's a good girl—

I run to the side of the aircraft.

Six, says my jumpmaster.

I look over the edge down through all those dishes the thick cold sky and now there's crayons all over the hard earth below and I recall that almost everybody in the early 1900s believed the air would be sucked from the jumper's body as he fell and he would be dead or unconscious within seconds and looking through hard darkness.

You were thinking about a star. A while ago. My jumpmaster hands me a memory of silver.

Yes but I didn't share it you see it
was wrong it's a bad
memory this star

> *of summer*
> > *my back*
> > *sunk into earth*

There's a dribble in here that looks like dog pee.

> *could hear her*

Smell it Fern, see if it is.

> *breathing as white*

I did and I can't tell.

ploughed my

Does it look like pee?

fallow

Sortof.

mind

Oh.

And from where I stand I start shouting *then bloody well clean it up Fern what's on your fallow no I mean foul mind that you'd sit and sniff at dog pee and just leave it?*

I'm reading.

You're what?

I'm reading.

You mean to say you're reading when Krystal and your grandmother are doing dishes what happened to my nice girl—

It's a great book Angelmom the best—

Put the book down before I plough you! Oh. Fern. I'm sorry.

I look at my jumpmaster. *Damn! I shouldn't have said*

that shouldn't have Oh and I am sorry.   Listen. I'll be right back.

I move to Fern give her a cuddle *I shouldn't have said that Fern shouldn't have said I'll plough you with my white oh what am I saying it's all getting a little confusing I should just give up the idea of jumping for the time being but we have to clean up Basil's pee and*

ANGEL! Hello. I just popped in for a quick cup to see you off.

Barbara and she's come such a long way what a kind *I'll put the pot on Barbie it'll just take a sec   have a seat my jumpmaster's*

I run back to her and can't contemplate the edge the motionless   distant and very marble hard

Your material, says my jumpmaster.

and Irvin, the world's first free-fall jumper, may have been the first to conclude that it isn't the fall that hurts
        it's the sudden stop
and wasn't that sweet of Barbie to stop in for coffee and who wouldn't want a cup right about

Your material—

It's Barbie. Barbie's here and she won't be here for long, I'd ask her to leave only she's come such a distance to see me

off if she were a closer friend I'd be able to say leave have you
seen Jemma? What's Jemma up to I haven't even

Five!! Whispers my jumpmaster holding out her palm
upon which rests a fleck/a flash/less than a moment of silver.
Now, you were thinking something.

Yes where did six go did I even hear seven Barbie! I'll
be right there.

Angel. You were thinking. About a star.

Yes and the memory
> *breathes*
> *on the burning*
> *I should have oh*
> *sally and I'm sorry*
> *jasmine:*

> *harvesting*
> *guilt*

like I said, is one of guilt. And how is harvesting guilt going
to help me now when my mother needs help oh god that's it
she'll be doing the Thanksgiving dishes she'll

Within the body of the aircraft my mother has just
finished the Thanksgiving dishes. She is ready to start on the
pile-up left over from Labour Day weekend. I grab a towel
from the laundry to soak up Basil's pee before the coffee's
made and Barbie's quite content fixing a snack for Don who's

come over to borrow a hammer but I know it's really because he's lonely   oh god how the laundry piles up I'll just throw in a load   *Fern* I shout. *Fern!*

I'm reading.

Fern! I'm trying to be nice I really don't want to—Fern!

Yes Angelmom!

Come here look at all this shake the sand from these shorts all these summer clothes are filled with sand will you you're such a good   you really really are

Mom!

Yes!

When am I going to get to read my book!

Later honey. Now there's a good girl so kind.

I'm sorting soiled ski clothes when my jumpmaster calls four. I wave my arm at her. I'll hurry and be back for three.

I've forgotten Basil's pee.

I grab a towel. Can't find his spot. *Krystal! Krystal! I shout you're not selfish. You'll help pick up the Barbie dolls won't you! I can't find Basil's pee on the floor with these Barbies all over the place. That's a good girl. What a good girl you are.*

I just want to finish my picture.

No. Help me now.

I want to finish!

Krystal. What a selfish girl you are here I am trying to make a night jump just one night jump the only night jump in my life and you won't even help clean up the Barbies.

My jumpmaster is waving her arms. *Just a second!* I shout.

What? says Don who can't find the hammer. *You're going to jump out of this airplane?*

I nod. *Yes*, I say. *I am.*

Wow. Can I come?

No.

I should not be so unkind should at least say sorry, but no, it takes some practice. Or, you'll have time one day, Don. It's not his fault he's such a   . But those are bad thoughts. I take a breath, *Sorry*, I say.

Three! shouts my jumpmaster. And beckons me.

OK, I shout. *Don't get impatient. The dog's peed and it's not really fair to the pilot to have dog pee all over his plane when all he bargained for was one skydiver.*

> *I am a star*
> *lying in some farmer's field*
> *harvesting*

I'm a star to clean up some farmer's field Krystal you put
your goddamn picture down now you can harvest it anytime
put it down it doesn't matter there's a good thought —

> *thoughts*

My jumpmaster waves her arms.

I run to her. She indicates that I am to put down the
Pledge and dust cloth. *Here,* she says, and hands me silver the
size of a sneeze. *You'd better get working it.*

I know. But there's a memory

> *a furrow of*
> *knowing*
> *of being above*
> *the breathing*

where the human body rotates at terminal velocity where
centrifugal force
> *the star*
takes over and the arms the legs are pulled away
> *my parachute   and I am*
from the body where blood and thinking and it's
> *suspended between heaven*

quite a mess in there with the dog pee and Don

> *and*

> > *I should have*
> > *oh sally only humans*

> > *do   want others*
> > *to like*

She takes my arm my jumpmaster holds me tight her hand clenching my upper arm. *I am a star, you just said to me I am a star say it   to me out loud.   I am a star.*

I am a star.

Right.   Now about some farmer's field.

I am a star
lying in some farmer's field
harvesting

thoughts.   I look down I can look down and in the slow sky

> > *there is a star*
> > *and*
> > *there is a but/then*
> > *but/   if i had oh sally*
> > */then the earth would breathe*
> > *beyond my hearing*
> > *do you see jasmine?*

> > *and in this—*

guilt
Two o o , Angel.

makes my moment
as brief as the falling

And while I'm thinking my hands pull moonlight roll stars: my material grows is now waist-high as high as *Jemma! Where's Jemma I haven't seen her just a*

share angel be
kind so others will
be good angel
my little

I move through the aircraft looking in cupboards *have you seen Jemma Barbie! Krystal where's Jemma!* behind the toaster in the linen closet calling *Jemma where are you Jemma my little*

immobilizedstar

immobilizedstar.

She is in the costume box with Basil curled up she's curled into his breathing. She is not sleeping. Her eyes are open *I'm   I'm not doing anything   but being kind   being good   I'm not making any   Am I being good!*

I lift her from the costume box *there is my star* I whisper *my little   * I whisper holding her still body. Why do we

immobilize our daughters why do we for the sake of good.
kind. share. immobilize ourselves?   Brief arcs of white
fizzle in moments of   oh sally look jasmine

>   do you see   I am

>   guilty

>   un

>   kind kindred   I am

>   kindled burning ignited.

One sings my jumpmaster.

I put Jemma down *don't worry Jemma about all that
stuff just get on with playing.* I fly through the aircraft
gathering Krystal Fern to me. *If there's reading/drawing then
go forget all that*

My jumpmaster waves her arms.

*don't let kind. good. share. put halting in your way. I've got
to go—come watch if you want but I'd read/draw if I were—*

I stand at the door beside my jumpmaster. I take the
filmy material in my hands and shake it out shake it hard
before me. Stars roll off it white and falling moments of
brilliance drift from it as dust. I hold it in front of myself ready
to plunge. My jumpmaster laughs *no not there, Angel* she
says. And harnesses it to my shoulders. *Jump!* she shouts.

And I am ploughing through the matt black   air

>   *falling angels*

a white arc my wings the night's Saran Wrap reflect

have this memory

ignited thoughts as I fall toward the vast and marble etched
yes, earth.

～

Catherine A. Simmons *writes poetry and fiction and is
currently working on a verse novella. Her work has appeared
in such journals and anthologies as* Alberta Bound *(1986)*,
Secrets from the Orange Couch, Vox, NeWest Review *and*
absinthe *as well as in the "What If" series published by
Second Wednesday Press. She lives in Calgary with her
husband and their two sons.*